# NO GREATER DUTY

A NOVEL

# ROBERT STEWART

BQB
North Carolina

*No Greater Duty, A Novel*
© 2022 Robert Stewart. All rights reserved.

Published in the United States by BQB Publishing
(an imprint of Boutique of Quality Books Publishing, Inc.)
www.bqbpublishing.com

Printed in the United States of America

978-1-952782-59-6 (p)
978-1-952782-60-2 (e)

Library of Congress Control Number: 2022933937

Book design by Robin Krauss, www.bookformatters.com
Cover design by Rebecca Lown, www.rebeccalowndesign.com
First editor: Caleb Guard
Second editor: Andrea Vande Vorde

# PRAISE FOR
# *NO GREATER DUTY*
# AND ROBERT STEWART

"*No Greater Duty* is a tour de force that plunges readers headfirst into a skillfully paced, intricately plotted ethics drama on par with *A Sense of Honor* by James Webb. Stewart captures the gritty, often paradoxical, essence of military service, expertly presenting one of the most omnipresent leadership challenges— how to balance 'doing what is right' against 'the rules.' A timely, riveting story by an author highly tuned into the Naval Academy and the naval service."

> – Steven Konkoly, USNA '93.
> Wall Street Journal best-selling author

"A powerful story that provides a multi-faceted leadership case study full of ethics challenges. The author does a great job developing the characters in a realistic context that displays their individual growth, and biases facing women service members."

> – RADM Margaret Klein, USN (Ret.), USNA '81,
> former Commandant of Midshipmen

"It sounds cliche to call *No Greater Duty* a page-turner, or a book that you can't put down, but it really is. I found myself not wanting the story to end. It keeps you engaged, immersed, and entertained with each page."

> – Commander David R. McKinney, USN (Ret.), USNA '98

"This story is a tale of leadership; the characters navigate the gray areas where leaders will tread during their career. Frequently the tough answers are not easy to arrive at, and the author tells the story masterfully. Entertaining read and excellent plot that is hard to put down!"

– Colonel Jon Aytes, USMC (Ret.), USNA '90

"Great book! A compelling and realistic story of modern American warriors. A unique insider's look at midshipman life and the ethical challenges facing leaders today."

– Lieutenant Colonel Amy McGrath, USMC (Ret.), USNA '97, author of *Honor Bound*

"*No Greater Duty* is an instructive tale of leadership and integrity, told by an author who knows the topics well."

– Major Nathaniel Fick, USMC (Ret.), New York Times best-selling author of *One Bullet Away*

"A masterful piece of work. The nation is ready for a tale of heroism and character, on the battlefield and beneath the ocean as well as the U.S. Naval Academy. I enjoyed every page."

– Commander Ronald H. Reimann, Sr., USN (Ret.), USNA '61

"This powerful, expertly told story, rich with meticulous attention to detail, is an intensely compelling tale of integrity and moral courage that allows you to stand in the shoes and see clearly through the eyes of some of America's most dedicated young men and women. Whether embedded in a Noncombatant Evacuation Operation (NEO) in Sierra Leone, in a tense standoff under the sea, or in the halls of the U.S. Naval Academy, this intriguing coming-of-age read deftly relates the very real hard ethical and professional decisions our service members face, and the deeply personal consequences our actions have."

– Wendy Phillips Piret, USNA '93,
MA International Relations,
American University, Washington D.C.

"A timely and timeless read about the character-forging experience of military service. The intense combat scenes will keep readers turning to the next page. But the 'moral' combat scenes are equally gripping, and showcase the loyalty of our service members to each other on battlefields abroad and at home."

– Major Frank "Gus" Biggio, USMC (Ret.),
author of *The Wolves of Helmand*

# DEDICATION

This story is dedicated to the memory and in
honor of selfless service to country:

**Colonel Vincent R. Kramer,**
United States Marine Corps (Ret.)
1918-2001

Recipient of:
Navy Cross, Air Medal, Commendation Ribbon with Combat "V"
(WWII Guadalcanal Campaign; China Burma India Theater;
Korean War; Vietnam War)

**Warrant Officer Mark A. Whikehart,**
United States Army
1948-1970

Army Aviator and recipient of:
National Defense, Vietnam Service,
Vietnam Campaign and Air Medals
Killed in Action, 17 March 1970

# PROLOGUE

**Commandant's Conference Room, Bancroft Hall**
**United States Naval Academy, Annapolis, MD**
**March 6, 2024 at 0845**

Midshipman Alex Kramer, United States Naval Academy Class of 2024, stood at attention—eyes front, chin forward, and hands by his sides with thumbs closed and rested against his uniform pants. It wasn't easy to try to stay calm and pay attention. He shouldn't have been called here in the first place.

Mids rarely set foot in this room during their four years at Annapolis. And most of them couldn't have cared less about a conduct hearing that didn't involve them. Beyond a classroom discussion, midshipmen seldom paid attention to conduct mishaps. That is, until they were the ones caught breaking regulations.

But Alex Kramer's case? His was different. He was different. Plenty of chatter floated around the Academy about his single situation. A recommendation rendered here would either uphold or tarnish the code he'd bled on a battlefield fighting for as a decorated Marine. No midshipman in the entire Brigade had ever performed under fire like he had.

Ahead against one wall were four flags posted in gold floor stands. From left to right, the flags in the colors of the United States of America, the Marine Corps, the Navy, and the Naval Academy hung with identical folds. Alex's respect for the first two flags ran so deep that he had nearly given his life to uphold the ideals sewn as vibrant symbols upon their silk fabric. The other two flags? He'd tell you to ask him later.

A composed bearing disguised his cynicism. He was royally pissed off. *They're really going through with this? Because I saved a man's life?* The twenty-six-year-old midshipman's throat felt like sandpaper when he swallowed. *Where's their goddamned honor?* he shouted in silence.

Alex's crystal-blue eyes aimed like lasers on the Marine Corps officer standing a mere few feet in front of him. Colonel Bruce Wettstone, the Deputy Commandant of Midshipmen, was in his mid-fifties and stood in uniform. The man's square jaw and weathered face mirrored a lengthy career of military service. The colonel had arrived to convene a hearing not yet begun, and called for him to show no pre-trial bias. But the officer's grim mouth, with its corners turned down, hinted that he'd already begun forming early opinions, and they weren't good ones.

Looking over the colonel's 'chest candy'—his many service ribbons—Alex's thoughts drifted back in time to First Platoon, Bravo Company when Gunny Westphal had lectured his Marines. "Service ribbons are your visible resume. We eyeball other Marines' decorations like dogs sniffing each other's asses," the battle-tested gunnery sergeant had said. "An enlisted Marine without a good conduct ribbon says 'conduct issue.' Silver Star? One of them ribbons ain't never missed by other Marines."

Alex's own service ribbons adorned the top row of his Service Dress Blue uniform. The deputy commandant would have to be blind to miss the midshipman's Purple Heart alongside the nation's third highest military decoration for valor, the Silver Star. Like Gunny Westphal had said, "That one ain't never missed."

The judicial inquiry had not yet begun and the mood was already unsettled.

All of the Naval Academy midshipmen in the room shifted

restlessly from one foot to the other as they stood. They were witnessing a major military tribunal levied against one of their own who'd been decorated for valor in combat. Several Mids had been ordered to testify. Curiosity lured others to show up, having heard that arguments attempting to separate right from wrong could become hostile.

The leaden winter skies beyond the windows forewarned two things: snow in Annapolis and a cruel outcome for the accused.

Moments earlier, Alex had followed Colonel Wettstone's authoritative entrance into the conference room. Everyone in the room, all naval service officers and enlisted personnel, had snapped to attention while the Marine officer stood erect and took his place behind a podium in the center of the room.

Careful not to let his eyes wander when he arrived that morning, Alex had known who would stand at attention on each side of the colonel. Right of Colonel Wettstone was the Commandant of Midshipmen's lawyer, a Navy lieutenant from the Judge Advocate General Corps (JAG). To the JAG's immediate right came Alex's chain of command at the Academy, from lowest to highest in rank: Two classmates and 19th Company's top midshipman officers. Next, Navy Chief Petty Officer Lisa Sorrel, 19th Company's Senior Enlisted Leader (SEL). He liked the sailor and believed she was an excellent role model of maturity for midshipmen. He smiled to himself. The lady would have made a fine Marine.

Next to the SEL stood Navy Lieutenant Tara Marcellus, Alex's company officer. Though she'd taken over 19th Company less than a year earlier, Alex had come to admire the good-looking lieutenant's poise. She had even tolerated his occasional impatience, maybe because he was prior-enlisted and she trusted his maturity.

Alex had also noticed a few times that Lieutenant Marcellus seemed slightly guarded around male officers, yet more open with female officers and enlisted personnel at the Academy. As though an incident from the past set her on edge. Something was going on there, and he had wondered what it was the lady wouldn't reveal.

Alongside Tara stood her boss, Navy Commander Ryan Griffa, the Battalion Officer. Alex didn't have any particular opinion one way or the other about him.

The Academy's conduct officer stood at Colonel Wettstone's left. Navy Lieutenant John Pollard was an enforcer who reviewed allegations of misconduct among the 4,400-member Brigade of Midshipmen who got caught coloring outside the lines. His job didn't win him any popularity contests. The Brigade Conduct Officer, a Midshipman First Class and classmate of the accused, was also present.

When Alex had entered the conference room, there were as many people present as there were members of the three fire teams of infantry Marines he had led into combat in West Africa in 2019. Five years had come and gone since the mission and firefight in Sierra Leone. But to him, it would always feel like yesterday. Images were sealed in his memory: Refugees mowed down by rebel gunfire like plastic ducks at a carnival shooting arcade. His blood-soaked hands holding Billy Whittington's dismembered leg, nearly blown off from the IED explosion. Directing attack helicopters to rain their automatic fire down on enemy positions hidden in the high grass.

On that fateful day, bullets flew in every direction. Some Marines suffered grievous wounds. Alex was one of them.

At this morning's hearing, he expected verbal bullets to fly. *This will be a different battlefield. And Marines fight to win every time they're called.*

The Marine colonel behind the podium studied the accused midshipman standing before him. "Today is 6 March 2024. I am Colonel Bruce Wettstone, United States Marine Corps, Deputy

Commandant of Midshipmen, United States Naval Academy," he announced. "This hearing is convened to present charges of misconduct against Midshipman First Class Alexander Kramer, 19th Company, that occurred on 13 and 14 February 2024." Colonel Wettstone did not remove his gaze. "You may stand at ease, Mister Kramer."

*Get on with it, Colonel,* a tense Alex muttered silently.

"Midshipman Kramer, you have been charged with the following major-level conduct offenses," the deputy commandant read aloud in an overly authoritative tone:

**04.14**—Unauthorized means of ingressing or egressing either Bancroft Hall or the Naval Academy grounds.

**07.01**—Intentional absence without authority from an academic class, military obligation, or formation.

**07.06**—UA after reporting for Taps.

The Administrative Performance and Conduct System manual states:

By pleading "guilty," a midshipman acknowledges that the offense was culpably committed as alleged, that the midshipman is liable for punishment, and that he/she relinquishes the right to seek consideration, or to appeal on the issue of guilt or innocence.

The deputy continued reading from the statement of conduct offense charges leveled against Alex: How the midshipman had left the Naval Academy's property grounds ten minutes before midnight on an unauthorized absence, or UA, and returned the following morning.

*Present charges of misconduct against you.* The very words burned Alex like a nasty rash. He listened without revealing any visible reaction. Being forced to suffer through a formal hearing that questioned his character disgusted him. *I went back for a wounded buddy, another Marine—for the second time,* he shouted in silence. *You're punishing me for doing my duty?*

"The elements of your offense are set forth in the investigating officer's report," the deputy commandant said, poker-faced. "Based on the Preliminary Investigation Officer's findings, the accused stated the reason for his unauthorized absence was, in his own words and I quote, 'To stop a good friend and Marine, whom I previously served with in combat, from taking his own life' end of quote," he added. A condescending quality in his words turned heads inside the room.

*You don't know the half of it, Colonel, so better watch your step,* Alex silently warned the deputy commandant. *You're judging my moral code now.* The very code that had been embedded in Alex's mind the moment he became a Marine.

**Commandant's Conference Room**
**United States Naval Academy**
**March 6, 2024**

Standing to the side in Standard Dress Blue uniform with proper military bearing, Lieutenant Tara Marcellus focused on Alex, who was still at attention and now a Naval Academy midshipman, yet forever a Marine.

In the past several weeks, Tara had come to understand this unusual young man better than he might reluctantly admit to understanding himself. She'd already dealt with foes determined to question her duty, her honor. He had fought well against enemies who wanted to end his life on a battlefield. The Navy lieutenant was prepared to stand up for this single-minded midshipman if the morning's judicial verdict went against him.

Her hazel eyes darted back and forth between Alex and the

deputy commandant as they sized each other up. Had the colonel already assumed his high rank meant the cards he held guaranteed him a winning hand during this standoff? Probably. *Guess what, colonel? You didn't reckon on facing a midshipman who won't fold his cards for anyone who questions his dedication to the uniform he wears*, she thought.

The day Tara had told her mother she was applying for an appointment to the Naval Academy, the announcement had invoked an icy reception.

"Really?" Laura Marcellus had contested with suspicion. "You want to prove yourself in a men's club that still has contempt for women?" Forty years had passed since women had officially become part of the Brigade of Midshipmen at Annapolis. Tara's generation had heard the disturbing stories about the first waves of female midshipmen. Those women had been confronted with open hostility and seething contempt the moment they set foot on Academy ground. Male midshipmen's caustic remarks had cut as sharp as a surgeon's scalpel: *You don't belong here. Go home. You don't have what it takes and you never will. Bitch.* Legions of older Academy graduates were enraged about the newcomers, insisting women were unfit to serve on the front lines of military conflicts, period. Case closed.

But the women weren't going away. Female Mids at the US Naval Academy had learned in a short time to take care of themselves. They'd watched each other's backs and had drawn deep from a reservoir of unprecedented stamina and personal courage. The women stood their ground against relentless, even malicious opposition.

In late August of her first year, Tara had joined her classmates and submitted her six top service assignment preferences following commissioning in May. Firsties could select from twenty-four different Navy and Marine Corps service communities as forthcoming career choices. Tara was confident about getting her first choice: assignment aboard a US Navy nuclear submarine. Everything looked good. Her Order of Merit placed her in the top ten percent of the class. Her latest Aptitude for Commissioning grade had been an A, and she served as her company's executive officer in the midshipmen chain of command.

One final test she had to pass, the admiral interview, awaited her desire to become a submarine officer. Despite a small case of stomach butterflies, Tara had earned the admiral's approving nod when she pleased him with her composed demeanor and modest confidence.

"Midshipman Marcellus, wouldn't you prefer the fleet, with more opportunities for women officers than aboard submarines?" asked a rear admiral with angular features behind eyeglasses resting on the bridge of his nose.

Tara nodded. "That's true, sir. But I have sought to serve as a submarine officer since I was a plebe," she had answered with self-assurance.

The admiral had smiled. "You have your mind set on this, don't you, Midshipman?"

"I do, sir," Tara had answered, her eyes bright and certain.

"The Navy needs more women who wish to serve as submarine officers," he had responded with a favorable expression.

A week before Thanksgiving holiday leave, Tara's smile beamed brighter than a lighthouse beacon when she received official word. The Navy approved her request to serve in the United States Navy's silent service.

When Tara was still a midshipman, her mother had questioned Tara's motivation to serve aboard a submarine someday. "You want to live underwater for months at a time?" she'd said with wide-eyed disbelief. But Frank Marcellus had spoken in Tara's defense.

"It shouldn't matter if she's on a submarine or a ship," he'd said to support his daughter's goal. "Tara can take care of herself."

The Naval Academy constantly asserted that midshipmen must demonstrate the highest principles of personal and professional conduct and honesty. *But we're all imperfect,* reflected Tara, *even when we judge someone else's integrity.* This hearing would display the Academy's disciplinary process as either neutral or leaning one way.

Lieutenant Marcellus looked at Alex for any visible reaction. Nothing. He didn't even stir. She admired his stoicism. But the company officer also grew concerned about Alex's potentially defensive reaction once the deputy commandant brought up the Preliminary Investigative Officer (PIO)'s detailed report, including recommendations from the conduct officer and the staff JAG. "You need to stay calm," she'd warned Alex ahead of his hearing, "no matter what the deputy commandant says or does."

Tara imagined Alex wanting to tell Colonel Wettstone where he could shove his hearing. She'd come to know the decorated midshipman well enough to expect he would absolutely defend his actions if push came to shove. Alex's dedication to duty couldn't be shaken by anyone, not even a Marine colonel.

Today was Alex Kramer's judgment day. It was Tara's too. Her path from commissioning to submarine officer and back to the Naval Academy as a company officer kept unfolding with unforeseen trials of conscience, including this one.

# PART ONE

# CHAPTER 1

Arlington, VA
May 2016

"Help me understand this. You're not going to college? Where's this coming from?" demanded an exasperated Olivia Kramer after her son had announced his plans to enlist. Even his girlfriend had disapproved, telling Alex he was making a big mistake by not going to college. Carolyn Hagerty was headed for one of the Ivy League schools, loaded with ambition about making a difference for mankind or womankind. The hard and plain truth was that Alex, the son of parents with professional careers, had been floundering without any direction his whole high school senior year. He would soon graduate, yet still struggled to figure out what he wanted to do with his life.

Then in early April 2016 his mother received an unexpected letter. That letter replaced Alex's aimlessness with a specific direction to follow—a purpose.

Standing in their townhouse kitchen, his mother ran a hand through her long auburn hair and peered down for several seconds at the hand-scribbled letter in her grip.

"What's going on?" Alex asked, pointing to the letter in her hand.

"A letter from an uncle," said his mother. "He up and vanished years ago. Now he's coming here because"—her eyes turned from the letter to her son—"because there's a place he wants to see."

"What's that all about?" said Alex, puzzled.

"Sit down and I'll explain," she said, gesturing to a kitchen chair.

"My uncle Gerry Rourke, my father's brother, enlisted in the Marine Corps in 1967 and went straight to the war in Vietnam. But after coming home from 'Nam, he refused to speak about anything that happened over there, not even to his own brother." She inhaled slowly, then let it out. "For all I know, he's never recovered from the war."

Olivia reached down and fiddled with a placemat on the table. "I could really use a cigarette right now."

"Keep talking, Mom."

"Anyway, that's when he vanished. No one's heard from him in years"—she lifted the sheet of lined paper scrawled with slanted handwriting—"until this letter. Somehow, he found out we lived close to DC, and he wants to visit. But he also wants to see the National Museum of the Marine Corps before he dies." Two words, "lousy health," were posted in the letter without any explanation. "You know about the museum? Down at Quantico?"

"Can't say I do. Why?"

"Doesn't matter." She dismissed it with a wave of her hand. "If he asks you to go with him there, please say yes. He might finally be ready to talk."

"Glad to, Mom."

Olivia sat herself down in a kitchen chair. "It was awful when he came home." Years back, she had eavesdropped on Rourke and her father talking outside the house. On the day he returned to the States, some people in the airport, upon seeing him in uniform, stared with visible contempt. They wanted him and other service members returning from Vietnam to feel shame. "For what?" Rourke had snapped with bitter indignation.

His humiliating homecoming was cemented in her uncle's memory. Visiting the museum might afford him the dignity he and other Marine veterans never received when they came home—if they even made it back alive or in a casket. He'd be surrounded by symbols of selfless service, sacrifice, duty. That might be enough to spill his guts. If going there would make the man whole, she was all for it.

True to his letter, Gerry Rourke showed up two weeks later. He asked Alex to accompany him to the museum, and Alex agreed. They stopped at a diner on the way home because the Vietnam vet was ready to unload memories of war he had tightly held onto until now.

"I was a boot Marine with 1st Battalion, 9th Marine Regiment," said Rourke. His voice was so quiet Alex had to lean in closer to hear him say, "To Marines it's always 1/9—not *the* 1/9." The unit's infamous nickname was the "Walking Dead" because it had suffered the longest sustained combat and had the highest killed-in-action rate in Marine Corps history. Rourke's opening words began an uninterrupted thirty-minute saga about relentless warfare.

Alex's plate of food sat untouched. "You saw a lot of men wounded? Killed?"

Rourke's aging body stiffened. "Both. And too many of 'em." He pivoted when the teenager wanted to know if he'd received any medals. "Every Marine in the fight was a hero, whether the Corps pinned a medal on his chest or not."

Alex later learned Rourke had been awarded the Bronze Star with a "V" device and the Purple Heart.

"Were you wounded?"

Rourke exhaled sharply. "I was shot twice. Still got pieces of some grenade fragments floating inside me."

The probing questions began to trample on sensitive terrain. The boy was jabbing Rourke without permission because he wanted to know more.

"Did you—" Alex waited, then blurted it out. "Did you kill anyone?"

"What do you think?" Rourke glared at the teenager. "It was war."

"Just one more question."

Rourke cringed. "You sure have a lot of those, don't you? Have at it."

"Why'd you enlist in the first place?"

The old Marine pursed his lips. "I wanted to be part of something greater than myself." He stared out the diner window. "You're just a kid, you can't understand."

Except the Vietnam vet was mistaken. When he visited the museum without any preconceived ideas, Alex had understood. His desire to find out if he had what it took was enough incentive to talk to a Marine Corps recruiter, then enlist.

Two weeks later, Olivia was home early from work and dressed casually in a fuchsia cotton sweater over denim jeans. She'd just finished pouring unsweetened iced tea into a glass when Alex walked into the kitchen. His awkward expression relayed that he had to get something off his chest.

"You all right?" she asked.

"I've got an announcement to make."

Olivia noticed Alex was holding what looked like papers and a multicolored brochure clutched in his left hand. The Marine Corps emblem was visible on a section of the brochure.

"Okay, I'm listening," Olivia said, iced tea forgotten, and turned to face her son.

He lifted the papers toward her. "I'm going to enlist in the Marine Corps," he said and stopped, anticipating the perplexed look that formed instantly on his mother's face. "But first I need yours and Dad's written permission because I'm seventeen."

There was benevolence in Olivia's eyes. "Are you sure about this?"

"Yeah, Mom. I'm sure."

She slowly set down her drink on the kitchen island. "Your father's going to try and talk you out of doing this."

"I know."

Olivia wrapped her arms over her chest and slowly inhaled a deep breath. "I'll sign the papers giving you my permission," she said. Her mouth twisted with a hint of knowing what else she had to do, and it wouldn't come easily. "I can't promise anything, but I'll try my best to convince your father to sign the papers."

Alex walked toward his mother and wrapped his arms around her. "Thank you."

She hugged him back, then withdrew to look into his face. "Is this what you really want?"

"Yes. I want to do this."

Captain David Kramer, US Navy, Alex's father and US Naval Academy Class of 1992, already had two sea commands and was designated for a third following his assignment with the Joint Chiefs of Staff at the Pentagon. Alex's dad wanted, practically expected, his son to apply for an appointment to the Academy. For David it was foregone, but not for Alex. Annapolis hadn't been on his radar. Even with solid high school marks, college wasn't in the plans. He wouldn't say why, either.

Two days before Alex signed his enlistment papers, he and his father exchanged tense words while they walked.

"Do you really think enlisting is better than going to college?" probed the Navy captain, looking at his son with eyes wide in disbelief.

"What makes you think it's not?" Alex shot back.

"You've got the intelligence and spirit to become an officer—if a military life's what you want." David inhaled sharply. "You could have gone to the Academy. I thought—"

Alex shook his head. "You thought I was looking for the same thing. But me at Annapolis? That was your wish, Dad. Not mine."

An eerie silence settled between them.

Alex finally spoke. "I could change my mind about the Academy someday, you know," he said, wanting to avoid an argument. "Right now, enlisting in the Corps feels right." The Marines had let Gerry Rourke be part of something greater than himself. Alex had been searching for something similar, for a purpose. "Give me some space here, sir. That's all I'm asking for, okay?" Alex asked, making sure to not beg.

Captain Kramer nodded but his mood was lukewarm. "All right. We'll see where this goes."

# CHAPTER 2

**Marine Recruit Basic Training**
**Parris Island, South Carolina**
**June 2016**

A Marine Corps drill instructor (DI), Caucasian and tall with chiseled chin, acne scars, and flared nostrils stood ramrod straight at the front of the bus. He was ready to bring a heap of verbal shit down on the new recruits who just arrived at Parris Island. Tapered like slits, his eyes were ablaze with a wordless warning: *You're mine now, maggots.*

"Get your cheese-dick asses off this bus *now!*" he thundered at them.

Alex leaped from his seat, joining jittery recruits piled up in the bus's aisle who couldn't move fast enough to satisfy the DI's rapid-fire orders. He finally made it down the bus steps to the street, nearly pushed from behind.

Parris Island's thick summer humidity smacked him in the face faster than his feet reached the pavement. It was a suffocating heat that felt like he was tied up in a soaking wool blanket and was struggling to breathe. Beads of perspiration broke out across Alex's forehead, turning into lines of sweat that slid down both sides of his cheeks like rain streaking down a window.

"Get on the yellow footprints!" bellowed a Black Marine DI, a short man with thick, muscular forearms. Hands on hips with his eyes narrowed, he stared menacingly at recruits who stood beneath bright lamp posts under the darkness of night.

Alex joined the other sweating recruits who scrambled to find untaken sets of yellow markings on the pavement. Heels together, eyes straight to the front, thumbs along the sides of their trousers.

"You're never bored at Marine Corps Recruit Depot, Parris Island, South Carolina," roared the Caucasian DI. "And you have just taken the first step to becoming a member of the world's finest fighting force, the United States Marine Corps."

It was pitch-black beyond the lamp post's glow. Alex's eyes followed the DI's index fingers stabbing the air like a machete. Left hand, right hand. He didn't dare divert his eyes from anywhere but a point straight ahead in the darkness.

"Starting now, you will train as a team," said the same DI. "You will eat, sleep, train, and live as a team. The word 'I' will no longer be part of your vocabulary." Alex watched him pace back and forth, glaring at the new recruits. "From now on, the only words that come out of your mouth are 'Sir, yes sir' or 'Sir, no sir' when somebody asks you a question. Do you understand?"

"Sir, yes sir!" they roared back.

A recruit next to Alex raised a hand to wipe sweat away from his wet eyes. Alex was tempted to do the same until the DI was instantly in the recruit's face, one foot too-close-for-comfort away from Alex. "Get your nasty face away from your hands, maggot!" the DI shouted. "Why are you eyeballing me?"

Alex felt spittle and the overpowering odor of coffee from the DI's breath smack him at full force, and he wasn't the one who raised a hand to wipe away sweat.

The start of Receiving Week at Parris Island was organized mayhem in assembly-line fashion. Still wearing their civilian clothes, recruits shuffled like androids into the barber shop. Barbers sheared the hair off so fast that some recruits walked away with missed patches of hair standing out on a completely shaved head. Alex looked down at his sheared blond locks on the floor when a DI was on top of him in a nanosecond. "Keep moving," he roared, "that haircut ain't making you any prettier, you nasty thing."

With his head now shaved, Alex shuffled in line and grabbed a bag for "bucket issues" such as soap, shaving cream, razor, socks, underwear, towels, and other bare necessities. Next, he and the others tossed uniform gear into sea bags to include boots, 'cammo' blouses and trousers, T-shirts, and eight-point covers because Marines never called them hats.

A DI ordered recruits to dress in twenty seconds: underwear, then boot socks, then bottoms, then tops. Many still scrambled when he yelled, "Strip down and do it again!"

The squad bay he'd call home for the next twelve weeks lacked any personal identification except for Marine Corps symbols and words posted in different places. Organized rows of perfectly aligned metal bunk beds, two-foot lockers on the floor at each bunk bed, and wall lockers. It wasn't scenery from a luxury hotel room on the French Riviera. More like a dressed-up penal colony.

After penicillin pills and anthrax injections at the medical unit, recruits returned to the four-story barracks and their squad bays, always holding up their sea bags, never letting them hang inches from the ground. "Put your stuff on your foot locker, then sit down and shut up!" one DI bellowed at them.

"Stand up straight! Get your eyeballs off me! Nobody cares about you, not even your mothers! You're pathetic!" DIs seemed to love delivering their words with flying saliva. Alex wondered whether the Marine Corps had a special wing at Walter Reed National Military Medical Center outside Washington, DC where drill instructors went to surgically replace their shredded vocal chords. Then they'd return to the Corps' two recruit depots ready to scare the living hell out of more recruits.

Next to Alex, a recruit named Bondurant sat atop his foot locker. Bondurant looked older than the average recruit. His hair was prematurely thinning so there wasn't much to shear off in the opening and early frantic hours of boot camp. Alex sized him up. He was not just another wide-eyed teenager. Maybe this guy heard a call to patriotism or hearing the Star Bangled Banner gave him goosebumps. Maybe he believed the Marine Corps would hold a mirror up to his face and he'd find out in real time what he was or wasn't made of. When the DI was momentarily out of earshot, Alex had heard Bondurant whisper to a recruit that he'd left college after three years in to enlist. Why? He could have applied for a Naval ROTC scholarship and earned a commission.

Alex stopped himself. Where do you get off judging another recruit? He hadn't applied for an appointment to the Naval Academy like his father had wanted. Instead, he'd enlisted and wound up here just like Bondurant.

"Hey buddy, why'd you enlist?" Bondurant's question interrupted the quiet squad bay.

*We're not supposed to open our mouths,* Alex wanted to tell him but it was too late.

The last word was barely out of Bondurant's mouth when, out of nowhere, a six-foot-plus DI appeared and erupted, "Who's opening his nasty mouth?"

Innocent or dumb or both, Bondurant stood and raised his hand, "This recruit, sir—"

Alex braced himself. *Oh shit, here it comes.*

The drill instructor's boot exploded against Bondurant's foot locker, its contents flying across the deck. A bulging vein on the side of the DI's neck looked like it would burst right through the skin.

Recruits learned right away never to call each other by their first names. Just "recruit last-name." Nor could they speak to other recruits or all hell would come down on them. But DIs created their own names for different recruits. Nicknames went from harmless to downright crude. Recruits who wore glasses were 'portholes.' Another recruit from a farming family in Virginia was 'cow turd.' Alex's name was 'Navy brat.' He figured DIs probably got wind of his father's military status from a note tucked in his recruitment file.

"If you're not good enough to be a Marine, then you should have enlisted in the Army or the Air Force," a sneering drill instructor told recruits. "They'll take anyone."

All recruits walked on eggshells almost every minute of the day and night except when lights were out. Eyes aimed straight ahead while walking, running, or during drill instructions. Wakened every morning by a DI banging on a trash can and shouting loud enough to shatter glass.

With trim waistlines and muscular bodies, DIs never seemed to sweat even in the dense Parris Island humidity. Their uniform shirts were bedecked with colorful service ribbons from deployments in Iraq, Syria, Afghanistan, and other places as part of the Global War on Terrorism; GWOT. They came from every corner of the Corps: Infantry, Intelligence, Logistics, even Explosive Ordnance Disposal (EOD). They stood for an eternal principle of the Corps: every Marine was and is a rifleman first.

Recruits endured twelve weeks of constant mosquito bites, sunburned necks and faces, sand in their boots and scalps, and the DIs' breath at their necks. They didn't dare breathe a word of complaint.

Every time a recruit was sent somewhere, his 'battle buddy' always went with him. DIs drilled that principle into recruits' heads: *Protecting other Marines is a solemn trust. You'll understand when someone tries to kill you on a battlefield.*

On the Sunday afternoon of his third week, Alex scribbled off a note. "Hey Mom, all's good here so far. Chow sucks but we eat anything they put in front of us because everyone's always hungry.

I'm starting to believe that being a Marine is cool. Maybe Dad will get on board with it someday."

One morning following a three-mile run in high humidity and early-summer heat, a DI pulled Alex aside.

"Hey, recruit," the menacing drill instructor said, standing a very uncomfortable three inches from Alex's face. "Is it true your father's an officer in the US faggot Navy?"

Alex suddenly felt the raw wound between him and his father split open again, and it stung.

"Yes, Staff Sergeant," Alex told him, standing rigid at attention, eyes locked straight ahead.

"Why are you here, maggot?" the DI goaded. "Didn't you want to be a pretty boy sailor like your old man? I bet that pissed him off."

"I want to become a Marine, Staff Sergeant," Alex answered, his words strong, beads of sweat forming along his forehead. He figured being a Marine had been among the most prized moments—the proudest—in Gerry Rourke's troubled life. He wanted the same experience.

The DI took a step back and cocked his head, looking sideways at Alex. "Then prove it, Kramer. One chance is all you get to be a Marine."

"I will, Staff Sergeant."

"Oh yeah? We'll see if you've got what it takes," the DI said and walked away.

When the dramatic finale for every Marine recruit's boot camp, the Crucible, got underway, Alex couldn't wait. He joined all the other determined recruits, ready to be tested morally, physically, and mentally until they had each earned the privilege to be called a United States Marine. All of them wanted to start their traditional fifty-four-hour marathon where recruits marched forty-five miles, conducted military exercises, and overcame battlefield challenges together. Filthy, covered with mud, soaked in sweat, deprived of sleep, and eating only bare rations.

Alex finished marching the final stretch to a replica of the historic Iwo Jima flag-raising statue. He and other recruits stood in close formation with eyes straight ahead. They were physically spent and chock-full of pride.

"Good morning, Charlie Company!" called out a gunnery sergeant, standing atop the base of the replica Iwo Jima statue amid breezy winds. The early morning sun's orange glow rose on the horizon.

"Good morning, sir!" the chorus of recruits thundered back.

"In a few moments your drill instructors will issue you the Marine Corps' most respected emblem of honor: the Eagle, Globe, and Anchor," the Gunny announced with a loud voice and spirited tone. "Think about those who came before you and the proud tradition you now join. You are Marines. Welcome to the Corps. Semper Fidelis, Marines. Always faithful!"

The platoon DIs moved down their squads' assembled lines one recruit at a time. Gunnery Sergeant Kellerman, Alex's DI, presented a hardened gaze that reflected a life dedicated to preparing young men for war. The veteran NCO handed Alex his hard-earned badge and shook his hand. "Congratulations and good luck, Kramer." Kellerman's words were barely audible but his intent clear.

"Semper Fi, Gunnery Sergeant," said Alex. He tried to look serious but couldn't resist a small smile. The DI saw it and nodded. Alex was a Marine now. He had arrived at Parris Island an individual. In short time there, he had become part of something greater than one. All of the recruits looked the same, thought the same, spoke the same because a fighting force had to operate as one team together or it would break down.

On graduation day before heading to the parade field, Alex

took one final check of himself in the squad bay mirror. Basic training left him twenty-five pounds leaner than when he arrived. He was now a taut 175 pounds with a thirty-two-inch waist and in top physical condition. He smiled seeing himself in enlisted blue dress uniform with a scarlet stripe down the outer seam of each leg of blue trousers. Firm creases ran down his short-sleeve open collar khaki shirt, and a white enlisted Marine Corps cover sat on his head. "You did it!" Alex shouted and grinned at his reflected image.

He had excelled in so many areas of basic training that he graduated E-2, the uniformed military rank of Private First Class (PFC) in the Marine Corps. The majority of recruits graduated as E-1, or Marine Private.

David and Olivia Kramer waited with hundreds of other parents and family members on the parade field's grandstands. After the final company of graduating recruits marched sharply under brilliant sunshine past the commanding officer and his staff, families and friends streamed down onto the parade field to greet their new Marine.

"I am so proud!" Olivia said and hugged Alex. He held his mother's embrace for a few seconds. Alex loved her for standing by him when others disapproved of his enlisting. Carolyn Hardesty, his girlfriend, had abruptly broken off with him right after his enlistment. "You'll regret not going to college," she had said, scolding him like a stern nun at parochial school. *Says you*, Alex now thought to himself.

Olivia pulled away and smiled at him. "You're handsome in your uniform," she gushed. Alex's smile shone as bright as the white cover he wore on his head.

"Congratulations, son," said David. He shook Alex's hand and nodded with more self-control than Olivia's enthusiastic reception. "You proved your point about enlisting."

Alex's jaw clenched. "Dad, did you think all this time I was trying to prove a point?"

"Where's that coming from?" Olivia's head spun toward her husband in confusion. "This is his day, not yours."

David raised one hand, ashamed of what he had said at this extraordinary moment in his son's young life. "You didn't deserve that. I'm sorry."

"This is about Alex defying you, isn't it? All because he didn't want to earn an appointment to the Academy just like you?" Olivia said, visibly upset.

"Let it go, Mom," Alex said and draped an arm around her shoulder. "It's okay."

"No, it isn't," she replied, glaring at David.

"He's apologized, okay?" Alex replied, taking his father's defense.

David Kramer's disappointment that his only son didn't choose to follow him to the Naval Academy now became Alex's burden to bear. The comment moments before had cut deep. Yet Alex still loved his father. Maybe someday they would patch up their differences.

Alex gazed across the parade field, his eyes taking in hundreds of new Marines with proud smiles brimming on their faces. Cell phone cameras were everywhere, taking scenes of family photos, mothers with wet eyes hugging their boys, and fathers shaking their sons' hands. It could have been scenes on post cards at the base gift shop. He pressed his eyes closed and saw the words printed on an old recruiting poster displayed at the National Museum of the Marine Corps that day in April when he and Gerry Rourke were there:

If everybody could get in the Marines, it wouldn't be the Marines.

*No, it wouldn't*, he had told himself. Today he became part of the Corps. But somehow his victory felt incomplete. Didn't he still have a point to prove to anyone who doubted his resolve? His father among them?

# CHAPTER 3

**Wardroom, USS *John Warner***
**Submarine Force Atlantic, South Atlantic Ocean**
**April 19, 2019 at 0815**

Lieutenant Junior Grade (LTJG) Tara Marcellus stood in the wardroom's tight quarters with other Division Officers (DIVOs) in US Navy-speak. She was one of six officers from the crew who were Naval Academy graduates, and one of the submarine's two female officers.

Her own objective was clear cut: to excel as a junior officer, *and one who also happened to be a woman.* Accept no special treatment because of her gender. Prove to sailors and shipmate officers they could trust her judgment. Stand up to any insults suggesting women officers aren't up to the job of command. And one other hard and fast rule: never back down when someone gets in your face for doing your duty.

Eighteen months had passed since Tara joined the crew of USS *John Warner* SSN-785, one of the Navy's Virginia Class fast-attack submarines operating with advanced technologies in underwater warfare. After Nuclear Power School and Prototype, she completed the Submarine Officer Basic Course. There she received her orders to report to *John Warner.*

The boat was designed to seek out and attack enemy submarines and surface ships through open-ocean missions as well as shallow coastal water, or littoral, missions. The Virginia Class submarine's advanced technology detected and identified radar plus communications signals faster and better from ships, aircraft, and other submarines. Each boat's payload supported forty torpedoes and cruise missiles, special operations forces, unmanned undersea vehicles, and an Advanced SEAL Delivery System. Virginia Class submarines carried out Intelligence, Surveillance, and Reconnaissance missions (ISR). They could support battle group operations and engage in mine warfare.

The USS *John Warner*'s most fearsome weapon? Acoustic and electronic signatures enabled the boat to move in almost absolute silence and with stealth using state-of-the-art technology for a fast-attack submarine. Clandestine warfare.

Lieutenant Commander Walter Arroyo, the Executive Officer, stood inside the wardroom near the hatch as the submarine's officers filled into the tight space.

Average height with brown eyes behind tortoise-shell-rimmed glasses, sections of his black hair already graying in a few places, he stood erect with hands clasped behind his back. Naval Academy Class of '03, his stoic expression swept the small room to account for department heads and division officers present. The man served as second in command of a US Navy nuclear-powered fast-attack submarine armed with non-nuclear medium-range ballistic missiles and torpedoes.

Tara watched the last two men enter the wardroom. The brief wouldn't begin without them: Commander Jim Whikehart, the Commanding Officer and Master Chief Kincaid, Chief of the Boat. The chief pulled the hatch shut behind them.

Almost two years into her first submarine tour, Tara was still fascinated how crews in the silent service conversed using their own language. At the Naval Academy, she'd quickly picked up on 'Navy speak' aboard submarines—how officers and senior enlisted recognized each other's titles and duties. Acronyms replaced first names. The commanding officer was CO, the executive officer XO. Aboard a submarine, department heads (DHs) were often addressed by their department name instead of their first names or rank: ENG (Engineering), WEPS (Weapons: Torpedo, Fire Control, Sonar, Missile, Combat Systems), NAV (Navigation and Communications, IT), and CHOP (Culinary and Supply). Chief of the Boat, a US submarine's highest rank enlisted sailor, was COB. Junior officers like Tara were JOs and DIVOs. Submariners called their vessel the 'boat'—never the 'ship.' Ships were maritime craft riding on the water, not under it. Once aboard, Tara had the dialect down cold.

Listening to Commander Whikehart, Tara's attention momentarily rewound back to seventy-two hours earlier when she had been summoned to the wardroom without knowing the reason. Why report on short notice? Had something happened? She stepped through the hatch and saw ENG, her boss, was there. So were XO and Lieutenant Kerr, the Weapons Officer or WEPS. The three men acknowledged her presence with blank faces.

*Presume nothing,* Tara had told herself.

In that meeting, her heart rate slowed down after Commander Arroyo had informed her that the Tactical Systems Officer (TSO) had suffered an acute appendicitis attack and had to be relieved of his duties. If his condition worsened, the submarine might have to surface to airlift the TSO to the nearest naval medical center.

"Lieutenant Marcellus, WEPS needs someone to serve as DIVO for Sonar and Fire Control Divisions now," XO had told her. Lieutenant Commander Mike Urbanick, the Engineer Officer—ENG—and Tara's Department Head or DH—had recommended she step in as acting TSO, and the CO had signed off. Tara was confident, knowing a submarine's primary weapons functions were torpedoes, fire control, sonar, and missiles.

"You're it. Any questions?" XO had asked in a manner expecting certainty in her response.

"No questions, sir," she had answered to his satisfaction.

"Very well. WEPS will brief you on your duties."

Now back in the moment, Tara listened to the CO address half his officer staff, some seated at the wardroom table and the others standing.

"*John Warner* has received orders for its next mission," said the Skipper, slightly over six-foot tall with a broad chest, a square face, and thinning chestnut brown-turning-gray hair. "XO will brief you."

"Thank you, sir," replied Commander Arroyo and took one step forward. "Commander, Submarine Force Atlantic has designated *John Warner* to conduct ISR in the South Atlantic Ocean. The National Command Authority has advised US European Command and US Africa Command of intel on *Russian* submarine movement in the region."

Tara noticed the officers' curious reactions when they heard the reference to Russia.

Russia had growing business interests in the region, diamond mining and fishing agreements, among others. When *John Warner* sailed out of Norfolk fourteen days earlier following a one-year stand down, its orders were to conduct ISR on friendly and hostile forces operating in the South Atlantic's waters.

"At this time, Intel does not point to naval forces encountering any hostile situations," Commander Arroyo told the alert officers. "However, Intel has identified the submarine *Severodvinsk* roaming under the sea on multiple occasions on the West African coast. *Severodvinsk* is Russia's newest Yasen-class nuclear-powered multipurpose attack submarine."

Yasen-class boats were successors to the Akula-class submarine. Their armaments were eight torpedo tubes: four standard-diameter 533-millimeter and four 650-millimeter. The tubes housed homing torpedoes and Klub missiles capable of anti-ship, land attack, and anti-submarine offensive warfare. The boats in Russia's newest sub class had twenty-four vertical launch missile tubes located behind the Sail. They could carry ramjet-powered anti-ship missiles.

"Mister Kerr?"

The Weapons Officer took over the brief. "Yasen-class boats are fast. They can do up to sixteen knots on the surface and thirty-one knots submerged, and remember this: they're capable of doing twenty knots running at quiet, *underwater.*" WEPS wanted his warning firmly settled in each officer's conscious and subconscious thinking. Later, COB would brief the senior chiefs, and they'd inform their sailors. "The *Severodvinsk* is the Russian Navy's most recent challenge to US naval superiority under the sea," warned the lieutenant. "Make no mistake. It presents a threat to us and our mission any time we're swimming around each other in the same ocean space. We will not underestimate its capabilities."

WEPS glanced at the CO. "Captain?"

"Surveillance and detection of Russian submarine activities will be our primary mission," Commander Whikehart addressed his officers. "It is important to stay alert. Keep your sailors informed." He studied their faces. "Questions?" There were none. "Dismissed."

Tara walked out with Mike Urbanick. ENG was several inches taller than her. But Tara didn't notice because his friendly smile put her at ease. She admired the man's pleasant manner with others, especially enlisted personnel. Serving on this submarine with this crew should be fine, she assured herself.

"I told XO and WEPS they could count on you," Mike remarked in the passageway.

"I'm good, sir," she said brightly. "My sailors and I will handle anything that comes up." Her voice was certain, her stride confident.

"Sounds good," he answered her with a smile.

Urbanick waved and left to take care of some business. Alone in the passageway and headed to Control, Tara pondered what awaited her, one of two female junior officers aboard a US Navy nuclear fast attack submarine. And a junior officer whose words and orders would be weighed closely by the crew's 135 officers and sailors. The most anti-female among them would probably pray for Tara and the other female to mess up. *We're not at war,* Tara reminded herself. *Just do your job the best you can. You're an officer, so act like one.*

Three days later, the second lunch period for officers had finished when off-duty watch standers and most officers reassembled in the wardroom. Lieutenant JG Tara Marcellus was among them. She saw the CO, XO and COB were already present. They were about to get busy, and Tara was ready.

"At 1400 we received updated orders that change our mission parameters. Commander, Submarine Force Atlantic has assigned our boat to join Expeditionary Strike Group Two and its reporting unit, Amphibious Squadron Six," Commander Whikehart told the attending officers. "We will escort security for USS *Wasp* and Marines of 24th Marine Expeditionary Unit while the MEU operates in northern Sierra Leone—that's Africa—to support a Noncombatant Evacuation Operation, an NEO. We will rendezvous with the *Wasp* in approximately fourteen hours."

The USS *Wasp* was one of eight Landing Helicopter Dock Multi-Purpose Amphibious Assault Ships in the fleet. It could transport close to 2,000 Marines, ammunition, and various air and landing craft for peacetime and combat operations.

"US Fleet Forces Command does not anticipate the Strike Group and 24th MEU will encounter opposition forces," he told the officers present. "I know the crew of *John Warner* will be vigilant during our mission."

Tara spoke up. "Sir, will *John Warner* still monitor Russian submarine activity?"

The CO nodded. "Our orders are two-fold, Lieutenant," he said and recognized her. "We will support the MEU as a secondary mission, our primary mission being to continue monitoring Russian submarine contacts."

The South Atlantic Ocean was also the submarine's Area of Responsibility, its AOR.

"I want to underscore that *John Warner* will be ready for Anti-Submarine Warfare and strike support during the MEU's mission," emphasized the CO.

He turned to Lieutenant Commander Arroyo, his second in command. "XO."

"Thousands of people are escaping widespread acts of genocide," said Commander Arroyo with a serious expression. "Given what we know from Intel on western Africa, trouble could definitely occur while the MEU is operational. That's anticipated anytime Marines and sailors are inserted into a hot zone." The XO paused to let his remarks settle in: widespread acts of genocidal murder, sailors and Marines potentially coming under attack.

"Both missions are higher priorities now," he continued. "Conditions for either or both could change on a dime. *John Warner* will be ready should anything happen. Captain?"

"In forty-eight hours, we'll meet up with Expeditionary Strike Group Two and the MEU's Reporting Unit, Amphibious Squadron Six," said the CO. "Chiefs and crew will be informed on our updated mission." Whikehart studied the officers' attentive faces. "It's important we stay alert. You'll get updates as soon as we have them. Thank you, dismissed."

Mike Urbanick waited for Tara in the passageway. "If we run into any Russian subs, you'll see some action," he said.

"I know, sir," said Tara. She needed no reminder of her

temporary duty assignment as Tactical Systems Officer working in the submarine's epicenter of activity. Nonetheless, she felt the pressure on her in Urbanick's comment.

"Nervous?" he said, teasing.

"Nothing I can't handle," she said, her face lighting up.

# CHAPTER 4

**First Platoon, Bravo Company, 24th MEU**
**USS *Wasp*, the South Atlantic Ocean**
**April 19, 2019 at 1745**

A descending orange sun signaled dusk on the Atlantic Ocean. Marines from 24th Marine Expeditionary Unit (MEU) who were scattered across the hanger deck cleaned, checked, and re-checked their weapons like musicians tuning their instruments before a concert. Marines wouldn't treat their weapons carelessly because rifles and sidearms could malfunction in combat. Then a misfired last round might result in a warrior's last rites.

Each MEU was composed of 2,200 Marines formed by a battalion-strength Ground Combat Element and Marine Quick Reaction Force (QRF) joined with Aviation and Logistics Combat Elements. Every Marine stood ready to be immediately deployed to any crisis spot around the world. Their missions were global incidents calling for jungle or mountain warfare, mass casualties from natural or man-made disasters, humanitarian assistance, Noncombatant Evacuation Operations or NEOs, and riot control. MEUs travelled with a flotilla of amphibious warfare assault ships and military transports unmatched by any other fighting force in the world.

Billy Whittington, revealing crooked teeth in his boyish grin, glanced in Alex's direction. "Hey Kramer, you know where we're headed?"

Seated with legs wide apart and weapons pieces spread out in between them, Alex wiped and rewiped his reassembled M4.

"Don't know, Whittington," he said with his typical carefree disposition. "I walked by Gunny, the lieutenant, and the captain a while ago when they were talking. Gunny was sayin' 'copy that, sir' a whole lot."

Ethan Crowell, seated with crossed legs and wearing a camo-green T-shirt that revealed a tattoo of a Marine bulldog on his upper right arm, chimed in. "You think Gunny's going to tell us our orders tonight?"

Alex paused from wiping the bolt carrier, laid the oil-soaked rag down on the deck, and glanced for a long moment at the guys from 2nd Squad, first fire team: Billy Whittington, Ethan Crowell, Anthony Camacho, and Eddie Cabrera. Four still fresh-faced boys—two of them not yet twenty years old—who'd been raised in very different surroundings from Alex, and with less opportunity. They'd come from the Tennessee mountains, Pennsylvania coal country, the south side of Chicago, and south Texas. His addresses growing up were more socially upscale residences along the eastern seaboard. Their families were blue-collar stock while Alex's family had been in white-collar professional ranks and the military as an officer. His words were more articulate and his opinions more informed. Theirs tended to be one-dimensional with viewpoints formed by something they'd heard and taken at face value.

Still, Alex had closed his eyes to what made their early-life experiences different from his own because they were all Marines, dedicated to the Corps together. They said harmless stupid stuff that made Alex laugh out loud. He'd do anything for them, and they for him, with unconditional support. That's how Marine grunts were: with and for each other. Being well off or hard up, socially graceful or awkward, was meaningless when they received new orders, grabbed their gear, and did their jobs. No one was better than anyone else. Alex trusted all of them with his life, and they felt the same way about him watching their backs. They were Marines. Trust always cut both ways. They wouldn't accept anything less from each other, period.

Alex, now a twenty-year-old Marine corporal, was in the final stretch of a four-year enlistment. Every Marine in First Platoon—forty-two plus one Navy Corpsman—was an infantry grunt. All of them were accomplished riflemen committed to their mission.

Alex reloaded the last two of six ammo magazines he always carried as part of his combat load. "I'm thinking we'll be boots on the ground somewhere in forty-eight hours."

Twenty minutes had passed and dusk started to settle on the ocean's horizon when Gunnery Sergeant Jerome Westphal stepped through a hatch and out on the hanger deck to check on his Marines.

"Hey, Gunny, we got new orders?" a Marine shouted out.

"Listen up," he announced with a baritone voice. Marines stopped what they were doing and turned their eyes to the Black Marine. First Platoon's senior Non-Commissioned Officer was all business. The NCO had been decorated for his actions under fire twice during four deployments. "We're goin' to Sierra Leone," he said, his firm bearing and chiseled features evidence of the drill instructor he had been for two years at Marine Corps Recruit Basic Training, Parris Island, SC.

"Where's that, Gunny?"

"Africa," he answered back. "Our mission will be handling some bad shit that could go down there. The lieutenant's coming to brief us."

Gunny no sooner had finished when First Lieutenant John Fontana, platoon commander of First Platoon, Bravo Company, stepped through the hatch.

Alex stopped cleaning his rifle and raised his head to follow his platoon commander's approach. John Fontana stood just under six feet tall with short-cropped black hair. Thick, muscular forearms stood out like rolling pins below the rolled-up sleeves on his camo utility shirt. He had the handsome looks usually spotted on a Marine Corps recruitment poster.

Alex and his brother Marines liked Fontana. He understood an enlisted grunt's life. He'd been there done that as an enlisted Marine who rose to staff sergeant. Fontana had humped the same gear and weapons, gone out on patrols, watched carefully where he stepped, and returned fire against enemy positions, just like them. Alex and the rest of the Marines admired his all-in-all-the-time attitude. And they respected Fontana because he had earned his second lieutenant's gold 'butter bars' *after* being enlisted. The man was an officer who knew exactly what brotherhood on a field of fire looked and felt like. His reputation was a take-no-shit Marine who fought against militant Sunnis in Iraq and violent insurgents in Afghanistan. Many of John Fontana's brothers had bled, some had died.

"We've received our orders, and it's an NEO," Fontana said, the words delivered in his soft southern drawl. Their NEO mission was to secure the safety of a few thousand refugees headed to Sierra Leone, Africa, not far inland from the Atlantic Ocean shoreline. Refugees were escaping unspeakable genocide attacks and ethnic cleansing from rebels of the Revolutionary United Front, known on the African continent as the RUF.

"UN observers on the ground report natives being slaughtered," the lieutenant said. "In-country rebel tribes are fighting for control of the region. Innocent men, women, and children are on the run. We're going there to make sure they get out alive."

Large areas of the region had been suffering from famine for several months. Starvation, poor health, and bare medical care had ravaged the population. Transporting refugees to the United

States was not a realistic option. US Department of State officials had arranged for rescued refugees that Marines referred to as IDPs—internally displaced persons—to be transported to the neighboring nation of Guinea-Conakry to seek refuge, shelter, further medical attention, and possible asylum.

"The whole MEU's getting in on this one," said Fontana. "After ground infantry units secure the area, Aviation Combat Element will transport the IDPs from designated departure sites to the USS *Wasp* waiting offshore," he continued. "Super Stallions will relocate IDPs from the *Wasp* to Guinea-Conakry."

"What's that place we're taking 'em, sir?" a Marine called out.

"Guinea-Conakry—that's a neighboring African country even more poor than Sierra Leone," he said and shrugged. "But they don't have a civil war going on. Our government has arranged for us to relocate the IDPs there."

He paused and met the eyes of all his Marines, who sat waiting for his next words.

"Second Platoon will be the assault platoon," Fontana continued. "Third Platoon will secure the area. Everyone in full combat load, inside and outside the relief compound." The platoon commander looked around at the young men, some still boys, alertly waiting for his next words. "Questions?" No one raised their hands or spoke up.

"This is important, so listen closely," he said. "First Platoon, you will stand by as the Quick Reaction Force, full combat load. The region where we're going has a history of violence and civil unrest. People are running for their lives away from ethnic cleansing."

Their mission for the NEO was twofold, he added. They would carry out security at a designated compound and evacuate fleeing refugees. "We could run into some resistance during the mission.

Trust your eyes, trust your instincts. Know where your brother Marines are at all times. And look out for each other." The platoon commander turned to the senior NCO. "Gunny."

"Sir." Westphal cleared his throat and trained his eyes on his Marines. "The ETA for reaching our operations base is seventy-two hours at 0845—maybe a day earlier," he said. "Super Stallions will transport First, Second, and Third Platoons from the *Wasp* to the evacuation staging area with logistics right behind. Our birds will stand by on strip alert for Close Air Support if we need to call them in." If Marines on the ground came under attack from hostile RUF forces, Cobra and Huey attack helicopters would go operational on short notice. Harrier jets also would stand by on the amphibious ship.

"Questions?" asked Westphal.

"Sir, will we also set up for riot control?" asked Alex.

"That's affirmative," said Lieutenant Fontana. "Attacks by tribal groups could form up fast. We will handle any tensions that develop at the evac site. Conditions on the ground could go south at any moment."

"All right, Marines, you heard the lieutenant," came Gunny Westphal's firm tone. "Prep your gear and stand by for a map brief. Initial inspections for gear in six hours."

"Use the next 48–72 hours well," Lieutenant Fontana told his Marines. "Review your jobs so well you could perform them in your sleep. Check and double-check your weapons and your gear. Get enough rest and don't skimp on chow. Any questions or issues, come see your squad leaders or Gunny Westphal. If they're not around, then come see me. We will reassemble four hours before the *Wasp* drops anchor, and all units proceed to the relief site." He scanned the faces of the men under his command. "First Platoon, dismissed."

# CHAPTER 5

**Northern Province Sierra Leone, West Africa**
**April 23, 2019 at 0835**

Corporal Alex Kramer stood in full battle load at the northwest corner of the compound his company had orders to secure. He was thirteen meters inside the checkpoint and front gate, where several hundred refugees began passing through two days ago, and more were flocking there every day.

Four days earlier at sea heading to their mission, Lieutenant Fontana had pulled him aside. "You're taking over as squad leader for 2nd Squad. You good with that?" Fontana had said.

Surprised, Alex nodded. "Very good, sir." The twenty-year-old would now be responsible for leading thirteen other Marines—and always having their backs.

"Marines in the platoon respect you, big time," the platoon commander had told him.

Alex's eyes swept the outside perimeter of the secure compound. Refugees, with fear and exhaustion written on their faces, walked past heavy concrete barriers set up to prevent unauthorized vehicles from breaching the gate and compound. Mothers held babies in one arm and a frightened-looking child's hand in the other. Elderly needed assistance to take even a few steps, and so did the disabled. Yet they all managed to shuffle toward what they believed was a far safer place.

Starting at early dawn, refugees escaping ethnic cleansing came in waves. IDPs were mixed with ECOWAS—Economic Community of West African States—peacekeepers whom the

rebels hunted down to maim and kill. Clouds of red dust surrounded weary refugees as they trudged along the dirt road
branching off the highway. The refugees were tightly packed,
anxious to process into the compound and its relative safety.
The line stretched so far that Alex couldn't see its end. Men and
women, old and young alike, and children. Most walked, some had
to be carried.

Two six-foot walls of protective sandbags were positioned one
on each side of the front gate. The sandbags were strategically
stacked to allow Marines a large open view they could use as firing
positions behind their cover.

Sweat formed at the back of Alex's neck, and his stomach and
back were damp under his Kevlar flak jacket. Alex had entered
adolescence with a screwy metabolism. Namely, he perspired
easily. When he had arrived for basic training at Parris Island with
its swarms of mosquitoes and oppressive humid temps, his drill
instructors had constantly ragged on him, calling Alex 'shower
head,' for sweating so much.

Boot camp was three years back in Alex's rearview mirror. It
had been grueling but his drill instructors taught him, trained
him, pounded it into him how to be the last one standing against
an enemy. How to be a Marine.

Now he was in Mambolo, the principal chiefdom in the District
of Kambia, Sierra Leone's northern province. Early morning
was uncomfortable—more like blistering hot—and it was only
April. The sun's orange ball rising in the east cast shadows across
the compound area as refugees massed at the front gate. Palm
trees, some of them 150 feet high, lined the widely paved Mange-
Mambolo Road, which ended at the dried red clay mud path into
the relief site. Two miles away, the Great Scarcies River flowed
into the Atlantic Ocean.

At 0545 Alex announced his first orders of the day to his three fire teams, each with four ground warfare-trained Marines. They were to begin their Pre-Combat Checks, followed by fire team leaders conducting Pre-Combat Inspections, which all of them would do automatically because it was drilled into every Marine as naturally as breathing. Double-check that all combat gear and weapons were in working order: M4s, M27s, and M203 grenade launchers. Ammo clips were packed and ready. They carried batteries for radios, then checked radio security. Ensure Kevlar helmets and flak jackets with heavy ceramic bulletproof plates were in good condition. And carry enough water to stay hydrated.

Through his sunglasses, Alex estimated at least 750 natives on the run had already passed through the checkpoint gate. He glanced at his watch: 0835.

Pre-planned air support and logistics for the NEO were in place and ready, which was Standard Operating Procedure or SOP for every MEU mission. Marines left nothing to chance. Pre-planning prevented unintended consequences. Otherwise, Marines got hurt. The company commander described the Aviation Combat Element (ACE)'s state of readiness at the last mission brief seventy-two hours earlier. CH-53E Super Stallion helicopters from the MEU's aviation squadron would be spotted on the USS *Wasp*'s deck for on-call support to the mission.

Once through the main gate's checkpoint and processed by Marines protecting and assisting UN representatives, refugees would be directed to a designated corner of the compound inside the wire. At that location, two Super Stallion choppers would rotate flying in to transport any refugees needing immediate life-saving care to the *Wasp* anchored not far off in the Atlantic. The 40,000-ton multi-purpose amphibious assault ship was equipped to provide all forms of emergency medical care for up to six hundred casualties with its four central and two emergency operating rooms.

Additional Super Stallions also rotated in and out of the compound's EXFIL or exfiltration area, ready to transport refugees to a controlled airfield, a designated holding area along the southwestern coast of Africa. From there, aircraft sat ready to fly escaping men, women, and children to the *Wasp* for medical triage and care before moving them to their final destination in neighboring Guinea-Conakry on the African continent.

Four Cobras and three "Venom" Hueys, the Marine pilots' and crews' steadfast helicopters and airborne weaponry that they called "skids," stood by to support the MEU's ground combat element with immediate Close Air Support (CAS). From the Command Element staffed by senior commanders down to the infantry platoon, they knew the mission posed a potentially dangerous trap door. It could open at any time on a field of battle confronting RUF rebels in Sierra Leone.

For almost a decade, RUF rebels had fought to replace democratic rule with tribal military control there. The national army finally captured and imprisoned their leadership three years ago, ending the rebels' uprisings and regional attacks. Now they were back. Their victims' faces and flesh bore the grotesque scars of acidic chemicals thrown at them by RUF soldiers. Whether blind or disfigured or both, these victims couldn't shake free of the terror that surrounded them.

A rising sun showed itself over the horizon line when the mission got underway. Marines and United Nation workers, operating under hot temperatures and high humidity, processed fleeing refugees and moved them efficiently to Super Stallion helicopters, waiting for refugees with engines running and propeller blades rotating. See-through fencing with rolled barbed wire on top surrounded and protected the transport zone buzzing with Marines and refugees.

Two times in the morning's duty tour, Alex joined his three fire teams to patrol outside the site's fence line. They'd encountered people laid on stretchers with ghastly wounds, awaiting surgeons to repair their mutilated limbs, heads, and faces. Genocide was an equal-opportunity murderer. Several times Alex needed to look away or he'd puke on his desert camouflage utility pants, his "cammies." The voice-activated satellite radio squawked with the platoon commander's voice. "Bravo One Actual to First Platoon, keep sharp. Do a once-over on anybody looking too healthy or doesn't look scared. We have reports of RUF trying to blend in with refugees. Bravo One Out," Lieutenant Fontana issued his order from the command post (CP) in the center of the relief area.

"Bravo 1-2, copy," Alex reported back with his call sign for 2nd Squad to follow 1st Squad, checking in with the platoon commander. 3rd Squad came in next.

From a position just outside the security fence, Alex's trained eyes surveyed the scene for anything that looked wrong to him. Four mud and brick huts with bamboo thatch roofs set close together were at two o'clock and faced the dirt road coming in. Barefoot children played outside. Thick, straw-like grass approximately three-to-four feet high rose up thirty to thirty-five meters behind the huts. At eleven o'clock and slightly more than twenty meters northwest of the front gate, he counted three one-story rusted metal-siding pre-fab buildings. Early morning sunlight reflected so brightly off their rusted corrugated tin roofs that he was forced to squint even wearing sunglasses. Like the thatch huts, the three buildings were in close proximity.

Alex saw no sign of equipment, machinery, or materials outside, or workers coming and going. The buildings appeared vacant. Some windows were intact, others were broken. He studied them while caution crept into his thoughts. On a battlefield, almost nothing was as it seemed. He imagined words printed on an automobile's side mirrors: objects may be closer than they appear.

Beyond and behind the abandoned buildings stood another area of four- to five-foot tall dense, straw-colored grass stretching back some 100–125 meters deep. It reached a grassy clearing a mile and a half wide. Where the grassy clearing ended, one quarter mile of sand bled into the Atlantic Ocean's shoreline.

Watching the refugee traffic, Alex took five steps and tapped Christian Aquino on the shoulder. Aquino's head spun toward the touch.

"What's up, brother?"

"Hey Aquino, I don't like what I see over there." Alex pointed a finger to the identical sections of thick high grass at the northwest and northeast corners beyond the main security gate. "I'm thinking nothing good is hiding in there."

"You expecting trouble?" Aquino, a PFC, cocked his head with eyes hidden behind sunglasses. The olive-skinned first-generation American from the Philippines was the Rifleman or "Ready" position on 2nd Squad, second fire team.

Alex removed his sunglasses and wiped the sweat from his forehead. "I've got a feeling it's coming to find us."

"How come?"

Alex aimed his chin toward hundreds more refugees waiting to be processed in. "Those people are on the run from killers, butchers. I'm thinking, 'where are the rebels now?' If you were them, wouldn't you follow those people and hunt them down? Stay alert."

"Copy that."

A gnawing feeling persisted in Alex's gut. Something wasn't right with those areas outside the fence line. His eyes didn't trust what they saw.

"Bravo 1-2 to Bravo One Actual," he said, referencing a Marine's immediate commanding officer as "Actual" in radio comms.

"Go ahead, Bravo 1-2," Lieutenant Fontana replied.

"Sir, a 180-degree sweep of terrain in 2nd Squad's Area of Operations, outside the security gate—that area can hide hostiles. Request permission to send a SITREP to Bulldog 1-4 for possible air assault-support, over," reported Alex, referencing the vital Situation Report.

"Roger that, Bravo 1-2."

Sergeant Cirko, call sign Bulldog 1-4, was the Joint Terminal Attack Controller, the JTAC or 'jay-tac' in Marine-speak. He was on patrol with 1st Squad on the opposite side of the evacuation compound. His job was to monitor all Close Air Support communications from pre-to-post air operations by the Aviation Combat Element.

"Bravo One Actual to Bulldog 1-4—"

"Go, Bravo One."

"Squad Leader 2nd Squad, Bravo 1-2 will be your Forward Observer for northwest sector outside the gate," said Lieutenant Fontana and named Corporal Alex Kramer as the FO.

"Roger that, Bravo One."

After removing his helmet and sunglasses, Alex withdrew two sections of baby wipes from a cargo pants pocket and wiped more sweat off his face and scalp.

"Bravo 1-2 to Bulldog 1-4, over," Alex called the JTAC.

"Go, Bravo 1-2."

"Bulldog 1-4, possible hostile areas are located outside west-to-northwest of the front gate—going from seven to eleven o'clock. Advise when ready for position and SITREP, over."

"Bulldog 1-4 to Bravo 1-2, ready for SITREP, over."

Cowboy-7, a Marine officer and aviator on duty as Forward Air Controller, called the F-A-C, and stationed at the command post, followed Alex's and JTAC's communications. His vital job was to directly support ground combat units the moment they came under fire or anticipated a hostile engagement.

Alex placed the helmet back on his sweaty head. Wearing a helmet always meant being safe than sorry anytime shit hit the fan.

"Bulldog 1-4," he said, scanning the area again. "Northwest of main gate at eleven o'clock are three one-story pre-fab buildings. No personnel or activity visible. Located three-zero meters behind them, four to five-foot-tall thick, straw-colored grass runs from seven o'clock to eleven o'clock—estimated 100 to 125—repeat, one-zero-zero to one-two-five meters deep, over."

"Roger that, Bravo 1-2. Continue," said Bulldog 1-4.

Cowboy-7 copied Alex's radio traffic and updated the battle board at the command post as he received the information.

Alex knew Sergeant Cirko, the JTAC now on patrol with 1st Squad, was already aware of the four small huts northeast of the front gate at two o'clock and with children observed on the ground. Also, a second, almost identical stretch of tall, straw-like grass behind and beyond the huts approximately one hundred meters deep. Another sector of would-be trouble where RUF rebel forces could hide and open fire on refugees, Marines, and UN workers.

"Second Squad, First Platoon is Oscar Mike on patrol," said Alex, noting they were on the move. "We will have eyes on those areas in our Area of Operations and report back with situation updates for possible CAS, over."

"Copy, Bravo 1-2," Bulldog 1-4 came back. "Cobras and Hueys are standing by on Strip Alert. One AV-8 will be dispatched for MIR over your position," he continued, citing the acronym for Multi-Imagery Reconnaissance. "Bulldog 1-4 out."

"Cowboy-7, copy that," the Forward Air Controller affirmed MIR conducted over the enemy positions and CAS target areas.

Ready to check on his three fire teams patrolling outside the fence line, Alex patted six extra magazine packs stuffed in his ammo pouches on his flak jacket. Reassurance.

# CHAPTER 6

**Northern Province Sierra Leone, West Africa**
**April 23, 2019 at 0915**

It was only a quarter past nine a.m. and Sierra Leone's humidity enveloped Corporal Alex Kramer like he'd stepped into a smothering sauna. It would only get hotter, so he and his brother Marines might as well sweat.

The squad leader from First Platoon's Quick Reaction Force looked out at the long, densely packed line of refugees at the security gate, forty meters out and beyond. He removed his helmet and, with one hand, wiped away the newest layer of perspiration dampening his hair and scalp, and heard his radio squawk.

"Bravo One Actual to Bravo 1-2, report 2nd Squad fire team positions," said First Lieutenant John Fontana.

"Second Squad, first fire team ready at eleven o'clock outside the wire near the front security gate," Alex reported back. "Second fire team at nine o'clock and third fire team at seven o'clock, over." Alex's Marines were armed and ready to engage any hostile contacts.

"Bravo One, copy" confirmed Fontana. "Bravo One Actual to Bravo 1-1, report your—"

He didn't finish his sentence before automatic rifle fire shattered the morning calm. Refugees packed thick in line fell right where they stood on the dirt road while a combination of semi-automatic and automatic rifle fire tore violently through their flesh.

Alex's head whipped in the direction of the gunfire coming

from the wide areas of tall, straw-colored weeds behind the thatch huts. His eyes locked on three persons standing erect in the tall weeds holding rifles and opening fire on the pack of crowded refugees: two adults and a boy who didn't look a day over twelve years old. Alex recognized two things instantly: the rapid, tin-can sounds of Russian AK-47 semi-automatic rifle fire, and the weapon's distinctly curved magazine under the stock—curved more than an M4's ammo clip. He also knew the sound of a Soviet RPK machine gun firing away.

The three shooters—two wore camo uniforms and the young boy, almost a child wearing a black T-shirt over jeans—were Black. He made out their facial features and skin color clearly enough to know they had to be African, likely RUF rebels. Not Caucasian Eastern European or dark-skinned Middle Eastern mercenaries. The scene around him transformed into rapid pandemonium outside the compound. The screams of refugees filled the air. As refugees waited to process in, they stood exposed and vulnerable like mechanical targets at an outdoor shooting range. They ran in every direction with eyes widened in terror.

Wounded men, women, and children thrashed on the ground. Agonizing moans of physical pain played out in a chorus of carnage. Then there were the silent ones, the dead, many of them. Blood penetrated their clothes, pooling and darkening the dried, red-clay dirt road underneath them.

Sergeant Jamison, Squad Leader for 1st Squad, ordered his Marines to advance. One fire team pressed forward in formation toward incoming fire from the tall, straw grass. The second team flanked the enemy on its most exposed side while the third fire team took up a position providing security and cover fire.

Radios echoed with Lieutenant Fontana's voice. He was sprinting from the command post to the front gate.

As the human massacre unfolded not too far from where he

stood, Alex knew he couldn't commit 2nd Squad's fire teams to any counterattack—not yet. Several hundred panic-stricken natives either stood frozen in fear or ran between him and the high grass while gunfire mauled them down.

For all intents and purposes, the Marines' starting point of attack was behind them at the compound security gate. Alex's fire teams needed to advance to an assault position and pursue the enemy—now. Contain, isolate, destroy, and secure the area.

Looking directly east as the sun rose in the sky made it difficult for Marines to see the hidden enemy and their weapons. They were silhouetted, almost hidden by the sun rising behind them. That was 1st Squad's sector. Alex was still concerned for their safety.

First Squad's fire teams were already engaged in returning fire. Shouting loud enough for his Marines to hear him, Sergeant Jamison called out for any preliminary info on hostile fire from the first Marine to see the enemy: direction, description, and range. Suddenly, the enemy gunfire went silent. The scene became spine-chilling, with only the sounds from terrified natives screaming and crying.

Twenty-five meters from Jamison's position, Alex took a knee alongside his Marines from first fire team. His thumb rested on the safety of his M4, ready to click it to fire mode. His index finger was primed to move to the trigger the moment enemy gunfire resumed. Shifting his eyes left then right, Alex felt relieved to see that none of his men had been wounded.

His eyes pivoted toward the other area of tall, dense grass from seven to eleven o'clock, the same location he told Christian Aquino had "bad shit hiding there."

AK-47 automatic fire resumed from the tall weeds to his right where 1st Squad had moved on the enemy's position. More terrified refugees were mowed down where they stood. Others ran for cover, ran for their lives.

Ethan Crowell, team leader for 2nd Squad, second fire team, advanced with his M4 raised and aimed to fire. Alex placed his face close to Ethan's and pointed at the adjacent tall, thick grass area to their left. "Eyes on that. The next attack will—"

"Agh!" Eddie Cabrera, the Assistant Automatic Rifleman from Ethan's team yelled out and dropped to his knees. A bullet struck his Kevlar jacket near the back of his left arm at the shoulder. Two inches to the left and the AK-47 round would have torn through Eddie's lung.

Ethan rushed over to check on the wounded Marine.

"Dammit," Cabrera cried out, flat on his back, his face contorted in pain.

Ethan rolled the wounded Marine over on his stomach and checked the area where the bullet struck. He tucked his fingers under the flak jacket and felt a lump the size of an egg. "Hit your flak, missed you by a couple of inches. You're one lucky—"

Gunfire suddenly erupted at the eleven o'clock position from what appeared to be the most distant of the three abandoned single-story warehouses. Ethan, Billy, and Anthony, along with Alex, opened up with a salvo of return fire at the enemy's newest position while 2nd Squad's other teams moved up to join first fire team.

Alex ordered his three fire teams to set up in a Squad Wedge Formation: first fire team advanced straight ahead, second covered the left flank, third covered the right flank. "Move out!"

On point for 2nd Squad, first fire team, Billy Whittington moved quickly and stayed low, spraying fire from his M4 in bursts from left to right across the one-meter-wide narrow alleyway between the warehouses. Ethan Crowell was behind him, followed by Anthony Camacho carrying an M27 Infantry Automatic Rifle.

The Marines advanced like football running backs taking handoffs and cutting past the line of scrimmage. They were stepping over and around dead and wounded natives spread motionless on the ground instead of offensive and defensive linemen. Except this was no game.

Alex took the rear position. His eyes scanned in a rapid yet focused 180-degree sweep. The earlier shooters who showed themselves had dropped below into the tall weeds and out of sight. He looked for them to reappear with AK-47s or a Soviet RPK or even a Rocket Propelled Grenade launcher rising above the tops of the weeds. Muzzle flashes or the smoke of hand-held weapons coming from the weeds. Anything.

Whittington was four steps away from reaching the closest warehouse when his right boot caught on something. All four Marines stopped at the sound of the trip wire's click, followed by a violent explosion.

Alex's head was turned away, watching their six when the planted Improvised Explosive Device detonated. The IED's blast lifted him off the ground and tossed him almost one meter, landing on his back. His M4 was knocked loose from his grip and fell away.

Stunned and raising himself up on his forearms, the twenty-year-old squad leader looked around in a daze. He couldn't make out where his Marines were through the dust and debris. His head hurt and his ears rang. The blast's wind had sent his sunglasses and helmet flying off his face and head.

Feeling a sudden warm and burning sensation on the right side of his neck, he ran his fingers across the area to see them smeared with blood. A piece of shrapnel had torn a gash across that area of his neck. A bloody trail ran down the skin behind his ear, soaking the top of his flak jacket and turning the collar of the Marine Corps issued green short-sleeved T-shirt he wore underneath a dark crimson.

Enemy fire kept coming at them, either from the backs of the vacant warehouses or the grassy area behind them. He couldn't confirm if it was coming from one or both areas. RUF rebels weren't showing themselves or their weapons.

"Whittington, Crowell, Camacho!" Alex shouted. He heard moans but didn't recognize the voice that called out.

RUF rebel gunfire continued in short bursts. His head throbbing like a jackhammer, Alex put on his helmet and crawled forward to find his men in the settling dust. He didn't have to go far. Two were wounded, lying close to each other on the ground of dried red clay.

Alex reached Billy first. The Marine lay motionless except for his head slowly rolling back and forth. "Whittington, can you hear me?"

The gravely injured lance corporal groaned some inaudible words.

Alex's hands and eyes quickly surveyed Billy's body. His head, face, and neck showed no visible injuries. But his lower left arm was grotesquely bent from multiple compound fractures. Part of one finger on his left hand was gone.

Alex kept triaging Billy's condition when a wave of nausea swept over him as his eyes traveled further down the wounded Marine's torso. The upper left leg was badly mangled. Alex shuddered to see deep, widespread tissue wounds and an exposed bone-shattered femur. Blood flowed everywhere. His thigh had absorbed the brunt of the blast, but his lower leg hardly fared any better. Almost a third of the young Marine's upper leg was partly severed and hung loosely, almost lifeless.

Alex ducked when more AK-47 rounds flew by inches from his head and tore into the rusted metal siding of the warehouse several feet to his right. He had to treat Billy fast, get him back inside the compound and then out to the USS *Wasp*'s hospital or the Marine would bleed out. "Hold on. I'm getting you the hell out of here."

Next, Alex crab-walked over to check on Ethan lying nearby, unmoving, his helmet laying ten feet away from him on the ground.

"Crowell, it's Kramer, where are you hit? Where's it hurt?" he asked.

From the wounded Marine came an unsettling silence. Then Ethan's mouth opened slightly, and one hand waved the air in front of his face. "I can't see," he said, his voice feeble.

Crowell had partly been shielded from the worst of the blast by standing behind Whittington . Blood wasn't visible anywhere on his combat gear or exposed skin. But the lance corporal definitely sustained serious wounds. Alex's guessed concussion, maybe traumatic brain injury. Rebel gunfire continued whizzing around them.

"I'm okay, brother," Anthony called out.

"Hold your position, Camacho. And keep your ass down."

Alex felt something moist on his upper lip. His fingers touched his nostrils. They were wet with blood running out of his nose. He could have been concussed from the IED blast. But he didn't have time for that now. Billy and Ethan had to be moved out of the field of fire ASAP.

"I'm taking you and Whittington to a safer place," Alex told Ethan. "Stay here, I'm coming back for you."

On his knees between the two wounded Marines, Alex lifted his head and looked around. In front of him was a door leading into the nearest warehouse. He had to get Billy and Ethan inside that building and triage them until it was safe to carry both wounded Marines back inside the compound for medical evacuation. Billy had to be MEDEVAC'd first.

Alex's 2nd and 3rd fire teams were already committed, flanking both left and right of the new enemy fire location. They couldn't help move Ethan and Billy. That left him and Anthony Camacho.

The tap on his arm made Alex spin around and aim the muzzle from his M4 toward what was his platoon commander's face.

"Shit, sir, I almost shot you."

"Report your casualties."

"Sir, Whittington's thigh is one-third blown open and one arm's busted up bad. Crowell's concussed from the blast." He pointed his chin toward the nearest empty one-story warehouse. "Sir, we need to get them inside until we can put down enemy fire. Then get Whittington out to the *Wasp* to save his leg—hell, save *him*—or else he'll die here. Get Crowell out, too."

"Copy that." Lieutenant Fontana pointed at Alex's face. "You're bleeding from your nose."

"I'm okay, sir."

Except he wasn't okay. But they were in a firefight for their lives and he wasn't letting up. Not with two members from his fire teams down and badly wounded.

"I'll kick in the door, you back me up, then we'll carry Whittington and Crowell inside," Lieutenant Fontana told him.

"Roger that, sir."

At that moment, the enemy's fire went silent again. The platoon commander and his squad leader knew it would be short-lived and that the RUF rebels would attack again.

With Alex kneeling and his M4 aimed at the warehouse door, Lieutenant Fontana raised his boot and struck the door handle with force. The instant his kick tore away the metal frame door from its jamb, he pivoted his body away from the open doorway and a possible second IED exploding. No second trip wire or blast followed.

His own M4 raised and aimed, the platoon commander stood ready at the doorway. Alex fell in behind him, the number two man of a short-handed fire team. They had to clear the building quickly, then get Billy inside and triage him as best they could.

Outside and watching over Billy and Ethan, Anthony Camacho stayed low to the ground. "Hurry up, guys."

Standing inside the doorway and looking past his platoon commander, Alex surveyed the scene in front of them. Two doorways on their right, and the rest of the narrow one-story building was all open space to their left. Just a few metal folding chairs and several empty white Styrofoam food cartons scattered on the concrete floor.

"Clear right, hold left," Alex called out to his lieutenant. He lifted his knee and lightly bumped Lieutenant Fontana on the back of the officer's thigh. The platoon commander responded instantly to the signal and turned to his right. He stepped into a small room with his arms and M4 raised and swept the area. "Clear," reported Fontana.

Now back in the hallway, the lieutenant took his place directly behind Alex. He bumped Alex to move ahead and clear the second and final room. They finished clearing the building in twenty-five seconds.

Things were still quiet outside. Too quiet. Alex hated the silence. He noticed the strip of single-panel window panes running the entire length of the left side of the warehouse. The windows faced the high grassy area to the northwest. RUF rebels could make out their images through the glass. The Marines were dangerously exposed.

With the warehouse cleared, Alex and Lieutenant Fontana rushed back outside. Alex grabbed a barely conscious Billy Whittington under both shoulders and carried him inside to temporary cover. Fontana lifted and held the critically wounded Marine's nearly severed leg. Together they quickly moved the rifleman through the doorway and inside, where they carefully laid him down on the concrete floor.

"I'm going for Crowell," Lieutenant Fontana called out.

"Copy that, sir."

Anthony was still outside, guarding Ethan.

Alex kneeled over Billy. It looked bad. The Marine's breathing was shallow and irregular. His eyes kept rolling back in his head. Blood still streamed from his deep, open thigh wound. Only the top section of Billy's camo trousers offered any temporary protection to exposed tissue, bone, and nerves open at the middle section of his upper left leg.

Alex went to work straightway in treating Billy. He opened the badly wounded Marine's first-aid kit and withdrew the Combat Applied Tourniquet (CAT). His fingers skillfully secured the tourniquet between the partially severed limb section and where Billy's leg attached to the pelvis, with three inches of still-intact leg above and below.

Alex withdrew the package of combat gauze from Billy's first-aid kit. With little wasted motion, he placed his index finger into two folds of the gauze, then pressed the hemostatic fabric down into the thigh's very large, open soft tissue wound. He continued packing the sections of treated fabric into the area until it reached the end of the bandage.

Next with the roll of Emergency Trauma Dressing, he wrapped the ETD around the wound site, tightly compressing the combat gauze. The following three to five minutes were critical if there was any chance of saving the wounded lance corporal's leg, let alone survive the IED blast.

"Stay with me, Whittington," muttered Alex, his face, neck, and arms covered with sweat-coated dust and dirt. Seconds counted now.

Thinking fast about what else he could do to help Billy, Alex removed his flak jacket, folded it like a thick pillow, and placed it under the Marine's severely injured leg. Any method to further reduce blood flowing out of the limb and body was worth trying.

Alex returned his attention to his sector's field of battle. He ordered second and third fire teams to clear the remaining two abandoned buildings, then report back.

"Whittington, open your eyes," Alex told the gravely wounded Marine while waiting to receive reports from second and third fire teams. "Look at me—"

Loud automatic gunfire suddenly exploded from the tall grass area beyond the three warehouses. Alex dropped to the concrete floor, carefully laying his body over Billy to protect him. Bullets whizzed across the row of glass windows above him. Rounds tore into the cinder walls inside, sending pieces of concrete and glass flying everywhere like tiny missiles. A glass shard ripped across the thin layer of skin above Alex's wrist. Crimson liquid dripped out of the laceration and flowed down his forearm.

Alex heard a stream of four-letter words shouted from outside the building, and recognized Lieutenant Fontana's voice.

"I'll be back," Alex said to Billy, ignoring his new wound and picking up his M4. Without his flak jacket, he was totally un-protected—against incoming AK-47 rifle fire, a Russian RPK machine gun, a Rocket Propelled Grenade—against anything.

Alex crawled on all fours toward the doorway, keeping his head below the windows. Once outside, he spotted his platoon commander lying on the ground some two meters away, writhing in pain. An arc of blood spewed from his right thigh like an outdoor fountain spewing red water.

A bullet had ripped into part of Lieutenant Fontana's femoral artery. Alex calculated the wounded officer's odds. His platoon commander's life expectancy could be as short as Billy's. Fontana could bleed to death if they didn't transport him back to the *Wasp* soon. He crawled as fast as he could to reach his wounded officer.

Lieutenant Fontana's hands attempted to open his first-aid kit and find the CAT. But lightheadedness from increased blood loss was setting in. The officer's fingers fumbled trying to open the kit.

Alex reached his lieutenant. The glassy-eyed stare showing in Lieutenant Fontana's eyes told him the platoon commander wasn't in any condition to administer self-aid. His wound appeared to be life-threatening. But Alex considered Fontana lucky. He saw three inches of undamaged limb between the tourniquet and the bullet's entry wound, and four inches above it to the lieutenant's hip. Enough space to stem bleeding as much and as quickly as possible until Navy surgeons could treat him.

Alex reacted instantly again, now treating the lieutenant's leg wound exactly as he cared for Billy minutes earlier. He swiftly applied and secured the CAT two inches above the gunshot exit wound on the front side of the platoon commander's thigh. Next, Alex pressed layers of treated combat gauze fabric from the lieutenant's first-aid kit, using all of it to pack the bandage deeply into the open bullet hole. Finally, he wrapped ETD around the wound site to compress and hold the hemostatic gauze in place.

With dressings pressed against the entry and exit wound points, the next several minutes were critical to stem further femoral artery bleeding and prevent Lieutenant Fontana from bleeding out.

"Camacho, get Crowell inside," Alex called out. "I'll take L–T–." "Copy that," answered Anthony, carrying Ethan in his arms and laying him down on the floor next to Billy.

Second and third fire teams reported in: the other two buildings were cleared. No enemy personnel.

Alex looked down into his officer's face. "Hold on, sir."

Fontana tapped Alex's shoulder. He understood.

Exposing both of them but forced to act fast, Alex lifted Lieutenant Fontana onto his shoulders in a fireman's carry. Moving quickly in a stooped position, he carried his wounded platoon commander into the warehouse when an AK-47 rifle shot grazed his upper left arm at the midpoint, ripping into the soft tissue.

"Dammit!" he screamed out, suddenly losing the grip on his left hand that held on to Fontana's arm. The six-foot distance to the doorway looked more like sixty yards.

# CHAPTER 7

**USS *John Warner*, Control Room**
**South Atlantic Ocean**
**April 23, 2019 at 1404**

Lieutenant Tara Marcellus marveled how Virginia class submarines were designed with more space for crew members
grouped together under the watchful eyes of the Officer of the
Deck; the OOD. The Sonar and Fire Control divisions were part
of the same space, not separate. Seated at a console, a lieutenant
junior grade operated a joystick to control the sub's photonics
masts. No periscopes penetrated the hull anymore.

On the port side of the dimly-lit, futuristic Control Room
filled with multicolored PC consoles, Tara stood watch as Contact
Manager. In front of her, Chief Petty Officer and Sonar Supervisor
Greg Drysdale, the third generation from a family of Navy chiefs
all in the silent service, stood watch over four sonar techs: two
Broadband Operators and two Towed-Array Operators. Their
eyes and ears monitored PC displays and headsets for all contacts
signaling either deep-sea life forms or submerged vessels of
unknown origin. The four sonar techs were not much older than
high-school-aged boys. But they were all well-trained sailors, and
committed to their jobs.

"Thanks for stepping in for Andrew."

Tara turned and saw LTJG Warren Mumma, the Assistant
Weapons Officer standing next to her. Warren and Tara joined the
crew at the same time as new DIVOs.

"How's he doing?" Tara inquired about the Tactical Systems Officer who'd been taken ill.

"Doc said he's stable," said Warren, "If his appendix bursts, there's medical services aboard the USS *Wasp* in our escort group." The crew had been informed the *Wasp* had two emergency operating rooms and could handle up to six hundred service members at a time requiring medical attention.

"XO and I will be in conference in the wardroom for fifteen minutes," Commander Whikehart announced in Control and turned to Lieutenant Donald Schrager. "It's your show, NAV."

"Aye, sir," replied Lieutenant Schrager, the Navigation Officer also serving as OOD and standing by the Ship Control Panel. He stood at an average height with coal black hair, fleshy cheeks, a slight paunch above his uniform belt, and was Naval Academy Class of '10. Tara and Schrager had made small talk on a few occasions since she joined the crew. Nothing serious. Their conversations leaned toward their recollections of being at Annapolis and nothing else.

Tara was still figuring Schrager out. Too often his expressions were fixed in a condescending smirk. Some officers called him arrogant behind his back. The man could be sloppy with his words and opinions, which didn't go unnoticed by officers and sailors. He was ambitious too, which drew occasional scorn from other officers. Schrager boasted openly of wearing an O-6's shoulder boards one day, the military services pay grade of a Navy captain and one step below a one-star rear admiral. Tara didn't object to any officer wanting to advance. She didn't have much patience with vain opportunists.

"NAV, make preparations to proceed to periscope depth at the top of the hour," Commander Whikehart ordered Lieutenant Schrager on his way out of Control with XO in tow. "I want to clear the broadcast a little early."

"Make preparation to proceed to periscope depth at the top of the hour. Aye, sir."

Tara watched Schrager on the other side of Control, talking with COMMO, the Communications Officer, and jabbing a finger toward him. *What's that all about?* she wondered of Schrager's intimidating hand gesture.

She heard Petty Officer Third Class Ruiz, one of the sonar techs, call out, "Contact Manager, gained new possible submerged towed array contact bearing one-five-zero or two-one-zero, designate Sierra 14." Ruiz and the other sonar techs promptly dissected through slices of high and low frequency signals to classify the Sierra contact.

Chief Drysdale stood behind Ruiz, focused on his sailors. The thirty-six-year-old salty sailor leaned over Ruiz's shoulder and stared with a second set of submarine-experienced eyes.

The atmosphere in Control was calm. But the crew inside was alert to the towed array narrow-band detection. Officers remembered the captain's mission brief: be alert to unidentified submerged contacts. Meanwhile, *John Warner* maintained its present course.

Ninety more seconds passed in the quiet room until the Sonar Supervisor announced updated data. "Contact Manager, Sierra 14 has been classified as a Russian Yasen-class attack submarine, bearing ambiguity resolved by correlation to hull-mounted sensor to the port side, bearing one-five-five," said Chief Drysdale.

"Attention team, redesignate Sierra 14 and Sierra 15," Tara called out in Control, "We have a contact of interest."

Chief Drysdale swiveled his head in the TSO's direction. "Ma'am, we have identified a Russian Yasen-class submarine. I believe it bears one-five-five, but I recommend we maneuver to verify. We also need to verify his range."

"Very well, chief. Give me bearing drift when you have it."

"Aye, ma'am."

Tara knew it was the time to think about what her next course recommendation should be. Her self-confidence as an officer was improving. But there were still moments when she hesitated, and she didn't like being that way. Indecision signaled weakness in leadership. She wasn't some immature DIVO who didn't know better.

"Pilot, right 10 degrees rudder, steady on course zero-seven-zero," came the order from the OOD.

Hearing Schrager's directive, Tara gritted her teeth behind pursed lips. *He's called to come right to 070, 10 degrees rudder. But not left? NAV ought to know coming left would be quicker. Then he steadies up to 180. He's changing his mind?* She also knew OODs rarely gave specific rudder orders on Virginia Class submarines. They'd simply say, "Pilot, all ahead standard, steady course one-eight-zero," letting the boat's automatic control algorithm determine the rudder angle. Not Schrager.

And if that wasn't enough for Tara to want to roll her eyes back in her head, his calling for 10 degrees was too small a turn—more like puny—with a Russian submarine stalking *John Warner*. Given the urgent situation at hand, he should have at least called for 15 or 20 degrees.

All crew members in Control heard Lieutenant Schrager's orders right after the towed-array operator's announcement of a hostile submarine present in the area. If they were paying attention, they also noticed the OOD remained stone-faced, not acknowledging the sonar supervisor's detection of a Russian sub in the immediate area. Schrager's next order was, "Pilot, all ahead standard on a course of one-eight-zero," followed by placing one of the contract traces within 30 degrees of the Russian boat's bow.

Tara's eyes darted back and forth to other officers and sailors in Control to follow their facial reactions. *We're speeding up?*

*That's it? I don't believe this. We'll lose the trace into end-fire with that maneuver. What the hell's he doing?*

Tara's warfare instincts kicked in. *John Warner* needed to maneuver and verify the contact's range so it could finish its initial Detection Leg Action for a submerged contact. Then, the submarine should come up behind the Russian, or at least track him. But Schrager's order directed the Virginia class sub to lay idle and exposed—wrong on all counts for offensive countermeasures.

Schrager crossed the room and stood alongside Tara—too close for her comfort.

"Any sign of counter detection?"

Tara braced herself. *Are you asking me or Chief Drysdale or Ruiz, the TA operator?* She detected a nasty edge to the OOD's words. "No indication the Russian has detected or is following us, sir," Tara answered flatly.

"Sonar should have picked up the Russian's position farther out than he is now, and sooner," Schrager's tone echoed with a sharp rebuke.

Tara wasn't buying it. Schrager was wrong. Her sailors weren't sleeping on the job. Out of the corner of her eye, she noticed all four sonar techs shift slightly in their seats, reacting to Schrager's stern tone. Officers and sailors inside Control heard it too and turned toward the commotion. "Your operators need to be more alert, Mister Drysdale."

Now he was going after the sonar supervisor. *This is bullshit,* Tara grumbled silently. *We're not on a wartime footing, and Schrager's out of line. Besides, Drysdale knows more about submarine warfighting operations in his sleep than Schrager would if someone had slipped him the answers to the test.*

She took a deep breath, unsure whether to speak or stay silent while conditions in Control grew more intense.

Lieutenant Tara Marcellus was certain of two things: First, she'd been a keen student of submarine warfare since joining the crew. She had pressed ENG and WEPS to pass along to her everything they'd learned as sub drivers. Schrager's order didn't stand up to the rules of engagement. Second, she was beside herself how he'd made her sailors convenient scapegoats for his irresponsible decision. They'd done their jobs. He had not.

The OOD's next words aimed at Drysdale caught everyone's attention—for the second time in forty-five seconds. "Sonar Supervisor, find a relief for this sonarman," Schrager demanded, once again jabbing an index finger but this time in Ruiz's direction.

Tara still couldn't believe what she was witnessing. Who was Schrager kidding? He ignored her initial warning about the Yasen-class sub and kept driving the boat. Now he accused one of her sailors of dereliction of duty.

"Petty Officer Ruiz has fully performed his duties, sir. I will take responsibility for any failure to track data quickly enough," Drysdale promptly yet properly answered a self-righteous Lieutenant Schrager.

Tara tasted bile in her throat upon hearing Chief Drysdale stand up to NAV. She was tempted to call Schrager out too. Yet, questioning the holier-than-thou OOD in front of enlisted personnel could be a dangerous miscalculation. Knowing Schrager's transparent protect-thyself attitude, CO and XO would eventually learn what happened. The fact was they'd insist on the truth. That was their job.

*Be careful,* Tara cautioned herself. *If you're going to contest Schrager's action against your sailors, make damn sure it's worth it. Once you speak up, you've crossed what Marines call your line of departure. Then there's no turning back.*

But that wasn't good enough and she knew it. Schrager's order for Ruiz to be relieved of duty caused her to grit her teeth so hard her jaw ached. The self-righteous jackass officer wanted to blame someone, anyone, except himself.

The lieutenant junior grade felt a wave of fury wash over her. She was pissed at herself for choosing to sit still, not speak, not challenge Schrager. Instead, Drysdale had answered and he shouldn't be taking heat here.

Tara remembered her Plebe Summer and attending Honor Concept instruction at the Academy: *Midshipmen are persons of integrity. We stand for that which is right. We tell the truth and ensure that the full truth is known. We do not lie.*

Wasn't it her duty as an officer to defend her sailors when they were right? Schrager was lying. Did silence make her an accessory to his lies? Was she following the path of least resistance? *Where's my integrity and my sense of duty now?*

"Ruiz, what's the Russian's latest bearing?"

Tara swung around quickly toward the sound of Commander Whikehart's question directed at the Passive Narrowband (PNB) Operator, whose job was to search for acoustic signatures beneath the sea.

Schrager's eyes grew wide when he saw CO step into Control along with XO.

"Sir, last bearing for Master 14 is one-six-five," answered Petty Officer Ruiz.

"Have you picked up any signs of counter detection?"

"No sir, the Russian's just dog paddling out there, from what I can tell," said Ruiz.

"NAV, what was your initial directive after Sonar identified the contact as a Russian sub?" Commander Whikehart wanted the facts, and quickly.

Now Schrager was on the spot. "Sir, I observed Contact Manager and Sonar Supervisor hesitate. That's when I ordered the pilot to remain steady on course zero-seven-zero, all ahead standard."

Hesitate? Tara was beside herself hearing the OOD's bold-faced lie. Chief Drysdale had to be thinking the same thing.

"Explain what you mean by 'hesitate,' Lieutenant Schrager," the skipper said in a suspicious tone.

"Sir, their body language gave me the impression that they were unsure of the contact." Schrager looked straight at the CO and purposely avoided eye contact with Tara and Chief Drysdale. "At that moment I chose to take action to analyze the data and make a decision how to respond to the contact."

*More bullshit from him,* Tara thought. She watched for the CO's reaction for any sign of disbelief with the OOD's order to maintain course at all ahead standard. But Commander Whikehart wasn't letting on. Not yet. "At that moment, was there any consideration to maneuver our position to verify the contact's range?"

Schrager showed his best smug expression. "Sir, I could tell immediately the contact was not very close—"

"How could you tell?" interrupted Commander Whikehart.

"It was based on my interpretation of the sonar data. Also, I determined Sonar should have picked up the Russian sub's position farther out than Contact Manager's announcement for a 'contact of interest'."

Still no reaction from the CO. Tara wanted to jump in but held her tongue.

"It looked like we had that data stream for a few minutes," NAV informed the skipper. "That's when I decided the proper course of action was to maneuver to a better position to track the Russian. We already had a decent solution on him." He cleared his throat loud enough for everyone in Control to hear it, then finished: "My next move was to watch the Russian sub, ready to order counter measures when you and XO reentered Control, sir."

"If I may, Captain—" Chief Drysdale surprised everyone with his interruption.

"Go ahead, Chief."

"Sir, pardon me. I request permission to present a different version of the events that occurred once Sonar identified the Russian submarine."

The atmosphere in Control was totally silent after the Sonar Supervisor finished. DIVO watch standers for Engineering and Communications, along with their sailors in the dimly lit confined area, were riveted to the rising tensions on the other side of area.

"Chief, I will expect your version of the events. Write it up and give it to COB for his review first."

"Yes, sir," replied Drysdale.

"Thank you, Chief."

Commander Whikehart exchanged looks with the officers and sailors involved in the incident. "Very well," he said and turned to Tara. "Lieutenant Marcellus, I want to know the instant that Russian sub so much as blinks."

"Aye, sir."

"And Lieutenant Schrager, I'll expect your report by 0800 tomorrow."

"Yes, sir."

Tara knew the CO's sudden presence and precise words exchanged in the past three minutes flustered Schrager. No doubt the sonar techs and Chief Drysdale also caught it.

"Your report too," the captain looked at Tara. "I want to know everything that happened."

"Yes, sir."

The CO motioned with one hand at the two officers, annoyance etched on his face. "Carry on."

Tara and Schrager turned to leave when the CO called out, "Lieutenant Schrager, stay." NAV stopped. "Chief Drysdale's served under my command for several tours," the CO said in slow, measured words. "COB's always had the highest confidence in the chief's judgment." He waited for some response but Schrager stood there stone-faced. "This will be the first time an officer or senior enlisted has suggested the chief's abilities were less than reliable. You should think about that from now on. That is all."

Tara returned to her duty station, annoyed yet composed. Words whispered from behind startled her: "You can't cut it in this man's Navy."

She spun around and saw arrogance in Schrager's eyes.

"With all due respect, it's not just a man's Navy anymore," she answered, her eyes tightened in open contempt. "And you're not much of a man, anyway. Sir."

# CHAPTER 8

**Northern Province Sierra Leone, West Africa**
**April 23, 2019 at 0925**

A river of blood ran down Alex's bare upper arm, a section of soft tissue blown away. He gritted his teeth in pain and shouted toward the warehouse, "Camacho, I need you out here now to get L—T—inside."

Anthony appeared immediately. Together they lifted up Lieutenant Fontana enough to half drag, half carry their platoon commander into the building.

Alex reached for the end of his T-shirt and pulled it up to wipe sweat from his eyes. He pointed at Anthony's flak jacket. "Roll that up and shove it under the lieutenant's ass. Keep his leg up."

Once they were inside and their wounded platoon commander was less an exposed target to gunfire, Alex opened and closed his fingers, testing the degree of his wounded arm. Intense pain but no sign of any nerve damage—so far. He retained more strength in his hand and finger control than expected.

He tore open the Velcro cover of his first-aid kit and withdrew the combat tourniquet. With the tourniquet in place and the band tightened above the wound site, he twisted the rod until bleeding appeared to stop and secured the rod to the band. Good enough for now.

Pain was written across Lieutenant Fontana's face and his glassy eyes. He seemed aware of his surroundings. The platoon commander turned his head and saw Lance Corporals Billy Whittington and Ethan Crowell lying nearby. Alex was leaning over Billy, trying to keep him awake so he wouldn't slip into unconsciousness.

"What's happening out there?" Fontana called out.

"Still under attack, sir," Alex reported without looking in the platoon commander's direction. At the same moment, he wrapped a trauma dressing around his upper arm, pressing combat gauze against the bullet wound. "Lots of casualties on the road coming in. It's bad out there. Can't see the conditions behind us in the NEO compound."

"You've been shot?"

Alex spun his head around. Lieutenant Fontana squinted at him.

"Missed the bone but took a hunk of flesh," he shouted, intent on fastening the trauma dressing to stay in place.

The lieutenant's condition was worsening and his decision-making abilities were diminished. Alex quickly thought he might need to step in and unofficially lead the platoon's operations. Someone had to protect his fire teams, and their wounded platoon commander might be unable to. *Let me do it.*

Seeing blood begin to seep through the trauma dressing on his arm, Alex unclipped the tourniquet rod and turned it one more time. His body trembled from the tourniquet's pressure against his arm. He bit down hard on his lower lip.

"Sir, we need to call in air support," Alex announced through short but calm breaths. "Let the Cobras and Hueys lay down fire on the enemy positions."

A still-weakened platoon commander nodded in agreement.

Alex watched Fontana's face suddenly twist into a grimace. The first lieutenant's whole frame shook, the pain from his torn femoral artery coursing through his entire body like a burst of electrical current.

Seconds later his pain had passed and Lieutenant Fontana was momentarily alert again. He took the radio handset Alex handed to him and called for the JTAC. "Bravo One Actual to Bulldog 1-4, we are taking enemy fire from two locations northwest of the fence line and front gate. Bravo 1-2, squad leader for 2nd Squad is your Forward Observer for CAS."

Alex's premonition where enemy fire could open up on his fire teams had been right, from two locations in his patrol sector. Refugees, Marines, ECOWAS peacekeepers, and UN workers were also under attack in 1st Squad's Area of Operations (AO) on the opposite side.

Cowboy-7, the FAC, was busy at the command post monitoring traffic on the terminal air direction net. When the shooting began, he radioed the ship and requested the skids move their posture from alert 30 to alert 5—five minutes to notification to launch, and ready to prosecute their attacks.

Two Cobras and two Hueys total had been ready to lift off and begin attacking the target areas in the northwest sector, following Alex's SITREP to Bulldog 1-4 twenty minutes earlier.

Once the first section of two gunships prosecuted their mission's initial round and then were either short of fuel—"bingo"—or radioed "mission complete" to the FAC, they'd switch with the second section of two gunships that were "holding" on the Landing Helicopter Deck (LHD) amphibious assault ship. After refueling, the first section would remain on the flight deck until the second section reported "mission complete" or "bingo." The two sections would, as Marine aviators often described it, "yo-yo" in that pattern until their mission was finished and ground commander's intent was met.

While pilots and crews awaited further orders, they received continuous situation updates from the FAC.

"Stand by, Bravo One," Bulldog 1-4 radioed back to Lieutenant Fontana.

Cobras and Hueys were on deck when the JTAC requested pilots and crews to launch. Pilots conducted their CAS "Check-In" with capabilities and ordnance the moment they were on-station in the holding area. Crews and aircraft were prepared to take off no fewer than five minutes from notification: 'no less than' or NLT 5.

Down on the ground, First Platoon's combat units, fleeing refugees, African peacekeepers, and UN workers were still under relentless attack from automatic gunfire. The pilots understood they were operating under "troops in contact" conditions.

"Corporal," a wounded Lieutenant Fontana called out. "You're Forward Observer for air support on the northwest sector now."

"Sir, we need to get you to the docs on the *Wasp* ASAP." Alex had been right. Fontana's tourniquet was, at best, a stopgap measure. It couldn't guarantee the wounded lieutenant would survive without surgery, and soon.

Alex called out to Anthony, standing post at the open doorway with his M27 in a ready-to-fire position: "Camacho, inform the QRF of our position and our wounded."

"Copy that."

Alex reached for his M4 and crab-walked toward the warehouse door, careful to remain below the windows or risk getting shot a second time.

"Where are you going?" Fontana called out as more rounds of gunfire passed through the shot-out windows. Both of them ducked while more concrete chips flew like tiny projectiles in every direction.

"Sir, I need to get my fire teams out of there before air strikes begin. Out of friendly fire." 2nd Squad's second and third fire teams had finished clearing the other two abandoned buildings and advanced a second time in Squad Vee Formation on the high grass area beyond the warehouses.

Fontana nodded. "Be quick. We need the helicopters laying down fire ASAP."

"Copy that, sir," he said and radioed to reach his other fire teams. "Bravo 1-2 to 2nd and 3rd fire teams, EXFIL now. Repeat, pull back. CAS is in-bound," he ordered. "Drop smoke—I repeat, drop smoke—on your way out for skids' eyes-on-targets."

Alex heard the squad leader for 1st Squad transmit a similar "exfiltrate" message to his fire teams in the northeast sector: "Pop smoke on your positions and EXFIL."

"Marine Corps birds are coming to rain hell down on you," Alex mumbled at the nearest location erupting with enemy fire.

# CHAPTER 9

**Northern Province Sierra Leone, West Africa**
**April 23, 2019 at 0931**

Alex leaned over Billy and shuddered at what he saw. The Marine's complexion moved a shade paler since he checked on him just a few short minutes earlier. Shallow respirations and a weak pulse were the only visible signs of life.

"Whittington, open your eyes, bro." There was no response. Alex pinched the Marine's chin. Still nothing. "This is bad," Alex told himself.

"Camacho, get in here!" Alex yelled as loud as he could. Anthony appeared in the doorway in a crouch to avoid being hit by gunfire.

Lieutenant Fontana, along with Billy and Ethan, were inside and protected for now. The three wounded Marines experienced increasing weakness from blood loss. They'd still have to wait on their EXFIL while the firefight raged on.

Inside the abandoned building, Alex straddled his body over Billy while Anthony did the same for Ethan. Wounded in four places, Alex waited for Bulldog 1-4 to conduct a CAS brief and correlation on the enemy target areas. The lieutenant, lying on his back, wounded and shaky from blood loss but still lucid, followed the engagement on his radio.

Alex radioed to the JTAC: "Bravo 1-2 to Bulldog 1-4, be advised, three abandoned buildings three-five meters northwest of front gate have been cleared by fire teams—repeat—buildings cleared, over."

"Copy that, Bravo 1-2," said the JTAC followed by Cowboy-7, the FAC, right after him.

The silence was suddenly interrupted by the unmistakable *whoop-whoop* sounds of helicopter rotor blades. A Cobra and a Huey flew by overhead, four hundred feet over Alex and the three wounded Marines inside the first abandoned warehouse with him. Alex could hear the copilot, also serving as the gunner, open up his weapon on the enemy's position below.

Abusive 2-1 and Abusive 2-2, the call signs of the two sections of Cobra and Huey skids, went to work prosecuting their targets. Opening up with 20mm guns from the Cobras, .50 caliber and mini-guns from the Hueys, and 2.75-inch rockets from both, the attack helicopters sprayed automatic fire down on the designated target locations. Their gunfire struck the wide, tall, and deep grass areas northwest and northeast of the front gate hiding RUF rebels.

His body still stretched across Billy for protection as he listened to comms over his radio, Alex followed as call sign "Abusive" crews attacked their targets:

"Left shoulder, right pull, send read back when able."

"Abusive 2-1 and 2-2 reads back left shoulder, right pull."

"Abusive 2-1 and 2-2, good read back, fire teams popping smoke. Call the smoke."

"Abusive 2-1 and 2-2 flight contact green and yellow smoke."

"Abusive 2-1, green smoke is your target. 2-2 yellow smoke is your target."

"Abusive 2-1 and 2-2 tally targets."

"Abusive 2-1 and flight, request immediate Time on Target."

"All players be advised: that mission is approved."

With green and yellow smoke clearly marking their target areas, the helicopter pilots descended their aircraft and launched the attack.

"Abusive 2-1: Abusive 2-2 pushing."

"Continue."

"Abusive 2-1 and 2-2 in heading 025."

"Abusive 2-1 and flight, cleared hot."

The air strikes concluded in approximately two minutes. With the whir of departing Cobras and Hueys flying away, there was an eerie silence outside. The sound of enemy AK-47s and a solo Soviet RPK were permanently quieted, their shooters dead.

Alex crawled outside into brilliant sunlight. His wounded arm hurt something fierce. He lifted his head and saw the lingering green and yellow smoke that had marked the target areas for the air strikes.

He'd know more after 2nd squad's second fire team went back out to check on the northwest high-grass area and report in to him—after he advised Bulldog 1-4, and Cowboy-7 passed a Battle Damage Assessment to the aircraft.

Lance Corporal Billy Whittington would probably lose some or all of his leg. The degree of damage to Ethan Crowell's brain from the IED blast was unknown yet definitely serious. Lieutenant Fontana needed immediate attention too, but he could survive and recover. The African refugees outside were defenseless, wounded, and murdered. Victims of a horrid slaughter.

The bleeding from his own gunshot wound appeared controlled. The tourniquet was doing its job.

Lieutenant Fontana raised himself up on his elbows and watched as Alex kneeled next to an unresponsive Billy. They looked at each other and knew it was bad.

Alex went to the doorway. The smell of cordite from gunfire filled his nostrils. He estimated one hundred, maybe 150 victims lay motionless on the ground. Contorted bodies on top of each other. He imagined the terror that filled their minds when the shooting started. Irony with tragedy. Hundreds of refugees were on the run escaping genocide. They traveled miles to reach a place offering them safety, only to discover death was already waiting for them when they arrived.

"Bravo 1-2 to Bravo 6, over," Alex called in to the command post.

"Go ahead, Bravo 1-2."

"Sir, I have three badly wounded Marines," Alex said. "Request assistance ASAP to get them to the aviation landing zone for MEDEVAC to the *Wasp*," and reported his location.

"Assistance coming to you now at the front gate," said Bravo Company's CO. "Are there other friendly casualties, Bravo 1-2? Do you require additional MEDEVAC?"

"Do we have more wounded?" Alex shouted to the rest of the Marines from his squad. No casualties out of second and third fire teams.

"Negative, sir, no more friendly casualties."

Alex pointed to the high grass to his left. "Is the target area in your AO clear of enemy?"

Christian Aquino, the rifleman from Alex's second fire team, nodded. "Affirmative, the area is secure. All Tangos are down."

"Report your count on enemy killed."

"Eighteen, repeat one-eight counted," answered John Rawleigh, also with 2nd Squad's second fire team.

"Bravo 1-2 to Bravo 6," Alex radioed to the command post.

"Bravo 6, over."

"Bravo 6, Bravo 1-2 reports eighteen enemy dead, that's one-eight. Four Tangos wounded and captured."

"Copy that, Bravo 1-2."

Wayne Armbrister, second fire team's leader turned to Alex. "What are our orders, Corporal?"

Alex flexed the fingers from his wounded arm. They were stiffening and the wounded area on his upper arm throbbed with pain.

He ordered the Marines from second fire team to carry Billy, Lieutenant Fontana, and Ethan to the front gate. Litters were waiting to take the three Marines to a MEDEVAC helicopter en route to fly them to the *Wasp's* hospital unit. "Hurry up, go!"

Second fire team's Marines departed with Billy, and Alex lifted his flak jacket off the ground. He looked at the garment and remembered Eddie Cabrera. The Kevlar in Eddie's jacket had stopped a bullet from tearing through his internal organs. Alex's flak jacket wouldn't have blocked the round that tore a wedge of flesh out of his upper arm a few minutes ago. Eddie was lucky. They both were.

A sudden lightheadedness landed on Alex. He stopped moving his feet, trying with difficulty to hold his balance. Marines from third fire team saw him wobble and moved in quickly to catch him before he dropped.

He motioned them away with one hand. "I'm okay."

He leaned back against the side of the warehouse and watched Marines depart to carry out his orders. Anthony Camacho walked up next to him.

"You think Whittington's going to make it?"

"Hard to say. His leg's really bad. He could lose it."

Alex closed his eyes, inhaled deeply and released the sound of exhaustion from his body. The squad leader slowly slid down the side of the building until he sat on the dirt ground with his knees drawn up.

The brief he had attended on "The Golden Hour in Trauma" during the MEU's last pre-deployment training flashed into his head. Navy Corpsmen and Marines in the field only had an hour or less to respond to a traumatic injury or medical emergency with prompt treatment that could prevent death. The instructor emphasized his words to make his point: "Each minute that passes without some treatment shortens the time you have to prevent death."

"What about L—T—?" Anthony asked his squad leader.

"We stopped him in time from bleeding out but he's not out of danger yet."

"*You* stopped him from bleeding out. If the lieutenant and Whittington and Crowell make it, it's because you saved them, Kramer." He wrapped his arm around Alex's shoulder and pulled him close.

Alex shrugged. "Don't know anything about it."

"I do, brother, and I guarantee you one thing—the three of them know it."

"Just doing my job."

Anthony noticed Alex's wound sites: all four of them. The tourniquet on his upper arm. The grazing gunshot that left a three-inch rip across his neck. The spot above his wrist where flying shrapnel tore into the skin. Dried blood under his nostrils from his concussion. His neck and hand wounds still oozed with blood.

"I'm going to drag your ass to the *Wasp* myself so the docs can treat you." He pointed at the tourniquet. "That arm's gotta be fixed now. And the dried blood out of your nose, that ain't looking good either."

Alex waved a dismissive hand and slowly rose to his feet. "Yeah, okay."

He aimed his chin at UN workers and locals on the scene, busy searching for refugees who survived the massacre. "Get our guys together. Those people need help finding anyone who might still be alive."

"Will do, Corporal."

Anthony reached down to retrieve his M4 when he heard the thud and turned toward its direction.

As he lay face down on the ground and unable to move, Alex thought he heard Camacho shout, "Corpsman over here, now!" It was the last thing Alex remembered before he passed out.

# CHAPTER 10

**Wardroom, USS *John Warner***
**April 23, 2019 at 1745**

Heading for dinner, Tara Marcellus spotted Donald Schrager exit the wardroom. Standing in the passageway, she waited to see which way he turned. If toward her, then passing by him was inevitable first, followed by an impulse to spit in his face.

But refusing to work with him would amount to insubordination, a dangerous move in military service. Both were naval officers aboard a US Navy nuclear submarine, and Schrager still outranked her. She held her breath, wanting to avoid an uncomfortable encounter. Schrager turned the other way and she sighed with momentary relief.

Reaching the wardroom door, she waited while the last of the oncoming watch standers and half the officers, finished with the evening meal's first serving, returned to their duty posts. The CO and the XO were finishing their coffee. They liked to stay for the entire meal hour and catch up with their officers. She eased herself into a chair and waited to be served.

"Want some company?"

Tara looked up. Mike Urbanick stood alongside her chair.

"Sure, sir."

Navy culinary specialists placed white ceramic plates with generous portions of meatloaf, garlic mashed potatoes, and steamed carrots down in front of the officers.

"Meatloaf smells good," said Urbanick. He lifted a ketchup

bottle, poured it on the warm meat, and dug in. Between bites, he noticed Tara push the food on her plate around with a fork, not eating. "What's going on?"

"Not much appetite."

"Let me guess," Mike said and put his fork down. "Schrager threw you and your sailors under the bus this afternoon over the Russian sub." The engineering officer spoke in a quiet tone so others in the wardroom wouldn't overhear him.

Tara shuddered at his comment. "You heard about that?"

"I heard he accused you and your sailors of taking too long to detect and identify the Russian boat—and the CO was standing right there," Mike said. "Submarines are small places. Word travels fast."

Tara grimaced. "Wonderful, the whole damn crew knows about it."

"Submarine life would be boring without some drama to break up the monotony," he said to put Tara at ease. "It's not the end of the world, Lieutenant. Shit happens."

"Pardon me sir, but the shit that happened was Schrager covering up his own mistakes," said Tara. She was taking a risk talking that way. Tara figured she could speak in confidence with her DH. They got along well. But calling out one DH to another could be messy. Not to mention Schrager was still senior to her.

Mike wiped his mouth with a white cloth napkin and pushed his plate away. "Explain what you mean."

Tara looked around the wardroom and didn't see any other officers eavesdropping. "Ruiz, the sonarman, did his job," she said in a subdued tone. "He notified Control the moment he caught the trace. Then he ID'd the Russian sub in two minutes. That's a sailor doing his job well—and it's not any reason to relieve him." Tara's pulse quickened just talking about the incident. Ruiz didn't deserve to be relieved of duty, and her sailors didn't need to be reprimanded. "What Scharger did was—" she suddenly stopped.

"Was what?"

Tara took a deep breath. "It was a cheap shot."

"You plan on doing something about it?"

The corners of Tara's mouth curved down in disgust. "I can't and I won't, sir. What's done is done."

ENG finished the last drops of coffee from the white ceramic mug, then turned his face slightly closer to Tara's and spoke quietly. "You'll work with some terrific people in the Navy, people of integrity. Sometimes you have to work with a jackass like Schrager."

"Do I have a choice?"

Urbanick crossed his thick forearms against his chest. "I wasn't in Control, so I don't make judgments after hearing submarine gossip. There will always be a few show horses who think they're smarter than the rest of us." He wrinkled his nose. "Makes you wonder what Schrager's classmates said about him at the Academy."

Dinner ended and officers rose to return to their stations with Mike and Tara in tow.

"Good officers learn to handle situations involving duty and character, like the one that happened to you," he told her. "Sailors see that and we earn their respect."

Tara was concerned. "You think my sailors believe I stood up for them?"

Mike Urbanick stopped in the passageway. "Yeah, I do. And make no mistake—your sailors saw right through Schrager's lies."

"I'm glad you see it the same way I do, sir," she said, relieved. "See you later."

Schrager's irresponsible orders, followed by his malicious

insult personally aimed at her, still occupied Tara's thoughts like an obscene video on auto-replay. Walking back to her cabin, the image of his self-righteous expression while he lied to the CO filled her with indignation.

# CHAPTER 11

USS *John Warner*
South Atlantic Ocean
April 23, 2019 at 1945

Massaging her temples, needing a break from writing her report to the skipper, Tara lay back on her bunk with her eyes closed. Schrager's malicious insult replayed in her head, and Tara recalled another time when she had taken care of herself.

Fall leaves had blanketed the Academy grounds. Darkness had already fallen when Tara left Nimitz Library to head back to Bancroft Hall. A male upperclassman from her company—she knew of him, little else—followed behind at an uncomfortable distance until his tall frame suddenly appeared in front of her and blocked her way. Then his hand tightened around her upper arm and yanked her toward him. Tara's reaction was swift. She used one hand to break free of his grip while her other hand slammed into his sternum, knocking him off balance. "You ever try that again and you'll be in handcuffs," she told him, her heart pounding against the Service Dress Blue uniform she wore.

Back in Bancroft Hall, Tara had sought out Kay, her upper-class mentor who was alone and studying in her room. Still shaken, Tara had spilled out the details. She'd brushed aside Kay's telling her to report what had happened to their company officer and the US Navy police. "Do it now. File charges against him," the sophomore-year mentor had sneered. "Watch him turn up dead someday for doing that to another woman."

Tara had considered the incident. She knew he wouldn't dare

approach her again, and never breathed a word of it to her parents. But she'd never forget what happened.

Tara never brought it up with Raymond Lydon either, not even while their friendship as classmates turned romantic and the Mid who assaulted her remained at the Academy. Ray would have found a time and place to "settle things" privately with her attacker.

Seeing his handsome image in her mind eased Tara's distressed mood. The last time they'd been together was US Naval Academy Class of 2016 graduation and commissioning three years ago. Ray's comforting presence in her mind, and her memories of that special day in both their lives, made it feel like yesterday.

The May skies had been cloudless and eggshell-blue. Thousands of family members and friends had filed into Navy Marine Corps Memorial Stadium for their midshipman's graduation and commissioning. Tara's Service White Dress cotton-blend uniform had absorbed more of the blazing sun's rays than it deflected them. A solitary bead of perspiration slid down the side of her face and ran along the curve of her chin. But she didn't raise a hand to wipe it away. Tara had loved the Academy but it was time to move on.

She glanced sideways at Ray Lydon, seated next to her in his Marine Corps Dress Blue uniform coat, and inhaled a self-satisfying deep breath.

"We earned every moment of this, you know it?" she said.

Ray leaned toward her. "Think you'd do it again?"

"In a heartbeat."

Tara stared straight ahead at the President of the United States and other senior military dignitaries seated on an elevated stage. She squinted against the bright sun and gently elbowed Ray. "Look around," she mused. "A tsunami wave could sweep through here and we'd lose the whole Navy and the Marine Corps leadership."

"Won't happen," he said, his brown eyes shining with amusement. "The Marines will save everyone. We're always pulling the Navy's pathetic ass out of trouble." He playfully jabbed her shoulder.

Ray was recruit-poster-handsome, a gentle man who, in Tara's opinion, would look better than fine whether outfitted in uniform or civilian clothes. Whenever something set her off—another Mid acting like a jackass at noon meal, a boring instructor, not rowing her best at daybreak crew practice—she'd go looking for him. Ray Lydon always made her feel good about herself.

Tara and Ray had been friends and classmates at the Academy. After the Brigade reformed the previous August and first class year started, their relationship had changed. The connection was deeper than sexual attraction. They were intimate. At Academy-sponsored events away from Annapolis and in uniform, Tara wanted to slip her arm inside of his but the regs said no. Yet neither was searching for anything permanent. Not yet. They were headed out on different career paths. For Tara, one thing was certain: part of her would always love and care about Ray Lydon, wherever he was stationed in the world.

"Listen, jarhead," she said, having fun teasing him. "You could have chosen submarines and been deployed on stealth missions under the sea." Tara always liked kidding with Ray. He gave as well as he got, and so did she.

"I'll be with warriors," he said. "You'll be with a bunch of computer nerds in tight quarters. Any one of 'em might hit on you."

"Nobody hits on me unless I say so," she said and a smile creased her cheeks. Yet beneath the smile, Tara's memory of the midshipman who had assaulted her outside Nimitz Library still upset her. But Ray Lydon was an honorable man and she trusted him. Her voice nearly a whisper, Tara said, "*You* never needed permission to hit on me."

"Think you'll come back here someday?" Ray asked her.

"Teaching ethics appeals to me," Tara replied. "And being a company officer," she mused, "I bet I'd like doing that, too. Mids need good officer role models to follow."

Her eyes scanned the spectator stands for her family among a sea of guests that filled the upper deck on the stadium's Blue Side. A sensation of unbridled pride swept over Tara. She was the first member of her extended family to join the military service *and* attend a US service academy.

With graduation and commissioning concluded, Tara looked into Ray's face and beamed a radiant smile. "Congratulations, *Lieutenant* Lydon," she said.

"You too, *Ensign* Marcellus."

Under an early afternoon's hot sun, the graduates tossed their midshipman covers high into the air, waiting to replace them with new ones worn by Navy and Marine Corps officers.

"Come here," Ray said, motioning to her. Tara moved into his open arms and hugged him.

"Who's pinning on your butter bars?" she asked with enthusiasm.

"My father's doing it," Ray told her.

"Same here. My dad's attaching my ensign boards," she said.

Tara's fist tapped the top of Ray's shoulder, the time-honored tradition of celebrating where a new officer's bars and shoulder boards would be placed. She waved a finger in his face. "You'll be great at TBS."

Ray Lydon's orders were to report to The Basic School at Marine Base Quantico in forty-five days. TBS was the Marine Corps' course where all new second lieutenants were taught to think and act as officers ready to lead Marines. *Every Marine a rifleman* was an eternal motto of the Corps. At TBS it was, *Every Marine officer a rifle platoon commander* aligned with timeless principles: Learn to lead Marines so they believe in you. Because they want to follow your orders. Because they trust you know what you are doing. Because an officer's solemn duty is *never* to betray their trust.

"Listen up, squid lady, here's rule number one." Ray mugged a wiseass grin and moved in closer to Tara. He peered into her face and rested his hands on her shoulders. "Launch your missiles at the enemy before they launch first."

The fingers from her right hand softly grazed his cheek, a gesture of affection she could never do when they were midshipmen and in public. "Is that an order?"

"It is," he answered and leaned in to kiss her softly. "Maybe I'll catch up with you later."

"Sounds good," she said and waved to him as he walked away. As Ray disappeared from view, Tara was struck with a sudden thought accompanied by a body-stiffening chill: He would be cut down in the prime of his life. She instantly shoved the horrid notion out of her mind and looked around for her family.

Tara rubbed her eyes, rose from her bunk, and worked for another twenty minutes on her report.

All crew members on duty in Control had seen and heard Lieutenant Schrager mess up. Tracking a Russian sub was a very big deal. But he had issued reckless orders, then looked for scapegoats—her sailors—to cover up his mistakes. She had failed to question Schrager's careless orders, and that pained her. Then she had failed to stand up for Chief Drysdale and her four sonar men. "This was as much on you as it was Schrager," she said aloud in the empty cabin. She'd chosen the path of least resistance, and the feeling made her sick to her stomach.

Who cared whether Schrager was a self-serving prima donna who didn't deserve to drive a nuclear submarine? She could have proposed a more aggressive counter-detection response. Officers and sailors in the room would have seen her respond to a potentially hostile force encounter and drive the boat. She'd had her chance but turned the other cheek. Tara pressed her eyes shut and swore never to stand down again from doing her duty—to do what is right—no matter the consequences.

The clock on her PC said 2120. The CO didn't mention a deadline for turning in her incident report. He probably wanted it in the next twelve hours. Tired and needing sleep, Tara placed her fingers back on the keyboard to finish up. "Tell the truth," she said quietly, "even when it hurts."

# CHAPTER 12

**The Pentagon**
**Arlington, VA**
**April 23, 2019 at 1549**

"Any questions or comments?" said the Army major general.

"No sir," the group of senior military officers answered in unison. They were seated around a table for the vice director's afternoon brief on current overseas US military operations.

"We're adjourned until 0845 tomorrow morning," announced VDJ3, Vice Director for Operations J-3 Directorate with the Joint Chiefs of Staff. "Thanks, everyone.

David Kramer, now US Navy Rear Admiral lower half, closed his notebook and headed for his office down in the Pentagon's National Military Command Center. Marine Colonel Anna Lombardi appeared alongside him, also on her way back to the NMCC.

"The MEU mission in West Africa," she said as they walked along the ground floor corridor. "Isn't that your son's unit, sir?"

"That's right, 24th MEU," answered David.

"I'll keep him and them in my thoughts, sir."

"Thanks, Anna."

Admiral Kramer had paid close attention to that update during the afternoon brief. His fingers tapped nervously on the table as descriptions of firefights between Marine infantry and rebel guerillas, followed by preliminary casualty reports about fleeing refugees *and* Marine ground forces, relayed over a live video feed.

In past months, David's mood more often drifted toward

disappointment with himself. He regretted that he hadn't told Alex how he'd been sorely mistaken. Military service as an enlisted member was always honorable, period. David had been wrong to let Alex's decision not to follow him to the Academy put uncomfortable distance between them.

"Alex deserves the chance to build his own life," Olivia had warned him several times. "You—a senior officer—more than anyone, should understand how wrong this is." But he had refused to heed her advice. Now he regretted it, and swore he'd apologize to his son . . . *if* Alex would believe his father meant it.

Departing the NMCC, Rear Admiral Kramer took the elevator up to the Pentagon's D-ring for a consult with the vice director. He had entered the corridor when his cell phone rang. Olivia was calling him.

"Hey, what's going on?" he said.

"I just got a call from Alex's command at Camp Lejeune," she answered, her voice tense.

David stopped. An unexpected call from command to a service member's loved ones usually meant something serious.

"Alex has been wounded," she told him. "He's in surgery now."

Her words made him stiffen. "Did they say anything about his wounds? His condition?"

"No."

David sucked in a quick breath. "I'll make some calls and get back to you in less than ten minutes with some information."

"Okay," Olivia said, subdued yet anxious.

David searched an internal online Department of Defense directory and dialed a number for 24th MEU headquarters at Camp Lejeune, North Carolina. He had to wait four long minutes before he had his answer.

"Thank you for tracking this down, Captain." David placed the landline receiver down and called Olivia on his cell phone. She answered before the first ring finished.

"Is Alex alive?"

"He's alive and going to be fine," he said with an upbeat tone to allay her fears. "The MEU mission was in West Africa. They were on an NEO mission evacuating refugees from local violence. Rebels in the area ambushed Alex's platoon and opened fire on them."

"Was he shot? How badly?" Olivia interrupted, her voice ringing high with worry.

"He was shot in the upper arm but he's out of surgery and expected to fully recover," David said, emphasizing Alex's recovery.

"Thank God," she answered and exhaled loudly into the phone line.

Believing she was reassured, David added, "He suffered other wounds, but the arm was the worst and he's going to be all right."

"Where is he now?" she asked.

"He's in the hospital unit aboard USS *Wasp*. The PAO told me that he and the other Marines he saved could be released and flown back to the US in maybe two weeks."

"Marines he saved?" asked Olivia, taken aback.

"Alex's command told me that he saved three Marines during the ambush, and they were badly wounded," added David. "Two of them could have died if Alex hadn't gone for them." He didn't hear anything for a few seconds. "Olivia? Are you okay?"

"I'm here," she answered, the sound of her voice resonant with relief.

"We haven't lost him," David assured her. "If I find out more information, I'll call you."

"Thank you, David."

David thought about a saying in the US Navy: *Ship, Shipmates, Self.* That was his son—carrying out his mission, then looking out for his brother Marines, then himself, in that order.

"Alex will get through this, Olivia. See you at home."

# CHAPTER 13

Aboard the USS *Wasp*'s Hospital Unit
South Atlantic Ocean
April 24, 2019 at 0820

The Corpsman's voice awakened Alex from a groggy sleep. "Morning, Marine."

Tired eyelids lifted just enough for him to notice two lines of clear fluids inserted into his veins, one in each arm at the elbow. The room smelled antiseptic. Florescent ceiling light tubes cast shadows void of any warmth. Multiple monitors near his bed, displaying colored numerals, letters, and electronic strips moving up and down, recorded his vitals.

"Where am I?" Alex looked up into the face of a Navy Corpsman. The cloth name tag sewn on his uniform shirt said *Dowrich*.

"You're in the patient ward, USS *Wasp*'s hospital." The Corpsman pressed a button on the medical device he held, and Alex felt the blood pressure cuff automatically tighten around his upper arm for several seconds, then release.

"128 over 74, that's good, really good considering what you've been through. How're you feeling?"

Fatigue coursed throughout Alex's body. His upper left arm was heavily bandaged below the shoulder to the elbow. The area throbbed with pain. Dry mouth made swallowing difficult. He pointed a finger toward a plastic cup of water laying on a hospital tray next to him. The Corpsman brought the cup and straw up to Alex's mouth so he could drink from it.

"What happened to me?" Alex said.

"You were in surgery last night and came through it well," Dowrich motioned to Alex's bandaged arm. "Your surgeon's doing her rounds now. She'll come by soon."

"How long have I been out of it?"

The Corpsman looked at the clock on the wall. "About eight hours. You want something else to drink besides water?"

The best Alex could present was a weakened grin. "OJ?"

"Coming up."

"My arm hurts like hell. How about something for the pain?"

"Tell the doc when she comes in and the pharmacy will get it to me."

Alex's last memory was talking to Anthony Camacho right after the Cobras and Hueys rained fire down on enemy positions where rebels launched their attacks.

Where was Lieutenant Fontana? And Crowell and Whittington?

Alex's jaw tightened as another surge of pain coursed through his upper arm. He pressed his eyes shut and waited for the pain to subside.

Nine hours had now passed since his transport to one of the *Wasp*'s two emergency operating rooms, then surgery, recovery, and lying here. He ached from sheer exhaustion: mental, emotional, physical. With eyes open or closed, Alex's memory spun as fast as a centrifuge, vividly recalling each brutal scene and sound during the ambush and firefights. He relived every moment of it again.

"How are you feeling, Corporal?"

Alex opened his eyes and blinked a few times. A female physician wearing a white doctor's coat stood at the side of his bed. Her blonde hair was tied back in a bun and she wore royal-blue frame glasses. Under her white coat, he recognized a Navy commander's insignia with silver oak leaves pinned to her shirt collars. "I'm Doctor Engberg, head of surgery."

"Ma'am, can you tell me about the other Marines from our platoon who were wounded?" said Alex.

"Of course, I will. But first, how do *you* feel?"

"Like I've been tossed around by an ocean riptide, and my arm hurts," he said. "Corpsman said you repaired my arm. Am I going to be 100 percent again?" He feared hearing her answer.

Commander Martha Engberg revealed a likable smile. "Surgery went very well. You're lucky. The bullet tore through mostly muscle tissue. It missed the brachial artery, the long bone of the upper arm, and I didn't find any nerve damage."

A sense of relief swept over Alex.

"I grafted tissue from your hip and used it to replace damaged muscle tissue," said the doctor with an encouraging air. "It should regenerate and function normally again."

Alex chuckled and looked at his uninjured right arm.

Commander Engberg looked pleased to see him in good spirits. "What's so funny?"

"Glad they didn't shoot me in my other arm and ruin my tat."

"What tat?"

Alex motioned with his head to his good arm's hospital gown. "Ma'am, pull up the sleeve and you'll see."

She did and revealed the small black Marine Corps eagle globe and anchor tattoo, the size of a half dollar, centered between his triceps and biceps. The Navy doctor squinted and smirked. "Pardon me, Corporal, but I need a microscope to see it."

That made him laugh. "Marines in my platoon ragged on me for making it small. Some guys have huge ones on their bodies." Alex turned toward the Navy surgeon. "Ma'am, when can I return to duty?"

"That's up to your doctors at Camp Lejeune," Dr. Engberg said. "I'm optimistic you'll recover without any physical limitations. Meantime, you need to heal. Understood?"

"Affirmative, ma'am."

"I'll order something for your pain as soon as I finish my exam."

Alex used his good hand to shift himself to sit higher on the hospital bed. "Ma'am, what about the Marines from my platoon?"

"Which ones?"

"Lieutenant Fontana, that's John Fontana," he began.

"The lieutenant's out of surgery and doing well." She smiled warmly. "He should fully recover from his gunshot wound. It was a close call but he's lucky."

"Lucky how, ma'am?" Alex noticed the doctor's blonde hair and pretty features. He imagined untying the bun and watching her hair fall to her shoulders.

"Lucky two ways. The bullet didn't shatter his femur, and it also did not sever his femoral artery."

Alex nodded, relieved hearing positive news about his platoon commander.

"You were lucky like your lieutenant," she said. Her words reminded him to be grateful. It had never crossed his mind when he was shot. He only cared about his lieutenant, Billy, Ethan, and the rest of his Marine brothers.

"Anyone else you want to check on?" she asked with one raised eyebrow.

"Yes ma'am, Billy Whittington. His leg was nearly blown off."

"I'm sorry, but the surgical team was unable to save all of his leg."

Alex shuddered involuntarily at the news.

"It was necessary to amputate a few inches above the knee. Part of his femur was badly shattered and we had to reconstruct it." Resignation lined her face. "At least he'll keep part of his upper leg. When he's stronger, we'll send him to Walter Reed where they'll fit him for a prosthesis and begin physical therapy." She watched Alex's reaction. "He should be able to lead a full and productive life."

"But not as a Marine?"

"Not necessarily." She raised a hand. "There's every hope he could return to active duty. But not in ground combat again. Anyone else you want to know about?"

"Yes ma'am, Ethan Crowell."

"He suffered a serious concussion from the IED blast," she said and her features grew serious. "It's too early to know his prognosis."

"Do you think he'll be allowed to return to active duty someday?"

The Navy commander shook her head. "That's hard to say right now. He'll require close monitoring, perhaps over a long time. Let's finish checking on you now."

Commander Engberg placed the ends of a stethoscope in her ears and listened to Alex's heart and lungs. Then she tested the grip strength of his wounded arm, and his bandaging for any signs of weeping from the graft site. Finally, she withdrew a pen light from her pocket and checked Alex's eyes for neurological reactions to stimuli. "You were also concussed but not as severely as Lance Corporal Crowell. That's another reason why your brain needs time to recover before any decision authorizing you to return to duty." She put the pen light away.

It wasn't the answer Alex wanted to hear, but he wouldn't question her medical judgment.

"So far, things look good, Corporal." Her tone was encouraging.

"Thanks, ma'am."

Martha Engberg remained silent for a moment, then said,

"Your company commander, Captain Rosen, told me your actions saved the lives of those three Marines you asked about."

"Commander, I'm just glad they made it back alive."

"If you hadn't reacted so quickly back there, Lieutenant Fontana and Lance Corporal Whittington would have bled to death. They owe their lives to you. Lance Corporal Crowell does too."

"I did my duty, ma'am."

"What happened to you and the other Marines will stay with you for the rest of your life," she said. "Be proud about what you did out there, Corporal."

Alex nodded. "Yes ma'am, I will."

"You and the others are scheduled for transfer to Walter Reed. But the timing depends on when your lieutenant and your two squad members are reclassified from guarded to stable condition. Now, you need to rest, Marine."

Alex nodded. "Understood, ma'am."

"The Corpsman will bring you something for your pain," she said. "I'll check back in an hour. Your progress looks good." She nodded with a smile and left.

Alex took a deep breath, then released it slowly. The fingers of his wounded arm still ached. At least he could open and close them naturally.

Then suddenly his body trembled. The impact of the ambush and the firefights, the carnage of slaughtered refugees, wounded Marines, his own wounds finally overwhelmed him.

He ran the back of his hand across his eyes to sweep away tears. Anyone who walked by his ward and gazed inside shouldn't catch him crying. Marines weren't supposed to cry. That would be wrong because they do cry. Alex turned his face away from the doorway and wept with relief. Lieutenant Fontana and Billy Whittington would survive and go on. Ethan Crowell had a tougher road ahead.

# CHAPTER 14

USS *Wasp*, Hospital Unit
South Atlantic Ocean
April 24, 2019

Alex winked at the Navy Corpsman who drew two vials of blood out of his arm. "I'm spreading a rumor that you torture Marines."

"You're a pussy, Kramer," Dowrich laughed. "The Marine Corps should reassign you to some easy billet like food taster for the base commander."

"Am I interrupting?" said a voice.

Alex, who was watching the second vial fill with blood, looked up and wanted to leap out of the bed to stand at attention. Captain Greg Rosen, Bravo Company Commander, 24th MEU's ground combat element of 1/6—1st Battalion, 6th Marine Regiment— stood in the doorway.

"All done, sir," announced Dowrich, placing the two dark-red vials in a small wire basket. "Pardon me, sir," he said, acknowledging the Marine officer before leaving the room.

"You taking visitors?"

"Of course, sir." Alex carefully shifted in his bed.

The Marine captain, with graying hair cut in a high-reg style, a slightly receding hairline, and brown eyes under thick eyebrows, stood slightly under six feet. Thick, muscular forearms bulged beneath the rolled-up sleeves of the officer's combat utility uniform shirt. Marines under Rosen's command liked knowing he was approachable. He talked effortlessly with enlisted, NCO, and junior officers alike and they connected easily with him.

A cheerful Captain Rosen approached the side of the hospital bed. "How are you feeling, Corporal?"

"I'm ready to return to duty as soon as the doc clears me, sir," Alex said, upbeat.

"Right now, your mission is to rest and follow doctors' orders so that arm heals completely."

"Understood, sir."

Rosen stood casually, his arms hanging comfortably in front of him with one hand crossed over the other. "Corporal, your quick-thinking and your actions under enemy fire demonstrated leadership and valor in the finest traditions of the Marine Corps." Respect for the wounded Marine resonated in his voice.

"Thank you, sir." Alex appreciated the company commander's gesture. "The Marine Corps prepared me well, sir."

"Son, Lieutenant Fontana and I will be recommending that the Marine Corps recognize you for valor during the mission in Sierra Leone."

"Don't know what to say, sir."

"Your courage that day said it all, Corporal." Rosen noticed Alex's worried expression. "Something on your mind, Marine?"

"Pardon me, sir, but maybe I'm not worthy of valor."

"What do you mean?"

"I could have done more so Whittington wouldn't be an AK AMP," Alex said, referring to the military acronym for an above-the-knee amputee.

"You saved his life while under heavy fire," Rosen reassured him. "There's no reason to second-guess anything."

Alex nodded and shifted his position in the bed. "The doc said Lieutenant Fontana should be good to go soon."

"Let's focus on getting you back to 100 percent." The company commander reached out and shook Alex's good hand. "Take care of yourself, Marine."

"Copy that, sir, and thank you."

---

Alex stood in the hallway in a hospital gown and his surgically-repaired arm in a sling. He peered into the hospital room where Billy Whittington lay on his back and stared at the ceiling, his lanky frame filling the full length of the bed. Fluorescent tubes cast a blue-white light down on him. Sunken cheeks, a chalky complexion, and dark rings under his eyes revealed the toll of being seriously wounded in combat and major surgery after. Alex's gaze turned to Billy's right leg. The heavily wrapped stump where the Marine's limb ended a few inches above the knee rested on top of the hospital bed's sheet, not underneath. Alex was confused and frustrated. What was he supposed to tell one of the brave Marines in his squad? A friend he trusted with his life? That everything's going to be okay? He could have been a double amputee, so be grateful?

He inhaled loud enough for Billy to hear it and glance his way. "Hey, Kramer."

The vacant look in his buddy's eyes concerned Alex. The wounds had to be torturing him. He'd never serve on active duty as an infantry Marine again. Alex stepped into the room and stood alongside Billy's bed. There were no chairs.

"The doc said I could come see you," he said, trying to sound positive. He kept looking at Billy's face and not down at the Marine's amputated stump.

Billy's weak smile couldn't match his melancholy expression. "Good to see you too."

Alex knew his good friend's smile was genuine. The warmth

shown in their faces confirmed they were two brother Marines who cared about each other. Maybe being there would temporarily distract Billy Whittington from dwelling on half his leg being blown away.

Tears welled up in Billy's eyes. "Listen Kramer, I don't know what to say except thanks."

"Say about what? Hey, we killed those rebel pricks before they could kill us. We didn't lose anyone from First Platoon."

"You saved me or I would have died out there," Billy replied, lifting one hand to his eyes to wipe away the wetness. "The lieutenant and Crowell, you saved them too. All three of us."

Alex still harbored doubts he hadn't done enough for Billy. But right now, he was satisfied seeing him alive and alert. He leaned over the bed and the two Marines hugged each other. Alex lifted his head away, looked into his buddy's face, and felt a knot in his throat. "I planned on getting you out of there no matter what happened. Doc said you came through surgery well."

Alex's caring expression masked a hint of regret that, unlike Billy, his wounds, physical and emotional, would heal. He would be whole again. Yet he felt good inside, knowing Billy's youthfulness was strengthened by maturity understood only by Marines who had bled on a battlefield.

He extended an open hand. Billy Whittington clasped it and they held each other's grip firmly. "I'm gonna go check on the lieutenant, okay? Then go see Crowell."

Billy waved a hand and tears streamed down both his cheeks again. "I love you, Kramer."

"Love you too, Marine."

# CHAPTER 15

USS *John Warner*
April 24, 2019

Tara Marcellus was walking through the passageway when Chief Drysdale exited the crew's mess and nearly ran into her. Twenty-four hours had passed since her confrontation with Lieutenant Schrager. But her mood was still prickly since it happened.

"Excuse me, ma'am. Need to pay more attention." The hand-some broad-shouldered Navy chief took one step back against the bulkhead and gave the lieutenant room to pass.

Tara waved a hand. "We're fine, Chief."

She felt an urge to say something, to apologize without saying the words "I'm sorry" because she didn't defend him and his sonar techs to Schrager in Control. Because she didn't have their backs. Because she deserted them instead of standing by her principles. Then there was that morning's critique of the event with the CO to go over what happened during the incident.

"Chief, in Control yesterday, I—"

"What about it, ma'am?" Drysdale's eyebrows lifted slightly. His face was otherwise stoic.

Tara's shoulders stiffened. She wanted to do this the right way. "Do you have some time to talk? Now?"

"Will ten minutes be enough, ma'am?"

"That works. Let's try the wardroom."

They stepped inside the empty wardroom. Tara wanted to speak privately but made sure to leave the hatch open. As they stood together, an awkward silence passed between them.

"Chief, about this morning's meeting with the CO . . ." Tara finally said.

She wanted to speak first. Chief Drysdale needed to believe she was telling the truth, every word. "Like I told the skipper and wrote in my report, you and Petty Officer Ruiz did your jobs correctly. By the book. I believe the OOD was wrong to second-guess yours and Ruiz's judgments. And Ruiz shouldn't have been relieved of duty."

Tara was going out on a limb. Drysdale nodded, a sign he was ready to hear more.

"Take a seat, Chief."

"I prefer to stand, ma'am."

Memories from the prior day's incident brief flashed through Tara's mind: With a straight face, Schrager had told the CO that he didn't trust Tara's and her sailors' confirmed contact with the Russian submarine. Insisting on his own verification, the order to maneuver *John Warner* placed the Navy's boat in a vulnerable position. The crew had been dangerously exposed to an enemy submarine.

Then the skipper had questioned Tara. "Lieutenant, did you suggest to Lieutenant Schrager any options for *John Warner* to change course and reposition the boat based on the Russian's position?"

"No sir, I did not," she had said, and her admission felt as if she told someone to punch her in the face. There it was. She hadn't said or done anything to stop NAV's irresponsible orders. Schrager was a liar and she didn't call him out on it.

The CO's final words to Tara and Schrager had played in her head like a repeating reel: They were both right and both wrong. The Russian did not make any aggressive moves and the Navy submarine caught a break. But both officers screwed up.

"I will not tolerate anything less than total concentration on mission and operations under my command," Commander Whikehart had said in a firm tone. "Learn from your mistakes. This is how we fix our boat and it must never happen again on my watch."

*Learn from your mistakes.* The words echoed in Tara's head now as she faced Drysdale in the wardroom. "Chief, I'll say it again. I disagreed with NAV relieving Petty Officer Ruiz from duty, and also singling you out."

Drysdale waited several long seconds, then spoke. "Ma'am, Ruiz is a very good sonarman. He doesn't deserve having this on his record." The Navy chief crossed his arms. "I've seen what right looks like, and that wasn't it. Pardon me, ma'am, but this whole business is total crap."

His voice held restrained fury. Tara was unsure how to respond.

"Ma'am, I've seen officers come and go. Most of 'em were stand-up people," he said, now calmer. "But a few acted like they got their dolphins on eBay. Officers like Lieutenant Schrager, they don't deserve to be officers—not in my book." The words spat out of him.

Drysdale's disgust was written across his face. The Dolphins badge was the United States Navy's submarine warfare insignia. Wearing Dolphins signified the highest privilege of every officer and sailor in the submarine service. Willful negligent conduct tarnished the badge's revered symbolism—an act of contempt. That's what Schrager did, and Tara and Chief Drysdale knew it.

"My point is, ma'am, you can spot them a mile away. They suck at command."

Tara chose her next words carefully. "I will express my disagreement about how you and Petty Officer Ruiz were treated to the CO and XO," she said. "And I will do it soon."

She hoped Chief Drysdale understood this was as close to an apology as she was going to make. Officers seldom admitted judgment errors to sailors. Schrager would never own up to his defective performance when he should have exercised proper command. The man was a weasel.

"You do what you have to do, ma'am." The chief's mouth tightened. "Permission to speak freely?"

"Of course."

"This whole business jammed you up." Drysdale hesitated, then finished. "I bet the CO sees through the lieutenant's lie. The Navy shouldn't hold it against you."

"Thank you, Chief," she said and smiled, grateful that he meant every word.

# CHAPTER 16

**CO's stateroom, USS *John Warner***
**May 9, 2019 at 0835**

Tara Marcellus rapped her knuckles against the metal hatch.

"Enter," said a voice inside the stateroom.

Tara entered and saw the skipper seated at a small desk.

"Come in, Lieutenant," said Commander Whikehart. "Please, take a seat." USS *John Warner*'s commanding officer pointed to the chair alongside where he was already settled.

"Thank you, sir."

When Tara had joined the crew, Mike Urbanick had told her that the CO was an accomplished senior naval officer. Many in the naval service called him one of the Navy's finest sub drivers. There wasn't anything officers and enlisted wouldn't do for him. Crew members considered it a privilege to serve under his command.

During her inaugural deployment a year ago, Tara had been satisfied with her first official Fitness Report (FITREP) the CO had delivered. She'd earned high marks. But a nervous stomach the past forty-eight hours raised her concerns this next report might not be so good. Would he announce that her actions during the Russian sub incident and her dealings with Lieutenant Schrager were handled badly? Bad enough that he and Mike Urbanick, her Department Head, wouldn't recommend her as "promotable"?

She winced at the thought that her still-young naval service career was about to sink. Then again, maybe she was leaping to conclusions before even hearing the CO's report. She knew the truth lay somewhere between possible and inevitable. *Okay, let's get this over with,* she thought with increased anxiety. If the incident with Schrager negatively affected how others perceived her, then she'd settle up with that pompous jackass later. What did she have to lose at this point?

"O2 Fitness Reports are normally due in February, but I am making official notes to yours sooner," Commander Whikehart said good-naturedly to relieve any worry the junior officer might have carried to their meeting. "After your recent incident in Control involving the Russian boat and Lieutenant Schrager, I believe the timing for this preliminary FITREP is more productive for you and your career as an officer now instead of later," he added and paused a moment. "Take as much time as you need to read the report." His tone was calm. "When you're done, we'll talk."

"Thank you, sir," Tara said and nodded. She inhaled slowly and started reading.

*Promotion status: Promotable.* All ensigns and lieutenants' junior grade only received "promotable" if their overall FITREP didn't indicate any royal screw-ups.

She relaxed at the boxes checked 4.0 Above Standards for six out of seven Performance Traits—Professional Expertise, Command or Organizational Climate/Equal Opportunity, Military Bearing/Character, Teamwork, Leadership, and Tactical Performance. So far so good.

Then she read her rating for the last characteristic: Mission Accomplishment and Initiative (taking initiative, planning/organizing, achieving mission). The box under 2.0 Progressing was checked. Officers understood that 3.0 was usually code for being a C student, average. Was the Navy telling her she's a C-minus officer? One less-than performance trait could stand out like flashing red lights on an officer's report.

She felt anxious about reading further but took in a quick

breath and continued down the page to the section titled "Comments on Performance."

LTJG Marcellus is one of my best junior officers. She works seamlessly with personnel at all levels to produce well-trained, highly disciplined, and mission-capable watch teams. She is one of the most trusted watch and duty officers. Lieutenant Marcellus has contributed to the development of the entire crew. One example was how she significantly improved qualification times. She expects the upmost in professionalism in all her endeavors. She works diligently to be a model of leadership by her example.

Her breathing slowed and she kept reading.

Lieutenant Junior Grade Marcellus is an up-and-coming officer in the submarine service. By demonstrating continued excellence in her performance traits with ongoing progress in Mission Accomplishment and Initiative, she receives my highest recommendation for selection as a submarine Department Head and promotion to lieutenant.

When she finished, Tara looked up at Commander Whikehart.

"Your reactions?" he asked. "Anything specific you'd like to discuss?"

"Overall, I'm pleased, sir," she said. "There is one thing."

"Okay, Lieutenant," he said. "I want to hear what my officers are thinking."

"Sir, I came here prepared to find that my actions on 21 April involving the Russian submarine caused you to question my leadership and my ability for command," she said evenly and stopped.

*Slow down, Tara,* she warned herself. *What you say next could affect whether he keeps trusting you as an officer under his command.*

Commander Whikehart stayed silent, waiting for her to say more.

"In your opinion, I properly carried out my duties that day," Tara went on but struggled to stay composed. "Sir, I believe how the sailors I supervise and I responded to the situation that day were in the best interests of our mission, of the crew, and of the Navy."

"They were," replied the CO. "The situation on 21 April was an important lesson in command for you, Lieutenant. I believe it presented you an opportunity to learn to trust your judgment and decision-making abilities," he said, now with a more serious tone. "But I also won't whitewash what occurred. During a critical moment, you suffered a serious lapse of indecision. You did not demonstrate decisive judgment while being responsible for tracking a Russian submarine in our AOR."

Tara was not about to argue that point.

"Lieutenant," he continued, "an officer should never be afraid to do what is right, even when a superior officer thinks differently. You'll be confronted by this important question about command again in your career," he said with calm reassurance. "All officers are. Each time it comes up, find the courage within yourself to act responsibly."

"Sir, I fully accept the 2.0 rating on Mission Accomplishment and Initiative," Tara said. "I am totally committed to earning a rating of 4.0 or 5.0 on my next FITREP." The 2.0 rating initially stung. But everything else on her report indicated he rated her a good naval officer.

"Tara, remember that the definition of 2.0 is 'progressing,'" said Jim Whikehart, leaning back in his chair and looking more at ease. "To advance in a forward direction. That's the duty of every naval officer, and that means the CO too. I do not foresee one 2.0 rating limiting future opportunities for you. It's part of an officer's overall development."

She released a quick breath, grateful for his fairness and his candor.

The CO cleared his throat. "That incident with the Russian submarine was a lesson in leadership. It should not happen again if you want to command your own boat someday as an executive officer—or even a commanding officer, if that's your goal."

"I understand, sir," said Tara and nodded.

"Something similar happened to me when I was a lieutenant JG," Commander Whikehart said, his tone relaxed and open. "My CO at the time said to me, 'Learn from this. Become a smarter, better officer.' He didn't punish officers without a fair hearing of the facts, and neither do I. I've followed his example ever since I received my first command."

Tara glanced at her watch. Her review had gone better than she expected when the meeting began forty-five minutes ago.

"When do you come up for promotion to O-3?" he asked, referencing the designation for a Navy lieutenant's rank.

"June 2020 sir, at my 4th commissioning anniversary."

The CO wrote some quick notes and set down his pen. "We're scheduled to return to homeport in September. That's the time to think ahead about options for a shore duty assignment. Your JO tours will be done midway through the next stand-down."

"I'm already working on them, sir," she replied eagerly. "I've talked with ENG and WEPS about a list of shore duty assignments to send to my submarine detailer at Navy Personnel Command."

"Sounds fine, Lieutenant," the skipper said, cracking a smile at the optimism in Tara's voice. "Mind if I ask what billets you're looking at?"

"Glad to, sir," said Tara. She mentioned two staff officer

jobs—reporting to the CO, Anti-Submarine Warfare, Amphibious Squadron 5, and Operations and Planning for SEAL Team One—and an assignment at the Naval Academy.

"All good ones," he said, his tone equally encouraging. "What's the Academy billet?"

"It's the LEAD Master's Program, sir. The first year is full-time in a graduate degree program, then years two and three at the Academy as a company officer."

"Which one's at the top of your list?"

Her eyes sparkled. "I'd like to go back to the Academy and work with the midshipmen, sir."

Commander Whikehart stroked his chin. "When your shore duty's finished, do you see yourself returning to submarine warfare?"

Tara nodded. "Absolutely, sir, that's my plan."

The CO stood and Tara rose too. "You have a positive future, Lieutenant Marcellus, and the silent service depends on fine officers like yourself. I urge you to continue on that course."

"Will do, sir, and thank you."

"You're welcome," he said and smiled. "Now go back to work!"

"Aye, sir," she replied with a satisfied grin.

It appeared her performance as a junior officer wasn't taking on water after all.

# CHAPTER 17

24th Marine Expeditionary Unit
Marine Corps Base Camp Lejeune, NC
October 21, 2019 at 0935

Alex examined himself in the squad bay mirror and grinned. He was squared away.

Three rows of military decorations were displayed on his uniform. The Purple Heart and Navy Marine Corps Combat Action Ribbon adorned the top row. Below them rested two other rows of ribbons, some representing unit operations overseas, which let other Marines know he'd "been there, done that."

Fifteen minutes from now, the Marine Corps would recognize him for valor. The Silver Star would decorate his dress and service uniforms, and shirts. Its ribbon would sit first on the top row of his awards, alongside the Purple Heart. Alex had been awarded the Purple Heart while he recovered at Walter Reed. He had been presented the Combat Action Ribbon the second week he returned to active duty back at Camp Lejeune.

He spotted Gunnery Sergeant Westphal behind him in the mirror.

"Everybody's waiting for you, Corporal. See you out there."

"Be there in five, Gunny."

Alex turned back to the mirror. The dark circles under his eyes reflected how he felt about the medal ceremony. He still questioned his actions and decisions that fateful day in Sierra Leone. He had to. He'd been the ranking squad leader for First Platoon when bullets started flying and hundreds of innocent men, women, and children, along with Marines, were gunned down in the crossfire. His orders had affected everything that went down.

He'd been going back and forth thinking about what-ifs. What if he'd taken "point" instead of Billy? What if he'd been the first one to go in and clear the vacant building? Shouldn't he have looked first and spotted the IED's tripwire before it exploded and cost the Marine half his leg? Before the same blast turned some of Ethan Crowell's brain tissue into pulp and forced mental and emotional shit upon him? And left Alex with his own physical and emotional wounds? Why did his superior officers think him a worthy recipient of the Silver Star, the nation's third highest personal decoration for valor in military combat?

Sergeant Major Cepeda, the senior enlisted Marine in his battalion, had paid him a visit forty-eight hours ago. Alex had opened up about second-guessing what happened in Sierra Leone. Doubt was a normal reaction before being decorated for valor, a sympathetic one, said Cepeda. Other brave Marines had struggled with the same questions following combat.

"But did I really earn this?" asked Alex.

"Absolutely, Kramer," said Cepeda, a native Puerto Rican who, though small in physical size, was a toughened veteran Marine seasoned by twenty years of active-duty service. "You thought above your rank. You showed leadership under heavy enemy fire, and you were seriously wounded at the same time." The senior NCO placed a reassuring hand on Alex's shoulder. "Trust me, everything you did that day made Marines everywhere truly proud."

The ceremony was about to start. Alex stepped outside to brilliant sunshine. Clear blue sky and no clouds in sight adorned a stunning October morning. A gentle fall breeze swept across Marine Base Camp Lejeune, carrying with it the subtle smells of the Atlantic Ocean. Marines of Bravo Company stood in formation at parade rest on one side of the roadway. He beamed at seeing his brothers from First Platoon, also at parade rest behind Gunny Westphal.

Standing upright across the road from Gunny was Alex's command. He saw Colonel Freeman, Commanding Officer, 24th MEU and Captain John Fontana, his former platoon commander who now wore the two silver bars of a Marine captain on his uniform. Shortly following Operation Swift Rescue, Fontana had been promoted.

Behind the command and standing under a scarlet and gold canopy of Marine Corps colors were his mother, Olivia, and his father, Rear Admiral David Kramer, in uniform. Tori, Alex's older sister, couldn't attend. But she sent her brother a heartfelt note of love and congratulations. She'd try to get out of Manhattan soon to visit him.

Then Alex spotted Billy Whittington and Ethan Crowell under the canopy. He'd seen very little of either once he'd left Walter Reed, took ten days' leave, and returned to Camp Lejeune and his unit.

Billy wore Marine Corps green Service "A" uniform. Inside his trousers, a new prosthetic leg allowed him to resume an attempt at a normal life. He was three months out of Walter Reed and still getting physical therapy. He'd told Alex he wanted to continue serving in the Marine Corps and asked his command about a possible restricted line billet with the MEU's Logistics Combat Element. His leaders wanted to accommodate the wounded and decorated combat Marine. They'd look into letting him continue serving the Corps and the nation. For the time being, he remained in the Wounded Warrior Battalion.

An ill-fitting shiny black K-Mart-style suit hung on Ethan Crowell's thin frame. His attire seemed to match his expression, which was an unfocused thousand-yard stare. His story? Far more disturbing than Billy's. The concussion and psychological trauma from the IED blast screwed him up neurologically, mentally, and physically. He was honorably discharged from the Marine Corps with a permanent medical disability. Now Ethan spent four days a week talking to a mental health counselor. He needed meds to fight off psychological demons and physical pain that afflicted him day and night. Alex tried to stay in contact by text and email. Once in a while, he'd call. But he often worried Crowell could jump over the edge anytime without forewarning. Though no longer Ethan's squad leader, Alex would be his lifelong friend.

Alex, Billy, and Ethan were each partially broken in Sierra Leone. Each was doing his best to find a route back to normality. Alex was doing well, and Billy too. Ethan not so much. Seeing Alex approach, Billy smiled. Ethan nodded as if he were lifeless. Alex gestured back to them with a low-profile wave. Operation Swift Rescue, the name for the MEU's NEO mission, had taken place six months before. But to the three men, the events that had transformed theirs and John Fontana's lives felt more like they had happened six minutes ago.

Alex was one month shy of his twenty-first birthday. Standing at attention in front of Colonel Freeman, he caught John Fontana wink at him.

"Ladies and gentlemen and Marines of Battalion Landing Team 1/6, we have an important piece of business to announce before today's award ceremony," stated Colonel Freeman. Stationed at a podium off to the commanding officer's right side, Sergeant Major Cepeda for the battalion announced "Attention to Orders," then read:

In recognition of your skills, dedication to duty, and having demonstrated the leadership qualities necessary to lead Marines by the authority vested in me as commanding officer,

I have today promoted Corporal Alexander M. Kramer to the rank of Sergeant E-5—

Alex's chest filled with pride at hearing the words.

—given at Marine Corps Base Camp Lejeune, Battalion Landing Team, 1st Battalion, 6th Marines, 24th Marine Expeditionary Unit, on this 21st Day of October 2019.

Colonel Nathan W. Freeman,
USMC Commanding Officer

Colonel Freeman nodded to the sergeant major, who called the assembled Marines to attention and followed by the sound of all Marines snapping into precise formation.

"Well done, Sergeant." Colonel Freeman shook Alex's hand.

"Thank you, sir."

Captain Fontana was next to offer his congratulations, followed by Sergeant Major Cepeda, who handed Alex his promotion warrant. When Marines and guests finished their applause and hoots of praise, the sergeant major read aloud Alex's award citation for all to hear: "Attention to Orders."

*The President of the United States takes pride in presenting the SILVER STAR MEDAL to CORPORAL Alexander M. Kramer, UNITED STATES MARINE CORPS for service as set forth in the following CITATION:*

*For conspicuous gallantry and intrepidity in action against the enemy as Squad Leader, First Platoon, Bravo Company, Battalion Landing Team 1/6, 24th Marine Expeditionary Unit, US Marine Forces Europe and Africa in support of Operation Swift Rescue on 24 April 2019.*

The sergeant major continued reading the descriptive statement of Alex's actions and heroism during the firefight, paused a moment, and finished:

*By his bold initiative, undaunted courage, and complete dedication to duty, Corporal Kramer reflected great credit upon himself and upheld the highest traditions of the Marine Corps and the United States Naval Service.*

*For the President,*
*Secretary of the Navy*

"Captain Fontana?" Colonel Freeman gestured to Alex's previous platoon commander.

"Thank you, sir." John Fontana stepped up, took his place alongside the commanding officer, and stood before Alex. An hour earlier, he had requested permission to present Alex's medal and Colonel Freeman agreed. Fontana removed the Silver Star decoration from his pocket. "Sergeant Kramer, it is my personal honor to present you with the Silver Star Medal, our nation's third highest military award for valor." Fontana paused while the only sounds heard were the American and Marine Corps flags flapping in the October breeze.

"On 24 April 2019, your leadership and heroism under fire saved many lives, Marines, and civilians. One life you saved was mine. I will forever be indebted to you." The captain's voice softened. "It is the highest privilege for me to serve with you."

Fontana pinned Alex's medal on the lapel of his uniform. Colonel Freeman stepped forward. "Sergeant Kramer, this medal forever represents your distinguished gallantry and the heroism of all Marines from 24th MEU who served with you that day in the highest traditions of the Marine Corps."

He gave Alex a moment to absorb what he said and finished. "You have brought high honor to your unit and yourself. Well done, Marine."

"Thank you, sir," said Alex as his chin quivered. His right hand snapped up to the brim of his cover to crisply salute his commanding officers and the sergeant major. Olivia wiped away tears through a smile for her son. Rear Admiral David Kramer stood upright with arms at his sides and hands closed in military tradition. The ceremony concluded with Colonel Freeman inviting all guests and Marines present to a reception honoring Alex and his decoration.

Olivia hugged her son, her eyes still moist. "I'm so proud of you, Alex." She pulled away, grabbed his shoulders and looked into his face. "Sergeant Kramer," the proud mother said and beamed.

"Sounds pretty nice, doesn't it?" Alex replied with a wide grin but noticed a mischievous-looking smile from Olivia. "What?"

"I emailed Carolyn Hagerty that the Marine Corps was honoring you for valor."

"Mom, I'm not part of her life anymore, you know?" Alex said, puzzled. "She's Ivy League Princeton and I'm a Marine Grunt."

"You're a decorated Marine, a hero." Olivia's expression was serious. "She's never known a man who displayed such courage."

Rear Admiral Kramer stepped forward and shook his son's hand. "I want you to know how truly proud I am of the outstanding young man, the Marine, you are." David pulled Alex toward him and hugged his son tight. This time paternal approval showed in his eyes and his embrace, much different than the flippant remark he had made at Alex's graduation from basic training.

Alex knew it wasn't easy for his loyal Naval Academy graduate father to acknowledge his son's enlistment. He hadn't yet said a word to his dad about Captain Fontana and Captain Rosen, the company commander, urging him to earn a commission. Getting himself into the Naval Academy could still be in play, and Alex no longer discounted the idea. The timing was too premature to say anything.

Alex waved a finger at Billy and Ethan, standing nearby. "You'd better be at my reception."

"Wouldn't miss it, Sergeant," said Billy, wrapping his arms around Alex in a bear hug.

"Me too," said Ethan, who cautiously extended a hand to shake.

Worried to see the dispirited look in his friend's eyes, Alex wrapped one arm around Ethan's neck and pulled him close for a brotherly embrace. "I love you, Ethan."

"You saved me, Alex. You saved all of us," Ethan answered in a near whisper.

"We saved each other, and I'd do it again."

# CHAPTER 18

**24th Marine Expeditionary Unit**
**Marine Corps Base Camp Lejeune, NC**
**April 1, 2020 at 1245**

Alex stepped outside the barracks for mail call. The platoon sergeant held up a large manila envelope, stared at the return address, and smiled in Alex's direction.

"Hey Kramer, you expecting something from"—he raised an eyebrow—"Annapolis, MD?"

Alex stepped forward and retrieved the envelope. His eyes darted to the printed return address in large letters:

Office of Admissions
Unites States Naval Academy

Back in the barracks and seated on his bunk, he held up the large tan envelope. Large suggested the news inside should be good. His pulse quickened as he carefully opened the envelope, withdrew its contents, and studied the object inside—a handsome padded blue folder with the Naval Academy crest affixed in gold on the front. His fingers opened it to reveal his official announcement of Appointment to the United States Naval Academy Class of 2024. On the left side behind the clear covering was a close-up color photograph of the Navy's Blue Angels flight team flying in tight formation.

His thoughts drifted back to a morning six months ago when John Fontana had pulled him aside.

"You should think about applying for a commission," the

platoon commander had said. "The company commander agrees. You're definitely officer material, Sergeant."

"That's kind of a touchy subject, sir," Alex had told him.

"Tell me why."

Alex had explained that not following his father to the Naval Academy had been a sore point between them. "The truth is, sir, it hurt him when I enlisted in the Marine Corps. Other people said I was making a big mistake not going to college."

"You chose an honorable path, Alex," Captain Fontana had reassured him. "Be proud."

"I am, sir. But I don't think my father's totally forgiven me," he had responded with an echo of regret in his words. "Following him to Annapolis meant everything—maybe too much."

"You can still apply to the Academy," the Marine captain had offered, "and return to the Marine Corps as an officer. Remember, the best thing about being a Marine is—"

"—leading Marines," Alex had finished the sentence.

Alex laid the folder down on his bunk, then pulled out his cell phone and texted:

*Hey Mom, just received a big envelope from USNA. It's my appointment to the Class of 2024. I'm headed to Annapolis. I'll text Dad.*

He took an iPhone snapshot of the appointment citation and sent the image as an attachment to his mother.

With his citation in hand, Alex went to find Captain Fontana's office. Fontana was awaiting orders to his next billet.

"Enter," the officer called out at the knock on his office door.

Alex, smiling, stood at attention in front of the officer's desk.

"Afternoon, Sergeant." Fontana pointed to the envelope. "What's that?"

Alex withdrew the folder and presented it. "Sir, I took your advice and applied. Here's my appointment to the Academy. Came today."

The captain studied the citation, then looked up with a wide smile and nodded. "That's outstanding. Congratulations! Your folks will be proud, especially your father. Do they know yet?"

"Just texted my mom. I'll text my dad later. Wanted to let you know, sir," Alex said with delight. "A question for you, sir, if you don't mind?"

"Ask away."

"Just curious, where are you headed next?"

Captain John Fontana's brown eyes shined brightly at the question. "My new orders are to join Fleet Marine Force as a FAST platoon commander with an anti-terrorism security team," he said.

"That's great news, sir." Alex smiled. He knew a FAST platoon was a fifty-member unit tasked with providing armed, combat-trained Marines who provided and restored security for vital naval and national assets around the world. "I'm eager to start," said Captain Fontana, who rose from the chair and extended his hand. "I'll inform the company commander. He'll be pleased to hear the news. Well done, Sergeant."

Alex nodded. "Thanks, sir."

The Marine captain crossed his arms and smiled. "The Naval Academy is damn lucky to get a hard-charging warrior like you."

# PART TWO

# CHAPTER 19

**Induction Day, I-Day**
**US Naval Academy**
**Annapolis, MD**
**June 24, 2020 at 0615**

"Your mind's made up? You're still going through with this?" Olivia Kramer asked quietly so others standing nearby wouldn't overhear her. But they were too busy talking with their own sons and daughters to pay her any notice.

Alex shrugged. "Yes, it's what I want, okay?"

The early morning humidity made her pull a tissue from her pocket and dab at her perspiring face. "Your appointment to the Academy has been your father's expectation all along." She shot her son a questioning look. "Is being here today really your choice, not his?"

Alex yawned and rubbed the sleep from his face. "My choice."

Another shuttle bus approached them outside the Navy-Marine Corps Memorial Stadium, ready to board its next round of passengers and drive the short distance to the Academy.

"You'll be fine at the Academy." His mother's eyes were moist.

"I'll follow orders and try to behave myself," he told her, wrinkling his nose and smiling.

"Tell me something, and I want you to be honest."

"Sure, what?"

"After serving in hot zones as a Marine, don't you think Academy life's going to be pretty dull?"

He shrugged it off. "I'll be fine."

"This place is different, Alex. You'll be among *kids* who don't have a clue what it's like to serve in combat."

He softly patted her upper arm. "I'm not worried about any ghosts from Sierra Leone following me, Mom. I know the triggers that set me off."

Alex thought he saw a touch of worry coupled with maternal admiration in his mother's face, and he loved her for always caring.

"Okay, see you in Tecumseh Court tonight." Olivia hugged him once more and waved as Alex boarded the bus.

The day before Induction Day (I-Day)'s annual throng of incoming plebes, or freshmen, arrived at the Academy, Alex had joined sixteen other prior-enlisted Marines and fifty-four prior-enlisted sailors for I-Day Minus One. Every June prior-enlisted for the new Academy class officially processed out of the Marine Corps and the Navy. On I-Day they would join all the other incoming plebes and become employees of the US Navy.

Prior-enlisted Marines like Alex graduated basic training at Parris Island, SC and San Diego. Sailors came out of Great Lakes in Illinois. Every one of them was already trained in how to salute an officer, wear their covers, execute the orders during drill, make a rack, and tell you the toilet was a head, not a john or a latrine. Each Marine could load and fire small arms and M4s, and assemble and disassemble a weapon blindfolded as naturally as breathing.

Alex and some of the Marines were also combat tested. They had engaged the enemy on battlefields, taken fire, been wounded, and killed the enemy before he killed them. I-Day was a formality they patiently endured as part of their new duties.

First came the bus ride. Feeling instant relief from the air conditioning system blowing at high speed, Alex settled into a seat near the front of the bus while others moved past. A continuous stream of buses transported approximately 1,300 soon-to-be-plebes on a half-mile drive through Gate 8 to the start of Induction

Day for the US Naval Academy's Class of 2024. Add an average of three loved ones per plebe, and nearly four thousand people would be at the Academy for 1-Day.

For some plebes, the goal of attending the Naval Academy or any of America's other service academies could feel larger than life. Alex came from a different place. Going to the Academy had been his father's plan. Being a Marine had been Alex's. He wanted to lead Marines again, the next time as an officer. From the essential to the mundane to the ridiculous, he understood what the Academy offered—and expected from him—in return for receiving a commission.

Could he endure four years at this well-ordered place when his objective in life was to return to an environment that was nowhere close to life at Annapolis? Would he have the patience to put up with overly ambitious upperclassmen shouting orders because rank has its privilege—and keep his mouth shut? Even when their only leadership experiences so far were mustering midshipmen to form up for announcements and meals, parades, and home football games?

Alex wasn't sure how much verbal abuse he was willing to put up with from upperclassmen in the Brigade. But he'd conform and take whatever they dished out. The Marine Corps taught Alex about dedication to duty and commitment to mission. He learned it in spades and would uphold those core values at Annapolis.

The bus came to a stop at Alumni Hall, and Alex followed the others off.

"Good luck, son," said the driver, a husky, older gentleman with wire-frame glasses and a close-cropped salt-and-pepper beard. Alex noticed a small Marine Corps emblem embroidered on the man's white knit golf shirt.

"Veteran, sir?" Alex asked him.

"Vietnam, '67 to '68."

"Semper Fi," said Alex.

"You too?" The driver's eyes brightened.

"Deployments in Africa and the Med."

"You look older than the others coming here today." The deep crow's feet around the bus driver's eyes creased when he smiled. "Maybe you'll teach some officers at this place a few things. Just remember that they still outrank you." He extended his hand and they shook. "Find your way back to the Corps, son."

"I aim to, sir."

The sun rose behind Alumni Hall, casting an early-morning orange glow over the Severn River. Alex looked out at approximately nine hundred parents and relatives standing in packs behind barriers near the sidewalk alongside Decatur Road and into the building. There were family group hugs with sons and daughters. Everywhere, cell phones were held high in the air for family selfies, and phone cameras flashed like a swarm of fireflies.

After Marine Corps Basic Training at Parris Island, Alex figured he could handle anything they threw at him during Plebe Summer. He knew what was coming for the next six weeks. He'd follow orders, keep a low profile, and hook up with other "Mustangs," the name for prior-enlisted sailors and Marines like him who were there to become officers.

He took his place in the line leading into Alumni Hall, the place where I-Day began for every new plebe. "Welcome to the Naval Academy," said a rusty brown-haired female Marine second lieutenant standing behind one of several long tables. Her cheeks dimpled when she smiled. "Name?"

"Alexander Matthew Kramer."

He knew she and the other junior officers were brand-new Academy graduates from the Class of 2020. Hardly one month ago, if that. They were temporarily assigned to the deputy commandant's staff until they reported to their first billets. Their ensign shoulder boards and second-lieutenant gold bars didn't have time to collect any dust or tarnish yet.

The Marine second lieutenant flipped through a cardboard box full of small envelopes. Pinned to each one was a black metal name tag with yellow border, with last name and class year etched on it in yellow script. She found Alex's packet, pulled it out, and handed it to him. He stared at the tag: Kramer '24.

A Navy ensign typed on a laptop. "Check this out," he motioned to her.

She read where he pointed and turned back to Alex. "You're a prior-enlisted Marine?"

"Yes, ma'am."

He could have answered 1/6 out of Camp Lejeune. It wasn't necessary. He didn't want to brag in front of a new second lieutenant. TMI for her.

"Did you deploy?"

"I did, ma'am. 24th MEU to Africa and the Med."

"See action?"

Alex looked right at her. "Affirmative, ma'am."

"Family in the military?"

"My father's a naval officer, Academy Class of '92."

A smile spread on the second lieutenant's face. "I'm sure they're proud of you, especially your father, following him to the Academy."

"I suppose, ma'am," he answered with detachment.

Too bad some of those in the Corps couldn't let go of a jarhead attitude that a woman can't be attractive and a Marine at the same time, thought Alex. He also noticed two rows of service decorations adorned her uniform shirt, including the Marine Corps Good Conduct ribbon. Like him, she was prior-enlisted.

"Try to be a model for other plebes," she said with a smile. "Good luck."

"Aye, ma'am."

The next hour passed with tension for incoming plebes but not for Alex. Male plebes got their heads shaved. A 2019 regulation change allowed female plebes to forego having their hair cut to a length just above the shoulders. They could pin it up and back instead. The new rule created some grumbling among male midshipmen. Each received a copy of Reef Points, the small handbook loaded with facts on the Navy and Marine Corps, the Naval Academy's history and traditions plebes had to commit to memory. Finally, they shed their civilian clothes and put on their White Works Echo Plebe Summer uniforms: jumper and trousers. Blue-rim dixie cover. White court shoes and athletic socks. Blue-rim T-shirt. Underneath, blue USNA PT shorts. Name tag.

With families now out of sight, Alex was among twenty plebes hurried into designated areas of the building by "detailers," the groups of upperclassmen assigned to Plebe Summer to work with the Academy's newest members of the Brigade. Sometimes detailers shouted orders in raised voices, weaving in and between plebes standing at attention. They reminded Alex of a swarm of yellow jackets, looking for something or someone to sting. Some plebes were perspiring from the hot, motionless air in the staging area. Others sweated from anxiety.

"There is a right way and a wrong way to wear your cover," one detailer called out. He grabbed the cover from the head of a plebe standing right in front him. "This is your cover. It is not a hat. Is that clear?"

"Sir, yes sir."

"I didn't hear you."

"SIR, YES SIR," all the plebes shouted louder.

For the next few hours, some 1,300 inductees inside Alumni Hall were instructed where to place dixie covers on their heads, the exact position of fingers and hands at the sides of their body when standing at attention, where to hold *Reef Points* when reading and standing, the only five acceptable responses permitted to answer a midshipman's question, and how to salute.

While detailers shuttled in and out of his peripheral vision, Alex's memory drifted back to another indoctrination environment five years earlier at Recruit Basic Training, Parris Island. Maybe the Marine Corps would rename it Devil's Island someday. For Alex, I-Day and Plebe Summer's versions of tough love couldn't come close to resembling Marine Corps recruit basic training.

"All right, pick up your bags and follow the detailers," one of the Firsties called out to the plebes. "You're in the United States Navy now. Let's try and look like it."

The plebes in Alex's unit collected their gear and left Alumni Hall. Ten minutes later they reached the doors leading into Seventh Wing of Bancroft Hall and ascended up four flights of stairs, sweat still streaming down faces and wet scalps under their covers. With White Works Echo uniforms removed, and in PT gear for the next ninety minutes, plebes learned to make beds; store uniforms; and prepare for inspections, reveille, morning formation, and other Academy routines.

Detailers shed their summer whites for sneakers, blue USNA PT shorts, and gold T-shirts with DETAILER on the back and the Class of 2021's crest in color emblazoned on the front. Their left sleeves displayed *'21.*

"You are now part of the US Naval Academy, not State U," said a male detailer assigned to 2nd Platoon, Hotel Company with a long-distance runner's thin build. "Think about the T-shirts on sale with a gold *N* that spells out: 'Not College'."

"Plebes do not walk across the decks of Bancroft Hall," announced a fire-hydrant-sized male detailer. Alex watched him swagger back and forth while plebes stood at attention with their backs braced against tiled walls. "You will jog in small steps, or 'chop,' every time you move from one place to another inside this building." He showed them how to square corners by pivoting on their feet to make sharp ninety-degree turns, then they did it. Rooms were cabins, floors were decks, and doors were hatches. Walls were bulkheads and ceilings were overheads. Stairs were ladders. And bathrooms were heads, not latrines, the name for bathrooms in the Army and at West Point.

At 1500, plebes from Hotel Company headed back outside. Humidity descended quickly on Alex and the others. Unprotected by any shade or cover, they stood at attention out on "Red Beach," a section of roof over King Hall. Sweat streamed down alongside their ears, streaked their cheeks, and dripped off chins. Even out of White Works and in PT uniform where the cotton material at least breathed, it was still as hot as an oven.

Staring straight ahead, Alex could follow a red-haired detailer who paced back and forth in front of them. "Your duty will be to honor the institution and thousands of graduates who came before you," he said. "Today you begin learning about the Naval Academy and the Navy. Read your Reef Points. Make it happen, people!" he shouted. Twenty hands moved at the same time, reaching down to the deck to retrieve their small books.

A nameless detailer, tall with a high and tight haircut—T-shirts didn't carry any name tags—approached the plebe standing to Alex's left and got right up in his face. "Are you uncomfortable with me standing this close?"

"Sir, no sir," the plebe stuttered, a new trail of perspiration running down next to one ear.

Alex watched the detailer walk away. "Shake it off," he whispered to the nervous plebe, but not quietly enough.

The detailer spun around and came up fast in front of Alex. Another detailer a few feet away, with sandy-colored hair and wearing black-frame glasses, saw what was going on and came over. Now two Firsties stood close to Alex, one on each side, trying to get under his skin. "Follow me, Mister Kramer," said the one with glasses. Alex followed them a couple of yards away.

"Is there something you want to say, Mister Kramer?" said the tall detailer.

"Sir, no sir."

"You seem pretty sure of yourself," the sandy-haired one jumped in. "You're prior-enlisted from the Marine Corps, aren't you?"

"Sir, yes sir."

"When you were on active duty, did you see any action?"

Alex fought a temptation to look him in the eyes. Though he would have bet that the toughest thing the detailer had ever done was riding a pony at his seventh birthday party without peeing in his pants.

"Sir, yes sir."

"Where?"

"I was a squad leader with 1/6. Deployed to Africa."

The detailer paused. It didn't go unnoticed by Alex that neither detailer pounced on him for referring to himself in first person.

"Were you only supporting other units operating in forward areas?"

The one with glasses was starting to piss Alex off. He felt an urge to drop the guy in one swift move. *You little prick,* Alex grumbled under his breath.

"We were operating *in* a forward area, sir, and—" he stopped there. *This jerk doesn't understand.*

"And what?"

"That's all, sir."

He caught the two detailers exchange suspicious looks.

"Why are you being inducted today?" This time it was the

high-and-tight detailer, the calmer one, doing the talking.

"Sir, I'm coming directly from the fleet," Alex answered. "I processed out of the Corps last night at Marine Barracks 8th and I, sir. Did my I-Day Minus One."

"Eyes straight ahead," the sandy-haired one shouted, scolding Alex for looking into the other detailer's eyes instead of forward. "What's your reason for coming to the Naval Academy? Why are you here?" he barked, clearly wanting to rattle Alex.

"Get a great education and earn my commission, then return to the Marine Corps—sir." *Earn my commission.* Those three words had lived in Alex's subconscious from the day he lay in a hospital bed aboard the USS *Wasp*.

"How old are you?" Again, the annoying detailer with glasses.

"Twenty-two, sir."

"You think you can take orders from a lot of people younger than you?"

Alex hesitated before answering. What could you possibly know, he thought, about giving and taking orders when bad people want to kill you? Kill you and other Marines? Your shipmates? Screw you, mister. You don't know what you don't know, asshole.

The detailer with the high-and-tight haircut frowned. "No need to go there." He placed himself between Alex and the irritating detailer. "Welcome to the Naval Academy, Mister Kramer. Your prior service will let you be a leader for other plebes. Just don't get a swelled head because you know your way around a parade deck. Come find me anytime if I can help you."

"Sir, thank you, sir."

"Go on, get back over there and learn your rates," the tall detailer said and aimed his chin in the direction where the other plebes stood.

Alex did an about face and returned to his spot, close enough to hear the detailers exchange whispered words.

"What was that all about?" High-and-tight turned on his classmate.

"Take it easy, it's I-Day." The sandy-haired and sporting glasses detailer with a prickly attitude pushed back. "No harm, no foul by anything I said to him."

"That plebe's been knee-deep in shit we've never seen and couldn't imagine," said the tall detailer in a ticked-off tone. "Show him some respect."

---

The sun turned from white-yellow to orange when the Class of 2024, in a wave of white uniforms, paraded into Tecumseh Court for the swearing-in ceremony. The midshipman candidates had signed their oaths of office earlier in I-Day.

Alex looked around carefully, aware plebes were ordered to keep their eyes "in the boat" or straight ahead when seated. He was five years older than almost all other plebes present. He'd entered military service and swore an oath of duty to protect his country at a Marine Corps recruitment office at a Virginia strip mall, and now he was about to do it again at the nation's second oldest service academy.

A large crowd of family members and friends swelled behind and just beyond the end of the Tecumseh Court, as close to their plebes as they could get. This ceremony they'd come to witness didn't occur at civilian universities. Everywhere mobile phones and cameras flashed like an excited rock concert crowd photographing the moment for posterity.

Vice Admiral Robert Lawrence, Superintendent of the United States Naval Academy, stood at the podium on the front marble steps leading to Bancroft Hall's entrance. Rows of colorful military ribbons and decorations marking a distinguished naval career on his shirt stood out against his white summer uniform. "Today you are starting a journey that promises to be more challenging, more demanding, more rewarding, and more extraordinary than you can possibly imagine," he told the assembly of plebes seated before him. Moments later, Alex and his plebe class stood, raised their right hands, and swore to defend the Constitution of the United States against all enemies, foreign and domestic.

The ceremony over, plebes had twenty minutes to empty out of their rows in search of family and friends spread out in designated areas along sections of lawn and brick walkways. Hugs and handshakes joined smiles and joyful tears. More cell phone cameras flashed. Alex moved through the crowd looking for his parents. He spotted Olivia Kramer's wave. She was alone.

"Where is he?"

The look on her face was an effort to allay her son's reaction. "The Directorate for Operations on the Joint Staff called an emergency meeting," she told him. "Dad reached me and said there's no way out of it. He wanted to come. You need to believe that."

"I do," he said, disappointed. "But it's not like we're declaring war somewhere and he can't leave. His superior officers should have understood. That's just a lot of Pentagon nonsense."

Olivia placed an arm around his waist and pulled him close. "I'm here for you, all right?" Her gentle touch managed to erase Alex's scowl. "What counts is how proud your father is that you've followed him to the Academy," she said. "He wanted to be here for you more than anything."

The prior-enlisted Marine decorated for valor, and now a Naval Academy plebe, nodded. "I know that." He glanced at his watch. "I've got to go."

The mother and son hugged a final time.

"You've already proven you're a leader of men, in peace and in war," said Olivia. "Let everyone here know that, too."

"Aye, ma'am," Alex waved and departed.

He intended to find out what separated cheap talk from making something of yourself at the Academy.

# CHAPTER 20

10th Company, 5th Wing, 4th Deck
Bancroft Hall, USNA
September 16, 2020 at 0335

"Whittington, your leg fell off!" Alex shouted. "You're fucking bleeding all over. Doc!"

Alex punctuated the air with a stream of short, rapid breaths. Beads of sweat on his forehead glistened in the partial moonlight.

His cries startled both of his sleeping roommates. Harry Stocks leaped off the upper rack and kneeled down alongside his roommate's bed below him. Alex flung himself upright, his hands thrashing in the space in front of him, and struck Harry in the side of the head. Alex's eyes were wide open.

"You're safe, no incoming." Harry struggled to grab his roommate's hands that swung wildly. He finally took hold of both wrists and pressed them down against the bed. Alex's pillow was damp with perspiration.

"Second time this week." Brian Tannehill, their other roommate, stood over Harry. The two had been classmates at the Naval Academy Preparatory School (NAPS).

"Get me a towel," Harry called out to Brian. Hearing Alex's rapid breaths begin to slow, he wiped the sweat off his classmate's face and remained kneeling next to the bed. Left alone, Alex could still injure himself. Harry wouldn't chance it.

Alex laid back down on the bed, let out a deep breath, and brought up his hands to cover his face. "What the hell."

"Brian, turn on your desk lamp," Harry said. The bulb's soft incandescent light was enough for the three roommates to see each other without the harsh, recessed overhead fluorescent tubes.

Alex lowered his hands and faced his roommates. "I'm sorry."

Brian looked at him. "Do you realize you're having a couple of nightmares a week? Sometimes you're shouting orders."

"You need to talk to someone at the Midshipmen Development Center," Harry said. "Get some professional help, Alex. Those nightmares have gotta be a living hell for you."

Alex pulled his covers back from the bed, put his feet on the deck, and sat up. His mouth was so dry it felt like his saliva had turned to desert sand. "I need to drink something, anything."

Making sure he wasn't seen, Brian hustled to the company wardroom's refrigerator and returned with a bottle of water. Alex twisted off the plastic top and downed two-thirds of the cold liquid in a few seconds. He rubbed his eyes with the heels of his hands. "Either of you told anyone about me yelling in my sleep?"

They both said no.

"You look like shit warmed over," Brian said. "You're not getting anywhere near enough sleep."

"My appetite's all screwed up. Been that way since Plebe Summer." Alex rubbed his face. "Make sure I'm up at reveille, okay?" he pleaded to his roommates. "I can't be late for formation and get written up for a Negative Form-1. My father's coming up on Saturday, and I want to get off the Yard for a few hours."

Harry climbed back into the upper rack. "We'll make sure you're up. Now, dream about something else besides combat. Think about getting laid."

"Just don't yell out how great it feels," Brian laughed and turned off the desk lamp.

"Thanks for having my back, guys." Alex tried to go back to

sleep but it was useless. The sights and sounds from Sierra Leone—semiautomatic rifle fire, refugees thrashing in pain from gunshot wounds and many dying before they even reached the ground, Marine Cobras and Hueys firing 20mm Gatling cannons down on attacking enemy positions hidden by high grass. His mind was loaded with these memories and he couldn't make them stop.

---

The white light from Alex's PC monitor illuminated his face inside the dark room. He rubbed his neck, rotating his shoulders to ease the stiffness from his working out earlier at the Wesley Brown Field House.

"Hey jarhead, how much longer you working?" Harry's words were muffled, half his face sunk into the pillow.

"Ten minutes."

Brian was sound asleep.

Alex yawned and shook his head to stay awake. He opened the Academy's secure website for Brigade information and resources and found a link to the Midshipmen Development Center (MDC). A quick search led to an online questionnaire for midshipmen interested in the unit's services. Simple enough: Name, gender, class year, company, cell phone number, alpha number, and some other personal information. He hovered his cursor over a text box that said:

Describe Your Request for Assistance

He paused for a moment, then typed:

Want help with moods bothering me since I was in ground combat operations as a Marine. A few flashbacks and nightmares. I get impatient. Loud sudden noises set me on edge big time. Other Mids who see it happen don't understand. Some get freaked out. My appetite's out of whack. Classmates say I can be too quiet. Mids in my platoon told me I need to find out what's going on inside me. I already know what it is.

The last section in the application presented several terms with a box next to each one to place a checkmark indicating the midshipman's status:

Emergency
Urgent
Standard Consultation
Nutritional Appointment
Sports-Related Consultation

Alex stared at his monitor for a moment, pondering his response. Was it an emergency? He wasn't sure. But it was time to punch back at the enemy messing inside his head and his body. He clicked a checkmark on the box next to Standard Consultation. Less than twenty-four hours ago, he had leaped out of the bed in a cold sweat yelling about Billy Whittington's leg falling off.

The tired midshipman shut his PC, rubbed his face, and crawled into the rack. Reluctant, yet feeling it was important seeking medical advice to deal with his mood changes, Alex closed his eyes and drifted off. If there was one thing Academy plebes never got enough of, it was sleep.

# CHAPTER 21

**Midshipmen Development Center**
**8th Wing, Bancroft Hall, USNA**
**September 18, 2020**

Alex grasped the door handle to the Midshipmen Development Center and stopped. *Go on in there, it's time you did this*. Then he turned the handle and entered the room.

A petite young lady with hair tied back in a ponytail, wearing stylish cobalt-blue frame glasses, greeted Alex at the MDC reception desk.

"Morning, ma'am," Alex said and withdrew a small sheet of paper from his pocket. "I have an appointment to see Lieutenant Commander Forgash."

"Your name, please?"

"Alex Kramer, 10th Company."

She smiled and pointed to seats nearby. "The commander is expecting you. I'll let her know you're here, midshipman. Please have a seat."

Alex settled himself in a standard upholstered office chair. He looked up from his cell phone and saw a female naval officer in Summer Whites uniform approaching from a corridor next to the reception desk.

"Alex? I'm Lieutenant Commander Forgash," she said in a welcoming fashion. She was a tall woman, maybe late-twenties, early thirties with pleasant features and inviting crystal blue eyes.

"Hello, ma'am."

"Come with me, please," she said and led him down a short corridor.

"I read the message you posted about coming here for assistance," she said as they walked. "Our staff has a lot of experience working with different forms of emotional trauma."

"Thank you for seeing me, ma'am," Alex said, still uncertain about doing this yet reassured by the naval officer's openness.

Inside her small office, she pointed for Alex to take one of the two arm chairs and settled herself in the other one opposite him. Alex's eyes drifted to academic diplomas hanging on the wall. One was a doctorate from Johns Hopkins.

"My background's in clinical psychology and psychological trauma," Commander Forgash said. "I like to start by asking about some personal and medical history: family, where you grew up, education, how you chose to come to the Naval Academy, information like that. It helps us begin an open conversation."

He told her what she wanted to know about his early years and enlistment in the Marine Corps less than a year out of high school. He mentioned that his father was an Academy grad. Alex also summarized his route from basic training to being deployed with the 24th MEU and Marine Fleet Force.

Then he briefed her about his deployments responding to humanitarian relief missions, NEOs, riot control, and other missions. He spoke with ease about everything until his final mission with 24th MEU. That's when he stopped and showed a pained expression.

"Do you need to take a break?" she asked.

"No ma'am, I'd rather continue if that's okay?" he replied willingly.

"Certainly. Tell me what's happening with you now."

For approximately twenty minutes, Alex described for her everything that had happened during the MEU's NEO mission to Sierra Leone. Next, he described symptoms that troubled him: flashbacks and waking up in cold sweats. Eating and diet all screwed up. Moments feeling indifferent to what's going on around him. It could be in a class, at morning muster, baseball practice, formation. Anywhere, anytime on the Yard. "Sometimes I'm just not in the moment, you know what I mean?" Alex stopped, and the lieutenant commander waited patiently for him to continue. "Pardon me, but when it happens I don't much give a shit about anything for the next fifteen to thirty seconds. It's like my mind and my body aren't in the same place."

"Do you think others are aware you're dealing with things you don't talk about?" she asked him in an observant voice.

Yes, he confirmed. His roommates were aware and so were other midshipmen in 10th Company. They knew he was prior-enlisted and had engaged in ground combat operations. "But no one's said anything to me. They give me plenty of space, and that's fine. None of my instructors or coaches have said anything either. They're probably not sure what to say to me when I suddenly get quiet."

"I understand," she replied, checked her watch, and closed her notebook. The time had gone fast. But he'd gotten a lot off his chest. "This was a good first meeting, Alex. I look forward to another session if you choose to have one."

She proposed talking once a week. If something urgent happened between sessions and he wanted to talk sooner, he could email her because she periodically checked mail. She handed him her business card.

"Thank you, ma'am."

"I will see you next week, and email or call if you feel like talking right away about anything," she reassured. "Good luck, midshipman."

Alex stopped at the front desk and made his appointment for

the following session. Maybe Lieutenant Commander Forgash could help him find his way out of those dark places inside his head. Maybe she could convince him to believe that he wasn't "broken gear" or "damaged goods," or one of the other perverted references he'd heard Marines say about brothers who'd suffered psychological trauma. He'd been injured, but he wasn't broken beyond repair.

Give it a chance, Alex told himself and headed for his next class.

# CHAPTER 22

**10th Company**
**Bancroft Hall, USNA**
**October 14, 2020 at 2138**

Alex and Harry were in the middle of finishing homework assignments when an upperclassman in Service Dress Blue uniform appeared in the open doorway to their room. They rose from their desks and stood at attention. By December of the first academic period during fourth-class year, plebes wouldn't be required any longer to call "Attention on Deck" when an upperclassman entered the area.

"At ease, you two," he said, "I've done that too." He pointed to Alex. "Are you doing anything important?" Carl Myers, Midshipman Third Class, was Alex's mentor in 10th Company. Each plebe had an assigned sophomore year midshipman mentor.

"It can wait, sir. Something you want to talk about?"

Myers motioned toward the door. "Let's take a walk."

Alex reached for his issued gray Navy sweatshirt and threw it on underneath his midshipman-issue dark blue nylon jacket. He grabbed his blue woolen pullover cap with GO NAVY! knitted in large gold letters across it.

The two Mids made small talk as they took the ladder leading downstairs to Zero Deck, then exited the door out of Bancroft Hall and on to Cooper Road. When they reached the street, a cold wind coming off the Severn River struck their unprotected faces. Alex pulled his knit hat down over his ears and buried his hands tightly into his armpits. Carl turned up the collar of his issued

Eisenhower-style waist jacket against his neck. They passed the entrance to the field house and headed for the seawall where the river's winds picked up and stung their faces.

"Things going okay with you?" asked Myers.

"Yes sir, I suppose," Alex answered, the air from his breath forming a cloud of moisture as it hit the frigid air.

"I've noticed you're quieter lately. Anything on your mind?"

Alex shrugged. "Just being a plebe, sir. Keeping my head down."

"Seems to me something's going on. Is there?"

They walked along the Santee Basin and passed Naval Academy sailboats, 44s and 26s bobbing in the water. No one else was around.

"I tend to go dark sometimes, Mister Myers." Alex wasn't expecting his mentor's question. "Excuse me, sir, is there anything I should know? Anybody in the company have an issue with me and they're keeping quiet?"

Myers dug his hands deeper into the jacket pockets. "Tell me your side of what happened on fourth deck two days ago."

"I'm not sure what you mean, sir."

"Two Mids were in the passageway. Their story was you shouted 'Take cover!' or something like that." The two turned down Brownson Road and alongside a silent Farragut Field. "Is that true?" asked Carl.

Alex lifted his cupped hands to his mouth and blew a warm breath into them. He knew the incident Myers spoke of, which had rattled him for the past couple of days. It had happened before at small arms marksmanship and rifle training during Plebe Summer. The sound of rifle fire made him shudder.

"Yes sir, it's true."

"Want to talk about it?"

"Sir, am I accused of doing something wrong?" Alex's voice turned defensive and he instantly regretted it.

"No, you're not accused of anything. The company commander pulled me aside right after morning meal and asked me if I knew what was going on. I told him I didn't. Then he said the company officer heard about it." Myers removed his hands from his jacket pockets and rubbed his cold ears. "The battalion officer knows too."

"Sir, I'd like to know who told the company officer." Watch your temper, Alex told himself. He wanted to give Myers the benefit of the doubt that he was ready to take Alex's side. Now he only wanted to get back to his warm room.

"Just give me your version of the story," Myers told him, impatience in his tone.

"I walked out of my room into the passageway and saw two Mids coming in my direction, one of them carrying several books. Right after they passed, I heard a loud bang and it shook me up. That's all it was, nothing more."

"A bang?" A curious look formed on Myers's face. They approached Lejeune Hall when a US Navy police cruiser on patrol passed them.

Alex nodded. "What happened was one midshipman dropped a book. It slammed flat and hard on the deck."

Carl rubbed his cold hands together. "What did you do?"

"I dropped into a crouch on the deck," said Alex.

"You thought you were taking fire?"

"That's where my head was when I heard it."

"How did the two Mids react?"

Alex shrugged. "Their eyes got really big like they were shocked. One of them came over to see if I was okay."

"Word spreads fast inside the company, Alex. The executive officer came to me because I'm your mentor." Midshipman Myers stopped walking. "If this is coming from some shitty things that happened when you were a ground warfare Marine—"

"Yeah, it is," Alex told him.

"I want to make sure you get some help." Myers wrapped his arms tightly around his chest. "Have you talked with anyone at the MDC?"

Alex hopped up and down, desperate to stay warm. "I've talked to a psychologist there about it, a lieutenant commander. Had three sessions so far."

"How's that working out?" Myers asked, sounding interested.

"She listens to me talk about my nightmares, how I can't sleep much, my reactions to sudden noises. I get it that she wants to help me." Carl remained quiet, waiting for the plebe to say more. "In my head, being out on patrol and in firefights still bothers me. But I'm dealing with it. That's all there is to it, sir." His hands rubbed up and down his sleeves to keep warm. "We need to walk because it's goddamn freezing out here."

"Keep going to counseling," said Carl. "They know how to help Mids deal with psychological trauma, and it sounds like that's what you've got."

Alex appreciated Myers wanting to help. "But what if going there makes things worse for me? The Academy could cut me loose for medical reasons." Alex shook his head. "Bad, sir, very bad."

"That wouldn't happen," Myers explained. "The MDC isn't part of the Naval Health Clinic, so it doesn't keep records of Mids whom it treats. There isn't any paper trail if someone wanted to hold you back from graduation and commissioning."

They turned the corner at King George Street by Halsey Field House and headed back to Bancroft Hall. Alex waited to speak until a few Mids jogged passed them. "My scars from combat are still healing," he said after the joggers were gone. "But it takes time. That still doesn't give anyone the right to point to me as some mental head case and toss me aside." The muscles in his face tightened with frustration. "I'm not what some in the Corps like to call 'broken gear'."

"Hold on, nobody's saying that about you," Myers added promptly.

Alex wasn't buying it. "Others who haven't gone where I have been, who saw their brothers wounded and killed—they shouldn't fucking judge me."

"Ease up, Alex," Myers came right back at his plebe. "Every midshipman in 10th Company respects your prior service. No one's judging you."

"Pardon my language, sir," Alex paused, "but Marine grunts say 'fuck' about every fourth word. It's a hard habit to break."

"I get it." Myers managed a smile.

They walked into Bancroft Hall, grateful to get out of the cold. "Anything else going on you want to discuss?" Carl asked as they made their way up the ladder to the fourth deck. "It's just us talking."

"You can't help with this one, sir."

"Try me anyway."

Alex winced and pressed his eyes shut. "This morning I got a text message about a buddy from our platoon in Sierra Leone. A good Marine, too. He—" Alex abruptly stopped mid-sentence and looked down for several seconds.

"He what?" said Myers.

"He put a .45 in his mouth and pulled the trigger."

"Shit, I'm so sorry."

"Yeah, well," said Alex, the feeling in his chest bouncing between grief and anger.

"Being in combat can raise you up one minute and then it tears you down the next. You know what I mean, sir?"

"I don't, but I know you do."

They reached the fourth deck and entered the passageway.

"You're a good midshipman, Alex," Myers said. "I believe you're here for a reason. Everyone in 10th Company looks up to you."

Alex nodded. "Thanks, sir."

"It's Carl."

"Okay, Carl."

"See you at morning formation," Myers said and departed.

Alone in the passageway, Alex crossed his arms and shook his head with frustration. If he'd only known his Marine brother had been in such a dark place, he'd have reached out to him. An unnecessary death that could have been prevented.

# CHAPTER 23

**10th Company**
**Bancroft Hall, USNA**
**November 2, 2020 at 1740**

The laptop screen illuminated Alex's face as he proofread his course report for political science. He glanced at the time displayed in the bottom corner of the PC: twenty minutes until evening meal.

"Anyone know what's for dinner tonight?" he asked his roommates.

"I hope it's something that doesn't give me the runs," Harry Stocks said, laughing.

"Can you be more graphic?" Brian Tannehill chimed in.

"Hey, just as long as it doesn't taste like something my dog would walk away from." Harry looked up from his book with a scrunched face.

The three roommates could be sarcastic with each other because they were plebes. Because they were friends. Because they trusted each other like brothers.

"When you see me on my knees right before Taps, I'm praying for care packages from my mother," Harry added, revealing a naughty smile.

Alex gazed out the window and watched sheets of rain battering the glass.

There was a knock at their door. Harry got up from his rack to answer it, then turned his head. "Hey Alex, someone here to see you."

Midshipman First Class Carla Speake stood in the open doorway. "I heard you were at the Academy and decided to drop by, say hi," she leaned her head in and looked in Alex's direction. "It's been a while since we deployed."

"Definitely a long time, ma'am. Good seeing you," Alex replied with a warm greeting and rose to meet her.

Carla stood slightly under six feet tall with posture so straight she appeared taller. Her blonde hair tied back in a bun shimmered under the overhead fluorescent light fixtures. Three shining gold bars were pinned on each collar of her Working Blue uniform shirt: Midshipman Lieutenant. Her midshipman rank could have been Company Commander or Battalion or Regimental Staff. Whichever one it was represented a highly regarded leadership position in the Brigade.

A few weeks earlier, leaving a baseball practice at Halsey Field House, Alex had spotted a tall blonde female midshipman who, from a distance, resembled Carla. But he wasn't sure until a teammate's comment made Alex's neck get hot with anger.

"See that tall blonde Mid on the far right?"

"What about her?" asked Alex.

"Last name's Speake. A plebe I know from 4th Company told me she was a bitch detailer at Plebe Summer. Wanted to show she was tougher than the guys. She's supposedly prior-enlisted, probably Navy. No way she could have been a Marine. I heard she's a lesbian."

Alex fixed his gaze at the midshipman in the distance and confirmed she was Carla. She'd been a Marine corporal, like him, assigned to 24th MEU; Carla with the Logistics Combat Element (LCE) and Alex with the Ground Combat Element (GCE). Others who had served with Speake called her a stand-up Marine.

"Be careful what you say about other people," Alex had warned, his tone hard-edged. "You don't know what you don't know."

"What's that supposed to mean?"

Alex had fixed a cold stare at the other midshipman. "I'm a prior-enlisted Marine just like her. We served together. If more women were in infantry, she'd have carried an M4 on one of my fire teams," he said. "I don't care who she wrestles with under the sheets. No more talking trash about her, understand?"

The other plebe had nodded in silence. He understood.

"How about we do rolling trays at evening meal and catch up?" Carla asked and smiled easily at Alex from the open doorway. She referred to the relaxed regulation letting Mids sit anywhere they chose in the dining hall instead of the entire Brigade usually seated with their respective companies.

"Sounds good, ma'am," he answered.

"Look at us. We've gone from enlisted Marines to the Naval Academy," Carla said with a tenor of satisfaction as they headed for the cavernous dining hall that seated the entire Brigade. "Who would have thought, you know?"

They merged anonymously into a streaming crowd of midshipmen converging into King Hall. "Listen," said Carla and stopped until there were fewer Mids walking near them. "You don't have to address me as 'ma'am' when no one's near us," she told Alex in a hushed voice. "You're a plebe and I'm First Class. You okay with that?"

"Works for me," he replied.

"Good, because the way I see it, we were two enlisted Marines who served together with a great unit. If things go right for us, we're both heading back to the Corps as officers; me first, then you." She nodded, a satisfied gleam in her eyes.

They took seats and reached for the platters stacked with fried chicken. Alex scrunched his face in protest. Catching his reaction, Carla chuckled. "C'mon, the food here's not that bad."

"Chow at Parris Island sometimes tasted better than this," he joked.

"Hey, you and every other maggot recruit would've eaten anything they put in front of you as long as it didn't move when you poked it," she said. Both of them laughed.

They sat at the end of a table. The closest Mids were far enough away that the two of them could say whatever they wanted to each other. Alex listened while Carla described her journey from enlisted Marine corporal to earning an appointment to the Naval Academy. She had enrolled at UCLA while wait-listed by Naval Academy Admissions. Before finishing her freshman year, an unexpected call from the Naval Academy had come; Navy was ready to extend an appointment. They were holding a place for her with the class of 2021. She had grabbed it faster than she could blink and had closed her affairs at UCLA.

"Did you think about the Marine Corps Platoon Leaders Course for your commission instead of coming here?" said Alex between bites of food.

"No. Why would I?" she answered, her voice incredulous.

Alex drained the remaining milk from his glass and reached for a napkin to wipe the milk moustache off his lips. "I'm thinking about grads who never wanted women admitted to the Academy. Now some of them have sons and grandsons here who don't like women being in the Brigade."

"I know all about 'em," she replied icily with a fierce look in her eyes. Carla Speake—for that matter, practically every female midshipman on the Yard—could tell you that women made up almost 15 percent of the Brigade. "They're old farts behaving like insecure boys who never grew up," she remarked. "Frustrated because they probably were born with little hands and tiny dicks."

"If you say so," Alex said and chuckled.

Carla leaned back against the chair and folded her arms.

"Don't get me wrong, but not every female who makes it here adapts well enough to Academy life, and some do it quicker and better than others," she said indifferently. "In four years here, I've never bilged another Mid. Every class has slackers and I don't care if they wear bras or briefs. But female Mids who look for an easy way out of doing their duties," she frowned, "they really get under my skin."

Alex picked up on the edge in Speake's words.

"I'm not saying women with a high unhappiness factor can't become good officers," she added, "but some of them might be better off at a Naval ROTC program than here. Being here is a privilege," she added in measured words, "and not everyone earns it."

The conversation moved to Carla's plans following graduation. She had stated her commissioning preference for Marine Air, then earning her wings and one day qualifying to fly attack aircraft, preferably helicopters. "Guess I'll find out in November at Service Assignment if the Marine Corps agrees with me," she said and let out a frustrated grunt loud enough that nearby Mids heard and looked over at her. "You know what I mean."

"I don't," said Alex, who picked up straight away on her suddenly dour mood.

Anyone looking her way couldn't miss the pinched expression on Carla's face. "The Corps still has too many anal chauvinist officers," she said with open cynicism. "You've seen and heard them—'Hey, women can support mission operations, but never let 'em serve in forward areas,'" she sneered. "That's a load of you-know-what."

"Yeah, it is," said Alex.

"You might be surprised," she said with her hazel eyes wide open. "One day a woman in uniform will stand up for you because you did the right thing. She'll take heat for doing it but she won't back away. She will defend you."

Alex did a double take. "That sounds serious."

"Put that idea in the back of your mind for now," Carla said, smiled, and turned the conversation to something more easygoing. "What about you? What turned you on about the Academy?"

"My platoon commander ordered me to get a commission, then come back to the Corps," Alex said, "Or he'd kick my ass."

"Marines who tell you they'll kick your ass mean it," Carla laughed lightly. "That's it? Your platoon commander pushed you here?"

"My father's a graduate, Class of '92. He wanted me to apply but I wasn't ready after high school," Alex said, taking on a slightly serious tone. "But my attitude about coming here changed after my enlistment."

Carla pointed a finger at him. "What's that scar on the side of your neck?"

"On our deployment after you left, the MEU did an NEO mission in Africa. Things went south when in-country rebels opened fire on refugees we came to transport out—" he paused a moment and looked away—"then they opened fire on us." His fingers ran gently over the scar. "IED shrapnel. I got hit in a couple of places during the firefight."

The Firstie fixed her gaze on him. "You did more than get hit in a couple of places," she said, her expression solemn. "I know you saved three Marines, and one of them was that same platoon commander. And two of those Marines are alive today because you kept them from bleeding to death in the field—the platoon commander being one of them."

Alex shrugged. "I did my duty."

"Do other Mids know what you did during that firefight?"

"I don't talk about it," he told her and took in a breath, then released it slowly. "I know what I did and that's enough, isn't it?"

She nodded. "I guess so. Marine officers and SELs on the Yard—trust me, they know what you did."

Alex rose from his seat and headed toward the dessert table. He returned moments later with two plates of cheesecake. They were finishing them when Carla popped another question.

"How'd you manage Plebe Summer being prior-enlisted and older than everyone else?"

"You know what's it's like," he answered. "Some detailers get carried away trying to show you how tough they are on I-Day."

She was curious now. "Did anyone single you out on purpose?"

Alex wiped his mouth with a napkin and told her about taking grief from one or two detailers trying to get under his skin. "On I-Day one of them got in my face with some cheap-shot remark that the Academy would test me."

Carla rolled her eyes. "That's a laugh. Plebe Summer would test *you*?"

"I said something to him I shouldn't. That's how it came out I was a Marine."

"What'd you say?" she asked with widened eyes.

"I told him I'd already been tested," Alex said and wrinkled his nose. "The guy's eyes blinked so fast it looked like he was sending morse code."

Carla laughed out loud. "I wish I could have been there to see that. Any detailers ask if you'd served in a war zone?"

Alex folded his arms. "I think one of them asked, but I didn't want to talk and they didn't push me."

Evening meal was done and they rose from the table. Carla pointed toward the doors in King Hall exiting onto Cooper Road. "I'm going that way, out to my car by the seawall. Hey, I enjoyed catching up. Thanks."

"Same here," he answered.

"Anytime you want to talk, I'm around," said Carla.

"Thanks, I'll remember that."

"The Academy's damn lucky having you in the Brigade. You know more about sacrifice than a lot of officers here ever will."

Alex smiled wryly and shrugged. "Maybe."

"Trust me, you do." She nodded, smiling, and waved as she walked away. "Semper Fi."

"Oorah," Alex called out and waved back.

# CHAPTER 24

**Nimitz Library, USNA**
**November 11, 2020 at 2140**

Alex had three exams left to take for the twelve-week academic period. Chemistry would be tough and he wasn't ready. He thought his instructor for Rhetoric needed to improve his own rhetoric. With Seamanship, the only thing he gave a shit about was wanting sailors to know how to steer an amphibious landing craft and deliver Marines on a beachhead.

At least thirty midshipmen were working quietly in the library's public area. Alex flipped open his laptop, checked for email, and saw several new messages in his inbox. One from his father. Rear Admiral David Kramer was coming to Annapolis Friday afternoon. Maybe they could meet for dinner at the Naval Academy Club. An email from his sister, Victoria. Four years older than her brother, Tori Kramer was an acquisitions editor with a major book publishing house in midtown Manhattan. She was in a slow-dance relationship with a New York City fireman and it sounded serious.

Then he opened an email from his mother, checking in on him the way she did every other week since I-Day: "Plebe life still okay?" wrote Olivia. "What about your flashbacks? Is there a place there where Mids can talk about problems? And nothing gets written up in their personnel records?" He'd answer her tonight. Alex had plebe life under control. Little fazed him. As for getting help with flashbacks and nightmares? He was still working on that with Lieutenant Commander Forgash, and appreciated getting her professional medical advice.

Alex smiled at one unexpected new message. The sender's email address was locknloadusmc@gmail.com—Eddie Arsenault checking in. A year ago, Arsenault made staff sergeant and received orders to Parris Island as a Small Arms Weapons Instructor. Alex opened Arsenault's email:

> How's life at the Naval Academy? Anyone there teach you what to do if a pigeon craps on your summer whites while you're saluting an officer? LOL. Life's good back here at recruit basic training Shangri-La. Remember boot camp when we took bets our DI, Gunnery Sergeant Lopez, was abused as a child? The female DIs here are scarier than Lopez. I'll get up to Annapolis sometime to check up on you. Remember, you promised our platoon you wouldn't go soft and take a commission in the Navy. If you do, I'm coming to kick your ass. Take care, Kramer.
>
> OORAH!

He stared at two new emails from Ethan Crowell and held his breath. One email subject line said "messed up". The other said, "holding on best I can." That was it: two subject lines, no messages. Alex's path as a young man seemed predestined, from decorated Marine corporal then sergeant to a midshipman at the Academy. His future appeared boundless. He could do anything he set his mind to. But Ethan Crowell hadn't been so lucky.

PTSD became too much for him to bear. Lack of sleep, acting moody and distant, even sudden reactions to a door closing loudly or a truck's backfire could knock his emotional stability off its rails at any time. Ethan had been honorably discharged from the Marine Corps with a medical disability ten weeks after 24th MEU returned to Camp Lejeune following its NEO mission in Sierra Leone. From the moment he was discharged, his life had slowly but steadily spiraled through periods of despair and difficulties—trouble holding jobs, inability to relate to people, and drinking too much, which added to his depression. Ethan had married and then divorced all within seven months. Alex figured whatever meds Ethan had taken kept him from losing every ounce of psychological control.

The library was quiet as Alex pulled out the water bottle from his backpack along with a peanut butter PowerBar. He'd been hungry one hour following noon meal. Now he couldn't wait for evening meal.

His own eating habits were erratic ever since he was laid up at a naval hospital recovering from his own combat wounds. He felt an urgency to comprehend what was happening inside his head and had researched how people react to psychological trauma.

He'd read about symptoms he recognized all too well: mood swings, sweats, self-blame, startled reactions, withdrawal, and apathy among others. They described him. Plus, the occasional nightmares that haunted him. Different triggers could set off a flashback in a split second, any time of day. An email from Ethan was one of them.

Alex was sympathetic to Ethan's situation yet relieved he wasn't so afflicted as his friend. He recalled being disgusted watching how some Marine Corps commands treated Marines who struggled with combat-related trauma. The Corps could do the very best for its Marines one minute, then push them to the side of the road a minute later. It encouraged psychologically wounded Marines to self-report their mental health burdens. But mustering the courage to speak up presented risks. Alex had observed certain macho types in the Corps react with cold-hearted indifference toward their emotionally struggling brothers. Those episodes had made Alex sick to his stomach. He'd agonize when wounded brothers became exiles, outliers. They would be stigmatized with humiliating labels that spread around the base about them. One of the worst ones was "malingerer." They were no longer worthy of the mission. Some Marines even went so far as to call them embarrassments to the Corps. For Alex, that was deepest human cruelty from one Marine to another.

Service members who openly sought assistance also risked seeing their careers end up in near ruin. Command would strip them of their present responsibilities and assign them useless work, often administrative crap. That's what had happened to Ethan.

The deepest cuts upon a Marine's self-esteem happened too often when they finally self-reported. Marines they'd served with, close brothers through training and operational deployments, now avoided being seen with them. He feared that could be him someday.

His eyes shut and head leaned back, Alex slowly released the air in his lungs. Today's Veterans Day and Ethan's a veteran, he reminded himself. But it felt like no one was remembering Ethan. *I won't forget you, brother,* was Alex's silent promise.

"Is everything all right, midshipman?"

The sound of a delicate voice startled Alex. He sat up and shook his head, his eyes open wide.

"Yes ma'am. I'm okay."

A slender Black woman with streaks of gray in her dark hair stood next to him. "Something appeared to upset you."

"All's fine, really."

"If you need anything, please let me know. I'll be over at the desk."

"Yes ma'am, I will. Thanks."

Alex reopened his laptop and returned to email. There was another new message, one he wasn't expecting.

Hi Alex,

How's the Naval Academy? Is life there different than the
Marine Corps? I can hardly believe I'm starting my senior year
at Princeton already! Is your mom doing well? Hope she is.
And how about Tori? What's she doing now? Thinking of you,
and know you're doing what you want.

Best,
Carolyn
Princeton University Class of 2021

Though Carolyn's decision after high school to end their
relationship had wounded him, Alex had been determined to get
over her. While on active duty, he'd followed her Facebook posts
from Princeton. Sometimes her posts pleased him. Other times
they made him jealous of people in Carolyn's privileged Ivy League
orbit. Emails between them were scarce. They shared Christmas
and birthday wishes. That was it.

She didn't know he'd been wounded in combat, thousands of
miles away from her cozy existence at an elite school. She didn't
know he had saved three seriously wounded Marines and had
been wounded himself. Or that his country had decorated him
for valor. Not until Olivia Kramer had told her about Alex's acts of
courage under fire.

Carolyn and his mother occasionally exchanged emails. Alex
had asked Olivia not to tell Carolyn what had happened to him in
Sierra Leone. Their lives and their priorities were set on different
coordinates. Now this confusing email from her.

Alex ran a hand through his close-cropped dirty blond hair,
collected his things, and headed back to Bancroft Hall at 2230. He
needed to email Ethan because he didn't like reading "holding on
as best I can." Any message from Ethan with those words sounded
desperate.

Back in his room, Alex checked his watch. It read 2245, fifteen minutes until Taps.

The Company Duty Officer would be sticking his head inside doors soon to check on Mids. He opened his laptop and tapped out an email back to Carolyn:

> Academy life is good. Being a Marine, then coming here makes a person different. Not better, just different. I've been in situations other midshipmen can't understand. Mom's fine and Tori's in New York City. She's a book editor. You're a senior at Princeton now. That's awesome! Maybe we'll catch up at Christmas if you're home. The Brigade will be on leave.
>
> I was meant to be at the Naval Academy.
>
> Alex
> NAVY '24

He tapped Send on the keyboard, locked his fingers together behind his head, and leaned back. Alex thought about one sentence he'd written: "I've been in situations other midshipmen can't understand." Carolyn wouldn't understand when she read it either. She wasn't aware of his valor, his wounds, his leadership under fire in West Africa. Part of him wanted to tell her. Maybe someday he could.

# CHAPTER 25

**A restaurant in Arlington, VA**
**December 23, 2020**

It was two days before Christmas and the restaurant was crowded. Alex observed young people standing almost shoulder to shoulder at the bar, a scene from civilian life he hadn't experienced for several years. But he felt excited being part of it again.

Alex hadn't seen Carolyn Hagerty in four and a half years. But who's counting? He was. His chin lifted high enough to see beyond the bar crowd, and he spotted her sitting at a table alongside a tall window.

Walking toward her, he felt goose bumps rise on his forearms. Carolyn was as attractive as the last time he saw her, the day before he left for Parris Island.

He was reminded of the first time he noticed her in high school, seated at the far end of the classroom. She was a transfer student returning to the US from Europe, where her father was a foreign service officer. Alex had been drawn in by the way her pretty features formed into a smile. Now it was happening again.

Carolyn, stylish with a cream blouse under a crimson-colored velvet sport coat over black slacks and black flats, put down her glass of white wine and rose to greet him. Her long chestnut hair fell across her shoulders when she stood up. Longer than their last time together, Carolyn's hair glistened under the restaurant's overhead lights. A lighter lipstick shade perfectly matched the color of her sport coat.

They stared at each other for a few seconds. She smiled and

extended her arms. He took one step forward and placed his arms carefully around her waist. She returned the gesture, pulling him toward her in a hug.

"You look great, you know that?" said Alex, pulling away and gazing into her eyes.

"That's kind of you to say," she said.

"It's true."

They sat and a server approached to take Alex's drink order. Even with a busy crowd surrounding the bar, warm lighting from artificial candle-style lamps on tables and in booths, the place had a relaxed feeling. Just enough noise so they could hear each other and still feel some privacy from other people near them.

"My turn now," said Carolyn after the server left. "You're as handsome as I remembered," she hesitated, "And you're different."

His eyes narrowed. "Different how?"

"You don't look like a kid anymore. You've seen the world and grown up—maybe faster than a lot of other men."

The server returned with his Guinness.

"When I got to the Academy, I already knew I was different from other plebes," he said and took a long drink of his beer. "So far it's working out."

"Different because you proved a kind of bravery other men can only imagine."

Her words surprised him. "Oh, and you know this because—"

"Because your Mom told me what happened in Africa. What you did over there with the Marines."

"I think you mean what I did *as* a Marine." Alex leaned across the table toward her and nodded with a smile. "I could have guessed she would say something about it to you."

"Do you have any idea how proud she is? That you saved the lives of three Marines?"

"Look, I did my duty," he answered and made a dismissive gesture. "Any Marine in my squad would have done what I did."

"But did you know that it affected your Mom in a big way?"

"How?"

"It hurt her not knowing you'd been seriously wounded until much later."

Alex sat quietly for a moment and looked away, then turned back to see Carolyn. "I didn't want her worrying about me, that's all."

"She was proud of you, and so was your father," Carolyn said and blushed. "So was I."

He didn't know how to respond to Carolyn's last words.

With elbows on the table, Alex rested his fingers under his chin and exhaled slowly. "I'm still dealing with what happened there. Getting my head straight about it, if that makes sense."

"Not exactly. Tell me."

He took a drink from his Guinness while Carolyn waited for him to continue.

"I felt like it was my fault one of my Marines lost part of a leg and another was badly concussed," he said. "I should have gone first into that building. Since then, loud noises can still set me off. I'm here but I'm not here, you know? Other times I don't care what's going on around me." He leaned closer toward her. "Midshipmen aren't supposed to bring that kind of baggage with them to Annapolis. But parts of me came back from combat kind of broken. It's not easy and it takes time."

Carolyn swirled the wine in her glass. "A lot of people believe in you. They'll do anything to make sure you heal, and you will. You have a purpose at the Academy, just as you had a purpose for enlisting and the heroism you showed in—where was it?"

"Sierra Leone, West Africa."

Carolyn sat quietly for a brief moment, then cleared her throat. "You're different from other men."

Alex shot her a questioning look. "How do you know that?"

"Because you've always seemed to know where you're headed, where you belong."

"Four thousand four hundred other Mids have a purpose too. I'm not special."

Carolyn shifted in her chair and looked discomfited.

"Are you okay?" Alex asked, studying her silent reaction.

"I have an apology to make to you," she finally said. "Four years ago, I said you were making a big mistake enlisting, that you should go to college. I—" She hesitated. "I was wrong and I'm so sorry." Her chin quivered so slightly anyone else would have missed the twitch. But Alex caught it.

"You don't owe me an apology. You followed what you believed in." He saw her relax ever so slightly at his words.

"Hey, we both went after what we believed in, okay? For me it was the Marine Corps and for you it was Princeton." He reached across the table and took her hand in his. She let him.

"Not to change the subject, but shouldn't you be in uniform?" Carolyn said, now more at ease and wearing an easy smile.

"Plebes can wear civilian clothes when they're on official leave, and Christmas break is official leave." He chuckled. "Personally, I looked cooler in dress blues as an enlisted Marine than I do in my Academy uniforms."

"I bet I could find Instagram photos of you in Marine Corps dress," she kidded him.

"Bet you won't," he beamed back.

"You look just fine in civilian clothes."

"Let's order. I'm hungry," said Alex and gestured for the server. They ordered dinner and another round of drinks.

"Enough about me," said Alex, lifting some stuffed flounder onto a fork. "Tell me about Princeton and the Peace Corps. How'd that happen?"

"Okay," she said. "Junior year I spent five months in South America. It was a Peace Corps internship. We helped poor native families with farming and finding food supplies. I loved doing it." She smiled. "After graduation, I'm joining a global foundation to work on food programs in developing countries."

Alex saw how she brightened just talking about it. "Food programs, huh? What's that, exactly?"

She talked excitedly between chewing forkfuls of salad. "Different projects. Reducing hunger, malnutrition, and food loss in third-world countries is one major area. Another one's fighting food waste in American cities. And there's technologies for developing better food production in Africa."

"Africa? Yeah, that's a place I know. Well, good for you," he said, pleased by her enthusiasm. "You'll do important work, something with a purpose."

"I hope to." She paused. "Just like you did."

They finished dinner and their coffee orders arrived.

"I know a food project you should work on," he said with a chuckle. "You'll save thousands of lives."

"And what's that?" Her eyebrows lifted with curiosity.

Alex stirred half-and-half into his coffee and up looked at her, pretending to be serious but finally giving in to a smile. "Your mission will be to improve meals and end hunger for Academy midshipmen."

"Oh yeah?" she chuckled.

"Midshipmen are desperate to eat three square meals a day, and some decent-tasting food. You'd be doing a patriotic duty," he said, trying but failing to keep a straight face.

"I'll see what I can do when I get to New York," she said and smiled. "Till then, midshipmen should suck it up and eat what's put in front of them. It's free after all, isn't it?"

"Easy for you to say."

Alex signaled to their server for the check.

"Can I ask you something personal?" Carolyn said. "And it's all right if you don't answer."

Alex leaned toward her. "You can ask me anything."

Carolyn blinked a few times as if mustering courage. "Are you in a relationship?"

Alex's eyes grew wide, and he smiled. "No, I'm not. There's almost no personal free time for plebes except Academy life. Total immersion. It'll get better in May when I make Third Class."

"What's Third Class?"

"Academy speak. That's what you call a midshipman who's a sophomore. Ask my Mom. She'll explain Academy speak to you."

"I'd rather wait for you to be my teacher," she told him, her face lighting up.

Alex paid the check. They pulled their coats off the backs of their chairs and stepped outside into a cold and dry December evening.

"I'm glad we did this," she told him.

"So am I."

"You know, I'd still like to see you in uniform sometime."

"That could be arranged." He winked.

"I enjoyed tonight a lot, thank you. Merry Christmas, Alex."

"Merry Christmas, Carolyn."

Alex watched her walk away. She turned to wave, and he waved back.

Seeing Carolyn again had been exciting *and* conflicting. He wasn't sure if being together mirrored the past or hinted at the future.

# CHAPTER 26

**Preparing to Lead—Leadership, Ethics, and Law**
**Luce Hall, USNA**
**February 23, 2021 at 1430**

"Attention on deck!" the section leader called out, and the all-plebe instructional class rose to attention.

"Good afternoon, take your seats," said Captain Hundley as he entered the classroom and placed a set of papers on the table up front.

In earlier classes, Alex had noticed Hundley's three rows of service ribbons resting beneath his Naval Aviator Wings. Ribbons displayed a service member's military resumé. Some decorations he recognized: the Air Medal with a Strike/Flight Device; campaign medals denoting service in Afghanistan, Iraq, and Syria; and the Navy & Marine Corps Sea Service Ribbon, among others. Two ribbons stood out: the Bronze Star with Combat "V" device and the Purple Heart. Alex wondered what this Marine captain had done as a military pilot to be recognized for valor. Was he OCS-commissioned or an Academy grad? He didn't wear an Academy class ring. What about the Purple Heart? Was his aircraft shot down?

Captain Hundley reached for a blue marker and wrote on the erasable board:

Is Leading in Combat Unique?

He turned around and asked the class how many agreed the question was true. Several hands shot up and the instructor pointed to a plebe seated alongside Alex.

"Things happen fast in combat, and officers—well, they don't always have time to take their time, sir," she commented.

"Ms. Hollenbach suggests that quick decisions in combat matter," said Hundley looking around at the Mids. "How many of you would agree with her?"

All the plebes raised their hands in agreement except one: Alex.

"You have a different opinion, Mister Kramer?" Captain Hundley called out.

"I do, sir. That type of leadership turns into Charlie Foxtrot," Alex answered without hesitation.

Other midshipmen looked confused. They didn't know what those two words meant in Marine Corps speak. But their instructor did. "Mister Kramer, do you care to explain to those here who don't know the meaning of Charlie Foxtrot?"

"You want me to say it, sir?" Alex asked with obvious reluctance.

"Yes, tell them."

"It, uh, means clusterfuck," Alex said plainly.

"Are you saying Midshipman Hollenbach's view of combat leadership is all wrong?"

Alex shifted slightly in his chair. "No sir, she's not completely wrong. It's just that—"

"Just what?" Captain Hundley asked.

"—that Marines and sailors lose trust real fast with officers who make fast but bad decisions." He waited a moment. "You do that in combat and people get injured. Service members could die."

The rest of the Mids watched in anxious silence for Captain Hundley's reaction.

"Back to Ms. Hollenbach's point," the instructor said, "aren't there times when officers in combat must decide quickly because they don't have a choice—Mister Kramer?"

"Yes sir, there are," said Alex and turned toward the female classmate. "You're right and I spoke too soon."

"We're good," she nodded.

"This has been a good discussion," the instructor announced twenty-five minutes later and prepared to dismiss the class. "We will pick up here in our next session. Thank you."

"Attention on deck!" A midshipman announced the official manner instructional classes opened and closed. He and all others rose from their chairs to stand at attention as Captain Hundley gestured dismissal. Then Hundley approached Alex after most other Mids had walked past and out.

"Mister Kramer."

"Sir?"

After serving together for a period of time, there were moments when enlisted Marines could feel more at ease speaking with some junior officers and still respect the chain of command. Those officers related easily to their enlisted personnel.

But Alex was no longer a Marine sergeant sharing a harmless comment with his platoon commander. He was a Midshipman Fourth Class and expected to conduct himself properly. Six months out of I-Day and he hadn't fully adapted to it yet. He felt constrained, being talked down to sometimes by some Firsties who gave themselves more credit for maturity than they deserved.

"You came down sort of hard on Hollenbach," Hundley said but without a criticizing edge to his words. "They don't yet know things you do, so you might cut 'em some slack."

"I understand, sir."

"How old are you?"

"Twenty-two."

"Who were you with?"

"1/6, Camp Lejeune."

Hundley nodded with approval. "That's a fine unit. I'm around if you'd like to get together and talk sometime," He collected his satchel from the table. "See you at Friday class."

"Afternoon, sir."

Alex exited Luce Hall to a chilly yet sunny February afternoon. His black waist jacket zipped up to his neck to block the cold, he crossed the road and walked along the seawall.

He had arrived at Annapolis with a different backstory and different scars than every other midshipman. They hadn't witnessed people wounded or dead in combat, or seen their own blood spilled. They hadn't struggled with psychological trauma suffered in battle.

Time would tell whether he was a good fit or a misfit at the Academy. Sheer will had gotten him out of Sierra Leone alive, and it would get him through four years at Annapolis.

# CHAPTER 27

**US Naval Academy**
**September 10, 2021 at 1535**

Tara Marcellus stood at the edge of Worden Field and looked across the spacious green grass. She delighted in wearing her favorite pair of blue jeans and deck shoes. A crimson cotton waist jacket fit easily over her white button-down collar linen shirt.

With her eyes closed, she inhaled a slow, satisfying breath. An early September breeze glided gently across her face and soft shoulder-length hair. A warm and comforting sun slowly began its descent in a cloudless sky.

In twenty-five minutes, the Brigade of Midshipmen would march onto the field in their Infantry Dress Foxtrot uniforms for the Naval Academy's first formal dress parade of the fall academic period. Academy graduates, who were back in Annapolis for class reunion weekends, their spouses, and spectators filled the reviewing stands. With welcoming expressions and self-assured postures, an assembly of Navy and Marine Corps officers and enlisted personnel—all in uniform—joined civilian and military guests and dignitaries to watch the traditional ceremony.

It was the Friday afternoon of Tara's fifth anniversary since she graduated and the Class of 2016's first reunion. She was thrilled about seeing Ray Lydon again. For Tara, five long years had passed since they had graduated and received their commissions. He sent her an email saying that his flight was scheduled to arrive that evening at BWI International Airport.

"Tara Marcellus? Looks like being under water for five years hasn't aged you a day since we graduated!" a pleasing voice interrupted her tender thoughts about Ray.

Tara opened her eyes and turned. Standing beside her was a Navy officer dressed in Summer Whites. An engaging smile added to the woman's sunny features. The name tag on the top right of the uniform shirt said, LT J.M. Wickersham, USN.

She recognized her instantly. "Joyce! How great to see you!"

Though not classmates, Joyce Wickersham and Tara Marcellus had been midshipmen at the same time. Joyce was Class of '14—two years ahead of Tara. She had been her platoon sergeant in 4th Company when Tara was a plebe. The two women had become good friends while together at the Academy, a relationship not common between plebes and upper-class midshipmen. They had also rowed women's crew for Navy. After graduation, Tara had reported to Naval Nuclear Power Training Command for Power School while Joyce had headed to flight training. Their careers had interfered with staying in contact.

Tara saw gold Naval Aviator Wings pinned to the top left side of Wickersham's white uniform shirt, over two rows of service ribbons. "Are you a jet jock?" she asked in jest, using the familiar term for pilots who flew US Navy fixed wing fighter aircraft.

"No, but just as good," said Joyce. "My last tour of duty was flying Seahawks with HSC-6 off USS *George H.W. Bush*." She was referring to a Helicopter Sea Combat Squadron assigned to the Navy's aircraft carrier honoring the nation's forty-first president.

"That had to be cool. What brings you back to Annapolis?" asked Tara.

"I'm company officer for 23rd Company."

"So that's why you're here, and in uniform," Tara said with keen interest in Joyce's current duty station.

"What about you? Still a 'squid'?" Joyce said with a cheerful lilt.

Tara nodded. An easy laugh showed dimples creasing her cheeks. "I finished up three tours as a DIVO aboard *John Warner*, a Virginia Class fast attack boat."

"You're on leave and back for your class's fifth reunion?"

"Yeah, that and something else too."

Joyce raised her chin, curious to hear more. "What's the something else?"

"I'm still active duty 0-3 but a full-time grad student. Next May I receive my degree from Georgetown. And when the Brigade reforms later in August, I will be here as a company officer," Tara told her. "Same as you."

"Now, that's interesting." Joyce approved.

"How do you like it so far?" asked Tara, awaiting the answer with particular attention.

"I like it a lot. Mids aren't too different than when we were here. Same aspirations, enthusiasm, different struggles, raging hormones, and occasional mischief. I like working with them, watching 'em grow up."

"What about your chain of command?"

"Overall, things are going pretty well." Lieutenant Wickersham looked away for a moment, then turned to Tara. "A new Dant and Deputy Dant were appointed last August."

Tara picked up on a hint of caution in Joyce's voice. "How's that working out for you as a company officer?"

Joyce breathed in and slowly released the air in her lungs. "The commandant's Navy O-6, Captain Brookshier, Class of '93. Mids seem to approve of him. The company officers and SELs too."

Tara wanted to hear more. "What about the deputy commandant?"

A furrowed brow created lines across Joyce's forehead. She lowered her voice not to be overheard as people walked by them. "He's a Marine 0-6 with a frigid personal style. Not only are the

midshipmen unsettled around him, but so are the company officers and SELs," she said. "Between you and me, he's the kind of
person you intentionally cross the street to avoid passing."

"What's his name?"

"Colonel Wettstone, Class of '94. He and Brookshier will probably still be here when you begin your two-year duty tour as
company officer."

The Naval Academy Band arrived at the edge of Worden Field,
a signal that the parade was about to start.

Joyce checked her watch. "Sorry, Tara, but I'm escorting two
visiting dignitaries this afternoon." She pointed to the canopy
seating area where senior military officers and guests awaited the
parade to begin. "I'll give you my cell number. Maybe we can meet
up sometime this weekend during your reunion, okay?"

Tara tapped the digits into her iPhone directory. "I'd like that,"
she said. "I'm so glad we ran into each other."

"Me too."

They shared a quick hug and Joyce Wickersham headed off.

*Brookshier and Wettstone, names to remember,* Tara said to
herself. *Next June they will be the senior officers in your chain of
command.*

# PART THREE

# CHAPTER 28

**Bancroft Hall, USNA**
**May 17, 2023 at 0845**

Tara Marcellus felt satisfied as she walked through Bancroft Hall. Life was treating her well. She had no complaints.

She'd accomplished a lot in two years since she left the crew of *John Warner*. Completing the eight-week Prospective Nuclear Engineer Officer (PNEO) training program went without a hitch. "You want to graduate before you get orders to your next boat," had been Commander Whikehart's advice. She had tested well, aced her interview, and qualified as a submarine engineer. Her confidence ran high about being selected to serve as a department head on her next submarine tour.

Now a graduate diploma in international affairs from Georgetown University hung alongside the Naval Academy sheepskin in her Annapolis townhouse. She had finished the first of her two-year billet as a Naval Academy company officer with very good fitness reports from the Commandant of Midshipmen.

Tara couldn't be any prouder as a Naval Academy graduate. She was dedicated to her work: Preparing midshipmen to become able Navy and Marine Corps officers and leaders. Encouraging them to know and do what is right—the first time, every time. Never flinching from doing one's duty. Always standing up for their sailors and Marines. The past year as a company officer had been a good experience for her. She had grown as a naval officer and wouldn't have traded this time back at Annapolis for anything else.

And then there was Ray Lydon. They had gone in separate directions after graduation: Tara to the submarine service, and Ray to earn his wings as a Marine aviator. But she longed to stay in touch with him. It had worked out well with email and Facebook until she'd joined the crew of USS *John Warner*. Serving in the Navy's silent service for three, sometimes six-month long deployments at one time, and no contact with the outside world, could strain personal relationships.

They had finally reunited two years earlier at their class's fifth reunion at the Academy. A Marine Corps captain's bars had adorned his khaki shirt's collars and atop the shoulders of his green uniform coat. Gold naval aviator wings pinned to his chest had sparkled as brightly as his dazzling eyes. And she thought he was still drop dead good-looking.

Their words and looks flowed naturally as two reunited graduates. Deployments—her adventures aboard a US Navy Virginia Class fast attack nuclear submarine, the buzz he got flying attack helicopters—barely allowed time for a personal life. But the physical and emotional connection they had once shared quickly returned when she saw him. Tara had also eyeballed the ring finger of his left hand. There wasn't a wedding band on it. That weekend, they had rediscovered the physical intimacy and love that was stolen from them as midshipmen when regulations had forbidden any open displays of affection.

The year Tara had begun graduate studies, she and Ray had managed to be with each other once a month. Ray would take leave from his aviation squadron in California and come east. At his last visit when they went out to dinner, she'd nearly choked on a glass of wine hearing Ray's totally out-of-the-blue question.

"How about we make this arrangement work a different way?"

"What did you have in mind?" Tara asked, unsure what his answer might be.

"Get married?"

"My God, I didn't see that coming." Tara's eyes had grown large with amazement.

Ray filled a momentary silence between them. "I've thought about you, about us, ever since we left the Academy."

"Me too," she'd sighed with relief.

Thoughts of Ray were interrupted when Tara reached her destination. The office door was open. "Good morning, sir," she called out.

Ryan Griffa, Battalion Officer (Batt-O) for the 4th Battalion, raised his head and peered over the top of his glasses. Gold Naval Flight Officer Wings were attached to his uniform shirt above two rows of service ribbons. "Morning, Tara," said her boss. He motioned to one of the chairs at a small conference table.

Tara took in the man's office space, which reflected that of a typical mid-level officer. A framed family portrait rested on the credenza behind his chair, showcasing him with his wife and three children. More framed photographs covered both walls: Griffa with three other men carrying rifles in hunting camouflage gear. Three more framed photographs of himself wearing a flight suit, one seated inside a helicopter's controls and two more standing in front of Navy helicopters along with other men in flight suits. Resting on the corner of his desk was a scale model replica of a Sikorsky Anti-Submarine Warfare (ASW) helicopter.

"How are things going so far?" he asked Tara.

"Good, sir. I've been meeting with the new midshipmen command from 16th Company," she replied. "I'm impressed."

The office phone rang. "Pardon me a moment." Griffa went over to see whose ID appeared on the display and promptly lifted the receiver. "Yes sir, we're about to discuss it," he said and listened for several seconds. "I certainly will, sir. Thank you." He hung up and rejoined Tara. "That was the commandant," he said and nodded at the telephone. "He asked me to extend his compliments for the fine first year you just completed as company officer." the Batt-O gave her an approving smile.

"Thanks, sir. I feel good about it." She was also having fun serving as the "O Rep" or officer representative for the women's volleyball team, but it didn't warrant mentioning now.

"I want to discuss an adjusted change of duty for you," he announced. "It comes down from the deputy commandant. The commandant's also on board."

Her face remained neutral while her stomach did a somersault. A minute ago, she was doing an outstanding job. Now a change of duty? "What would that be, sir?"

"Colonel Wettstone's instructed me to reassign you as the new 19th Company Officer starting a month from now, on I-Day."

His announcement startled her. "With all due respect, sir," she said carefully, "have you been dissatisfied with my performance?"

"No, nothing like that, Lieutenant," he said and waved a hand in the air to ward off any sudden undue concern by her. "The situation we're dealing with is that the midshipmen discipline in 19th Company has been substandard the past couple of months. We've seen excessive conduct offenses. Mids showing up late in too many places—to class, at different required activities, close-order drills, muster, noon formation, and even classwork turned in late." His mouth formed into a displeased frown. "You name it, they're late."

"I understand the colonel's concerns, sir." Tara nodded.

"He's beyond annoyed." the Batt-O grimaced.

Tara suspected Griffa was personally feeling heat coming from the Deputy Dant about the situation, and it probably wasn't pleasant.

"Colonel Wettstone's selected you to straighten them out, and soon." His open hands gestured to emphasize his predicament.

"I'm depending on you to provide the direction they need when the Brigade reforms in August."

"I look forward to the opportunity," was her best answer at the moment. Her new orders delivered two messages: she had earned their confidence, and they'd be watching her closely.

"I'll advise the deputy commandant that it's a go," said the battalion officer. He stood and she followed. "Any further questions for me, Lieutenant?"

"Not at this time, sir."

"We're aiming for zero tolerance on misconduct," he affirmed with her. "Thanks for stepping up, Tara."

"Aye, sir."

*Prove to the commandant and deputy commandant that they made the right choice in you taking over 19th Company,* Tara told herself as she headed back to her office.

# CHAPTER 29

**Dewey Field, USNA**
**August 16, 2023 at 1849**

Alex parked his Toyota truck along the sea wall off the Severn River. The two front windows were down because the AC stopped working on another insufferably hot August evening. Outside, a swamp-like humidity was as oppressive as aiming a hair dryer set at "hot" right in your face.

He reached down to the front passenger seat floor, flipped open the cooler lid, and pulled out an iced Michelob. Using the tail of his green T-shirt with "Marines" printed across the chest, he twisted the bottle cap off, lifted the bottle to his lips, and let the brewed beverage slide smoothly down his throat. Being caught bringing alcohol on the Yard, and drinking it, would get him in a shitstorm of trouble. But taking the chance didn't faze him. Besides, Navy police had no pretext to search his truck. What would the commandant do to him, anyway? Restrict him to Bancroft Hall for one month without weekend liberty?

Leaning back against the driver-side door and feeling the comfort of the cold bottle against his forehead, Alex closed his eyes.

Third and Second Class years at Annapolis—sophomore and junior—were behind him now. Two more Army-Navy games had come and gone with one win and one loss. But Navy grounded Air Force twice in football. Graduation was coming up in May. At the end of Second Class, he and several classmates were reassigned to 19th Company, which was led by a company officer known for being too lenient about conduct offenses. It made no sense to him why the Dant would put up with an officer being nursemaid to some Mids with cocky attitudes. But the company officer was Navy. No Marine company officer would have tolerated any nonsense, period.

Alex opened his eyes and spotted his weathered baseball glove lying on the floor of the truck. He'd swung a pretty good bat and fielded well for Navy's baseball team the past two years. He had earned the starting job at third base for the upcoming fall season.

Summer military trainings had been awesome: Ten days aboard a ballistic missile submarine. A three-week stretch on Yard Patrol boats out of the Academy. Training with Marine NCOs in San Diego aboard a Navy cruiser for thirteen days, and ending up at Naval Station Pensacola to fly T-34s and a fixed wing aircraft. Best of all had been this past summer with a four-week training evolution at "Leatherneck" training at Marine Base Quantico: navigation, offensive combat tactics, mission evolutions, basic weapons knowledge and application, night patrols, getting sweaty and filthy with hard-ass instructors eyeballing them. A lot of the training was déjà vu for him, a veteran. But he still relished every minute. Most other Mids couldn't understand how much and how fast he wanted to wear a Marine's second lieutenant bars.

He ended the past spring's academic period with a 3.8 academic rank after finals. More than respectable. He had an Overall Order of Merit of 114th in his class and an Aptitude for Commissioning grade of A going into the final year. Brian and Harry would still be his roommates. The three of them shared an indelible bond of friendship.

Alex reached for the beer bottle and took another long drink when Carolyn Hagerty entered his thoughts. They'd lost contact with each other soon after their dinner together back home during his plebe year. Was that his doing? It seemed like it was.

He regretted not letting go of some stupid notion he wasn't good enough for her—she the Princeton graduate, he a former grunt Marine. Carolyn's last email a year ago mentioned getting married in the spring to some guy who, like her, worked for a global nonprofit. The news gnawed at him because he hadn't stopped thinking about her, about them, despite his self-doubts. He'd ask his mother. Olivia would know because she and Carolyn kept in contact.

Carolyn Hagerty had wanted to know how things were going at the Academy, if he still planned on being a Marine officer after graduation. Like that was ever really a question? If there was any one thing in life Alex was damned certain of, it was going back to his Marine Corps.

Last year he and his classmates had marched into Memorial Hall, wrote their signatures on the large rolling sheet of paper spread across several tables, and pledged to the Naval Academy's tradition of "2 for 7." Two years left at the Naval Academy followed by a five-year active-duty commitment in the Navy or Marine Corps. The annual ritual for Second Class Mids was called "The Point of No Return."

He thought back to his final week at Leatherneck when Colonel Geoff Burlingame, the Academy's Senior Marine, came over to speak with him. He had wanted Alex to join some Marine officers scheduled to brief midshipmen on careers in the Corps. Alex had agreed with one reluctant request: "Sir, I prefer that officers at the briefs not say anything about my decorations if they introduce me."

Colonel Burlingame, USNA '96, smiled with his square jawline. "Son, your quiet pride is a credit to your service as a Marine. I'll pass along your request to all my officers from the Marine Detachment."

"Thank you, sir."

Alex closed his eyes, inhaled deep and slow, and thought about his visit to the Marine Corps National Museum one week ago.

The first time he'd toured the hallowed building was with Gerry Rourke. Now he had wanted to return and honor Rourke's service.

His last stop had been to view a portrait gallery of Marines awarded the Medal of Honor, the nation's highest military decoration for valor. They numbered almost three hundred. Their photographic expressions were rather ordinary. But individually and as one, their respective acts of gallantry during battle had been extraordinary.

His eyes had rested on a display he hadn't paid close attention to the first time. Behind the glass rested the Medal of Honor and other decorations presented to Marine Corps Gunnery Sergeant John Basilone for conspicuous gallantry in the Pacific during WWII. Next to it lay the gunnery sergeant's Navy Cross, the naval service's second highest decoration presented for extraordinary heroism. For a long moment, Alex had reflected on the meaning of the two awards. He understood Sergeant Basilone's decorations and the Medal of Honor portrait gallery more than he ever could have before his own experiences in a war zone.

On his way out, Alex had stopped to watch two older men talking to a young Black male Marine lance corporal. Precision creases ran down the enlistee's long-sleeve khaki shirt with matching colored necktie and a gold tie clasp. A single row of service decorations stood out on the uniform shirt. A scarlet stripe from waistband to bottom hem marked the outer seam of each leg of his blue trousers. The red "blood stripe" commemorated the Marines who were killed—their ultimate sacrifice—while storming the castle of Chapultepec in Mexico in 1847.

He had noticed the deep lines of aging that creased the two older veterans' features. One steadied himself with a cane.

Another wore a red baseball cap with "Korea Veteran" inscribed in gold letters across the front. He guessed the two veterans had to be in their mid-eighties.

"Semper Fi, Marine." One of the elderly men had slowly extended a trembling hand with gnarled arthritic fingers for the young lance corporal to shake.

"Semper Fidelis, sir."

Semper Fidelis: two words displayed prominently throughout the museum. This place had been Gerry Rourke's marble, brick-and-mortar testament to brotherhood. Now he, too, was part of this honorable tradition.

The lance corporal had turned on his heel and walked in Alex's direction. As he passed, the young Marine had nodded to Alex and said, "Sir." Alex had nodded back, "Lance Corporal."

That exchange further motivated him to press on and get back to the Corps.

Alex placed the empty beer bottle in the cooler and shut the lid. The Brigade reformed tomorrow at 0730. He grabbed two duffle bags from behind the front-seat bench, locked his truck, and walked toward Bancroft Hall. His priorities for the final year at Annapolis were set: Help Mids who come to you, just like Marines take care of each other. Stay in your own lane, or at least try to. Don't do stupid shit that will piss off senior officers. Most of all, never retreat from doing your duty, no matter what.

All signs pointed to the next ten months being trouble-free. He didn't foresee any incoming fire. Graduation, commissioning, and Marine Corps second lieutenant bars pinned on his shoulders awaited him. It was all his to win or lose.

# CHAPTER 30

Bancroft Hall, USNA
August 19, 2023 at 1735

Tara Marcellus lifted her special-ordered navy colored ceramic mug with "USS *John Warner* (SSN-785)" prominently etched in white on its side, and finished the last of her coffee.

Seated at her desk, she rotated stiffened shoulders and continued tapping out the first draft of her report on Plebe Summer Training for 19th Company. The detailers had done well and the results pleased her. Only one plebe had quit, packed up, and went home out of forty in the company. The plebes had regularly scored high on spot quizzes from *Reef Points*.

Tara's features opened into a meditative expression as she leaned back in her not-built-for-comfort office chair. It wasn't that long ago she and every plebe in her class had carried with them everywhere their own pocket-sized encyclopedia of Naval Academy and naval service history and facts, from I-Day in June through Plebe Summer's end in mid-August. Plebes didn't dare be caught without *Reef Points*.

She returned to finish her report when she heard three raps against the half-open office door. Tara lifted her head to see a midshipman standing in the doorway. He wore a Navy Baseball T-shirt over blue USNA gym shorts. Laces from baseball cleats hung from the fingers of one hand, and his glove and baseball cap gripped in the other.

"Midshipman Alex Kramer reporting as ordered, ma'am. You

requested me to come at 1745." His arms opened like he was ready for a security pat down by an airport TSA agent. "Excuse the clothes, ma'am, but I just came from baseball practice."

"Thanks for coming, Mister Kramer," she told him in an amiable fashion and pointed to a chair across from her desk. Alex placed his gear on the floor next to the chair while Tara sat in an adjacent chair. "I've taken over as 19th Company Officer and wanted to get acquainted."

Alex didn't reveal any facial reaction. But midshipmen in 19th Company were informed that Lieutenant Romanowski, the prior company officer, had been relieved of his duties in Fourth Battalion.

Tara already knew of Alex's distinguished service as a Marine veteran. Major Mark Anderegg, 19th Company's Marine mentor at the Academy, had briefed her. He'd also told Tara how the midshipman was tight-lipped when anyone asked about his acts of valor. "He's always putting others first, keeping them safe," Anderegg had told her. "If Alex Kramer had a second middle name, it would be 'duty.' He's the whole package for becoming a fine officer."

In a neutral tone, she laid out the directive from the deputy commandant's office. Nineteenth Company had to cut down its rate of conduct offenses starting yesterday, period. Being one of four midshipmen platoon commanders, it was now Alex's job to tell the thirty Mids he led to get their act together, and fast.

Alex ran one hand through his thatch of straw-like dirty blond hair and shrugged. Marines never trained for babysitting, and they weren't nursemaids or nannies. Didn't matter. Lieutenant Marcellus had her orders, and now he had his.

Tara changed the subject. "Major Anderegg tells me Mids look up to you like you're a rock star," she said with an easy smile. She was tempted, but resisted asking what he'd done for the Marine

Corps and the nation to decorate him with the Silver Star. "What unit did you serve with?"

"Bravo Company 1/6, ma'am. 24th MEU."

"Where were you deployed?"

"Different places. Last mission was West Africa, Sierra Leone."

"When were you in Sierra Leone?" she asked, now being especially attentive.

Alex repositioned himself in the chair. "April 2019," he answered but didn't add anything else.

"I deployed aboard a fast attack sub in the South Atlantic Ocean around the same time."

"I bet that was interesting, ma'am," said Alex.

Tara nodded, ready to talk. "Our mission parameters changed, and we received orders to provide escort security for USS *Wasp* and a MEU," she explained while Alex listened intently. "I recall the MEU's mission was an NEO, in Sierra Leone. Maybe your unit?"

"Could be, ma'am."

They talked a few more minutes until it was time for her to finish her report.

"Good to meet you, midshipman, and thanks for coming." Tara rose from her chair and Alex collected his gear. "Remember, clean up those conduct offenses in 19th Company," she reminded him with an easygoing tone.

"Copy that, ma'am."

Tara watched the midshipman disappear under the fluorescent-lit passageway.

He was older, more mature than the others. He had been through wartime conditions other Mids and many staff officers at the Naval Academy could not image, and still came out standing. He'll make sure any undisciplined midshipmen get their acts together, she thought. *That Marine won't need me watching his six.*

# CHAPTER 31

**19th Company**
**Bancroft Hall, USNA**
**February 13, 2024 at 2345**

Alex's legs stretched out across the top of the desk. Hands clasped behind his head, he stared at his image on a Navy baseball team poster taped to the wall. "Dark Ages" at the Naval Academy were nearly over. Next week ended winter's annual period of cold and gloom across the Yard, a bleary stretch from early January until mid-March when the Brigade bolted from Annapolis for spring break.

He'd enjoyed Christmas leave. His older sister, Tori, and her husband, a fire department lieutenant in New York City, had driven down from Manhattan. His parents had struggled through a recent rough patch over stuff he didn't know about but wanted to understand. He had tried to get his mother to open up. Yet she would change the subject the few times he had asked. Tori didn't know anything either. Before Christmas his folks had seemed to straighten out their differences. Alex hoped it stayed that way because he was especially close to Olivia. The whole thing reminded him of other people saying that marriage takes work.

It had been great catching up with one or two high school buddies. As they talked about themselves, Alex didn't have any regrets about his own choices. Being a Marine had been awesome, and he liked being a midshipman at the Academy. He sighed with satisfaction because his life had purpose.

He'd thought a lot about Carolyn Hardesty when he was home, wondered how her life had turned out after getting married. His mother probably knew but Alex wasn't going to ask her. From the day he left for Marine Recruit Basic Training at Parris Island through this moment, part of him always felt unfinished without Carolyn. Almost nine years. Move on, he told himself.

After his fistfight at a local tavern off the Yard last fall, his first major conduct offense, Alex had resolved to obey naval service and Academy regs. Graduation and commissioning were three months away and he intended to be there. Nothing could get in his way. Color inside the lines and keep out of trouble, he kept telling himself.

The pinball-machine chimes from his cell phone startled him. He raised his head off the desk where it had fallen to rest on top of his folded arms. A half hour ago he couldn't keep his eyes open so he'd given in and let them close.

What time was it? The heels of his palms pressed against his eyes to rub them open. His eyes tried to focus on the luminescent hands on his Navy SEAL watch. Almost midnight and well past Taps at 2300. His phone replayed its tones, and Alex read the incoming text from Ethan Crowell.

"Alex, where are you, man? I'm in my shithole of life again and it sucks. Another firefight gone bad. I've had enough. I'm done, brother."

Alex stared at the message. "Ethan, don't you do what I think you're talking about," he muttered in the quiet room. The firefight in Sierra Leone had really messed with Ethan's head. The last time they saw each other was at a restaurant in Annapolis last May. Alex had been ready for First Class summer to start with Leatherneck at Quantico. Ethan was between jobs again. He had a new female friend and had sounded better on the phone. But the friend didn't stay long, like other women before her who couldn't deal with his erratic mood swings. He was never violent or abusive. But Ethan's dark moods and depression were too much to handle.

Now Alex's Marine friend was alone again, getting by on a small military disability check to pay rent for an apartment, and a few bucks left over for food and other essentials. Alex guessed the only items sitting in his refrigerator would be a carton of spoiled milk, orange juice, and some six packs of beer.

Ethan Crowell's ongoing battle with psychological trauma had him riding a psychiatric roller coaster. Prescription drugs helped manage depression, but his buddy still suffered from a hairline trigger reaction when he heard sudden noises. His mind would flash back to the IED blast that left him neurologically injured and psychologically disabled, messing up his head.

Managing anxiety and depression with meds required someone looking out for him. When he wasn't meeting with his mental health counselor, Ethan was stranded. He had attempted suicide once before in the five years since he was medically discharged from the Marine Corps.

The text sounded suicidal. Something must have set him off. Alex texted a reply:

"Coming now. Leave door unlocked. Do nothing until I get there."

Harry and Brian, Alex's roommates, were asleep in their racks with Brian snoring. All three midshipmen had signed the Taps Muster Sheet around 2230 before study period ended. Alex was reading up on Marine Corps fire team tactics when the Company Duty Officer checked in on the three of them. All midshipmen were required to be "sighted" by their CDOs thirty minutes prior to Taps. Only then were they officially confirmed as being in quarters.

Alex kneeled down and gently shook Harry's shoulder. "Wake up." It took a second attempt for Harry's groggy head to lift off the pillow.

"What time is it?"

"Almost midnight."

"This better be good," he slurred his words.

"I need to borrow your car. It's important."

Harry tried to shake the sleep out of his head. "Where's your truck?"

"It's in the shop, getting new brake pads."

Harry propped himself up on one elbow and cocked his head to the side. His squinted eyes searched Alex's face. "Why do you need my car?"

"I have to help a buddy who's in trouble."

"Who?"

"He's a Marine I served with."

Harry pressed on his wristwatch crown and saw the hands illuminate in blue. "For cryin' out loud, Alex, it's after Taps."

"Listen, this guy's attempted suicide before. His text sounds bad and I want to get there *before* he tries anything."

"So call the police right now and they'll go check on him," Harry said and rubbed more sleep out of his eyes. "Then go see him after Friday liberty starts."

Alex objected, vigorously shaking his head. "Police knocking on his door will make him wig out. He needs to see someone he trusts. That's me."

Harry threw the bed cover back and sat up. "He's one of the Marines you saved?"

"Yeah."

"You're going now?"

"I want to be out of here in three minutes."

"All right," said a still drowsy Harry. He got out of his rack, retrieved the remote key fob for his car, and handed it to Alex.

"Listen, Harry," Alex whispered so Brian wouldn't wake up. "If I don't make it back for morning muster, Hannigan's gonna ask where I am," he added, mentioning their platoon commander in 19th Company and another Firstie. "You do not lie for me, understand? I'm going UA," he said, referencing Unauthorized Absence, a serious violation of Naval Academy and Navy regulations.

"I'll just say you left while I was sleeping."

"Not good enough," Alex said and gripped Harry's shoulders. "I don't want you lying and risk an honor offense three months before graduation."

"Then what do you want me to say?" Harry asked nervously.

"Tell him the truth."

"What *is* the truth anyway, Alex?"

"I woke you up and said I was going over the wall to help a friend, a Marine, in trouble, and I borrowed your car." He fixed his gaze on Harry in the dimly lit room. "You have no idea when I'm coming back."

Harry interrupted in a desperate voice. "I'll stuff clothes under your blanket. The Battalion Officer of the Watch will think you're asleep if he does a random spot check."

Alex shook his head. "Not good enough. That makes you party to my offense and you can't lie your way out of that one."

Brian stirred in his rack and looked over at them. "What's going on?"

"Go back to sleep," ordered Alex and turned back to Harry. "Something else. Tell the company commander that you told me to self-report for breaking regulations, and I refused."

"Are you crazy? You'll be in more trouble."

Alex didn't care. "Go ahead, tell me to self-report."

"You're committing a big-time conduct offense." Urgency rang in Harry's whispered words. "I'm telling you to self-report to the Officer of the Watch. Shit, Alex, don't do this. Find another way to help your Marine buddy but don't go UA."

Alex knew Harry was right. But Ethan needed him, not cops banging on his apartment door. He trusted his instinct to go back for his friend, just as he'd gone back for Ethan in Sierra Leone.

"You've done your duty and I ignored you," Alex said. "Now you've covered your bases."

"Hey, it's your funeral," Harry warned him. "I sure hope to hell you know what you're doing."

"Two final things," said Alex.

Harry's eyes grew wide with suspicion. "There's more?"

"This one's really important," Alex said with an unmistaken urgency. "Tell Lieutenant Marcellus I went UA to bring back a Marine brother of mine before he stepped off the edge. She's got to know why I left the Yard," he said and sucked in a quick breath. "She'll understand. And also tell her that you told me to self-report but I wouldn't do it." Alex glanced quickly at his watch then back at Harry. "Will you tell her for me?"

"Tell her yourself," Harry pushed back. "She might still be up."

"I don't have time."

"Yes, you do," his concerned yet frustrated roommate shot back.

"Yeah, okay. Anything else?"

"Go see Major Anderegg, the Marine mentor for 19th Company and give him the same message you give to Lieutenant Marcellus. He'll understand—just like she does—why I went UA."

"Why him?"

"Just do it and in person at his office. No email. I'll text him you're coming." Alex stood up. "Where's your car now?"

"Along the sea wall, close to Rip Miller Field."

"I'll be back when I know Ethan's safe," he said and took off.

Alex knew that leaving on an Unauthorized Absence would land him in a shitstorm of trouble. The Naval Academy would come down hard on him. Being a Firstie made his situation a lot worse. There'd be no mercy for a senior midshipman who went UA. He didn't care, though. His instincts ordered him to go back for Ethan, just as he'd gone for his wounded brother during their NEO mission. It had been Alex's duty the first time, and it was his duty once again.

# CHAPTER 32

**Morning Meal**
**King Hall, USNA**
**February 14, 2024 at 0739**

Harry gripped two paper bowls of cold cereal and headed back to his table. The high-decibel noise of 4,400 midshipmen eating ricocheted off the thick wooden beams all across the high ceiling in King Hall.

He was chewing a mouthful of Cheerios when a tap on his shoulder startled him. He turned, nearly choking, and rose to his feet with wide eyes to find Lieutenant Tara Marcellus standing behind his chair. Other Mids seated at the table stopped whatever they were eating and watched. After morning muster, most could guess why the 19th Company Officer showed up.

"Relax," The lieutenant told him. "Finish up and meet me in Smoke Hall."

"Yes, ma'am." Harry attempted to finish the cereal but the somersaults in his stomach killed any appetite left.

"What's going on?" a female classmate seated alongside him asked after the lieutenant was out of earshot.

"I'm handling it," Harry said and pushed back his chair.

Smoke Hall was empty save for Lieutenant Marcellus, standing and checking her cell phone. She heard the Mid's footsteps approach and turned to face him. "Take a seat, midshipman."

Harry hesitated then followed her order. She sat as well.

"The company commander informed me Alex Kramer was

missing from morning formation," Tara said, her statement left unfinished for two long seconds. "Do you know where he is?"

News travelled at the speed of light in the Brigade. "Yes, ma'am, I do," Harry answered. He felt her stare lock on him. "He told me just before he left the Yard."

"When was that?"

"A few minutes before 2400 last night."

Tara ground her teeth. A midshipman, a Firstie, and a midshipman leader in 19th Company—her company—had just committed his second major conduct offense in less than six months. She expected the deputy commandant would go batshit when he found out. "Where'd Midshipman Kramer go, Mister Stocks?"

Harry explained the text message from a Marine Alex had served with who'd suffered TBI during combat operations. Alex thought his buddy might try and kill himself, something he'd attempted before. Harry noticed the female officer's features tighten hearing the word "suicide."

"Ma'am, Alex saved that Marine's life once before in a firefight," Harry said. "This morning at zero dark hundred, he believed he had to save him again."

"Did he say when he was coming back?"

"No, ma'am."

Lieutenant Marcellus stared out Smoke Hall's huge windows at the early-morning sunshine rising over the Severn River, then back at the visibly uncomfortable midshipman. "What else do you want to tell me?"

"I tried talking him out of going UA," pleaded Harry. "Told him to call the police where his buddy lives and let them take care of it. But he refused."

"I appreciate you telling me what you know," Tara rose to leave the ceremonial hall. "You should go now."

"One more thing, ma'am."

Tara stopped and turned.

"Alex asked me to give you a message."

"What is it?"

"He said, 'Tell Lieutenant Marcellus I went to bring one of my men back.' Alex told me you'd understand what that meant."

"Thank you, Mister Stocks." She checked her watch. "Don't be late to class."

## Sampson Hall, USNA
## February 14, 2024 at 0950

Harry Stocks climbed the winding white marble steps to the second deck in Sampson Hall. He reached the landing and glanced at his watch—he'd be marked late to third period class in Michelson Hall, and a conduct violation would follow. As though he wasn't walking on thin ice already for letting Alex go UA. Telling the company commander would mean bilging his roommate, but Alex had told him to do it anyway. If a conduct offense hearing determined Alex should be restricted to the Yard from now until graduation, he wouldn't appeal it.

Alex's claim that his roommate was off the hook wasn't true either. Harry telling Alex to self-report last night wasn't enough. He, too, could be twisting in the wind for letting Alex take off without official permission.

Midshipman Stocks started down the corridor and found the office. A nameplate alongside the closed door said *Major Mark Anderegg, USMC,* with a US Marine Corps Eagle Globe and Anchor emblem decal affixed next to it. Harry heard someone talking on the other side, so he rapped twice, hard.

"Enter," called out a voice inside. Harry pushed open the door to see a Marine officer place the telephone receiver down. The midshipman's eyes quickly took in the office. Several group photos hung from two walls: Marines posing together in the desert and different base camps. The settings looked like Afghanistan or Iraq, maybe both. Combinations of smirks, smiles, and I'm-one-mean-hard-charging-sonofabitch expressions pasted on their faces. They were dressed in full battle load minus Kevlar helmets, with sunglasses and holding M16s against their chests.

"What can I do for you, midshipman?"

"Good morning, sir. I'm Harry Stocks, 19th Company, and Midshipman Alex Kramer's roommate. He sent me to see you."

"Okay, take a seat."

Mark Anderegg, a Naval Academy grad and one of the few prior-enlisted then commissioned officers or "Mustangs" at the Academy, studied the discomfited midshipman seated in front of him. This unscheduled visit was most curious. "Is Alex all right?"

"Sir, the answer is yes and no," Harry said with a frown.

The Marine major uncrossed his arms so the Mid might relax. "You've got my attention, so take your time."

"Excuse me," Harry said and pulled out a half-filled water bottle from his backpack and drank some. "Sir, last night, a few minutes past midnight, Alex went UA."

"He literally went over the wall?"

"Not literally, sir. He borrowed my car."

Harry told Major Anderegg everything that happened, including Alex wanting the major to know that he'd gone back for one of his men. Mark Anderegg tried to read Harry's still uneasy features. "Did he say anything about coming back?"

"Negative, sir."

"Of course he wouldn't." The major reached over to his desk to grab a notepad and pen to write down Alex's mobile number as Harry recited it.

"Your company commander's already been informed?"

"He was, sir, at morning muster."

"What about Lieutenant Marcellus? Does she know?"

"She knows, sir. I just came from informing her."

Mark Anderegg stood and Harry followed. "Thanks for reporting this to me."

Harry sighed. "You know, it's strange, sir."

"What's strange?"

"At muster I heard another Mid say, 'Alex better have a good reason for going UA.' It's like they're doubting him before they even know anything."

"Going back for one of your Marines or your sailors is always a noble reason, isn't it?" The Marine officer waited for the midshipman to answer, then filled in the quiet space. "You can speak freely. Our conversation doesn't leave this room."

"Yes, it's a noble reason." Harry felt relieved from Alex's heavy load on him. "Thanks for your time, sir."

"You're welcome."

As soon as Harry departed, the major tapped out a text message:

MIDN Stocks told me what's going on. Call if you want to talk. I will be available 24/7. Semper Fi.

# CHAPTER 33

Bancroft Hall, USNA
February 14, 2024 at 1037

"Thanks, I'll get back to you."

Tara Marcellus finished the phone call when she looked up and noticed Alex Kramer standing in her doorway. She saw fatigue imprinted in his weary features and somewhat pale complexion.

"Excuse me, ma'am."

She'd had a hunch the midshipman would show up. He wasn't a Marine any longer. But she reminded herself that he was eternally devoted to the military ethos of unconditional loyalty. She believed Alex's devotion to duty was absolute. It propelled him to defend others who, at any given moment, couldn't defend themselves.

The Navy lieutenant also knew the decorated Marine had an impatient streak. She remembered their talk after his fistfight at a local tavern last fall. "That drunk shit bag—excuse me, ma'am—he started it," Alex had said, his eyes narrowed into slits, the corners of his mouth twisted with disgust. "I was protecting Hannah from that foul-smelling pecker head," he'd said through rapid breaths. "I defended myself when he put his hands around my throat." Tara had knitted her brow when she heard the fury in his words.

Earlier she'd called on him to model good behavior other Mids could follow. "I told you to avoid conduct offenses and you go start a brawl outside the Yard," she had scolded him. He had it coming. "That was a dumb thing you did, and you know it."

Yet she had also wanted the headstrong Mid to learn from his mistakes. "A good officer looks at options before reacting," she had urged him to remember. "Didn't you make critical decisions under extreme pressure when you were an NCO?"

"I did, ma'am, when I was an E-4 corporal," he had answered.

Now, Alex's latest conduct breach presented grave consequences for his future. The Academy expected Midshipmen First Class to know right from wrong. Alex Kramer didn't need anyone teaching him the difference. Shit happens and individuals react differently. His conscience—not Naval Academy regs—influenced the path he'd follow.

"Come in and close the door," she waved at him to enter.

The Mid plopped down in a chair, still dressed in Navy Working Uniform Type I he wore when he left the Yard moments after midnight. Dark circles under his eyes revealed the strain that burdened him. "Midshipman Stocks—Harry—already knows that I went UA."

"He told me about it at morning meal," said Tara. "Now I want to hear it from you. By the way, have you had anything to eat and drink since you left?"

When he shook his head no, the lieutenant told him to go into the officers' wardroom where he'd find muffins and small bottles of OJ in the refrigerator. Alex lifted his exhausted body from the chair and returned moments later. Tara watched him drink half the bottle of juice in three swallows. Next, he broke off a section from the top of a blueberry muffin and shoved the whole piece in his mouth.

"All right," she said. "Tell me what happened and don't leave anything out."

Alex gulped down another piece of muffin and stopped to rub his face. He described the chain of events that began ten hours earlier. He took several quick breaths and looked intently at his company officer. "I went to stop Ethan from doing it."

---

"Was he trying to kill himself?"

Alex nodded. "When I got to his apartment"—he mentioned how a Virginia State Trooper had followed him there—"he'd already swallowed meds from three prescription bottles."

"My God," Tara said and blinked with disbelief.

"The trooper and I took him to the nearest ER. He's under psychiatric care now." Alex shrugged with a bleak expression. He leaned forward in his chair, his shoulders hunched over and his head down. "Ma'am, I couldn't do any more for him, so I came back here to face the consequences."

"Do more?" she said, her eyes large. "You saved his life, that's what you did."

Tara understood that Alex went back because saving Ethan a second time had been his duty. She understood that, in his mind, Alex was still engaged in the firefight from his NEO mission. Now she had to tell him to prepare for a mess that could come crashing down on his life at the Academy. Going UA after Taps was a major conduct offense. Her duty was to give this midshipman the plain, unvarnished truth. There would be an investigation and it would start soon.

But this wasn't the time to further upset him with details on how the Academy's conduct offense process played out. Yet Tara knew that if the deputy commandant came down hard on Alex and recommended separation, his case would get pushed up to the Commandant of Midshipmen for a second open hearing. If the Dant also upheld the first recommendation for separation, there would be a third and final review by the superintendent. Midshipmen offenses under review seldom traveled that high in the Naval Academy's chain of command.

She attempted to explain what adjudication meant while Alex looked out the window, anguish in his features. *For crying out loud, Alex, what were you thinking before you went UA?* Tara asked herself. Why hadn't he thought to call the police? A patrol car and EMT unit would have reached his buddy in under ten minutes and this whole messy business would have been avoided.

As soon as Tara learned Alex had gone UA, she went online to the Midshipmen Information System (MIDS) to find out about any prior honor offenses in his personnel jacket. It turned out Alex had been tagged for an honor offense plebe year. He'd known his roommate thought about cheating on a professional knowledge or "pro know" quiz, which all plebes took regularly. Alex hadn't told the roommate to turn himself in or to self-report. A midshipmen-led Honor Board had charged Alex with a Negative Form-1 because he knew his roommate's intentions yet stayed silent until the other plebe owned up.

Conduct offenses at the Academy could have serious consequences. Tara knew that officers could recommend lighter sanctions if the accused was a plebe or third class, depending on the conduct violation. But Mids like Alex were held to a higher, less forgiving standard. They'd been members of the Brigade long enough to know how to behave, period.

Tara needed to know everything in Alex's history before she might intervene on his behalf, especially any attempt by her to influence the deputy commandant's recommendation for punishment. She was certain the deputy would want to trim Alex's sails, make an example of him.

"Something else to consider," Tara informed him. "If the deputy remembers the brawl you had, then it could make your going UA look worse. You've committed two major conduct offenses too close together," she stressed. "First Class aren't supposed to make those mistakes."

"I know that," Alex said, his face reddened. "Excuse me, ma'am, but I don't give a flying"—he began and caught himself—"you know what I mean."

He rose from his chair and paced around the small office. "I wasn't going to let Ethan commit suicide," he said with a steely glare. "Not after his life got so royally screwed up after our last mission."

Alex stopped pacing and dropped down into the chair. He didn't say anything but Tara read the disgust etched on his face.

Tara grew uneasy. Committing two major conduct offenses in five months placed Alex's status as a midshipman in jeopardy. Recommendations to separate him would shatter everything he had believed in and had so bravely fought for as a Marine. He'd be wounded all over again, devastated. But this time with psychological cuts penetrating deep. Not being commissioned would be the fatal blow.

"Ethan was one of my Marines and I went back for him," said Alex, his words and face strained with tension. "I will defend what I did to anyone at the Academy," he said loud enough for someone walking by in the passageway to overhear. "Doesn't matter how high their rank."

"Sit down, Alex," the Navy lieutenant calmly yet firmly advised him.

Alex ignored her order and spun around. "Any officer who hasn't bled on a battlefield, who hasn't seen his Marines and sailors bleed, has no right to lecture me about doing my duty."

"You're talking about me, you know," she replied, aiming a stern glance at him.

"Present company excluded, ma'am."

Tara needed to calm the angry midshipman down. "Go back to your room, wash up, put on your uniform, and go to your next class." She instructed Alex to tell his instructors for classes missed that he'd left on an Unauthorized Absence. "Make sure you tell them that everyone in your chain of command already knows,"

Tara told him. "I'll do my best to give you some guidance while all of this plays out."

"Thank you, ma'am." Alex excused himself and left.

Tara rubbed her temples. Taking sides with a midshipman accused of a major conduct violation could land her in dangerous territory with her command. Yet if push came to shove, she was prepared to stand up in his defense. She recalled her sailors aboard *John Warner* when she stopped short defending them with more conviction. Alex had done his duty in the morning's early hours. *You've got a second chance to do the right thing,* Tara told herself. *Defend him if it's necessary.* She wouldn't listen to anyone who tried talking her out of it. Not even Ray Lydon.

Tara checked her watch. The time was 1055. The Batt-O's Friday morning staff meeting for company officers and SELs started in five minutes. She grabbed her notebook and took off.

# CHAPTER 34

**Midshipmen US Marine Corps meeting**
**Dahlgren Hall, USNA**
**February 29, 2024 at 1930**

Alex was delighted with what he saw. Scenes of poised, confident faces from at least two hundred classmates who, like himself, had received their first choice for post-graduation warfare at Service Assignment last November. In three months, all of them would receive their commissions as Marine Corps second lieutenants. "Oorah," he said softly yet triumphantly.

A buzz of comfortable talk, binding military ties, and shared national purpose echoed through Dahlgren Hall, one of the Naval Academy's oldest buildings. Hanging from its walls were large old black-and-white photographs—many of them decades old—of midshipmen at parade, close order drill, and graduations when they had been held inside the historic building. Both of the long balcony walls displayed oil portraits in exquisite frames of past Academy superintendents going back at least a hundred years.

Marine officers and NCOs were spread across the balcony area wearing the distinctive MARPAT, or Marine Pattern camouflage uniform with its digital-patterned fabric. They spoke to Firsties one-on-one and in clusters, relaxed and showing easy smiles more than the hard-charging warrior expressions seen on online recruitment videos.

A Marine captain with a chiseled jaw and a kind face came toward Alex. Missing his glasses, he squinted at the midshipman's name tag. "Congratulations on being selected to the Corps, Mister Kramer," he announced in a pleasant baritone voice.

"Thanks, sir," Alex answered with a simple nod. He spotted the officer's gold Naval Aviator Wings pinned to his camo uniform.

"You're prior enlisted?" the captain asked, his eyes widened with closer interest in the midshipman standing before him.

"1/6, 24th MEU, Camp Lejeune, sir," Alex noted with admiration.

Knowing Alex had deployed with a Marine Expeditionary Unit, the captain could easily have guessed the midshipman's former Military Occupational Specialty. But the officer chose to hear it from him. Marines liked to brag about where they had served. "What was your MOS with the MEU?"

"O311, sir," said Alex, at the ready with the four-digit code for Infantry Rifleman. The pride in his eyes mirrored the emotional accomplishment he would forever display as a prior grunt Marine. "I deployed with the MEU's Ground Combat Element."

"Marine Ground, America's first and the best when it's time to hit a beachhead!" the captain proclaimed, and his fingers tapped the gold wings pinned to his chest. "I fly Vipers, plus I instruct on DAS and CAS offensive operations," he said, using the military-speak acronyms for Marine pilots and crews delivering Deep Air Support and Close Air Support to infantry and weapons units engaged against enemy positions.

Alex caught the aviator eyeballing the two rows of decorations showing the Silver Star's red, white, and blue ribbon displayed on Alex's Service Dress Blue uniform. He'd seen many others, both in the Marine Corps and Navy, who had picked up on the ribbon representing "conspicuous gallantry and intrepidity in action." They had all nodded to acknowledge his service.

"What MOS are you aiming for after you graduate from The Basic School?" the captain asked.

*I like this guy, not some 'full of himself' officer.* "Well, sir, I could definitely return to 03," he said, naming the MOS code for Infantry. Then he pointed a finger at the captain's gold wings. "Aviation's a possibility," he smiled.

"We'd be pleased to have you contract for Marine Air," the captain told him with buoyant charm. "It's been a pleasure meeting you, midshipman. If you do request aviation, look me up anytime and we'll talk." He offered his hand.

"Appreciate that, sir," said Alex and they shook. "I might take you up on that before graduation."

"Pardon me while I go talk up the Marine Corps with other midshipmen," the officer announced and pivoted to leave. "Enjoy tonight's meeting." He nodded with a friendly smile.

Alex waved to a few classmates he knew from the Fourth Battalion. Then the always-hungry midshipman lifted a slice of pizza off a platter with one hand and a plastic cup of cold beer with the other off a nearby table when a voice from behind him called out.

"Mister Kramer—you ready to wear the Eagle, Globe, and Anchor on your uniform again?"

He spun quickly to find Marine Staff Sergeant Ernie Ortiz, the SEL from 17th Company. Alex smiled broadly at the good-looking Spanish-American NCO with broad shoulders and his famous gap-tooth smile. "I'm ready *now*, Staff Sergeant," he replied and they laughed together.

From different companies in the Brigade, they had become acquainted after Alex learned Ortiz had served with 22nd MEU's Aviation Combat Element, Marine Corps Base Camp Lejeune, the same military base where Alex had been stationed with 24th MEU. Another SEL staff sergeant named Berenson joined them.

Ernie pointed discreetly in the direction where Colonel Burlingame, the senior officer of the Naval Academy's Marine

Corps Detachment, stood thirty feet away talking with a group of Mids. "You didn't hear this from me," he told Alex, "But when all of us in MARDET reviewed personnel jackets of 1/Cs who chose the Corps at Service Selection, you were in the first ten out of 265 who made the cut."

"Thanks for telling me that," Alex said and raised a joyful fist pump in the air for the good feeling coursing through him. The three of them chuckled until Berenson's face turned serious upon seeing Colonel Wettstone, the Deputy Commandant of Midshipmen, headed in their direction. "Hey, 'Polar Bear' incoming at ten o'clock," he said, mentioning the nickname Brigade staff officers and SELs spoke carefully among themselves to describe the deputy's icy personality.

"Evening, gentlemen," the Marine colonel addressed the midshipman and the two SELs with a plastic expression that lacked any warmth.

"Evening, sir," the two staff sergeants replied together and returned awkward smiles.

"Sir," Alex nodded with a small smile for the chain of command. *This Marine is odd man out in a room full of fine people. Who chose him to lead over four thousand midshipmen at the Naval Academy?*

Without returning a genial face, the colonel showed Alex a hard stare for a few seconds. "Mister Kramer, I believe you're scheduled to appear before me next week about a Class A conduct offense," he said in a lifeless voice that darkened what had been a warm conversation before he showed up.

"That's correct, sir," Alex said squarely, pivoting from the colonel's apparent move to catch him off balance.

"Are you any relation to a David Kramer, Academy Class of '92?"

Alex's entire body tightened hearing his father's name suddenly dropped into an already hostile conversation. Now it was personal and he didn't know why. He warned himself to be careful with his answer or he could be in the deputy's sights before next week's hearing. But Alex wouldn't let the arrogant Marine officer off easy because the man he named outranked him. "You're referring to *Rear Admiral* David Kramer, sir. He's my father."

Colonel Wettstone's lip curled up on one side of his mouth. "Small world, isn't it?"

Alex simmered at the remark. *What's that supposed to mean?* He had no clue.

"Gentlemen," the deputy commandant nodded at the three men and walked off.

Ernie Ortiz waited until the colonel was out of earshot. "Maybe it's not my business, but what was that all about?" he asked, incredulous.

"I'm thinking the same thing," added Berenson.

"I don't know, but I'm going to find out," Alex answered, the heat from his brief exchange with the colonel still burning in his throat.

Ernie's head swiveled around, not wanting those standing nearby to overhear, then turned to Alex. "You're up for a Class A offense in front of him next week?" he said, with a curious look.

Alex waved a hand in dismissal. "It's a long story, so let's leave it there."

A solemn-faced Ortiz leaned in closer to the midshipman. "Watch your back, Mister Kramer."

Alex knew the condescending deputy commandant had caught the NCO off guard too. "Good copy there, and thanks, Staff Sergeant," he told his friend and raised one hand while he pulled out his cell phone with the other. "One moment, okay?"

"I'm going for another beer. You want one?" Ernie Ortiz asked.

Alex nodded and tapped out a text to his father:

"The deputy commandant, a Marine, just got in my face at a

USMC meeting in Dahlgren Hall, and said something strange to me. You'll want to hear this. Talk soon."

# CHAPTER 35

**Commandant's Conference Room**
**Bancroft Hall, USNA**
**March 6, 2024**

Colonel Wettstone had read the completed Preliminary Investigative Officer's Report on Alex Kramer going UA: Sneaked out of the Academy without permission in early morning darkness and drove into northern Virginia. Found his Marine buddy nearly comatose after a second suicide attempt. Alex and a Virginia State trooper transported the former Marine to a local hospital ER. The delinquent midshipman returned to the Academy several hours later.

"At this hearing, you have the right to testify or remain silent," Colonel Wettstone addressed the accused midshipman in a clipped voice. "You have the right to examine all evidence or records, to object to evidence, to call witnesses, present evidence on your behalf, and to present oral or written argument on your own behalf." The Marine colonel lifted his eyes from the papers he read and studied Alex. "Do you understand these rights?"

"Yes sir, I do," said Alex, his voice measured without revealing any annoyance.

Colonel Wettstone, USNA Class of '94, had arrived at Annapolis in early June 2021 before Induction Day—and the summer before Alex's sophomore, or Youngster Year, at the Academy. In short time, gossip around the Brigade about the deputy pictured a man who, at times, acted uncomfortable among large groups, namely midshipmen. The past September at a spirit rally before the football team's home opener, the commandant had called Colonel Wettstone over to address the Brigade in Tecumseh Court. It was an awkward moment for a dense crowd of midshipmen standing near the front of the rally and watching the deputy. One of Alex's classmates had whispered to him, "The poor guy acts like the spiritless trying to rally the spirited. Is that weird or what?"

"I have considered the following evidence," the deputy commandant continued, poker-faced. He had reviewed the PIO's report, the Negative Form 2 applied to Alex's offense, and statements taken from his roommate, Lieutenant Marcellus, and ER staff at the hospital who treated Alex's Marine buddy. Colonel Wettstone announced loud enough for all to hear that his decision would be based on the evidence, Alex's performance and conduct records, and any other information presented during the hearing. The deputy paused a moment, then asked if the accused midshipman had been granted ample opportunity review the evidence package. It was his right.

"Yes sir, I had time to read it," replied Alex.

"I, too, reviewed it thoroughly and decided the findings presented a conduct offense serious enough to convene this hearing," said the Marine colonel and the hearing resumed. "Choosing to leave the Yard on an Unauthorized Absence is a significant conduct offense, particularly by a Midshipman First Class. Do you wish to challenge any part of the charges and the investigative report? Do you have any objection to my consideration of this evidence?"

"I choose to challenge the PIO, sir," said Alex. "I will also object if you believe it's an accurate report of what happened," he paused, "because it is *not*."

Everyone in the room picked up on the irritation in Alex's voice.

Colonel Wettstone looked displeased by Alex contesting his authority. "You may proceed."

# CHAPTER 36

Commandant's Conference Room
Bancroft Hall, USNA
March 6, 2024

"The report states Harry Stocks, my roommate, had prior knowledge I was going UA and didn't warn me of what could happen if I did," Alex said, determined to correct the record. "That is a"—he was about to blurt out "lie" but stopped himself—"a falsehood, sir."

Lieutenant Marcellus had warned Alex to hold his temper during the hearing. If it turned into a battle of wills between him and the Deputy Dant, Alex stood to lose everything. Being correct wouldn't matter because while his intentions were right, his attitude would land him in the deputy's crosshairs. Colonel Wettstone wouldn't stand for it.

"Explain, midshipman," Wettstone probed Alex.

"Sir, I asked Harry to do three things early that morning," Alex said, no emotion in his words. "First, he should report my absence at morning muster. Second, he was to go find Lieutenant Marcellus and tell her where I'd gone and why because I wanted her to know ASAP. And the third person to tell was the Marine mentor for 19th Company, Major Anderegg."

"Why did the major need to know?" Colonel Wettstone asked with skepticism dripping in his tone.

*Why do you think, asshole? You know why!* Alex seethed at the charade going on. He'd done his duty. He went back for a Marine whose life was in danger. "Because the major knows I'm returning to the Corps after commissioning, sir."

"Go on," said the deputy, looking down and not at the accused.

"Something else, sir," Alex interjected, and Colonel Wettstone finally looked up at him. "Midshipman Stocks did not purposely violate the Honor Concept. I told Harry not to lie for me or withhold any information from our command, sir."

The Marine colonel's gaze turned toward Tara Marcellus. "Lieutenant, is Midshipman Kramer correct?"

"Yes, sir. I was notified of Midshipman Kramer's unauthorized absence right after morning muster," Tara calmly stated. "I went and found Midshipman Stocks at morning meal. He described everything they discussed before Midshipman Kramer left, including Mister Stocks warning him to self-report that he intended to take an unauthorized absence. Alex refused to self-report."

"Very well," said the deputy. He finished writing more notes and put his pen down. He sighed loud enough for everyone in the room to hear it and turned to Alex. "Are there any other findings in the PIO's report you wish to contest?"

"Yes, sir."

"Go ahead."

"The former Marine I went to help suffered a traumatic brain injury on the battlefield and he's never been whole since combat. He was trying for the second time to kill himself and that's why I went UA, sir." Alex stopped to compose himself but his voice rose and everyone in the room picked up on it. This was personal for him. "Sir, I would like to know why those important facts were left out of the report." He felt the heat rise in his face.

"Your concerns will be taken into consideration," said the deputy, writing more notes.

Alex was certain Colonel Wettstone intentionally ignored his challenge that the PIO's report was incomplete either by intention or carelessness. *Stay frosty,* he told himself. *He's baiting you.*

"The purpose of this hearing is to allow you to present evidence or to make a statement on your behalf," said the Deputy Dant. "You are advised that you may remain silent regarding your offense during this hearing if you wish, and I will not draw any adverse inference from your silence. Do you understand?"

"Yes, I understand sir."

"I will now take your plea, Midshipman First Class Kramer. Of the three conduct offense charges stated in the PIO, how do you plead?"

"Guilty, sir."

The deputy nodded. "Do you wish to make an opening statement?"

"Yes, sir."

"Continue, midshipman."

Alex inhaled, then slowly let his breath out. "I intentionally left the Academy on an unauthorized absence because I was that Marine's last hope. That's why he texted me. I went back for him because it was my duty. Just like I went back five years ago when an IED explosion left Ethan Crowell in broken pieces."

Tara spotted a line of perspiration slide down Alex's cheek. He was nearing an explosive point. "I will not apologize for what I did," Alex said, his voice defiant. "That's what an officer is *supposed to do* for his Marines and his sailors."

The conference room was eerily silent for several seconds, everyone waiting for the deputy commandant's response to the accused midshipman's statement. Colonel Wettstone turned to face the persons in Alex's chain of command and addressed them. "Do any of you wish to make an opening statement?"

They did. "Sir, there's no doubt that Alex is respected more than any of the other 145 midshipmen in 19th Company," said

Jordan Haviland, his classmate and company commander. "Every midshipman will tell you that Alex Kramer knows what it takes to lead sailors and Marines," added Chief Petty Officer Sorrel, the Senior Enlisted Leader. "He proved it under fire on the field of battle."

Tara's turn came next. She wanted her words to reach every person in the room, but the deputy commandant most of all. Midshipmen in the Brigade saw in Alex the highest ideals of the Naval Academy, and they would say so. "Duty, honor, and loyalty are etched in Alex Kramer's character and in his values," she said.

Colonel Wettstone blinked but was otherwise unresponsive to any of the character statements delivered. "Mister Kramer, do you have any character witnesses who would like to appear on your behalf?" An accused midshipman was allowed up to three witnesses to attest to the person's character in the open hearing phase.

Alex had wanted Lieutenant Commander Forgash, the clinical psychologist from the Naval Academy's Midshipmen Development Center, to speak up for him. But she'd left the MDC to join the Behavioral Health Unit at Walter Reed a year ago. Character witnesses had to be actively serving or working at the Naval Academy at the time of a conduct hearing, so that didn't work.

Tara had gone out on a limb and contacted the Center's director. "Think carefully before mixing mental health and disciplinary matters," he'd cautioned her. "That's a very slippery slope." She'd advised Alex to keep his counseling sessions out of the hearing.

"Why should I, ma'am?" Alex had answered back defensively. "I was concussed in combat but my head's still screwed on tight."

"Because if the deputy finds out you received counseling for post-combat trauma, you're giving him an opening to question your emotional stability," she had said.

"You think he'd stoop that low, ma'am?" Alex had responded.

"I'm saying don't give him a reason to question whether you're psychologically stable to be a Marine officer," had been her warning.

Tara knew Colonel Wettstone would crucify Alex if he got hold of that information. *You cannot let that happen, Tara.*

# CHAPTER 37

**Commandant's Conference Room**
**Bancroft Hall, USNA**
**March 6, 2024 at 1005**

Tara Marcellus sensed a subdued yet unsettling restlessness in the room. She followed Colonel Wettstone's facial expressions, the slightest gestures, even the tenor of his voice signaling how he might rule for or against the midshipman before him.

If she had to guess, it would be the latter and she wanted to be wrong, for Alex's sake.

"Mister Kramer, before I meet in private with other officers present, do you have any final words in your defense?" said the deputy commandant.

"I do, sir," Alex answered, still standing at attention. "I went UA because"—he waited a moment—"because one of my Marines needed assistance. He was in an unsafe situation, sir, and I went back for him."

The conference room grew quiet again while the eyes of those present flicked back and forth between the deputy commandant and the accused. Their faces didn't reveal anything. But Tara thought if expressions could speak, she'd predict many in the room approved of Alex's explanation for his conduct. Tara still couldn't get a better read on the deputy commandant's intentions.

"In the days since your offense, have you reflected on your actions?" Colonel Wettstone asked him. "In hindsight, were there other options available to address the difficult challenge you were confronted with?"

Alex waited a brief moment, then answered. "Sir, I've thought about it every day since. Maybe there were other options I could have chosen. But when it happened, I felt it was my duty to go get him, so I did." Alex paused, sucked in a quick breath, and finished. "I still believe going back for him was the right thing to do."

The deputy noisily cleared his throat. "It is my judgment that the accused is guilty of intentionally leaving the Naval Academy by unauthorized means and in violation of midshipman conduct regulations," he said. "His actions on 6 March and 7 March 2024 constituted major violations of midshipman conduct."

Alex inhaled deeply and slowly released the air from his lungs.

Tara's chest tightened.

Colonel Wettstone gathered the papers in front of him. He straightened his shoulders and lifted his chin. "The battalion officer, conduct officer, and JAG will remain for a closed-session deliberation with me. When we are finished, this hearing will reconvene," he declared. "Dismissed."

Tara glanced at her wristwatch. Sixty minutes for the Deputy Commandant to return and announce his recommendation on Alex's case. She shuddered, fearing the news wouldn't be good.

# CHAPTER 38

**The Rotunda**
**Bancroft Hall, USNA**
**March 6, 2024 at 1010**

Alex anxiously shifted his stance from one leg to the other beneath the high ceiling of the Rotunda's majestic architecture. Attendees from his hearing walked by. Most nodded, others stared straight ahead, and a few smiled.

Standing impatiently inside the entrance to Bancroft Hall, one of the largest university dormitories in the world, he looked beyond the wide white marble steps leading up and into Memorial Hall. A large group of people, many in dress uniform, were assembled for some official function.

"There, it's done," Alex uttered to Tara, exasperation in his voice. They were finally alone except for a few Mids going in and out of Bancroft Hall. "The deputy wants to make an example of me, doesn't he? He's got some self-righteous stick up his ass."

"We'll know his recommendation soon enough. You represented yourself well in there," Tara tried to reassure him.

Alex frowned, "I tried, ma'am."

"If the deputy recommends retention, the Batt-O will propose sanctions that won't cramp your life too much with graduation and commissioning coming up."

He lowered his eyes, then looked back up at Tara and shook his head in a defensive motion. "The deputy didn't even ask me if Ethan survived the suicide attempt. Does he have ice in his veins, or what?"

"His job is to pass judgment on your conduct, not whether your friend lives or dies." Tara's answer was neutral.

"He's a Marine officer, and we were talking about another Marine who was psychologically broken in war," Alex shot back, his voice rising.

"It doesn't matter now, Alex," Tara insisted. "I know you're upset but try and take it down a notch, okay? Let's hope for the best when he returns with his recommendation."

She'd been concerned for the midshipman prior to his hearing. Then came the deputy commandant's transparent dislike toward Alex this morning that had troubled her. So far, things didn't look good. She feared the colonel's official recommendation for Alex's punishment could devastate him when announced in approximately one hour's time. But she kept that thought to herself. The lieutenant was hoping for the best possible outcome, but she feared the deputy would render moderate to severe sanctions as punishment for Alex's misconduct.

Tara had grown to admire the courageous midshipman for several reasons, one of them being he never wavered about a person's character. His inspiring story of honor and dedication to duty was a reminder of how her own military story had some tarnish. Perhaps standing up for him before the military's unforgiving culture would finally cleanse her past and restore her self-esteem. For Tara, that moment couldn't come soon enough.

They stood without speaking for a few moments when Alex broke the silence. "Okay if I ask you a personal question, ma'am?"

"Go ahead," she said.

"Why are you doing this?"

"Doing what?"

Alex looked directly at his company officer. "Standing up for me, ma'am," he said and furrowed his brow. "Taking on a lot of risk. Why do it?"

Lieutenant Marcellus ran one hand through her thick brown hair and took in a long breath. "Because I believe in what you did and what you stand for, midshipman." She yearned to say something about her past encounter with courage, but the words didn't form. "Let's leave it at that, all right?" she said in a friendly tone.

"Yes, ma'am, and thank you." Alex said with obvious gratitude in his voice.

"You're welcome," she answered. *The difference will be convincing others to believe in you as strongly as I do. That's what I will do for you.*

Then Tara grimaced. The bloody tavern brawl against local townies that Alex and a few classmates had back in November could come up during the hearing. Even if it did, she wouldn't be deterred from defending him for going UA to save Ethan Crowell.

# CHAPTER 39

Deputy Commandant's Conference Room
Bancroft Hall, USNA
March 6, 2024 at 1015

Three officers—Commander Griffa, the Battalion Officer; Lieutenant Pollard, the Conduct Officer; and Lieutenant Commander Letterle, the commandant's JAG—stood near the deputy commandant like boarding school students waiting for instructions from their headmaster. Colonel Wettstone took a seat at a round table and the others followed.

The deputy turned to Griffa. "Commander, except for his conduct offense, summarize Midshipman Kramer's record."

Ryan Griffa, Naval Academy '04, who served as a Surface Warfare Officer (SWO) in the fleet, briefed the colonel and the others. Alex Kramer was one squared-away midshipman. The prior-enlisted Marine carried a 3.8 academic rating, was a platoon commander in 19th Company, and recorded top Physical Readiness Test scores all four years at the Academy.

"He's never received less than an A grade on his Aptitude for Commission, sir," noted Griffa. The Batt-O cited what many at the Academy considered the most vital personal character evaluation each midshipman receives from classmates, the company officer, and the SEL. Alex had consistently earned the highest ratings reflecting what those others considered his moral, mental, and physical traits—his "aptitude"—to lead sailors and Marines when he graduated.

"Another point, sir," Ryan Griffa continued. "This midshipman's military performance scores for professional training and Marine Practicum instruction have always been in the top 2 percent. He also earned the second highest performance scores at Leatherneck last summer." Griffa also mentioned that Alex's shipmates in 19th Company voted him in the top 1 percent for leadership. The commander flipped to another page in his notebook, then looked up at Colonel Wettstone. "Midshipman Kramer's Overall Order of Merit ranks him 137th in his class," he said and paused. "Sir, for all intents and purposes, Midshipman Kramer has had a spotless record."

"Very well," the colonel answered, expressionless the entire time he listened to the battalion officer's report, and turned toward the conduct officer. "Lieutenant, I recall the accused was involved in another conduct offense a few months ago."

"Yes sir, a 6K infraction," Lieutenant Pollard answered, noting a major conduct offense.

"Remind me of the incident," said the deputy commandant, looking out of sorts.

Pollard described Alex's fight at the local tavern the prior November.

"I remember now," said Colonel Wettstone. A scowl on his face revealed his disdain for the midshipman who didn't meet the colonel's standards of military comportment.

---

**Annapolis, MD**
**November 2023 before Thanksgiving leave**

A white haze of cigarette smoke floated above the crowd of patrons at Reef Points Bar and Grill. Every tall seat at the bar was taken. Neon tube lighting for Corona, Blue Moon, and Yuengling formed an illuminating rainbow of colors at the corners of the large mirror behind the bar. There were few empty tables or seats available.

Platters loaded with food covered the two rectangular tables that were pushed together in the back where 19th Company classmates from the Class of 2024 had gathered to celebrate. For them, liberty started after Service Assignment finished some four hours ago. The Army-Navy game was two weeks away. Christmas leave arrived in five weeks. They'd happily shed uniforms for civilian clothes and fit in like a group of locals on a Friday night after work or college classes.

But a few Naval Academy and military identifications were visible. Carol Youngblood's blue windbreaker with "USNA" in large gold letters printed across the back was slung over her chair. Hannah Foreman and Malik Monroe wore gray Academy-issue sweatshirts. Alex wore his favorite beat-up Marine regulation sweatshirt with "USMC" and the eagle, globe, and anchor emblem imprinted on the left breast.

Three men, probably late twenties or early thirties, finished up at the billiard table several feet away from where Hannah and Carol were preparing to play. One man stood out. A John Deere cap turned backwards sat on his head with dirty, unkept locks of hair flattened against his neck. A dark flannel shirt with its sleeves rolled up to the elbows revealed sleeve tattoos covering his forearms. Alex winced, listening to the man's loud and obnoxious voice mixed with frequent traces of slurred speech. All three men lifted beer bottles to their mouths more frequently than they raised pool cues to play a game.

"Those guys are leaving. Let's shoot some pool." Hannah said to Carol, pointing to the billiard table.

Carol nodded. "You're on."

Hannah and Carol approached the pool table. Hannah racked up the balls and Carol pulled out two cues from the wall rack.

"Carol, Hannah, get over here," Alex called out. The two midshipmen placed their sticks down on the pool table and joined their classmates.

"A toast to Firsties from 19th Company." Alex beamed. The classmates applauded when he rubbed one hand back and forth across his close-cut scalp, exactly the way it was shorn off his head on I-Day and boot camp at Parris Island. This morning, Alex and every First Class Mid whose service assignment had been the Marine Corps or Basic Underwater Demolition/SEALS or Explosive Ordnance Demoli-tion (EOD) went through the traditional Brigade ritual of Service Assignment to get their heads shaved. "Here's to our first billets as officers." They raised their glasses and toasted one of the highlights of every midshipman's lifetime at the Academy.

Then Hannah and Carol returned to the pool table to play. Carol sent the cue ball smashing into the rack. "Here we go," she said. Watching Carol line up her next shot, Hannah was suddenly startled by the presence of a man standing closely next to her—the man in the flannel shirt and the John Deere cap.

"Hey, how 'bout I buy you a drink, then you and me shoot some pool?" he said, the words spoken into her right ear.

Hannah cringed, feeling hot breath on her skin and smelling the odor of beer and stale cigarette smoke.

"No thank you, sir," she managed to say, the man's foul breath making her gag. "I'm with friends." She pointed to her classmates at the table.

"What's a matter? You from that Navy Academy place?" His words were so slurred she strained to understand them. Hannah quickly retreated two steps back to put distance between them. "Like I said, no thanks, sir," she said with growing anxiety.

The local closed the distance, standing directly in front of Hannah's face again. "I ain't good enough to drink with you?" He pointed a shaky finger at her classmates and friends ten feet away. "But they are?"

A male voice interrupted them. "Is there some problem here?"

The local whipped his head around and found himself facing Alex.

"Mind your own business. This here's between me and her," said the belligerent drunk.

"This *is* my business," Alex shot back. "Go back to the bar," he said. His eyes turned to slits. "Don't come near those two ladies again."

Hannah stood next to Carol for more protection.

"And what if I don't? Who the fuck'r *you* tellin' me—"

Alex didn't flinch. "Final warning, get lost."

In the next instant, Alex felt the drunk's fingers around his throat. He pressed his right palm into the local's face and pushed away. At the same time, the fingers of his other hand gripped the local under his chin. In one swift motion, Alex lifted the drunk off his feet and flung his body through the air. The man fell hard, slamming onto the hardwood floor.

The drunk's two friends seated at the bar turned to see their buddy moaning and cussing. They jumped off their bar stools and moved toward Alex when Malik Monroe and Ted Wisecarver, another classmate, leaped out of their chairs and blocked the path to Alex.

"Sit your asses down or you'll end up like him," shouted Malik, who stood at 6'3, 220 pounds, and as solid as a steel girder.

The two locals grumbled and started to retreat. Ted looked away for a split second and one of them sprinted past him, holding a beer bottle by its neck with payback flashing in his eyes.

"Alex, behind you!" Malik shouted.

Alex spun to his right and blocked the beer bottle coming down on him. A split second later, his right fist slammed into the local's mouth. The punch lifted the attacker's feet off the ground and projected him against a wood-paneled wall. The man pressed his hands up to his injured face, crimson blood oozing between his fingers, and yelled something indiscernible.

Country music blared while patrons rose from the seats to watch the brawl.

"All of you stay right here," said a middle-aged woman with a chain-smoker's leathery face, who appeared from behind the bar. "I called the police." She surveyed the mess in front of her and shook her head. "I don't need any fightin' in my place." She turned to the Mids. "All you from the Academy?"

"That's correct," answered Malik.

"I bet you all don't need trouble like this happening."

"There's your trouble, lady." Alex pointed at the two locals lying injured on the floor. One of them smeared his shirt sleeve across a mouth still bleeding from two cracked teeth. "You let drunk bottom feeders into your goddamned place." Alex put his face right in front of the woman's. "They're deadbeat losers, white trash."

Carol Youngblood grabbed Alex's sweatshirt and pulled him away to put distance between him and the bartender. "It's okay, Alex," she said to calm him down.

"No, it's not okay," Alex called out, his face twisted in anger, and rolled his eyes. "There goes my fucking commission."

---

Colonel Wettstone's dislike for the accused midshipman was contaminated with jealousy. Both Marines had experienced combat. But Alex Kramer had selflessly saved the lives of three seriously wounded Marines while suffering from multiple battle wounds himself. The Silver Star on his uniform represented "conspicuous gallantry and intrepidity in action." The colonel's uniform displayed the Combat Action Ribbon, but no decoration as significant as valor. That got under Colonel Wettstone's skin, and it burned. Not to mention a bug up his ass that went back years when he and David Kramer, Alex's father, had been assigned to the same company in the Brigade.

"What else?" asked the deputy commandant with apparent impatience.

"Midshipman Kramer was found guilty of one conduct offense in the Naval Academy's administrative guidelines on midshipmen conduct," said Lieutenant Pollard. "Local authorities didn't file any charges against him after they took his report, and a breathalyzer proved negative for alcohol."

The three officers exchanged furtive glances as the deputy commandant's expression made clear to them that he wasn't through judging the accused midshipman. The Marine colonel asked Lieutenant Pollard to remind him of the sanctions imposed on Midshipman Kramer from the fight because he didn't recall them. The conduct officer spelled them out: Sanctioned with forty-five demerits. Restricted to the Yard for thirty-five days. Loss of privileges including overnight liberty, not able to wear either "Spirit Gear" on the Yard or civilian attire during weekend town liberty for three months. And he had been placed on conduct probation through graduation.

Lieutenant Commander Eleanor Letterle, the commandant's JAG was the last to speak. "Commander, has Midshipman Kramer been charged with any honor offenses at the Academy?" the deputy commandant asked her. Honor offenses were very serious violations, especially for Firsties, and the colonel wanted to know.

Letterle reviewed her notes. "No, sir. He received a Negative Form-1 plebe year. It involved a classmate's honor offense, which he had knowledge of." The JAG described the 2020 honor offense where Alex received an Aptitude grade of C for being implicated, and ordered to be mentored by 10th Company's Senior Enlisted Leader.

Reflecting on Alex Kramer's fate, which lay at that moment in the deputy's hands, Colonel Wettstone remembered being in Afghanistan commanding a battalion strength of 1,200 Marines. One of his platoon commanders had ordered Marines to advance on an enemy position. The lieutenant's fire teams were ambushed by Taliban-backed militants waiting in the wooded mountainside— one Marine killed, two seriously wounded. Wettstone had been responsible for many Marines. It didn't matter whether they were infantry grunts or ones serving an aviation squadron. He thought back to General James Mattis telling Marines of 3/2, "Mistakes are forgivable, but a lack of discipline should be met with zero tolerance." As the conduct hearing progressed, Wettstone grew concerned that Alex's instincts as an officer might tell him to follow his gut more than his training. That mindset could have unintended consequences.

The deputy commandant refused to be swayed by one prior-enlisted midshipman having received the nation's third highest award for valor. Yet, he grudgingly acknowledged Alex could also turn out to be an outstanding Marine officer. Colonel Wettstone felt obligated to consider options for sitting in judgment on the brave young man's future. What if he recommended reversing Alex's service assignment? What if the Navy told the midshipman he'd serve as a naval officer in the fleet or aboard a submarine but not a Marine officer? He would still be retained, graduate, and receive his commission. Colonel Wettstone's own instincts told him that Alex would never accept those terms. He was determined to return to the Corps wearing the gold bars of a Marine second lieutenant, not a Navy ensign.

The deputy commandant cleared his throat loudly, as though he wanted the three officers to sit up straight. "The accused has been a good midshipman on several levels. I am bound to only consider the facts of the specific case, not prior offenses a midshipman has committed." The deputy shifted in his chair and the three officers waited silently for him to finish. "But Midshipman Kramer's already on probation for one serious conduct offense, the bar fight he engaged in four months ago."

The Marine raised his hands with a gesture of submission.

"Two major conduct offenses close in time present me with a clear decision. A Midshipman First Class is supposed to know better. Apparently, this one doesn't."

# CHAPTER 40

**Commandant's Conference Room**
**Bancroft Hall, USNA**
**March 6, 2024 at 1045**

Lieutenant Pollard opened the conference room door and signaled Alex Kramer, Lieutenant Marcellus, and Chief Petty Officer Sorrel to return.

Colonel Wettstone stood with erect posture, his thick neck bulging slightly beyond the sides of the uniform shirt collars. "Your overall record as a midshipman is very good," he said to Alex. "I reviewed it along with the Preliminary Investigating Officer's report, all testimony and character witness statements. I also reread your objections. Do you understand the gravity of the offense you committed?"

"I do, sir," Alex answered.

Looking straight ahead with eyes fixed like lasers on the deputy commandant, Tara pondered the hypocrisy of his question. *What about you, Colonel? Do you understand the gravity of why this midshipman went UA? Didn't you pay attention when he explained that he went to save another man's life?* Watching the deputy's body language and following the tenor of his voice and his words so far during the morning's hearing, Tara was convinced the man understood nothing about dedication to duty.

"Midshipmen First Class are held to the highest standards of the Brigade," said the colonel. "They are expected to know right from wrong on all matters involving honor, conduct, and personal character." He paused and waited for a reaction from the accused.

There wasn't one to find. "Midshipman Kramer, I've made my decision concerning your offense. It is my recommendation that you are to be separated from the United States Naval Academy."

The silence across the conference room was louder than cannon fire. No one stirred.

Tara shuddered and whispered the words in her head: Whisky Tango Foxtrot—*What the Fuck*. She mumbled something inaudible under her breath. Next, she glanced sideways at the JAG and the conduct officer and found no reaction from either one. Her eyes darted quickly back toward Alex.

"Mister Kramer, do you wish to say anything?" the deputy commandant asked.

"Yes, sir." Alex purposely waited several seconds just to piss off the colonel. "Separating me from the Academy is a dishonor to the Marine I was and the midshipman I am—*sir!*" he answered with controlled force.

Colonel Wettstone's face twitched for anyone looking to notice.

"I will appeal your recommendation because it's wrong," Alex said before the deputy could respond. He glared at the Marine officer who wanted to kick him out of the Academy.

"Mister Kramer, I believe your reasons for leaving without official authorization *appeared* honorable," the deputy said in a patronizing manner. "But you failed to consider all reasonable options for your situation. You willfully—"

"Excuse me, sir, but I willfully did what the Naval Academy teaches midshipmen a naval officer *must always* do," Alex sharply interrupted the visibly startled colonel. "We never leave our sailors and Marines behind," said the accused midshipman, his voice louder with rage. "That's the code of duty we follow, sir."

Tara's gaze jumped back and forth between the defiant midshipman and a Marine colonel whose expressions, words, and overall demeanor hinted that no one should question his opinion. Her throat constricted listening to Alex attempt to embarrass the deputy in an open hearing full of service members.

"You willfully disregarded more options that could have saved the individual you knew and served with." The colonel's face still flushed at the midshipman interrupting him, a senior officer, in mid-sentence. "It is my judgment that while your intentions *might* have been sincere, your actions that followed were clearly wrong," he said without taking his eyes off Alex. "I will present my recommendation forthwith to the commandant and the superintendent for their reviews. You're dismissed."

"Sir," Alex said in a near shout, then pivoted about face and exited the room without turning to look to his right or his left.

Watching Alex pass by, Tara's jaw clenched so hard her entire face hurt.

# CHAPTER 41

**Wardroom, 19th Company**
**Bancroft Hall, USNA**
**March 6, 2024 at 2030**

Sitting on the vinyl couch with his fingers interlocked behind his head and his legs spread wide out like a rag doll, Midshipman First Class Paul Munoz's angular features displayed abject disgust. "The Academy wants to crucify Alex," he practically spit out the words. "What they're doing is horseshit."

Back from a workout at Wesley Brown Field House, Malik Monroe unzipped the navy blue USNA issue windbreaker he wore and collapsed into one of the wardroom chairs. An offensive lineman on Navy's football team, the African-American Midshipman First Class was popular among his shipmates. "I went to the first day of Alex's hearing. The Deputy Dant walked in and looked around like he'd arrived to order an execution," he vented with a sense of fatalism.

"The Academy's taking the wrong side," said Jane Emmer, hands planted on her hips. "Alex stopped a suicide. Now they're going to hang him because he went UA?" She eyed her two classmates. "Where's the honesty in the system?"

The three 19th Company classmates, with just two months left before their graduation and commissioning, reflected silently with gloomy expressions for a few seconds. The wardroom's only sound radiated from a college basketball game shown on the wall-mounted flat-screen TV.

"Am I interrupting?"

Their heads turned at the same moment and saw Lisa Sorrel, 19th Company's Senior Enlisted Leader, standing in the doorway. The Navy Chief Petty Officer, her hair pinned back and chocolate brown eyes seeming to light up her face with an easy smile, strolled into the wardroom.

"Evening, chief," Malik Monroe rose from his chair and greeted her with a slight hesitation the others picked up.

"I'm supposed to meet Midshipman Harvath here at 2030," Sorrel said with her calm yet authoritative demeanor. The SEL was well-liked and respected by Mids in 19th Company. "Any of you seen him?"

"Sorry, chief, haven't seen Willie," answered Munoz.

Walking further into the wardroom, Chief Sorrel searched the three midshipmen's grim faces and lifted one eyebrow. "What? Did all of you just come back from a funeral?"

"More like the funeral is still going on, chief," Jane Emmer answered, the bridge of her nose wrinkled with a scowl.

The SEL muted the volume on the TV, then seated herself at one end of the couch opposite Munoz. "Okay, who's having the funeral?"

"It's Alex Kramer's funeral," said Malik Monroe.

Sorrel heard weariness and wrath in Monroe's voice, and figured he spoke for the three of them. "I had a feeling this was about your classmate," the chief petty officer said.

She'd already eavesdropped on other 19th Company midshipmen talking about the prior-enlisted Marine's conduct offense. Her impression was that a lot of Alex's classmates and shipmates in the company were sweating it out along with him while he sat in judgment by the Naval Academy.

Lisa Sorrel wasn't certain where this conversation might lead. But with sixteen years of service in the fleet before coming to the Academy, the veteran sailor warned herself to choose her

next words carefully. Naval Academy midshipmen talked freely—
sometimes too much—about things going on inside their company. If she dared to express her opinion about one midshipman's troubled situation and his fate at Annapolis, word would
get out to 145 midshipmen of 19th Company in less than twenty-
four hours. Then Lieutenant Marcellus would definitely hear that
her SEL had spoken out of turn, and she wouldn't like it. If the
battalion officer got wind of it, he'd come down hard on her too. *Be
careful what you say here.*

Midshipman Emmer  bit her lower lip. "Pardon me, Chief,
don't you think this whole business is looking more like a per-
secution than a fair trial?" she said, her voice rising in exasperation.
"Okay, he went UA. But he left the Yard to keep someone from
taking his life. Isn't that acting with honor?"

*I'm not disagreeing with you,* Lisa Sorrel thought. Alex
Kramer's conduct hearing had sounded openly prejudiced. It
favored the deputy commandant, the Academy's opening pro-
secutorial power. She'd watched Colonel Wettstone closely. The
man's menacing looks and his cold tone implied he was out for
blood and wanted Alex's type. But the Senior Enlisted Leader
couldn't say aloud what she perceived.

"I respect Midshipman Kramer's dedication to duty," she
said in an even voice. "But he had options that night. He could
have helped his Marine buddy without going UA." She waited a
moment. "And that's where he jammed himself up."

"But what's more important?" Malik Monroe blurted out
in frustration. "Saving someone's life or wasting time getting
permission to leave the Yard?"

Sorrel raised an open hand at the Navy football player, warning
him to check his emotions before he said something he couldn't
take back. "Saving a life is. But your classmate could have called
local police to go check on his friend—and he didn't. He could

have called EMS but he didn't." She waited for some reaction from them. "See what I mean?"

"I get what you're saying, Chief," said Munoz. "We're not trying to put you on the spot."

*Yes you are, but I understand,* Chief Sorrel thought silently. "The process for your classmate is still going on. Try and have some faith it will be fair and end well for him." She rose from the couch. "If you see Mister Harvath, remind him he didn't show up for our meeting, and he still needs to find me."

On her way out, the SEL spotted a piece of paper pinned to the bulletin board and went over to read its printed message: *Alex Kramer is a warrior who did his duty. The Academy is WRONG to punish him!*

She removed the paper and showed the three midshipmen a hard stare as she held up the note. "I don't care who put this here, but it hurts your classmate's cause," she said sternly yet without anger in her voice. "I understand what you're doing, but this isn't the way to go about it." She waved the paper at them.

"With all due respect, Chief," Malik interrupted her, "then what *is* the way?"

A few uncomfortable seconds of silence followed. Chief Sorrel inhaled a long, slow breath. "Trust that the system will find greater duty in Alex's character than his act of disobedience."

# CHAPTER 42

**Alexandria, VA**
**March 9, 2024**

Shoppers, sightseers, and DC metro residents filled the sidewalks of Old Town Alexandria. Sun mixed with clouds amid temperatures in the high forties signaled winter hadn't ended yet.

With her hands tucked into her denim jeans pockets to keep warm, Tara Marcellus strolled along King Street. A gray Naval Academy-issue midshipman's hooded sweatshirt helped block out the chilly temps.

Walking alongside her, Ray Lydon pulled Tara in close to him. The Marine pilot pointed to the Irish goods store window they were passing. "I'm buying you an Irish cable-knit sweater, navy or white. You'll be beautiful in either color," he said.

Tara's face lit up in a loving smile at Ray. He was handsome from any angle and the last time she checked, her uncorrected eyesight was 20/30.

"Let's get some lunch. I'm hungry." Ray wrapped an arm around her waist and pulled her to him. "Then we'll come back to the Irish store."

"I'll just have a glass of wine but you should eat, okay? I don't have much of an appetite."

"What's going on?" he asked her. "You're suddenly a hundred miles away."

"It's a midshipman from my company. He's in a rough situation, and it's been on my mind 24/7 lately."

"Something bad happening to him?"

"It could, and I want to try and stop it."

"Stop what?"

"The commandant's upheld the deputy's recommendation for separation," said Tara. "I've asked for a meeting with the Dant and Deputy Dant."

"Why?"

"To plead my case that he shouldn't be separated," she said, "and try to stop it from going as far as the superintendent."

"Why are you going out on a limb for this midshipman?" Ray asked with an unconvinced air. "You know that going around your chain of command will cause problems for you. Then it's a lose-lose deal for you and this midshipman." He shook his head. "Might as well forget about the commandant also reversing his recommendation. He'll never admit he could have been wrong—neither of them."

Tara stopped walking. "I have to, Ray. They want to hang him out to dry, and it's wrong. Those two men don't have any friggin' idea what real courage is. Not like this midshipman. He showed incredible bravery under fire."

"Can't this Mid fight his own battles?" Ray appealed in an earnest voice. "Why do you have to be in the middle of it?"

"Because—I just do."

"Then convince me."

They continued walking while Tara, for the first time, described to Ray her own trial under fire aboard USS *John Warner*. And while they'd kept on-again, off-again contact in their early years as junior officers, the embarrassment of bringing it up had been too much for Tara to bear. Yet the incident still haunted her. "I didn't stand up to do my duty when I should have," she said. "I have a chance to make right what I failed to do before." She was relieved to say it out loud.

"Couldn't this Mid have helped his friend without going UA?" asked Ray.

"Yeah, he could have called the police and given them the address," Tara said.

Ray cocked his head to one side. "Except he didn't, and that's why he's jammed up now."

"All he cared about was doing his duty," she answered defensively. "To go back for one of his men. I'm standing with him. Someone has to do the right thing here. I have to."

Ray reached out and gently held her face in his hands. "Be careful what you wish for."

"Thanks for understanding why I need to do this," she said and wrapped her arms around his chest.

# CHAPTER 43

**Annapolis, MD**
**March 10, 2024 at 1430**

Rear Admiral David Kramer entered the Fleet Reserve Club in downtown Annapolis. Dressed in a Naval Academy windbreaker over a white button-down collar dress shirt and burgundy crewneck sweater, he peered across the indoor bar and restaurant area. He spotted Alex in blue jeans and a flannel shirt, sitting alone at a booth. David signaled to him.

"Thanks for coming, Dad." said Alex, who rose to greet him.

David picked up on Alex's subdued disposition. The young man's typical optimism wasn't on display. An attempted smile couldn't hide what looked like discomfort written on his face. "Your voicemail said it was important," David answered as he removed his jacket and sat opposite Alex. "I'm just glad to see you," he said warmly, yet curious to find out the burden his son appeared to carry. "Mom wanted to come too—"

"It's better for just you and me to talk for now, okay?" Alex interjected. The weak smile had disappeared.

"Sure." David raised one hand when Alex began to speak. "I'm gonna get us a couple of beers and we'll talk, then get some lunch. How's that?" he asked with a reassuring uplift in his tone. "What are you drinking?"

"Blue Moon on tap," Alex replied, nodding in David's direction.

"Got it," David said and glanced at a menu. "If a server comes, order me any burger medium-well and whatever you feel like."

"Sounds good."

David looked past the glass doors at the merchant stores along the downtown Annapolis dock while the bartender poured two beers from the tap. He thought about the voicemail Alex had left yesterday that only mentioned he wanted to talk.

Olivia used to be the parent Alex would turn to for advice. By pressing Alex in high school to apply for an appointment to the Naval Academy, then disapproving when he enlisted in the Marine Corps, David had driven his son away. But things changed when Alex was wounded in Sierra Leone and decorated for valor. David had been chastened by the oral citation of his son's courage under fire. Then came Alex's appointment to Annapolis.

His son's selfless dedication to duty, his loyalty to the others he served with, and his urge to protect them from perceived and real harm brought David a profound sense of pride.

He returned with two tall glasses of beer and placed them down. "What's going on?" he asked Alex.

"The deputy commandant's recommended I should be separated," Alex said slowly.

"What happened?"

The corners of Alex's mouth curled down, he met his father's alerted gaze. "One of the guys I saved—Ethan—he tried to kill himself two weeks ago," he said, his voice low. "It was the second time he's tried suicide, and I went out to his place in Alexandria to stop him."

Watching Alex relive something difficult, David leaned forward in his chair. "How did you know your buddy was trying to take his own life?"

Alex anxiously drummed his fingers on the table. "He texted me about ten minutes before Taps. I sensed he was going to try to kill himself again. I couldn't let him do it, Dad, so I went to stop him."

"Of course, you couldn't," said David, wanting to sound reassuring. "Did you get there in time?"

"Barely," Alex told him, relief now evident in his voice. "But he's alive and a psychiatrist is watching out for him."

"Good," said David.

There was a momentary silence while the flag officer and Naval Academy graduate studied his midshipman son and decorated Marine. Too much time had passed since David had told Alex how much he loved him, believed in him. David wouldn't let that happen again. "Did you notify your command?"

Alex's head shook back and forth, "I went UA."

Immediately knowing the gravity of Alex's offense, David slid his glass to the side. He'd lost his thirst. "The recommendation for separation happened at a conduct hearing?"

Alex lifted his glass of beer and downed half of it, then wiped his mouth with his shirt sleeve. "Two days ago."

"Who's the deputy commandant?"

"A Marine O-6. His name's Wettstone."

Hearing the name, David's facial reaction took on a mix of amusement and disdain. "Doesn't surprise me."

"What doesn't?" said Alex.

"He was Third Class when I was a Firstie in 21st Company," David said with a sarcastic expression. "I'll tell you a story about him. Then you'll understand," he said and began. "Wettstone had planned a twentieth birthday party for himself off the Yard. He convinced two classmates to pick up alcohol for the party. Then he was stupid enough to invite a couple of plebes. Well, they showed up and got shit-faced."

"That's it?" Alex asked.

"No, things went downhill from there," David said. "When the plebes returned to their wing in Bancroft Hall, they ran into their company officer and he smelled the alcohol on their breath."

"What happened after that?" asked Alex, now very attentive.

"There was an investigation and Wettstone was charged with a conduct offense, just like you were. But he wouldn't admit to anything or mention any other midshipmen's names. Meanwhile, the battalion officer wanted to nail somebody to the wall. When the recommendation was announced to slam Wettstone with a ton of sanctions, he decided to save his sorry ass. He ratted out the other Mids who'd been involved, *but*"—David stopped in mid-sentence and raised an eyebrow at Alex—"he never talked to them first before he gave them up."

David knew Alex would view the colonel implicating his former shipmates as an unforgivable betrayal by a midshipman. Wettstone had bilged other Mids connected with the party. From that moment on, he became a pariah to every midshipman in 21st Company.

"How'd they find out Wettstone set them up?" Alex asked.

"Internal messages to them from the commandant's office."

"What came next?"

"Sanctions plus restrictions for all of them," answered David. "Nobody was separated. But everyone in the company knew what Wettstone did. I heard the guy was radioactive for at least a year, even when the Brigade reformed after summer training. Also heard that none of his classmates would sit near him in King Hall." The admiral leaned in toward his son and took in a slow, deep breath. "I hadn't left for my billet yet and was in town when I ran into a Firstie from 21st Company. He told me, 'Sailors or Marines will turn on that prick one day. They might put a bullet in him.'"

David waited while Alex finished his beer and a server brought their lunch orders.

"If I could say or do anything to help you, I would," he pleaded. "But my interference would hurt your case, and I'd never do that."

Alex smiled, appreciative for the offer and his father's desire to help. "It's all right. I think my company officer wants to stand up for me if she can. She's good."

"She?"

"Lieutenant Marcellus, a sub driver," Alex said between bites of food.

"Then she'll need to watch her step if she tries in any way to support your actions."

They ate their lunches and talked about other things. David picked up the check and they walked outside to a breezy sunshine.

"Going for Ethan followed a dedication to duty you believe in," said David with sincerity. "A lot of Academy officers—the deputy too—they've never been called to do what you did during your NEO mission. They can only imagine what it means."

"I suppose," said Alex with some resignation.

David smirked. "Navy SEALs have a name for military officers who've been sitting behind desks for too long. They call 'em 'cake-eaters'."

"It figures," said Alex.

"I love you, son," David said and gathered Alex close to him in an embrace. "You make me proud."

"Love you too, Dad," Alex responded in kind.

"Keep me informed about what's happening with your case. Call or text me anytime, day or night."

"I will," Alex replied. "Thank you, sir."

David pulled away and held his son's shoulders. "This is a fight to win?"

"Definitely a fight to win," said Alex, his spirit brightened.

# CHAPTER 44

**Bancroft Hall, USNA**
**March 15, 2024 at 1910**

It was the end of a long Friday and the end of a long week. Tara was hungry and spent. Time to go home, do something, anything this weekend.

She scribbled some final notes about presenting an appeal to Alex's separation and cleared up the papers scattered on her desk when her PC chimed with an inbox message. It was an online news bulletin from *Marine Corps Times*.

Tara froze seeing the headline: *Deceased Marine aviators identified.* Two Marine officers were reported killed during a helicopter training mission in the California desert. Ray Lydon's face appeared in front of her while she speed-read the bulletin.

Her heart racing, she clicked the link to read the news story:

The Marine Corps identified the two aviation crew members killed when their Bell AH-1Z Viper attack helicopter crashed during a training mission out of Marine Corps Air Station Camp Pendleton, California early Monday morning 25 March. Major Jonathan L. Rusk, 35 and Capt. Raymond D. Lydon, 29—

"No, please, not him," she gasped, the words bursting forth. Pools of tears filled her eyes.

Tara shuddered, thinking of her graduation day omen that Ray's life would be snuffed out prematurely. She hadn't said a word about it to Ray when they'd caught up at their class's fifth reunion because it was ridiculous. Except now it wasn't. She had been so happy to see him that mentioning the omen would have disheartened their time together.

Tara tried reading more about the fatal crash, but it was useless. She immediately shut her office door so no one walking by would observe her in a state of shock. In private and overwhelmed with grief, she fell into a nearby chair and wept.

Ray Lydon, her classmate and best friend at Annapolis, was gone. He had dedicated himself and his life to the Marine Corps and to his country. He had been an intimate companion and tender lover who had spoken just four days ago of being her fiancé and wanting to be her husband. Now he had been struck down in the prime of his life.

Tara took a deep breath while she tried to process her shocking loss. Just when it felt as though she was physically calming down, bile rose swiftly up into her throat. Gagging and without enough time to reach the head, she lifted the metal trash can off the tile floor and vomited into it.

# CHAPTER 45

**Bancroft Hall, USNA**
**March 19, 2024 at 0755**

Above the large wooden doors were the words inscribed in gold letters: OFFICE OF THE COMMANDANT. Tara was relieved the Rotunda was empty. Four thousand and four hundred midshipmen were in first-period class.

Major Anderegg walked down the opposite stairway and crossed the Rotunda to join her. His handsome features cut an imposing figure. Yet a warm smile and generous personality made him one of best-liked officers of the Academy's Marine cadre among the midshipmen.

Tara and Mark were intent on stating their positions on Alex Kramer's fate in person to the commandant. And both knew they were starting a conversation that could lead to retaliation against them. Most senior officers didn't take well to subordinates questioning their decisions. So far, Tara hadn't personally contended with either the Dant or the Deputy Dant. She couldn't gauge whether they would be long on forgetting and short on forgiving anyone who challenged their judgment, let alone their authority.

"Lieutenant, tell me we're not about to cut our own throats going in there," said Anderegg, aiming his head toward the Dant's office doors.

"I still want to do it, sir," Tara said. "I told the battalion officer that separating this midshipman would be a serious mistake."

"What'd he say?"

Tara's pursed lips revealed a premonition that trouble awaited her and Major Anderegg on the other side of the large wooden doors. "He told me this meeting could backfire on us, but he'd arrange it."

The Marine major looked down at his cell phone and shook his head. "Mids are all over social media about the commandant's and the deputy's recommendations. Here, read this tweet," he said and raised the cell phone's screen for Tara to see.

*@callsigntomahawk Separating Alex Kramer is a shit sandwich. The Silver Star he wears on his uniform didn't come from a Cracker Jack box. Shame on the Dant and Deputy Dant for doing this to a brave Marine and a solid midshipman.*

"You feeling all right?" asked Mark, noticing dark circles and lines of weariness under Tara's eyes.

"I lost a close friend last week," she said. Her jaw quivered slightly.

"Oh, I'm very sorry," Mark said with sympathy. He checked his watch. "It's 0755. Time to go in there."

Through the double doors, a Navy lieutenant pointed to the open office door and directed them to go in.

Captain Adam Brookshier, Commandant of Midshipmen, was seated at the conference table in his expansive office. Commander Griffa, Tara's boss and Batt-O, sat on the commandant's right. Tara nearly tripped over her own feet when she spotted Colonel Wettstone seated on the Dant's other side.

"Major, Lieutenant—take a seat," Captain Brookshier told them in a near frosty tone, pointing to chairs on the other side of the table. "Commander Griffa explained your reasons for wanting to discuss Midshipman Kramer's conduct offense and my recommendation."

After Colonel Wettstone had rendered his recommendation

to separate Alex from the Academy, Tara had met with Griffa. She would wait for the commandant's hearing and judgment. But if it was another separation recommendation, she would firmly yet respectfully insist on meeting with the two senior officers to state her reservations.

Griffa had reluctantly agreed. "I'm willing to let you 'discuss' your concerns, Lieutenant. But I will not allow you to challenge the commandant and the deputy commandant directly," he had warned her with a stern nature.

Tara interpreted the commandant's crossed arms to mean the man had little interest in a company officer's opposing views. Namely, hers. She picked up right away how Colonel Wettstone refused to make eye contact with her. *What's your problem, colonel? You won't even acknowledge I'm in the room? How dare an officer lower in rank question your holier-than-thou judgment?* Tara bristled inside.

"This conversation serves no purpose, Lieutenant," the commandant said in a firm yet composed demeanor. "The deputy commandant and I have made our recommendations, and they are final."

"Sir, we believe that separating Midshipman Kramer would be a serious mistake," Tara said, keeping her criticism and her tone respectful.

She had no intention of backing down, even after their recommendation for separation. Maybe her appeal could persuade them to reconsider their judgment. Whatever she might pull off with these two men before Alex Kramer's conduct case came before the Naval Academy's superintendent for its third and final hearing was worth trying.

Captain Brookshier and Colonel Wettstone looked at each other. Brookshier's raised eyebrows showed his disbelief. Wettstone's mouth twisted into a sneer.

"How's that?" the commandant asked, looking piqued. "I

thought through my recommendation very carefully." Tara felt Captain Brookshier's eyes on her like a jaguar surveying its prey. "Tell me why you *believe*," he emphasized the last word, "that I made a mistake." Then he gestured with one hand at the deputy seated next to him. "That *we* made a mistake."

Both of them were mistaken recommending separation, Tara thought. Yet she exhibited calmness toward them. She wasn't about to strenuously disagree because she could lose. "Sir, Midshipman Kramer's offense was going UA to save a Marine— someone he saved once before, along with two other Marines on the field of battle."

"I know that, Lieutenant. But his conduct offense happened here at the Academy, not on any field of battle," said Captain Brookshier.

"I suggest the two are linked, sir," she answered back and squared her shoulders. For Tara, there was no turning back now. Either she was all in or all out. Surrender meant feeling shame a second time for not standing on principle. She chose her next words and her temperament carefully. "The Academy would be separating Alex Kramer because he followed the timeless principles of duty and honor that we've always taught midshipmen: officers never leave their sailors and Marines behind."

"Seems I've heard this sermon before," Colonel Wettstone said with unhidden sarcasm in his voice. He leaned forward in a menacing gesture toward Tara. "Tell me, Lieutenant, are you parroting the midshipman who already lectured me that we never leave our own behind?"

Lieutenant Donald Schrager's chubby face and misogynistic words suddenly flashed in Tara's mind: "You can't cut it in this man's Navy," the lying navigation officer had mocked her with sailors in earshot aboard *John Warner*. Questioning her judgment and demeaning her sex without saying it out loud had cut into her like a jagged blade. Now the deputy commandant's high and mighty words that fired at her carried the same condescending tone she'd heard before.

"Sir, no one ever tells me what to say or think," she told the colonel, keeping tight control in her voice while she clenched her fists hidden underneath the table.

Captain Brookshier reacted with visible discomfort to the exchange he just witnessed between the deputy commandant and the company officer. He turned to Major Anderegg. "Do you agree with Lieutenant Marcellus's opinion?"

"I do, sir, completely," said the Marine officer.

"Have you discussed this with Colonel Burlingame?" Captain Brookshier said next, referring to the highest Marine Corps officer serving at the Academy.

"Yes, sir."

Tara shot a glance at the deputy. The corners of Wettstone's lips turned down again with open displeasure.

"And what was the Senior Marine's response?"

"Colonel Burlingame urged me to think twice about requesting this meeting. But he also supports my position, sir," the major answered, then lightly cleared his throat. "Gentlemen, isn't it enough that Midshipman Kramer admitted his offense and be sanctioned with remediation? He's a recipient of the Silver Star. In his mind, the Marine he went back to retrieve was gravely wounded *again*. Alex Kramer acted exactly as we would expect an officer to react—Navy or Marine."

"Midshipman Kramer's prior service record isn't on trial here," the commandant said.

Tara's body tensed while the room got quiet. Alex was her midshipman the same way Petty Officer Ruiz and Chief Drysdale were her sailors. Do not turn away this time, she told herself. She was doing this for Ray Lydon, too. The Marines needed to replace his loss with other dedicated, even occasionally irreverent officers like Ray had been and Alex certainly would be.

"Sir, I'm also thinking about the Brigade's reaction." Tara broke the silence and addressed Captain Brookshier. "Word will spread fast. Some Mids already believe Alex went back to save one of his men. Yet now they witness the Academy wanting to cut him loose. What do I tell a midshipman who asks me, 'I thought we're supposed to stand for honor'?"

Her chest grew tight. Ray had warned her to tread carefully. But holding herself back from speaking truth would betray her own oath of duty. She would see this through no matter what happened. "Gentlemen, I suggest that's what this midshipman's offense comes down to. Do we or don't we uphold our dedication to duty?"

"Of course we do, Lieutenant," the deputy interrupted, still a sharp edge to his words. "But you're confusing duty with insubordination."

Tara felt Mark kick her foot under the table—a signal it was time to quit. The men sitting across from her were two somewhat stubborn senior officers sticking by their unwise recommendation, she told herself. They wanted to make Alex their midshipman poster boy for punishment. They couldn't care less about the true story behind his conduct offense.

"Pardon me, Lieutenant, are you feeling all right?" Captain Brookshier thought he noticed physical discomfort in Tara's face.

Tara inhaled softly and returned the commandant's gaze. "I attended a classmate's funeral two days ago, sir. He was a Marine aviator."

"Gentlemen, we appreciate your allowing us this opportunity to express our views," Mark Anderegg announced quickly to give Tara some cover.

"Thank you," added Tara, her words void of any emotion.

"You're dismissed," the commandant said to the two officers. Everyone stood to leave.

Captain Brookshier called out as the two officers reached the door. "Major, Lieutenant—this recommendation was a very difficult one. But I believe it is in the best interests of the Brigade."

"Yes sir," the two officers answered at the same time and exited into the Rotunda.

"That could have gone better," Mark said with sarcasm. "Watch me get reassigned in twenty-four hours." He pulled out his cell phone and Googled something. "4130, that'll be my new MOS," he laughed.

"What's 4130?" asked Tara, curious since she was unfamiliar with Marine Corps Military Occupational Specialty codes.

Mark rolled his eyes. "Marine Corps Exchange Officer for Morale Welfare and Recreation. They'll put me in charge of the children's Christmas party and Easter Egg Roll at Quantico, or somewhere else."

"Sir, they needed to hear us out."

"But they're not changing their minds, Tara," said Mark. "Something wrong?"

"I have to find a way to break the news to Midshipman Kramer that they're not changing their recommendations," said Tara with trustration. "Thanks for joining me in there, sir."

"You couldn't keep me away, Lieutenant," he replied. "I'm not surrendering yet."

"Neither am I, sir," said Tara, her words slow and even.

Mark Anderegg waved and departed to instruct a class. Tara exited Bancroft Hall's front doors and walked down the marble steps into warm spring sunlight. She stopped in Tecumseh Court for a breath of fresh air, fresher than the suffocating attitude from the commandant and the deputy commandant moments ago. As they headed to their next instructional classes across the

Academy, the growing number of midshipmen saluted her as they passed.

Tara gazed down Stribling Walk's long red-bricked path and thought she recognized Alex Kramer walking with other Mids, fifty yards away. She grew pensive seeing him and weighing his predicament. In short time, the case would ramp up for its final review with the Superintendent of the Naval Academy. Alex's fate and his future now rested in the hands of one admiral's recommendation.

Tara wasn't keen on prayer but said one anyway. What the hell, she thought. For all she knew, God had intervened to save Alex in Sierra Leone, so he'd live to fight another day. *Maybe God will step in and do it again,* Tara thought, and went for a walk to clear her head.

# CHAPTER 46

**McGarvey's Saloon and Oyster Bar**
**Annapolis, MD**
**March 26, 2024 at 1845**

Dan Bregman stood when he saw Robert Lawrence, the Naval Academy's superintendent, walk through the restaurant's front doors and head right toward him. Robert and Dan, a retired Navy captain and CO, had been classmates and also roommates at Annapolis. The two men shook hands, and exchanged smiles that reflected their lasting connection as two trusted friends.

"I'm not used to seeing you out of uniform," Dan said in jest.

"I like wearing civilian clothes when I'm off duty," said Robert, revealing a wry smile.

"Sir, would you like something to drink while you look at the menu?" a server approached and asked Robert.

"Vodka tonic, please," the Navy three-star admiral said, and settled into a chair next to his former roommate. "Thanks for coming on short notice."

"Good timing," answered Dan. "Samantha's at a concert downtown and I didn't have any dinner plans."

The server returned with Robert Lawrence's vodka tonic and took their dinner orders.

"Your text said you wanted to discuss something," said Dan.

"An unusual situation involving a midshipman landed on my desk," Robert said and sipped his vodka tonic. "I knew it was coming to me. But knowing doesn't make this one any easier."

"What's going on?" Dan asked, curious.

"The deputy commandant, and then the commandant after him, have recommended separating a Firstie." The admiral's mouth twisted into a gesture of frustration. "This one's complicated, Dan."

"Why's it complicated?"

Their table was in a quiet section and it was Tuesday night. Robert Lawrence wouldn't have to shout over the otherwise loud Friday and weekend restaurant noise.

Dan listened intently while Robert described Alex Kramer's service record as an enlisted Marine, including his decoration for valor, followed by his arrival at Annapolis. Then he explained how the Midshipman First Class had gone UA to aid a troubled former Marine buddy, someone whose life he'd already saved once before during a mission. Two conduct hearings for the offense had ended with the most severe sentence recommendation: the accused midshipman should be separated from the Naval Academy.

The server arrived with their dinner orders. "Eat your dinner before it gets cold," Robert said. "I'll catch up."

"What else about this midshipman's case?" asked Dan as he began eating his food.

"I'm meeting with the commandant and the deputy commandant early next week to discuss it," said Robert, still not touching his dinner.

"What for?" Dan asked. "Haven't you read the summaries of their hearings?"

"I need to know how they formed their decisions about this midshipman."

"Why would you need to know that?" Dan asked and put down his fork. "You're supposed to review the midshipman's case based on the facts," he cautioned, "not the commandant's and the deputy's opinions."

"Because I might see things differently than they did," Robert said, arms folded across his chest. "Because this midshipman's story is different from many others."

Robert Lawrence wasn't yet aware of Alex Kramer's comments in his own defense at either of his two conduct hearings. But the commandant had informed his boss in person that the accused midshipman's company officer, along with a Marine mentor, had appealed to him and Colonel Wettstone. *Reconsider your recommendations for separation,* they had urged the two senior officers. Robert Lawrence only had Captain Brookshier's version of what they had discussed.

"Do you know what the two officers told the Dant and the Deputy Dant during that meeting?" Dan asked.

"No."

Dan looked surprised. "Don't you want to know? They must have thought it was important enough to stick their necks that far out for a midshipman."

Robert picked up a piece of blackened salmon with his fork, then set it back down. "My asking could look like I'm undermining the commandant," he said and gestured to his friend's plate. "Go on, eat."

Dan swallowed a mouthful of stuffed shrimp and wiped his mouth with a white cloth napkin. "We've been friends for a very long time. I've never steered you in the wrong direction on anything."

"That's why I called out to you," Robert said, his dinner still untouched.

Dan signaled to their server and ordered another Corona. He pointed to Robert's vodka tonic. "Bring him another one of those."

"Just tonic water with a lime," Robert told her, then looked back at Dan. "What do you think about what I've said so far?" he asked.

Dan rubbed his hands together and studied his friend. "You

need to be on the right side of this. That's what I think," he said in a firm yet counseling voice. "Separating this midshipman puts you on the wrong side. You don't want to be there."

Dan's warning bothered Robert. "Why do you say that?"

"Because he saved three Marines while they were under enemy fire, and he was decorated for valor. That's why."

"What's your point?"

"My point is, he went UA *because* he wanted to aid another Marine he already saved once. This time, to stop a suicide."

Robert Lawrence still hadn't touched his food. "Mids are speaking out anonymously on social media at #RetainAlex Kramer," he said. "The Brigade is standing with him."

Dan started to lift his glass of beer but put it back down. "You're in your final year as superintendent. You'll retire soon and finish a distinguished career." Dan paused, then continued. "Separating this Mid could stick a marker alongside your name, a symbol you wouldn't want and would definitely regret."

"What are you talking about?" Robert said, his tone protective for himself.

"I'm talking about when four thousand plus midshipmen are asked what they'll remember most about Admiral Lawrence when he was superintendent—and what you *do not* want them to say."

"Go on, tell me."

"They could say, 'The Supe recommended separating a decorated prior-enlisted Marine and a very good Mid because he helped someone in danger—because he did his duty. I thought the Supe was wrong and that's how I'll remember him'."

Robert rested his elbows on the table and crossed his arms, thinking over the stark caution his friend had just presented to him.

"Is that how you want the Brigade to remember you?" Dan broke the momentary silence between them.

"No, it's not," answered Robert, his tone certain and his features showing the burden of soon making a difficult decision about a midshipman's future. "I ran into Colonel Burlingame at the Officers Club two days ago. He's the Senior Marine on the Yard. I said, 'Tell me something I should know about this midshipman.'"

Dan raised his head, intent to hear. "What did he say?"

Robert lifted and swallowed a morsel of now cold salmon and placed his fork down. "He told me, 'Infantry Marines believe in two forms of courage: physical and moral. Alex Kramer showed physical courage in combat. When he went UA to help his Marine buddy, that was pure moral courage.'"

"Anything else?"

"Yeah. He also said, 'This midshipman doesn't see any daylight between those two forms of courage. To him, they're the same.'"

"There you go."

Robert folded his hands and sighed. "Do you believe the nation needs this midshipman leading sailors and Marines?" he asked. "If we cut young men of valor like him loose, then the country loses?"

"It's what you believe that counts for the nation, not what I might think," Dan said with care. "I believe in you to make the right recommendation."

Robert drank the last of the tonic water. "I have a few days before the midshipman's hearing with me. You've told me what you think. I'm going to get Abigail's thoughts on it too," he said. His wife always spoke the truth to him. He trusted her counsel as much as he believed in Dan's.

The server cleared the plates and took their coffee orders.

"Thanks, Dan," Robert said.

"I have no doubt you'll do what's right," Dan reassured him.

The server returned with their coffees. Dan poured cream and sugar in his cup and exchanged looks with Robert.

"This case makes me think about something I read in a

newspaper column. I cut it out and put it in my desk drawer," Dan said.

"What did it say?"

"It said, 'Character is the sum of one's hardest choices.'"

Robert nodded with a wrinkled brow. "Sounds like a choice *I* have to make."

"Like I said before, you'll know what to do," Dan replied.

# CHAPTER 47

**Superintendent's Office**
**Larson Hall, USNA**
**April 4, 2024 at 1015**

"Captain, Colonel—please, take a seat," Admiral Robert Lawrence directed Captain Brookshier and Colonel Wettstone to chairs at his conference table. "Gentlemen, I've gone through the JAG's legal opinion based on your summaries of Midshipman Alex Kramer's conduct hearings. I read her opinion twice," he said. "Before I render my recommendation, I would like to know how you came to similar decisions."

"Sir, with all due respect, do you have reason to question my recommendation?" Captain Brookshier responded with lifted eyebrows.

"No, Captain," said Admiral Lawrence, opening his hands on the table to invite a gesture of cooperation. "But after I read each summary," he said, then took a pregnant pause that invited curious looks from both the Commandant and Deputy Commandant of Midshipmen, "I wasn't convinced that this case is so clear-cut to retain or separate."

"I believe this case *is* clear-cut, sir," the commandant answered with a respectful nod. "This midshipman had other options than taking an unauthorized absence to deal with his situation, and he didn't take time to think through them. Given all the facts and his being First Class, I concluded his actions failed to meet the Naval Academy standard of knowing better."

Admiral Lawrence turned to Colonel Wettstone. "Colonel, what influenced your decision?"

"I agree with the commandant on all points," the deputy commandant said and shook his head vigorously. "I wouldn't trust the midshipman with the responsibility to lead Marines."

Captain Brookshier's body stiffened hearing the colonel's words. It wasn't the first time the commandant's second-in-command had suggested to others, and in a vindictive manner, that Midshipman Alex Kramer couldn't be trusted to lead Marines.

Admiral Lawrence waited a moment, then rested one hand over the other on the tabletop. "Here's where I'm coming from," he said to put them at ease. "I've read the circumstances of this midshipman's misconduct three times. I do not view Midshipman Kramer's separation from the Academy as clearly as both of you already have recommended. Not yet."

He exchanged glances with the Academy's second and third senior officers, looking for any reactions. Captain Brookshier remained poker-faced. But Colonel Wettstone's narrowed eyes studied the Naval Academy's highest official with suspicion. "Sir, my only comment is that the Brigade will expect you, just as they expect us, to be absolutely impartial," Wettstone said.

Admiral Lawrence thought for a brief moment. Did he need the deputy commandant to remind him how to conduct himself as superintendent? "The Brigade should, Colonel," he said. But he certainly hadn't missed the deputy challenging his fairness. "I will also keep an open mind that some cases are more than they appear to be at face value. This might be one of them," he finished. "Thank you, gentlemen."

Alone in his office, Robert Lawrence leaned back in the tall chair at his desk. He replayed the difficult conversation he just had with the deputy commandant. *I will keep an open mind about this case no matter what you believe*, he thought to himself. He took in a cleansing breath, flipped open Midshipman Alex Kramer's personnel jacket in front of him, and reread every page for the third time.

# CHAPTER 48

**Luce Hall, USNA**
**April 4, 2024 at 1045**

Alex reached for his cover, placed a notebook in his backpack, and blended into the sea of other midshipmen dressed in Working Blue Uniform who filled the decks of Luce Hall, on their way to fourth period morning classes.

Though he didn't bump into anyone, he was distracted from his surroundings. The second conduct hearing had ended with the commandant also recommending Alex's separation from the Naval Academy. His spirit had suffered another blow. He kept up with all of his duties as a midshipman. But each day, time crawled at an agonizingly slow pace. He slept poorly. Fear of being denied graduation and commissioning, one month away, hung on him like a curse he couldn't cast aside.

The sound of his name over the din inside Luce Hall snapped Alex out of his momentary funk.

"Mister Kramer!"

Alex spun around. Major Anderegg stood in a classroom doorway and gestured for him to come over.

"Good morning, sir. You want to speak with me?" said Alex, his manner pleasant yet apathetic at the same time.

"How are you holding up?" the Marine officer asked. He quickly spotted the midshipman's brooding expression.

"Permission to speak freely, sir? Marine to Marine?" Alex said with some reservation in his words.

"Absolutely. Marine to Marine."

Alex shrugged. "Ever since the deputy commandant and the commandant after him recommended the Academy should throw me overboard, each day feels like I'm in a holding cell waiting to be sentenced for a crime I didn't commit." He grimaced and shook his head. "It sucks, sir, and it's wrong."

"I can't imagine how you feel," said Major Anderegg. "But your conduct case isn't finished. There's still your hearing with the superintendent coming up. He could reject their recommendations outright." He was gladdened that a hint of optimism in his words seemed to erase some of the gloom upsetting the midshipman.

"You really think that's possible, sir?" said Alex. His mood momentarily brightened. He still had one final chance to survive his ordeal and remain at the Naval Academy.

"I do, and so does Lieutenant Marcellus," the Marine officer said in a convincing fashion. "Now, I'll tell you something, Marine to Marine."

"What is it, sir?"

Anderegg waited for a couple of Mids to walk by, then spoke in a subdued voice. "The lieutenant met with the commandant and the deputy, and she defended you." He paused a moment. "She even told them they were wrong."

Surprise formed across Alex's features. "Excuse me, sir. How do you know that?"

"I was there."

Alex checked his watch. "Pardon me, Major, but I'm late for class. Thank you for talking, sir."

Major Anderegg showed a reassuring smile. "This isn't over yet. Keep the faith, okay? Semper Fi."

"Semper Fi, sir," Alex replied, his mood brighter now.

# CHAPTER 49

**Superintendent's Office**
**Larson Hall, USNA**
**April 8, 2024 at 0835**

Robert Lawrence finished writing some talking points for an upcoming external address he was scheduled to deliver when he heard two raps against his partially open office door. He looked up and saw his flag aide, Liam, a Navy lieutenant.

"Sir, the commandant and deputy commandant have arrived," said the aide.

"Thank you, Liam. Show them in."

As the two senior officers entered the room, Admiral Lawrence thought he detected resignation on Captain Brookshier's unexpressive round face. His good-natured disposition sat well with the Brigade. Midshipmen liked him. But one glance at Colonel Wettstone's furrowed features warned the admiral of pushback coming his way.

"Gentlemen, I called you here to personally tell you my recommendation for Midshipman Kramer's conduct case," said Admiral Lawrence.

The day before, he had purposely instructed the staff JAG not to report the recommendation to either Captain Brookshier or Colonel Wettstone. He wanted the news to come from him first.

"A recommendation for separation will not move forward from me to the Secretary of Defense's office," said Admiral Lawrence. "Midshipman Kramer will be retained at the Naval Academy. He's staying right here."

"I understand, sir," said Captain Brookshier, his response lukewarm.

"Sir, I want to express my objection," Colonel Wettstone said with flared nostrils, almost interrupting the commandant.

Admiral Lawrence didn't miss spotting the deputy commandant's adversarial attitude.

"Your objection is noted, Colonel," he answered and cast a steely look at the deputy. "I have imposed tough sanctions against him." His words were aimed more at a verbally combative deputy commandant than the even-tempered commandant. "Two are significant. First, Midshipman Kramer must complete a remediation program. And second, the harshest penalty will be delaying his graduation and commissioning until August." He studied the two officers' faces. "He's not graduating with his class. That one will especially hurt."

"Sir, may I ask how you came to *your* decision to retain this midshipman?" said Captain Brookshier, calmly probing the admiral's judgment yet with proper restraint.

The admiral regarded both men. "Certainly. Midshipman Kramer demonstrated a selfless commitment to duty and honor when he went UA, even knowing it broke regulations. I believe he showed the full measure of dedication we expect of every Marine and Navy officer who graduates from the Naval Academy."

Colonel Wettstone shook his head. "Sir, we don't let Marines off that easy," he said. Captain Brookshier visibly recoiled with disapproval while Wettstone went on. "This midshipman did what the Marine Corps calls good initiative, bad judgment."

The admiral clenched his jaw. "Colonel, I do not believe it's bad judgment to save another man's life—twice."

"Sir, I don't disagree about saving someone's life," the deputy commandant replied hurriedly. "And I'm familiar with Alex

Kramer's decorated service record. But we're judging his conduct as a midshipman, not his service as a Marine corporal. He knew going UA was wrong but he did it anyway. I'm not convinced he's officer material, even though he was awarded the Silver Star."

The conference room fell silent. But the belligerence and discomfort on all sides were as loud as ever.

Admiral Lawrence rose from his chair and walked over to the credenza behind his desk. He returned and placed a natural wood picture frame face up on the conference table in front of Colonel Wettstone. The deputy commandant studied the military medal resting on navy blue cloth behind the frame's glass. "It's the Silver Star," he said with a dismissive air.

The admiral took his seat. "It was presented to Corporal Thomas Lawrence, my father—3rd Force Reconnaissance Battalion, 3rd Marine Division—for bravery fighting North Vietnamese forces, 17 January 1967. Six weeks later he was killed while out on patrol. The Marine Corps presented this medal to my mother. I was two years old at the time. It's all I really have from my father, that and his citation."

Colonel Wettstone returned Admiral Lawrence's stare.

"No one here is a recipient of that respected decoration," said Robert Lawrence with rising impatience. "The same one Midshipman Kramer wears on his uniform." The Naval Academy's highest-ranking officer exchanged looks with his two direct reports. "I believe that—"

"Excuse me, sir," Colonel Wettstone interjected. "Wearing the decoration doesn't—"

"Doesn't what, Colonel?" Vice Admiral Lawrence said at nearly the top of his voice. His eyes widened as Colonel Wettstone glared back at him.

"It doesn't give him a free pass to become a Marine officer!"

"That's not your call anymore. It's mine now," the super-intendent fired back, heat rising in his face and his neck. "This midshipman did his duty."

"His duty was to think before he went off half-cocked and broke regulations," the colonel snapped, his cheeks reddened. "He makes a habit of getting himself into jams, and that's dangerous in an officer."

The admiral rose out of his chair and stood erect. The two officers followed him. "Colonel, it appears to me that you harbor outright bias against this midshipman." Robert Lawrence spit out the words, still incensed by Wettstone's disobedience. "What is it? I want to know."

"Sir, I resent that remark," said Wettstone with his fists clenched at his sides.

"Answer the question, Colonel," Admiral Lawrence fired back. "Is it something personal no one else knows?"

"None of that is true!" said Wettstone.

The Naval Academy's superintendent shook his head. "Anything else either of you want to tell me?"

"No sir," the commandant and deputy commandant answered together.

"Very well," said the admiral, his irritation somewhat subsided. "Training Alex Kramer serves a greater duty to our nation and our mission. Sending him home is a mistake. We're done here."

With the two subordinate senior officers now gone, Robert Lawrence texted a message to Dan Bregman:

*"I chose to be on the right side. You'll understand. Will call later."*

# CHAPTER 50

**U.S. Naval Academy**
**The Alley Restaurant**
**April 9, 2024 at 1915**

"Good evening, ladies."

Captain Brookshier appeared unexpectedly in front of their table inside the Alley Restaurant. It was a convenient and popular place where officers, graduates, and civilians with ties to the Naval Academy dined and socialized.

Under warm recessed ceiling lights, Captain Brookshier's distinctive widow's peak of salt-and-pepper hair around the temples and deep crow's feet at the corners of his eyes made him easy to recognize around the Academy without his cover.

"Is this a celebration?" the commandant asked with a gracious lilt to the group of four female naval officers, relaxed and drinking wine under the restaurant's soft incandescent lighting. Lieutenant Tara Marcellus was as surprised as the other women to see the senior officer standing over them.

"Just some company officers winding down another week with the Brigade, sir." Lieutenant Nicole Immanuel's brown eyes glistened and the dimples in her cheeks creased with a cute smile. "We're drinking to winter finally leaving town, sir," she laughed.

"Sounds good," he said to the four women in uniform and held his gaze a moment longer with one in particular. It was Tara, and her fellow officers and friends noticed.

"Hello, Lieutenant," he nodded casually at her.

"Hello, sir," said Tara, polite but tentative at being singled out.

Chatter across the Brigade about Alex Kramer's Class-A conduct offense was growing. Comments from midshipmen appeared on social media apps where they could say whatever they wanted. Their identities were hidden and the most outspoken ones took Alex's side.

But the ladies with Tara tonight hadn't followed the controversial case, which had turned into a hot debate throughout the Brigade of Midshipmen. They weren't aware that Tara was busy working behind the scenes on Alex's defense. They did not know the professional jeopardy she had entered by openly questioning two senior officers—one who now stood by their table—after they had recommended Alex's separation from the Naval Academy. Colonel Wettstone had been so incensed by Tara's appeal at the meeting that he wanted to charge her with insubordination.

"Ladies, will you please spare Lieutenant Marcellus for a few minutes," he said with a relaxed air. "We have some Brigade business to go over."

The three other women looked at each other and motioned to him that it was fine.

Tara's mouth suddenly tasted as dry as desert sand, and her shoulders stiffened.

"Lieutenant?" Captain Brookshier motioned to her.

"Certainly, sir," she said but took her time getting up and showed her friends an uncomfortable smile. "I'll be back soon," she announced to end the quiet and her friends' curious looks. She had no idea what was coming to her.

Tara followed the commandant, who walked up to a place at the bar where the other women could clearly observe the senior and the subordinate officer talking in a manner that wouldn't appear improper. Tara and Captain Brookshier each settled into tall chairs. He ordered two glasses of ice water with lemon. She sat silently and waited for him to speak.

"The meeting you had with myself and the deputy command-ant where you opposed our recommendations to separate Mid-shipman Alex Kramer," he said. "You remember that?"

Tara felt a knot the size of a softball tightened in her stomach. "I certainly do, sir," she answered. "What about it?" She instantly regretted her last three words. He could interpret them as dis-respectful.

"By the way, Admiral Lawrence has made his recommenda-tion on that case but it isn't official yet. Midshipman Kramer will hear it soon, and so will you."

Tara kept a straight face and repositioned herself in the tall wooden chair. Captain Brookshier wasn't going to tell her the superintendent's decision. Alex would twist in the wind somewhat longer, and she would anxiously await the result with him.

"But that's not why I wanted to have a word with you," Captain Brookshier said. "You took a chance meeting with me and Colonel Wettstone, didn't you? You told us we were wrong."

Tara's heartbeat started racing. "Pardon me, sir, but I think it was more my suggesting why your recommendations could be wrong," she said in a slightly raised tone yet remained unfazed. "It was not my intention to *tell* you and Colonel Wettstone your recommendations were wrong."

"Point taken, Lieutenant," he said and drank from his ice water. Tara had not touched her glass yet. "I didn't agree with your opinion," he added, "but I respected your courage to express it—to our faces and not behind our backs."

Trying to read his expression on whether he was being sincere or setting her up, Tara sighed softly and took a long drink of ice water. "I appreciate your saying that, sir."

"The military doesn't do forgive and forget very well, Lieutenant," said Captain Brookshier, "and questioning a senior officer can have unintended consequences. Do you follow what I'm saying?"

Tara braced herself. *If you're trying to scare me, I'm not having any of it.* She flashed back again, for the second time in recent memory, to the moment when Lieutenant Schrager had torn into her in front of their CO to cover his errors in the submarine warfare command. First Schrager had put her down. Then three weeks ago, Colonel Wettstone had uttered his own cutting remark because he wanted to put the female lieutenant in her place. "Pardon me, sir, but I'm not following," she answered with care, then waited for Captain Brookshier to explain himself. She grew very concerned where all this was leading.

The commandant rested his arms on the counter and took a relaxed posture. "You're finishing your final year as a company officer?"

"I am, sir."

"And where do you see yourself serving next?"

"As a department head on my next submarine tour—that is, if the Navy agrees," she threw it out there with uncertainty about the Navy's intentions.

"Good for you, Lieutenant," he said with clear encouragement. "If your final company officer performance evaluation comes in as 'not promotable,' and I suspect it's because you disagreed with a certain senior officer whom we both know," he said and waited a moment, "then I'll send it back down with orders for him to rewrite it. Do you follow?"

"I do, sir," Tara said and exhaled with relief. She scolded herself for having jumped to conclusions, for thinking the commandant was just one more smug male officer who looked down on women in uniform. He wasn't, and she was wrong to prejudge him. He could also be right about the deputy commandant. It hadn't crossed her mind that Colonel Wettstone might strike back at her because she had openly questioned his fairness. A punitive FITREP would harm any career prospects she had in the Navy.

"You're a good officer, Lieutenant," he said with a reassuring smile. "Now, go join your friends and have a nice evening."

"Aye, sir," Tara said with relief. "Thank you."

# CHAPTER 51

**Superintendent's Conference Room**
**Larson Hall, USNA**
**April 12, 2024 at 0900**

Alex, wearing Service Dress Blue uniform, paced anxiously outside the superintendent's second floor conference room.

Two grueling conduct hearings had ended with the same recommendation: separation. Just saying the word raised a bitter taste of bile in his throat. Then last week, life had flipped *for* him, not against him. At Alex's third conduct hearing, the superintendent had announced his recommendation: The midshipman would receive tough sanctions for his conduct infraction. He was staying, not leaving, to graduate and receive his commission. Going back for Ethan had not been in vain. Alex had smiled so much the past few days that his face hurt.

Alex's appetite had been AWOL starting with his first conduct hearing three weeks ago. Since the Supe's recommendation, the prior-enlisted midshipman ate as though he hadn't seen food in weeks. Last night at evening meal, he had been finishing a dessert when his cell phone buzzed. He'd looked down and read a text from Lieutenant Marcellus:

"The superintendent wants you in his office at 0915 tomorrow. I'll be there. Do not be late!"

*What happened?* he had thought with some alarm. Why did Admiral Lawrence want to see him? Had the deputy or the commandant pleaded with the superintendent to reverse his recommendation and send Alex packing? What did those two cake-eaters know about real dedication to duty, anyway—the kind stained by blood on a battlefield?

The conference room door finally opened. Lieutenant Novak, the admiral's flag aide, smiled and motioned to Alex. "Admiral Lawrence will see you now, midshipman."

Robert Lawrence sat at a long mahogany conference table with black high-back leather chairs. Also seated were the staff JAG, a Navy captain whom Alex did not know; Colonel Burlingame, the Senior Marine on the Yard whom Alex had met before at a Brigade brief; and Lieutenant Marcellus, who smiled brightly as he approached.

The midshipman's eyes swept the superintendent's meeting room. Different US Navy and nautical items rested on end tables and bookshelves. Framed citations and photographs on walls and credenzas represented a lifetime of service to country. The admiral's flag of three white stars against a field of navy blue, and the American flag in gold stands were posted on each side of a fireplace. Several large half-moon light fixtures made of frosted white glass hanging from the ceiling cast a soft incandescent glow in the room.

Looking at Admiral Lawrence's personal items reminded Alex of his combat field citations, personal mementos, uniforms, and photographs of his life as an enlisted Marine. They remained packed in boxes in his parents' house.

"Midshipman Kramer, please take a seat," Admiral Lawrence said in a friendly greeting. "Have you met Colonel Burlingame?" he asked, nodding toward the Marine officer seated next to him. The colonel commanded all Marine Corps commissioned officers and enlisted personnel below his O-6 rank at the Naval Academy.

"Yes sir, we met at a Brigade brief."

Colonel Burlingame reached across the table and extended

his thick hand to Alex. "Good to see you again, midshipman." The senior Marine knew Alex's history in the Corps. The "fruit salad" ribbons adorning Alex's uniform—among them the Silver Star, Purple Heart, and Combat Action Ribbon—had long ago earned Colonel Burlingame's respect.

"Midshipman Kramer, how does it feel looking back on the events tied to your conduct offense throughout the past few weeks?" stated Admiral Lawrence, his manner relaxed.

"To tell you the truth, I'm exhausted, sir," Alex answered with a small grin. The officers nodded and smiled with understanding.

"What did you think about during the experience?" the admiral pressed on.

"Sir, before I came to the Academy, being a Marine taught me when to take charge. My command trusted me with weapons and materials. They thought I used good judgment. I proved I could lead Marines to fight and win." He paused. "They trusted me to protect the lives of Marines who followed my orders. I thought a lot about that."

"And what did you learn from your hearings?" Admiral Lawrence asked, leaning forward.

Alex inhaled slowly, then let it out. "Two things, sir. First, good leaders think through what they're preparing to do because there are consequences." He met the admiral's gaze. "The second one I already knew and always believe in: No choice in duty, sir. That's why I went UA, why I went back for Ethan. I stand by that code."

Robert Lawrence stared at the red, white, and blue ribbon indicating the Silver Star that was affixed to the midshipman's uniform. "Both of those are important lessons each naval service officer should believe in and think of often," he said in a serene voice. "Normally the commandant's office notifies midshipmen of sanctions to be enforced following a major conduct offense," added the admiral. "I've chosen to inform you in person because we're here to discuss a subject far more significant to you—your remediation program."

"Yes, sir." Alex answered, then listened closely as Admiral Lawrence explained the sanctions. He was stripped of his leadership billet as platoon commander. He could not represent the Academy in sports or extracurricular activities. That meant he wouldn't be in the baseball team's starting lineup for the 2024 Patriot League Tournament. It was disappointing but he'd get over it.

"You will be restricted to the Yard," the admiral continued. "You will receive ninety demerits for committing a major conduct offense, and an Aptitude grade of D." Admiral Lawrence finished describing the sanctions: No overnight liberty. Alex could not park or drive his truck on Naval Academy property. He would not be allowed to wear civilian attire during weekend liberty, or "spirit gear" in Bancroft Hall. Loss of privileges would start today and continue until his extended graduation and commissioning date in August. "Do you have any questions about what I've just explained?"

"No, sir."

The superintendent cleared his throat. "There are two additional and final sanctions, midshipman."

Alex steadied himself for what would come next. It sounded ominous.

"Your graduation and commissioning date will be extended to August 2024. Between now and August when the Brigade reforms, you must successfully complete your remediation program. Colonel Burlingame will supervise your work," the admiral noted, "and I can't think of a finer senior officer to work with."

Out of the corner of his eye, Alex saw Lieutenant Marcellus

nod. It wasn't so bad. If he completed his program with the colonel's approval, he'd be on his way to Quantico for The Basic School.

"An important job you will be doing during remediation will be mentoring the incoming Class of 2028's prior-enlisted Marines," the admiral informed him. "It will start on I-Day and continue through the summer until the Brigade reforms in August."

"I will do that proudly, sir," Alex said, gladly accepting the admiral's directive.

Robert Lawrence turned to the Marine officer. "Colonel, please."

"Remediation will be in two parts," Colonel Burlingame began. "First part, you and I will work on a critical gap that occurs in leadership and command. It's the difference between an officer doing what *he* believes is right versus thinking first about all available and reasonable options."

"Do you understand how that ties in with your conduct offense?" Admiral Lawrence asked.

Alex nodded. "Yes sir, I went UA for a Marine brother because I still saw him as being one of my men. But I reacted ahead of thinking it through, knowing my options. Being an officer means having a larger duty—"

"—a duty to think through how orders for one Marine or one sailor could affect your personnel and the mission, all at the same time," Colonel Burlingame finished Alex's sentence. "In war, officers make split-second decisions. That will be you soon enough."

Alex nonchalantly turned to Lieutenant Marcellus. She raised an eyebrow, signaling him to listen, and show that he was ready to learn and lead.

Colonel Burlingame made a few introductory remarks about

Alex's remediation program mentoring prior-enlisted Marine plebes with the Class of 2028. "Let's meet on Monday to discuss it further," he said. "Call my office."

"Yes, sir," Alex replied eagerly.

"Midshipman Kramer, do you have any final comments?" the admiral asked as everyone else waited.

"No, sir."

"Very well then, we're adjourned." Admiral Lawrence rose from his seat and the others followed.

"Trust me, all of this will be good for you in the long run," Tara said to Alex. "Colonel Burlingame will be an outstanding mentor too."

"Thank you for standing by me, ma'am."

Watching Alex's features brighten for the first time since his first hearing weeks earlier, Tara heard his gratitude and smiled kindly. "You'll come out of this better than you think."

Alex noticed Admiral Lawrence standing nearby and turned to him. "Thank you for believing in me, sir."

"We all believe in you, Alex. Most of all, Lieutenant Marcellus." The admiral gestured to Tara. "She believed enough in you to challenge two senior officers' recommendations for separation." Robert Lawrence exchanged looks with her. She had stood by a brave midshipman whom she believed deserved a second chance. "Make the most of this opportunity Lieutenant Marcellus made possible for you."

Alex offered a grateful look to Tara, then to the admiral. "You have my word, sir."

# CHAPTER 52

Memorial Hall, USNA
August 19, 2024 at 1014

Alex walked up the white marble steps two at a time from the Rotunda to the entranceway entranceway to Memorial Hall.

Dressed in Marine Corps Blue Dress "Alpha" uniform coat adorned with his individual and unit ribbon decorations over white trousers and glistening black shoes, just two final items awaited to make him whole: a pair of gold second lieutenant bars and a white Marine Corps officer cover.

He stopped to view a diorama honoring Colonel John Ripley, US Marine Corps and Naval Academy Class of '62. The miniature figures and recreated scenery displayed Ripley's battlefield performance when he single-handedly prevented twenty thousand North Vietnamese Army troops and tanks from advancing across a bridge into South Vietnam. The colonel had been awarded the Navy Cross, Silver Star, Bronze Star and Purple Heart for his valor under fire. The fingers from Alex's right hand came up and brushed across his own Silver Star and Purple Heart ribbons affixed to his uniform coat.

Alex stepped away from the diorama and surveyed the crowd of attendees, some standing and others sitting in rows of chairs in the center of Memorial Hall. Three large fans blew warm circulated air in the non-air-conditioned expansive and historic hall, and it was already warm inside. He was one of six classmates with an extended graduation and commissioning ceremony this morning, and the only one being commissioned a Marine Corps officer.

His eyes grew large with delight seeing his parents and Tori, his sister, among the crowd. Harry and Brian, his roommates and two best friends at the Academy, were there with a few other classmates from 19th Company who lived and were stationed locally. And Chief Lisa Sorrel, 19th Company's SEL was there. Her asking his permission to attend pleased him. He spotted Captain Brookshier, the Commandant of Midshipman in the vast, high-ceilinged hall. The program listed the Dant's name under "Remarks."

Alex did a quick count of several Marine Corps officers there, and two whose presence honored him: Colonel Burlingame and Major Anderegg. Alex exchanged glances with the colonel, who motioned to join them.

On his walk over, he noticed another Marine standing a distance away: Colonel Wettstone. Alex recoiled seeing the person who had recommended separating him from the Academy. Where did he get off coming here today for my graduation and commissioning? Alex thought. If the deputy commandant had any words for him, Alex would acknowledge them. He would respect the rank but never the man.

"We were about to send out a search party for you," announced Colonel Burlingame with a welcome greeting and handshake. "Marine officers always make it a point to be on time for commissioning and promotion ceremonies," he kidded.

"I'm here, sir," Alex answered, enjoying the humor and savoring the moment.

Suddenly, Alex spotted Carolyn Hagerty. She looked beautiful in a sleeveless dress with a V-neck. Three years had passed since he last saw her, before she married. He had no idea Carolyn was coming, let alone that she knew about today. Then he figured it out. Olivia Kramer had invited her and didn't tell him.

"Excuse me, gentlemen, my family's here." Alex left to greet his family and Carolyn. He beamed at his sister, Tori, and wrapped his arms around her in a brotherly embrace. "It's great seeing you, sis."

"I wasn't going to miss this day for anything," Tori said, hugging Alex tightly.

Martin, Tori's husband and an officer with the New York Fire Department, was attending a mandatory training in Brooklyn and sent his regrets.

Rear Admiral David and Olivia Kramer greeted their son with hugs and handshakes. Then Alex turned to Carolyn. "Thanks for coming. I had no idea," he said, almost stuttering.

"I wanted to be here because I know what this day means to you."

"This is my surprise," interrupted Olivia, a mischievous smile revealed underneath high cheekbones that highlighted her natural beauty.

Alex was tempted to say, "Some surprise, Mom," but didn't want to embarrass Carolyn. The unanswered question for him was why her husband let her attend the ceremony or if he even knew about it.

"At this time, I would like to welcome families, friends, and honored guests," announced a Navy lieutenant standing behind the podium, "to this extended graduation exercise for the Class of Two Thousand and Twenty-Four, United States Naval Academy. Please take your seats and we will begin in just a few minutes."

All stood as the official party—the vice academic dean and members from his staff, the commandant, and the senior Marine, followed by the graduating midshipmen—entered the hall and walked between the rows of seats to the front. Everyone remained standing as musicians from the Naval Academy Band played the National Anthem followed by an Academy chaplain, a Navy lieutenant commander, who gave the invocation.

After brief remarks from Captain Brookshier, the Commandant of Midshipmen, Alex and his five other classmates approached, one at a time, to receive their diplomas. The vice academic dean handed him a navy blue leather folder decorated with the Naval Academy crest in gold with his diploma inside. Alex moved two steps to his left to receive congratulations from the Dant—the second officer who'd recommended his separation. Despite Captain Brookshier's recommendation at his hearing, Alex had decided the man's gesture right now was sincere. Next, Colonel Burlingame extended best wishes. With his diploma raised above his head in a gesture of victory, Alex turned toward his family and revealed a radiant smile.

Following the commandant administering the US Navy Oath of Office to the five other graduates, it was Alex's turn. "Raise your right hand," directed Colonel Burlingame. "I, state your name, having been appointed a second lieutenant in the United States Marine Corps, do solemnly swear that I will support and defend the Constitution of the United States against all enemies, foreign and domestic; that I will bear true faith and allegiance to the same; that I take this obligation freely, without any mental reservation or purpose of evasion; and that I will well and faithfully discharge the office upon which I am about to enter. So help me God."

"I do!" Alex's shout echoed in Memorial Hall and applause followed. "Congratulations, Lieutenant Kramer," said the colonel, shaking Alex's hand. "Semper Fidelis."

"Semper Fidelis, sir," Alex answered joyfully.

With the ceremony concluded, Alex joined his group of family members assembled near one of Memorial Hall's tall majestic windows. They watched as David Kramer pinned Alex's gold second lieutenant bars onto the shoulders of his blue dress uniform coat. It was official.

"Words can't express how very proud I am of you, and for this day," David told his son, then embraced him.

"Thank you, sir."

Her eyes sparkling with joy, Olivia handed her son the box holding his white Marine Corps officer cover in it. "No mother on earth has a finer son," she said, wiped the wetness from her eyes, and hugged Alex with deep affection.

"I love you, Mom," he said, holding her embrace.

Several officers from the Academy's Marine detachment came to see and support Alex, the ceremony's only graduate being commissioned into the Marine Corps. They warmly welcomed him into their ranks with handshakes and backslaps. Then one by one, each raised a clenched fist and tapped down firmly on one of the gold second lieutenant bars pinned to Alex's shoulders.

As Alex looked past the officers gathered around him, Colonel Wettstone stood in civilian clothes, away from any groups or families. The former deputy commandant had retired in June after thirty years of active-duty service. They exchanged hard stares across Memorial Hall. Alex thought Wettstone's deadpan expression could have been mistaken for a callous sneer. *You tried to steal this day from me,* Alex thought. *I won, now leave.*

Lieutenant Marcellus had sent Alex a heartfelt apology for missing the ceremony. Alex owed so much to the officer who stood by him during his darkest days at the Academy. Tara had emailed to say she might be back to the DC area in a few months and would look him up at Quantico after he began at The Basic School.

"Sir, I request your presence to meet me outside the front doors of Bancroft Hall," said Chief Sorrel with an admiring look on her face. Alex knew what she was up to. "I'd be honored, Chief." He winked. "I'll meet you in Tecumseh Court in ten minutes."

"Aye, sir," she said and smiled.

Carolyn Hagerty stood alone at the distant right corner of Memorial Hall. She looked up at the Operational Loss Panels listing the names of Academy graduates killed while on active duty performing military operations, and was surprised when Alex approached her from behind.

"You coming here today means a lot," he told her. "I want you to know that."

"Your Mom emailed and asked if I would like to come and I wrote back 'yes,'" she said, her eyes smiling affectionately at him.

Eight years had passed—four in the Marine Corps and four more at the Academy—and Alex still cared for her. "Mom said you're married now," he told her carefully. Be careful where you go with this, he warned himself. "Your husband didn't mind you being here? Because we used to be friends or something like that?"

She looked away and sighed. "I'm divorced, Alex. Olivia didn't tell you?"

Her announcement confused and pleased him at the same time. His mother had never mentioned it. "What happened?"

"My husband had no direction, no purpose," she answered plainly. "He was adrift and we weren't happy. That is, I wasn't happy."

"I'm sorry."

"Don't be, because I'm not." Carolyn wrapped her arms tightly around herself. "It's taken me this long, too long, to finally realize you found a purpose for your life." She took one of Alex's hands resting along his side and held it. "You may not believe this but—" she started then stopped.

Alex waited and, looking down, noticed her hands shake. "But what?"

"I never stopped caring about you," Carolyn added. "I suppose I needed time to find out what I'd been missing." She raised a hand and gently touched his cheek. "It was us."

Alex drew a quick breath. "I'm a Marine again. You sure that's a lifestyle you can adapt to? Me serving in places that could put us far apart?"

"I'm willing to try," she answered without skipping a beat. "Are you?"

"Yep." He kissed her gently. "Excuse me, but someone's waiting for me outside," he said and chuckled. "It's a military tradition. I'll explain later."

"Go on," she told him with an affectionate smile, and waved him away.

Alex retrieved his cover from Olivia and stepped outside into a hot summer morning. He squinted against the brilliant sun looking for the SEL and spotted Lisa Sorrel standing below in Tecumseh Court wearing her Service Dress Whites. When Alex approached, she saluted smartly and he returned it.

"Sir," she announced and showed him a perfect set of smiling white teeth.

"You're my first salute, Chief. Thank you." Following the tradition of a newly-commissioned officer's first salute, Alex withdrew a silver dollar from his pocket and handed it to her.

"Thank you, sir, and best of luck," said the sailor.

"Can you make the reception?" he asked.

"I'll be there, sir."

"That's great."

Guests from the ceremony exited Bancroft Hall on their way to graduation-commissioning receptions at the Naval Academy Club nearby on the Yard. Colonel Burlingame was among them and approached Alex. "I'm late for an important meeting, Lieutenant. Sorry to miss your reception," said the colonel, sounding genuinely apologetic.

"It's okay, sir," Alex answered and straightened himself. "Thank you for helping me get ready to become an officer."

The Naval Academy's senior Marine withdrew a small cream-colored envelope from his uniform pocket and handed it to Alex. The Marine Corps Eagle, Globe, and Anchor emblem was printed on it. "This is for you. Good luck, Lieutenant."

"Thank you, sir," said Alex, accepting the envelope. His right hand lifted swiftly to his cover and saluted the Marine colonel, who returned the gesture.

Alex opened the envelope and withdrew a card carrying a handwritten message:

Second Lieutenant Kramer,

The Academy said you erred in judgment going UA to aid a Marine. I welcome an officer with such commitment serving under my command . . . one who will always protect his Marines and sailors.

Semper Fidelis!

Colonel G.A. Burlingame, USMC

# EPILOGUE

**The Basic School, Camp Barrett**
**Marine Corps Base Quantico—Triangle, VA**
**September 19, 2024 at 1019**

Tara Marcellus looked around the sprawling military base in northern Virginia forty miles south of Washington, DC. She crossed the road and was surrounded by Marines going about their business. The grounds, littered with multicolored hues of red, amber, yellow, and orange from fallen autumn leaves, resembled a 1950s Norman Rockwell magazine cover.

She recognized Alex Kramer standing in front of Lopez Hall, dressed in Combat Utility Uniform with the sleeves rolled above the elbow and that same confident manner with which he presented himself, even as a midshipman. The last time they'd met had been five months ago at the Naval Academy. Tara approached Alex, and he saluted.

"It's great to see you, ma'am."

"Great to see you too, Lieutenant," she said, returning his salute.

"You still at the Academy, ma'am?" Alex asked her.

"Not anymore. I'm at Naval Submarine Base New London, and halfway through Submarine Officer Advanced Course," she said with an easy smile, her hazel eyes glistening. "Submarine officers call it DH school."

Alex eyes widened. "You came all the way from Connecticut to check up on me?"

"I came to visit friends in Annapolis. But then I thought I'd hop down to Quantico to make sure you're staying out of trouble," she said with a chuckle.

Alex laughed with her. "Appreciate that, ma'am. We're so busy at TBS there isn't time to get into trouble." Then he changed the conversation. "When you graduate from DH School, does that mean you make O-4?" he asked, referring to a promotion to lieutenant commander, the next rank on Tara's career track as a naval officer.

"If I'm designated the engineer officer for my next boat tour, then I'll be O-4. But I'm satisfied to continue wearing a lieutenant's bars and be assigned DH for either combat systems or navigation and operations."

Alex picked up on Tara's optimism. "You'll make a great DH, ma'am. Sailors on any Navy submarine crew will be fortunate to have you lead them."

The creases along her cheeks formed by her smile complimented her creamy complexion. "Thank you, Lieutenant," she said.

They made their way inside The Hawkins Room at Camp Barrett, home base of The Basic School for new Marine Corps second lieutenants, for a late morning meal. Alex grabbed two breakfast sandwiches, and they found a table and settled in to eat.

"Listen, our boat was out for an underway certification last month, and I couldn't make it to your graduation and commissioning," Tara reminded him. "But I wanted to be there."

"I know, ma'am, and it's okay."

She drank from a large Starbucks coffee cup, then asked Alex if TBS was what he expected. Alex nodded eagerly between bites of his greasy bacon and egg sandwich. "I know it sounds dumb, but I love it."

She turned the conversation to his delayed graduation and commissioning in August. "Everything go okay at the ceremony?"

"It was a great day all around, ma'am."

"Any surprises?"

Alex nodded. "Yeah, two of 'em," he remarked and downed the last of the orange juice from its wax carton. "One very good, but the other was kind of strange," he said and wrinkled his nose.

"I'm listening," she gave him a curious look. Alex's voice lifted as he explained reconnecting with Carolyn Hagerty after being separated from each other for several years.

"That's the good one that happened," he said. "We've talked about being together. But that'll wait until I get my orders after TBS and find out where I'll be stationed."

Hearing Alex speak those words, Tara felt fleeting sadness. Ray Lydon had said almost identical words during the final weekend they were together last April. He'd told Tara he loved her, and then said, "How would you feel about making us permanent?" Two weeks later, Ray had proposed and Tara had joyfully accepted.

"You okay, ma'am?" Alex asked, noticing Tara's sudden sadness.

"I'm all right," she said and waved one hand in the air. "Where's your girlfriend now?"

"She lives and works in New York City."

"That's a very good story," added Tara, her mood lifted again by Alex's news. "What was the strange thing that happened?" she asked and watched his expression turn to displeasure.

"Colonel Wettstone showed up but he didn't come over to me," he said with resentment.

Tara's eyes grew big. "Not even to congratulate you?"

"He eyeballed me across Memorial Hall, then did an about face and walked out." Alex leaned forward in his chair. "Between you and me, ma'am, he wore the uniform but I never thought of him as an officer any Marine would want to follow."

Tara heard Alex's words loud and clear. "Copy that."

They finished eating, collected their covers, and stepped outside into a stunning late September morning.

"We've covered a lot of ground since our deployments," re-marked Tara when they reached the street, "but we always re-membered to do our duty." She looked away, then at Alex. "You inspired me to be a better officer—and you reminded me what dedication to duty truly means. Thank you."

"That goes both ways, Lieutenant," Alex told her. "I was up against the wall at the Academy. You stood by me, you and Major Anderegg. That took real courage."

Tara saw seriousness in the young Marine officer's face, reliving the emotionally-taught experience he had borne in his final year as an Academy midshipman.

"I'd be proud to serve under your command, anytime," Alex said. Then his serious face turned into a grin.

"What?" Tara said.

"A Marine recruiter once asked me if I had what it takes," he said.

"You've always had it, Alex. Twice over."

Alex took one step back and saluted her. "Semper Fi, ma'am."

Tara raised her chin, smiled, and returned the salute. "Good luck to you always, Lieutenant Kramer."

**END**

# CHARACTERS

**Alexander Matthew Kramer**
Midshipman, US Naval Academy Class of 2024
(prior-enlisted); Sergeant, USMC, 24th MEU

**Lieutenant Tara Marcellus, USN**
19th Company Officer, US Naval Academy
and USNA Class of 2016

**Rear Admiral David Kramer, USN**
Father of Alex Kramer and USNA Class of 1992

**Olivia Kramer**
Alex Kramer's mother

**Commander James Whikehart, USN**
Command Officer, USS *John Warner*

**Lieutenant Commander Walter Arroyo, USN**
Executive Officer, USS *John Warner*

**Lieutenant Commander Mike Urbanick, USN**
Engineer Officer, USS *John Warner*

**Lieutenant Hugh Kerr, USN**
Weapons Officer, USS *John Warner*

**Lieutenant Donald Schrager, USN**
Navigator/Operations Officer, USS *John Warner*

**Chief Greg Drysdale, USN**
Sonar Supervisor, Weapons, USS *John Warner*

**Lieutenant Commander Ann Forgash, USN**
Clinical Psychologist, Midshipmen Development Center, USNA

**Major Mark Anderegg, USMC**
Marine Corps mentor for 19th Company, US Naval Academy

**Carolyn Hagerty**
Alex's high school girlfriend

**Lance Corporal Billy Whittington**
2nd Squad, First Platoon, 24th MEU, USMC

**Lance Corporal Ethan Crowell**
2nd Squad, First Platoon, 24th MEU, USMC

**First Lieutenant John Fontana, USMC**
Platoon Commander, First Platoon,
Bravo Company, 24th MEU, USMC

**Captain Greg Rosen, USMC**
Company Commander, Bravo Company,
24th MEU, USMC

**Vice Admiral Robert Lawrence, USN**
Superintendent, US Naval Academy

**Captain Adam Brookshier, USN**
Commandant of Midshipmen, US Naval Academy

**Colonel Bruce Wettstone, USMC**
Deputy Commandant of Midshipmen, US Naval Academy

**Colonel Geoff Burlingame, USMC**
Senior Marine, USNA Marine Detachment

**Ray Lydon, USMC**
Marine Corps aviator and USNA Class of 2016

**Daniel Bregman**
Vice Admiral Lawrence's classmate

**Brian Tannehill**
Alex's Naval Academy classmate and roommate

**Harry Stocks**
Alex's Naval Academy classmate and roommate

*Fire teams from 2nd Squad, First Platoon, Bravo Company,*
*24th Marine Expeditionary Unit*

**2nd Squad, first fire team**
Billy Whittington, Rifleman
Ethan Crowell, Team Leader
Anthony Camacho, Automatic Rifleman
Eddie Cabrera, Assistant Automatic Rifleman

**2nd Squad, second fire team**
Christian Aquino, Rifleman
Wayne Armbrister, Team Leader
John Rawleigh, Automatic Rifleman
Brian Schuler, Assistant Automatic Rifleman

**2nd Squad, third fire team**
Todd Womack, Rifleman
Diego Zambrano, Team Leader
Michael Chu, Automatic Rifleman
Earl Kathy, Assistant Automatic Rifleman

# ACKNOWLEDGEMENTS

I was indeed fortunate to learn from, listen to, and form friend-ships with many outstanding US Naval Academy, US Navy, and US Marine Corps active duty, retired, and civilian personnel while I wrote this book. Their unlimited generosity with time and advice ensured that the storyline's characters and scenes presented realism as well as compelling fiction. They trusted me to fairly portray the US naval service and its service members. It was a privilege working with them. Individually and together, they deserve credit for making this unique tale of moral courage and a dedication to duty come to life.

**Commander David R. McKinney**, USN (Ret.) and US Naval Academy (USNA) '98—Naval Aviation; former PAO (Public Affairs Officer), US Naval Academy

**Lieutenant David R. Rodriguez**, USN and USNA '12—Naval Submarine Forces; former Brigade Training Officer and faculty, US Naval Academy

**Major Michael Kuiper, USMC and USNA** '06—prior-enlisted, Marine Infantry; former Brigade Training Officer, US Naval Academy; Executive Officer, 3rd Battalion, 6th Marine Regiment, US Marine Corps

**Lieutenant David C. Phillips**, USN—Department Head, Naval Submarine Forces; former Company Officer, US Naval Academy

**Commander Gregory Chapman**, USN (Ret.) and USNA '93—Surface Warfare Officer; former Honor Officer, US Naval Academy

**Major Kevin Boyce**, USMC (Ret.)—prior-enlisted, Marine Aviation Command and Control; former faculty, US Naval Academy

**Lieutenant Jenna Westerberg**, USN and USNA '16—Division Officer, Naval Submarine Forces; Company Officer, US Naval Academy

**Lieutenant Colonel Jeremy Cothern**, USMC—prior-enlisted, 24th MEU Aviation Command Element; Fighter Pilot and Air Warfare Instructor

**Lieutenant Scott Clark**, USN and USNA '09—Naval Aviation; former Conduct Officer, US Naval Academy

**Lieutenant Michael (Mike) Wallace**, USN and USNA '11—Surface Warfare Officer; former Conduct Officer, US Naval Academy

**Captain John Ralph**, USN—PhD Clinical Psychology; Director, Midshipmen Development Center, US Naval Academy

**Major Frank Biggio**, USMC (Ret.)—Civil Affairs Group; Marine Infantry

**Lieutenant Commander Alex Dietrich**, USN—Naval Aviation and faculty, US Naval Academy

**Captain Ross Pospisil**, USMC and USNA '10—Marine Infantry; academic administration, US Naval Academy

**Captain Robert Kay**, USMC (Ret.)—Marine Infantry; former instructor, US Naval Academy

**James Hanley**—former Consultant, Office of Admissions, US Naval Academy

**Major Thomas Zohlen**, USMC (Ret.) and USNA '88—Marine Corps Armor Division

**Major Shannon Roos**, USMC (Ret.)—Marine Corps Armor Division

**First Lieutenant David Laszcz**, USMC and USNA '18—prior-enlisted, Marine Infantry

**Captain Christopher R. Harrison**, USMC PAO Headquarters, US Marine Corps

**Captain Thomas W. Jones IV**, USMC PAO Headquarters, US Marines Corps

**Yvonne Carlock**, Deputy Communications Strategy (COMMSTRAT) Officer, US Marine Corps Awards Unit

**Major David R. Haines**, USMC and USNA '06—Marine Infantry; instructor, US Naval Academy

**Major Ryan Curry**, USMC (Ret.) and USNA '03—prior-enlisted, Marine Aviation; former academic administration, US Naval Academy

**Gunnery Sergeant Joel Moreno**, USMC Marine Infantry; former Senior Enlisted Leader, US Naval Academy

**Commander Sarah Flaherty**, USN—Naval Aviation; staff officer, Chairman of the Joint Chiefs of Staff, Pentagon

**First Lieutenant Jacob Baldus**, USMC and USNA '20—Marine Air Intelligence

**Captain Chad Wheeley**, USMC—Marine Infantry; instructor, US Naval Academy

**Commander Michael Murnane**, USN—Surface Warfare Officer; former Battalion Officer, US Naval Academy

**Justin Crevier**, USMC (Ret.) and USNA '93—prior-enlisted; Marine Expeditionary Unit, Ground Combat Element

**Steven Konkoly**, USN (Ret.) and USNA '93—Surface Warfare Officer

**Wendy Piret**, USNA '93

**Sarah Kovel**, USNA '82

**Vice Admiral Jan Tighe**, USN (Ret.) and USNA '84

**Major Serena Tyson**, USMC and USNA '06—Marine Aviation; former instructor, US Naval Academy


I also wish to extend my gratitude to Boutique of Quality Books (BQB) Publishing Company, my publisher, and the skilled team of professionals who support their authors so well. From editing and marketing to cover design and especially publisher-author relations, it is an outstanding group. They are Terri Leidich, President and Publisher; Glenn Leidich, Vice President and BQB author liaison; Caleb Guard, my developmental editor; Julie Bromley, Marketing and Audiobook Manager; and others there who assisted me to progress from nonfiction writer to novelist.

# GLOSSARY

The glossary provides additional information on certain acronyms and terms for the US Navy submarine service, the US Marine Corps, and the US Naval Academy that often appear in the novel.

## United States Navy submarine service

### Officer of the Deck (OOD)

This is a watch-standing position performed by a commissioned officer on a US Navy submarine's crew. The OOD is the direct representative of the commanding officer of the submarine or "boat," and is responsible for the safe operation of the submarine at sea. The OOD controls boat operations through commands to junior officers, enlisted supervisors, and operators who comprise the OOD's watch team. Both DIVOs and DHs (with the exception of the CHOP) can stand OOD, but typically a DH will stand OOD on mission.

### Contact Manager (CM)

This is a watch-standing position performed by a commissioned officer or senior enlisted sailor on a US Navy submarine's crew. They are responsible to the OOD for providing a clear and accurate picture of the "contacts" (i.e., other surface vessels and submarines) operating near their submarine. They work closely with the Sonar Supervisor and the Fire Control Technician of the Watch (FTOW) to develop an accurate picture and provide recommendations to the OOD on how to maneuver the submarine.

Typically, Contact Manager is stood by a senior DIVO while on mission.

## Towed Array (TA)

A towed array sonar is a system of hydrophones designed to detect and track faint contacts—for instance, low frequency or seismic signals—emitted from sources such as a potential submarine threat or unidentified entity. The TA is towed behind a submarine on a cable and long enough to prevent the array's sensors from picking up the boat's own noises. It also covers the baffles, which are the blind spot of hull-mounted sonars.

## Photonics Mast

Older submarines have optical periscopes which penetrate the submarine's pressure hull. Some newer submarines, to include Virginia Class submarines, have photonics masts which use sophisticated high-resolution cameras to provide situational awareness while at periscope depth or on the surface.

## Intelligence, Surveillance, Reconnaissance (ISR)

ISR's principal functions are to a) locate and track friendly and hostile forces, and b) assess damage to hostile targets in a boat's Area of Responsibility, or its AOR. ISR is an important element in submarine warfare strategy, and military command and control.

## Endfire

A submarine towed array term. The region directly behind or in front of the long stream of the towed array where it is hardest for the array to pick anything up. It's easiest to pick up contacts on the beam of the towed array versus the pointy ends. Not an ideal place to put the contact.

### Commanding Officer (CO)

The senior commissioned officer directing a US Navy submarine and crew. The CO holds the rank of Commander (O-5) or Captain (O-6). Crew members refer to their boat's commanding officer as CO, captain, and skipper.

### Executive Officer (XO)

The second highest commissioned officer aboard a US Navy submarine crew, holds the rank of lieutenant commander (O-4).

### Department Head (DH)

Each department on a submarine is led by a Department Head who reports to the XO and CO. With the exception of the Supply Officer ("CHOP"), every DH is on their second submarine tour and has previously completed a tour of duty as a DIVO. They are responsible for all matters directly involving their department's operations and performance. There are four DHs on a submarine:

- The Engineer Officer ("ENG") is always a Lieutenant Commander (O-4) and is responsible for the following divisions: Auxiliary, Electrical, Reactor Laboratories, Machinery, and Reactor Control.

- The Combat Systems Officer or Weapons Officer ("WEPS") is a Lieutenant (O-3) or Lieutenant Commander (O-4) and is responsible for the following divisions: Torpedo, Sonar, Fire Control, Missile (on SSBNs or ballistic missile submarines only), and the ship's SCUBA Divers.

- The Navigator/Operations Officer ("NAV") is a Lieutenant (O-3) or Lieutenant Commander (O-4) and is responsible for the following divisions: Communications, Information Technology, Electronic Warfare, and Navigation.

- The Supply Officer ("CHOP") is the only officer onboard not trained in nuclear power, and can be an Ensign (O-1), Lieutenant Junior Grade (O-2), or Lieutenant (O-3). They are responsible for the Culinary and Logistics divisions.

## Division Officer (DIVO)

Each department on a submarine is organized into divisions of between five and fifteen enlisted sailors who all have the same specialty. Division Officers, who report to and serve as assistants to Department Heads, are in charge of the optimal operation of their assigned division within their respective department. Division Officers are always officers assigned to their first submarine. They are typically Ensigns (O-1), Lieutenants Junior Grade (O-2) or Lieutenants (O-3), and work with their Leading Chief Petty Officer to run the division. It is common for DIVOs to lead various divisions throughout their time onboard their boat.

## Junior Officer (JO)

A Junior Officer in the US Navy is any officer who is a lieutenant commander (O-4) or below. On submarines, the term "Junior Officer" is typically used synonymously with "DIVO."

## Control

The Control Room inside a US Navy Virginia Class fast attack submarine is the central command-and-control location for the boat's sonar, photonics, navigation, fire control, and ship control system. This is where the OOD stands watch, along with the majority of the watch team.

## Chief of the Boat (COB)

The Chief of the Boat is the senior enlisted advisor to the Commanding Officer (CO) and the Executive Officer (XO) aboard a US Navy submarine crew. The COB holds the rank of Master Chief Petty Officer (E-9) or Senior Chief Petty Officer (E-8) and is responsible for the welfare, discipline, and morale of the entire crew.

## United States Marine Corps Marine Expeditionary Unit (MEU) and Ground Warfare Offensive Operations

### Expeditionary Strike Group

The Expeditionary Strike Group (ESG) is a US Navy concept introduced in the 1990s. An ESG combines the combat strength of three surface warships and one submarine with an Amphibious Readiness Group (ARG), Marine Expeditionary Unit (MEU), and Special Operations Capable (SOC). Its Navy and Marine Corps warfare components are:

- a US Navy Amphibious Assault Ship (LHA or LHD)

- an Amphibious Transport Dock (LPD) Ship

- a Dock Landing Ship (LSD)

- a US, Navy guided missile cruiser, a guided missile destroyer, and a frigate

- a fast-attack submarine

- a Marine Expeditionary Unit (MEU) capable of conducting special operations

- an AV-8B Harrier II jet fighter (Marine Corps)

- CH-53E Super Stallion helicopters (Navy), CH-46D Sea Knight helicopters (Navy), and AH-1W Super Cobra helicopters (Marine Corps)

### Marine Expeditionary Unit (MEU)

An MEU is a forward-deployed, self-sustaining force that

combatant commanders can order to carry out different special opera-tions and standard missions. MEUs are among the smaller air-ground task forces (Marine Air Ground Task Force or MAGTF) in the US Fleet Marine Force. Each MEU is a quick reactionary force of approximately 2,200 service members and commanded by a Marine Colonel O-6 who leads the Command Element. Each MEU is made up of three elements under its commanding officer: Ground Combat Element, Aviation Combat Element, and Logistics Combat Element. MEUs are deployed for missions that respond to:

- Conventional operations (amphibious assaults and raids)
- Tactical Recovery of Aircraft and Personnel (TRAP)
- Humanitarian Assistance (HA)
- Noncombatant Evacuation Operations (NEO)
- Security operations

## Rifle Platoon

A Marine Corps rifle platoon is made up of forty-two Marines:

- The Platoon Commander, either a second lieutenant O-1 or a first lieutenant O-2
- The Platoon Sergeant, a Staff Non-Commissioned Officer (NCO) staff sergeant E-6
- The Guide, a sergeant E-5, sometimes called the senior squad leader
- Three rifle squads with three (3) fire teams in each squad. Each fire team has four (4) enlisted infantry Marines—privates first class, lance corporals, corporals. Each squad is led by a squad leader, a Marine sergeant E-5 (39 Marines)

- One US Navy corpsman (not counted among a forty-two-member Marine rifle platoon)

## Forward Observer (FO)

A Forward Observer in the Marine Corps is an enlisted Marine who is trained to call for and direct artillery fire on enemy positions. He can also be an officer, especially in artillery. FOs accurately plot coordinates so that Marine Corps field artillery and rifle platoons can engage enemy targets. In the Corps, FOs are called "the eyes and ears of indirect fire support."

## Line of Departure (LD)

The line of departure represents a phase line that's crossed at a specific time by Marine units preparing to initiate an offensive operation. Its purpose is to coordinate the Marines' advance so they can strike enemy positions at a preferred time and order.

## Noncombatant Evacuation Operation (NEO)

An NEO is the mandatory (an official order from a governmental authority) or authorized yet voluntary evacuation of civilians called "noncombatants," and nonessential military personnel from dangerous conditions in a foreign land to a predetermined safe location. Noncombatants and nonessential personnel are usually transported to the continental United States. But when a USMC Marine Expeditionary Unit deploys for a NEO mission, it is an emergency action used specifically outside of the continental United States (OCONUS). Evacuations carried out overseas tend to involve situations of civil unrest, military uprisings, environmental dangers, and natural disasters.

### Forward Air Controller (FAC)

Marine Forward Air Controllers are mid-level commissioned officers and qualified Marine aviators. FACs are tasked from aviation units to directly support ground combat units when they are under fire or anticipate a hostile engagement. FACs direct Close Air Support (CAS) and other offensive air operations. One of their most vital duties is to ensure that Marine infantry, weapons, and armor units engaged in offensive operations are safe during CAS and not at risk from friendly fire. FACs may also have completed the rigorous Marine Corps Infantry Officer Course (IOC).

### Joint Terminal Attack Controller (JTAC)

Marine Joint Terminal Attack Controllers are qualified service members, operating from a forward position on the ground, allowed to direct combat aircraft engaged in close air support and other offensive air operations. They must hold an enlisted noncommissioned rank of sergeant E-5 or higher. JTACs are either enlisted riflemen or artillery Marines. They must earn a certification but also a Military Occupational Specialty (MOS 8002). JTACs must complete the JTAC primer course, and have graduated from the Special Operations Spotter Course (SOSC). In unusual warfare situations, a Marine does not need to be JTAC-certified or an FAC for an officer to assign that service member to make radio requests for CAS.

### Close Air Support (CAS)

Close Air Support is defined as detailed coordination of aviation and fires within *close proximity to friendly troops*. CAS provides flexibility to the maneuver commander, and it allows operations beyond the range of other supporting arms, such as artillery. CAS allows a light, expeditionary force to conduct violent, successful combined arms warfare. In future battlefield maneuvers, the Marine Corps will be more dependent on CAS than in past military operations.

## MEU Aviation Combat Element (ACE)

An east coast MEU (24th MEU is based at Marine Corps Base Camp Lejeune, NC) will typically deploy with:

- four (4) CH-53K Super Stallions

- seven (7) AV-8B Harriers (now being replaced by the F-35B with vertical/short take-off and lift capability)

- twelve (12) MV-22 Ospreys

- four (4) AH-1Z Viper or "Zulu" and three (3) UH-1Y Venom "Huey" attack helicopters (in 2020, the Marine Corps retired the AH-1W Super Cobra and replaced it with the AH-1Z Viper). Vipers and Hueys deliver ordnance against hostile targets.

For a MEU NEO mission as portrayed in the story, the aircraft will either hold overhead or hold away from the "target area(s)" in a holding area (HA) or battle position (BP). One section—a Viper and a Huey—will be on-station at a time, yo-yoing with a second section while the first returns to refuel back aboard USS *Wasp* or another amphibious assault ship (AAS). The attack helicopters can provide Multi-Imagery Reconnaissance (MIR), using their targeting pod to provide situational information to infantry units on the ground and for aviation-delivered fires. Having an aircraft from a MEU's Aviation Command Element on-station/strip-alert will be a mission-dependent decision, and can launch when ground warfare units are engaged against hostile or enemy positions. The MEU ACE also consists of small unmanned aerial systems (SUAS) and counter UAS capability to support the Ground Combat Element (GCE).

## NATO 9-Line Medevac Request

A coordinated process, in peacetime and war, that is followed to prepare casualties for evacuation and medical treatment. The nine (9) lines of a medical evacuation (MEDEVAC) request are:

1. Location of pick-up site.
2. Radio frequency, call sign, and suffix (N: no enemy troops present; P: possible enemy in area, approach with caution; E: enemy troops in area, approach with caution; X: enemy troops in area, armed escort required).
3. Number of patients by priority following triage.
4. Specific equipment required.
5. Number of patients by type.
6. Number and types of wounds (peacetime).
7. Security of pick-up sites (wartime).
8. Method of marking pick-up site.
9. Terrain description (peacetime).

## The Silver Star

The Silver Star medal (SSM) is the United States' third highest military decoration for valor in combat.

### The Purple Heart

The Purple Heart (PH) is a United States military decoration awarded to service members wounded or killed while serving on active duty.

### The Navy Marine Corps Combat Action Ribbon

The Combat Action Ribbon (CAR) is a military decoration awarded to United States sea service members of the United States Navy, United States Marine Corps, and United States Coast Guard "who have actively participated in ground or surface combat."

Recipients of the three military awards display their service ribbons alongside each other on the top row of decorations, or "ribbon rack," worn on their uniform coat and uniform shirt when the coat isn't required for regulation dress. The three decorations for valor are the same ones the United States Marine Corps awards Alex Kramer in the story, and are displayed on the book's front cover left to right: Silver Star, Purple Heart, Combat Action Ribbon.

*United States Naval Academy*

### The Brigade of Midshipmen

The Brigade of Midshipmen is approximately 4,500 under-graduates. Its military structure and chain of command are

represented by two regiments, six battalions, and thirty companies—five per battalion. There are between 135 to 145 midshipmen, or Mids, in each company. In almost all areas of Brigade
and Academy life, midshipmen identify themselves by their
company's numeral. They are not called students but instead:

- Midshipman Fourth Class (MIDN 4/C) or 'Plebe'
  (freshman)

- Midshipman Third Class (MIDN 3/C) or 'Youngster'
  (sophomore)

- Midshipman Second Class (MIDN 2/C) or 'Junior' (junior)

- Midshipman First Class (MIDN 1/C) or 'Firstie' (senior)

## Superintendent of the US Naval Academy

The Superintendent is the Naval Academy's highest military
officer and senior university administrator. He holds the US Navy
rank of vice admiral, a three-star flag officer O-9 and, by tradition,
is an Academy graduate. The superintendent, or 'Supe,' oversees
all military, academic, athletic, and other functions. However, he
does not manage those day-to-day operations unless situations
require his participation. He reports to the Naval Academy's
Board of Visitors.

## Commandant and Deputy Commandant of Midshipmen

The Commandant and Deputy Commandant of Midshipmen
supervise all daily military, professional training, honor process,
and conduct program activities for the Brigade of Midshipmen.
Active-duty commissioned and noncommissioned Navy and
Marine Corps officers and senior enlisted personnel assigned
to the Naval Academy report to them. Those personnel are the
regimental officers, battalion officers, company officers, and
senior enlisted leaders who direct a range of Brigade operations.

The 'Dant' and 'Dept or Deputy Dant'—as midshipmen sometimes informally refer to them—do not direct the academic faculty or their course development and presentation. They traditionally have been Naval Academy graduates, and are Navy and Marine Corps senior officers with the ranks of Navy captain (O-6) and Marine Corps colonel (O-6).

## Battalion Officer

The Brigade's six battalion officers, or "Batt-Os," are active-duty Navy and Marine Corps officers. Each is responsible for managing the performance of approximately 750 midshipmen assigned to assigned to the Batt-O's five companies. While they sometimes interact directly with midshipmen, they communicate daily with the five company officers under their command. The battalion officers hold ranks of commander (O-5) or captain (O-6) in the Navy, and lieutenant colonel (O-5) or colonel (O-6) in the Marine Corps. All Battalion Officers have previously served as commanding officers of a sub-marine, surface ship, aviation squadron, or Marine battalion.

## Company Officer

The company officers are considered the Naval Academy's most influential active-duty officers with responsibilities for the Brigade of Midshipmen. They represent the first line of officer supervision in the chain of command between the Commandant's staff and the Brigade. They interact daily with individual and teams of midshipmen on different issues that include but are not limited to: military performance and training; character and conduct on and off Academy property; academic issues; personal difficulties that interfere with a midshipman's physical safety, emotional health, general attitude; and overall relations with other Mids. The company officers advise and mentor midshipmen officers

elected by classmates and shipmates to lead each company: the
company commander, the executive officer, platoon commanders
and sergeants, and squad leaders. Company officers are Navy
lieutenants (O-3) and Marine Corps captains (O-3) in rank.

### Senior Enlisted Leader (SEL)

The Senior Enlisted Leaders are Marine Corps Staff Non-
Commissioned Officers (NCOs); typically, Marine Staff Sergeants
or Gunnery Sergeants, and Navy Chief or Senior Chief Petty
Officers. With significant military experience behind them, one
SEL is assigned to each company in the Brigade and reports to
the company officer. SELs teach midshipmen the importance of
the essential relationship between junior officers and their senior
enlisted leaders (e.g., the platoon commander and their platoon
sergeant in the Marine Corps, and the DIVO and their chief in
the Navy). Midshipmen must understand that senior enlisted
leaders become trustworthy mentors, leaders, and teachers they
will rely on to learn leadership skills. SELs teach midshipmen
the importance of mutual trust that must exist between senior
enlisted leaders whose rank places them between the junior
officers—Navy ensigns and Marine second lieutenants—and the
sailors and Marines those officers will soon lead and issue orders.
That same trust continues as Navy and Marine officers rise in
rank, and the NCOs and chiefs under their command also assume
greater responsibilities directing sailors and Marines.

### Overall Order of Merit (OOM)

The Overall Order of Merit is the significant numerical ranking assigned to each Naval Academy midshipman in relation to all
others in their class. OOM influences a midshipman's ability to
receive assignment to a desired Navy or Marine Corps community

during senior, or "first class," year at commissioning and graduation. OOM is a collective measurement based on numerical scores received in specific and equally important categories:

1. Academic Order of Merit (grades and academics)

2. Military Order of Merit (military performance, athletic performance, physical education, professional courses, conduct)

A midshipman's OOM is updated at the end of each spring and fall academic period.

## Midshipman Aptitude for Commissioning

During four years at the Naval Academy, a Midshipmen Aptitude for Commissioning letter grade rating is as significant as each midshipman's Overall Order of Merit. Specific Midshipmen Development Traits (MDTs) are evaluated by "raters" and "senior raters" representing: a) active-duty Navy and Marine Corps officers on the Commandant of Midshipmen's staff, and b) the midshipmen chain of command across the thirty companies that make up the Brigade of Midshipmen. The traits are:

1. Leadership

2. Character

3. Professionalism

4. Team-Driven

5. Judgment and Tact

Aptitude for Commissioning is closely tied to the Brigade's Conduct System and its Honor Concept process.

## The Yard

The US Naval Academy's campus in Annapolis, Maryland

is officially called "The Yard." The term dates back to the Revolutionary War, and refers to the word "dockyard."

# ABOUT THE AUTHOR

Robert Stewart is the author of four nonfiction books. Two of them include military works presenting the full four-year experiences for midshipmen at the U.S. Naval Academy and cadets at the U.S. Military Academy at West Point. His other two books cover national athletics: the competitive sport of rowing or "crew," and the biographical memoir of a former NCAA Division I Big Ten Conference athletic director.

*No Greater Duty* is his debut novel.

*The Brigade in Review: A Year at the U.S. Naval Academy*
(Naval Institute Press, 1993)

*The Corps of Cadets: A Year at West Point*
(Naval Institute Press, 1996)

*Rowing, The Experience*
(Boathouse Row Sports, 1988)

*An Athletic Director's Story and the Future of College Sports in America* (Rutgers University Press, 2020)